The Life of the World to Come

The Life of the World to Come

KAGE BAKER

TOR®

A TOM DOHERTY ASSOCIATES BOOK
NEW YORK

THE LIFE OF THE WORLD TO COME

Copyright © 2004 by Kage Baker

A portion of this novel originally appeared as the story "Smart Alec" in the September 1999 issue of *Asimov's Science Fiction*.

This book is printed on acid-free paper.

Edited by David G. Hartwell

A Tor Book
Published by Tom Doherty Associates, LLC
175 Fifth Avenue
New York, NY 10010

www.tor.com

Tor® is a registered trademark of Tom Doherty Associates, LLC.

Library of Congress Cataloging-in-Publication Data

Baker, Kage.
    The life of the world to come / Kage Baker.—1st ed.
      p. cm.
    "A Tom Doherty Associates book."
    ISBN 0-765-31132-1
    EAN 978-0765-31132-0
    1. Dr. Zeus Incorporated (Imaginary organization)—Fiction.
  2. Woman botanists—Fiction. 3. Immortalism—Fiction.
  4. Time travel—Fiction. 5. Cyborgs—Fiction. 6. Pirates—Fiction.
  I. Title.
    PS3552.A4313L54 2004
    813'.54—dc22

                           2004049574

First Edition: December 2004

Printed in the United States of America

0 9 8 7 6 5 4 3 2 1

This one is dedicated,
with reverence, respect, and heart's regard,
to my mentors temporal and spiritual:

Michael Kandel
(Eminent physician of prose)

Stiofan Ui Giollain
(Saint. Scholar. Man about town . . .)

The Life of the World to Come

THE BOTANIST MENDOZA

150,000 BCE (more or less)

Rain comes on the west wind, ice out of the blue north. The east wind brings hazes, smokes, the exhalation of the desert on the distant mainland; and hot winds come out of the south, across the wide ocean.

The corn and tomatoes like the west wind. The tall corn gleams wet like cellophane, the tomato leaves pearl and bow down. The onions and garlic, on the other hand, get sullen and shreddy and threaten mold in the rain. Poor old cyborg with a few screws missing—me—sits watching them in fascination.

When I find myself giving my vegetables personalities, it's a sign I've been sitting here watching the rain too long. Or the bright ice. Or the hazes or the hot thin stripes of cloud. Accordingly then, I put on a coat or hat, depending on which way the wind is blowing, and walk out to have a look at the world.

What I have of the world. When I rise, I can walk down the canyon to my brief stony beach to see if anything interesting has washed up there. Nothing ever has. Out on the rocks live sea lions, and they groan and howl so like old men that a mortal would be deceived. I ignore them.

Or I can walk up the canyon and climb high narrow hills, through the ferny trees, until I stand on rimrock in the wind. I can look along the spine of my island in every direction. Ocean all around, the horizon vanishing in cloud. No ships ever, of course—hominids haven't yet progressed beyond clinging to floating logs, when they venture to sea at all.

And I begin my day. Much to do: the planting or the harvest, all the greenhouse work, the tasks of replacing irrigation pipes and cleaning out trenches. A little work on projects of my own, maybe planing wood to replace such of my furniture as has fallen apart with age. I take a meal, if I remember to. I wander back down to the beach in the evening, to watch the little waves run up on the shore, and sometimes I forget to go home.

One day a small resort town will be built on this stony beach, palm trees and yellow sand brought in on barges, to make a place as artificial as I am. The water will be full of excursion boats, painted bright. Out there where that big rock is, the one that looks like a sugarloaf, a great ballroom will stand. I would dearly love to go dancing there, if he were with me.

Sometimes I torment myself by walking along and imagining the crescent of street lined with shops and cafés, gracious hotels. I can almost see the mortal children with their ice cream. I can almost hear the music. I sit down where there will be a terrace someday, complete with little tables and striped umbrellas. Sometimes a waiter has materialized at my elbow, white napkin over his arm, deferentially leaning from the waist to offer me a cocktail. He's never really there, of course, nor will he ever be.

But the other man *will* be here, the one I see only in my dreams, or behind my eyes as I watch the quiet water in the long hours. I have waited for him, alone on this island, for three thousand years. I think.

I'm not certain, though, and this is the reason I have bound more paper into my book, vandalized another label printer cartridge, cut myself another pen: it may be that if I write things down I can keep track of the days. They have begun to float loose in an alarming way, like calendar leaves fluttering off the wall.

I walked out this morning in the full expectation of thinning my tomato seedlings and—imagine my stupefaction! Row upon row of big well-grown plants stretched away as far as the eye could see, heavy with scarlet fruit. Well-watered, weeded, cared for by someone. Me? I swear I can't recall, nor does my internal chronometer record any unusual forward movement; but something, my world or me, is slipping out of time's proper flow.

What does it mean, such strangeness? Some slow deterioration of consciousness? Supposedly impossible in a perfectly designed immortal. But then, I'm not quite mechanically sound, am I? I'm a Crome generator, one of those aberrant creatures the mortals call psychic, or *second-sighted*. I'm the only one on whom the Company ever conferred immortality, and I'll bet they're sorry now.

Not that they meant to do it, of course. Somebody made a mistake when I was being evaluated for the honor of eternal service, didn't catch the latent flaw, and here I am like a stain in permanent ink. No way to erase me. Though marooning me at this station has undoubtedly solved a few problems for them.

Yet my prison is actually a very nice place, quite the sort of spot I'd choose to live, if I'd ever had a choice: utterly isolated, beautifully green, silent in all its valleys and looming mountains, even the sea hushed where it breaks and jumps up white on the windward cliffs.

Only one time was there ever noise, terrible sounds that echoed off the mountains. I hid indoors all that day, paced with my hands over my ears, hummed to myself to shut out the tumult. At least it was over in a few hours. I have never yet ventured back over into Silver Canyon to see if the little people there are all dead. I knew what would happen to them when I sent that signal, alerting Dr. Zeus to their presence. Were they refugees from Company persecution? Did I betray them? Well—more blood on my soul. I was only following orders, of course.

(Which is another reason I don't mind being an old field slave here, you see. Where else should I be? I've been responsible for the deaths of seven mortal men and unknown numbers of whatever those little pale things were.)

What the eyes can't see, the heart doesn't grieve over, isn't that what they say? And no eyes can see me here, that's for sure, if I generate the blue radiation that accompanies a fit of visions, or do some other scary and supposedly impossible thing like move through time spontaneously. I am far too dangerous to be allowed to run around loose, I know. Am I actually a *defective*? Will my fabulous cyborg super-intelligence begin to wane? It might be rather nice, creeping oblivion. Perhaps even death will become possible. But the Company has opted to hide me rather than study me, so there's no way to tell.

I have done well, for a cast-off broken tool. Arriving, I crawled from my transport box with just about nothing but the prison uniform I wore. Now I have a comfortable if somewhat amateurish house I built myself, over long years, with a kitchen of which I am particularly proud. The fireplace draws nicely, and the little sink is supplied by a hand pump drawing on the well I drilled. I have a tin tub in my back garden, in which I bathe. Filled before midday heat rises, the water is reasonably warm by nightfall, and serves to water the lawn afterward. So very tidy, this life I've built.

Do I lack for food and drink? No indeed. I grow nearly everything I consume. About all I receive from the Company anymore are its shipments of Proteus brand synthetic protein.

(Lately the Proteus only seems to come in the assortment packs, four flavors: Breakfast Bounty, Delicate and Savory, Hearty Fare, and Marina. The first two resemble pork and/or chicken or veal, and are comparatively inoffensive. I quite like Hearty Fare. It makes the best damned tamale filling I've ever found. Marina, on the other hand, is an unfortunate attempt to simulate seafood. It goes straight into my compost heap, where it most alarmingly fails to decompose. There has been no response to my requests for a change, but this is a prison, after all.)

Have I written that before, about the Proteus? I have a profound sense of déjà vu reading it over, and paused just now to thumb back through the book to see if I was duplicating a previous entry. No. Nothing in the first part, about England, and nothing in the afterword I wrote on my trial transcript. More of this slipping time business. Nothing has again been so bad as that day I paused in weeding to wipe my sweating face and looked up to see the row just cleared full of weeds again, and the corn a full foot taller than it had been a moment before. But nothing else out of whack! No sign of dust or cobwebs in my house, no conflicting chronometers.

Yes, I really must try to anchor myself here and now. It may be a bit late for mental health, but at least I might keep from sinking into the rock of this island, buried under centuries, preserved like a fossil in a strata of unopened Proteus Marina packets. I suppose it wouldn't have come to this pass if I'd seen another living soul in three thousand years who wasn't a dream or a hallucination.

If only he'd come for me.

I don't know if I should write about him. The last time I did that I was depressed for years, roamed this island in restless misery end to end. Not a good thing to summon up a ghost when you're all alone, especially when you'd sell your soul—if you had one—to join him in his long grave. But then, perhaps misery is what's needed to fasten me securely to the world. Perhaps this curiously painless existence is the problem.

If I look across the table I can see him standing there, as I saw him first in England in 1554: a tall mortal in the black robe of a scholar, staring at me in cold and arrogant dislike. We weren't enemies long. I was very young and so fascinated by the mortal's voice, and his fine big hands . . . I wake at night sometimes, convinced I can feel his mortal flesh at my side, hot as the fire in which he was martyred.

So I look away: but there he is in the doorway, just as he stood in the doorway of the stagecoach inn in the Cahuenga Pass, when he walked back into my life in 1863. He was smiling then, a Victorian gentleman in a tall hat, smooth and subtle to conceal his deadly business. If he'd succeeded in what he'd been sent from England to do, the history of nations would have been drastically different. I was only an incidental encounter that time, entering late at the last act in his life; but I held him as he lay dying, and I avenged his death.

Barbaric phrase, *avenged his death*. I was educated to be above such mortal nonsense, yet what I did was more than barbaric. I don't remember tearing six American Pinkerton agents limb from limb, but it appears I did just that, after they'd emptied their guns into my lover.

But when he lay there with blood all over his once-immaculate clothes, my poor secret agent man, he agreed to come back for me. He knew something I didn't, and if he'd lived for even thirty more seconds he might have let me in on the secret.

I really should ponder the mystery, but now that I've summoned my ghost again all I can think of is the lost grace of his body. I should have let well enough alone. The dreams will probably begin again now. I am impaled on his memory like an insect on a pin. Or some other metaphor . . .

I've spent the last few days damning myself for an idiot, when I haven't been crying uncontrollably. I am so tired of being a tragic teenager in love, especially after having been one for over thirty centuries. I think I'll damn someone else for a change.

How about Dr. Zeus Incorporated, who made me the thing I am? Here's the history: the Company began as a cabal of adventurers and investors who found somebody else's highly advanced technology. They stole it, used it to develop yet more advanced technology (keeping all this a secret from the public, of course), and became very very wealthy.

Of course, once they had all the money they needed, they must have more; so they developed a way to travel into the past and loot lost riches, and came up with dodgy ways to convey them into the future, to be sold at fabulous profits.

Along the way, they developed a process for human immortality.

The only problem with it was, once they'd taken a human child and put it through the painful years of transformation, what emerged at the end wasn't a human adult but a *cyborg*, an inconveniently deathless thing most mortals wouldn't want to dine at one table with. But that's all right: cyborgs make a useful workforce to loot the past. And how can we rebel against our service, or even complain? After all, Dr. Zeus saved us from death.

I myself was dying in the dungeons of the Spanish Inquisition when I was rescued by a fast-talking operative named Joseph, damn his immortal soul. Well, little girl, what'll it be? Stay here and be burned to death, or come work for a kindly doctor who'll give you eternal life? Of course, if you'd rather die . . .

I was four years old.

The joke is, of course, that at this precise moment in time none of it's even happened yet. This station exists in 150,000 BCE, millennia before Joseph's even born, to say nothing of everyone else I ever knew, including me.

Paradox? If you view time as a linear flow, certainly. Not, however, if you finally pay attention to the ancients and regard time (not eternity) as a serpent biting its own tail, or perhaps a spiral. Wherever you are, the surface on which you stand *appears* to be flat, to stretch away straight behind you and before you. As I understand temporal physics, in reality it curves around on itself, like the coiled mainspring in a clock's heart. You can cross from one point of the coil to another rather than plod endlessly forward, if you know how. I was sent straight here from 1863. If I were ever reprieved I could resume life in 1863 just where I left it, three thousand years older than the day I departed.

Could I go forward beyond that, skip ahead to 1963 or 2063? We were always told that was impossible; but here again the Company has been caught out in a lie. I did go forward, on one memorable occasion. I got a lungful of foul air and a brief look at the future I'd been promised all my immortal life. It wasn't a pleasant place at all.

Either Dr. Zeus doesn't know how to go forward in time, or knows how and has kept the information from its immortal slaves, lest we learn the truth about the wonderful world of the twenty-fourth century. Even if I were to tell the others what I know, though, I doubt there'd be any grand rebellion. What point is there to our immortal lives but the work?

Undeniably the best work in the world to be doing, too, rescuing things from destruction. Lost works by lost masters, paintings and films and statues that no longer exist (except that they secretly do, secured away in some Company warehouse). Hours before the fires start, the bombs fall, doomed libraries swarm with immortal operatives, emptying them like ants looting a sugar bowl. Living things saved from extinction by Dr. Zeus's immortals, on hand to collect them for its ark. I myself have saved rare plants, the only known source of cures for mortal diseases.

More impressive still: somewhere there are massive freezer banks, row upon row of silver tubes containing DNA from races of men that no longer walk the earth, sperm and ova and frozen embryos, posterity on ice to save a dwindling gene pool.

Beside such work, does it really matter if there is mounting evidence, as we plod on toward the twenty-fourth century, that our masters have some plan to deny us our share of what we've gathered for them up there?

I wear, above the Company logo on all my clothing, an emblem: a clock face without hands. I've heard about this symbol, in dark whispers, all my life. When I was sent to this station I was informed it's the badge of my penal servitude, but the rumor among immortals has always been that it's the sign we'll all be forced to wear when we do finally reach the future, so our mortal masters can tell us from actual persons. Or worse . . .

I was exiled to this hole in the past for a crime, but there are others of us who have disappeared without a trace, innocent of anything worse than complaining too loudly. Have they been shuffled out of the deck of time as I have been, like a card thrown under the table? It seems likely. Sentenced to eternal hard labor, denied any future to release them.

What little contact we've had with the mortals who actually live in the future doesn't inspire confidence, either: unappreciative of the treasures we bring them, afraid to venture from their rooms, unable to comprehend the art or literature of their ancestors. Rapaciously collecting Shakespeare first folios but never opening them, because his plays are full of objectionable material and nobody can read anymore anyway. Locking Mozart sonatas in cabinets and never playing them, because Mozart had disgusting habits: he ate meat and drank alcohol. These same puritans are able, mind you, to order the massacre of those little pale people to loot their inventions.

But what's condemnation from the likes of me, killer cyborg drudging along here in the Company's fields, growing occasional lettuce for rich fools who want to stay at a fine resort when they time-travel? The Silence is coming for us all, one day, the unknown nemesis, and perhaps that will be justice enough. If only he comes for me before it does.

He'll come again! He will. He'll break my chains. Once he stood bound to a stake and shouted for me to join him there, that the gate to paradise was standing open for us, that he wouldn't rest until I followed him. I didn't go; and he didn't rest, but found his way back to me against all reason three centuries later.

He very nearly succeeded that time, for by then I'd have followed him into any fire God ever lit. History intervened, though, and swatted us like a couple of insects. He went somewhere and I descended into this gentle hell, this other Eden that will one day bear the name of Avalon. He won't let me rest here, though. His will is too strong.

Speak of the fall of Rome and it occurs!

Or the fall of Dr. Zeus, for that matter.

He has come again.

And gone again, but alive this time! No more than a day and a night were given us, but he *did not die*!

I still can't quite believe this.

He's shown me a future that isn't nearly as dark as the one I glimpsed. There is a point to all this, there is a reason to keep going, there is even—unbelievably— the remote possibility that . . . no, I'm not even going to think about that. I won't look at that tiny bright window, so far up and far off, especially from the grave I've dug myself.

But what if we have broken the pattern at last?

Must put this into some kind of perspective. Oh, I could live with seeing him once every three thousand years, if all our trysts went as sweetly as this one did. And it started so violently, too.

Not that there was any forewarning that it would, mind you. Dull morning spent in peaceful labor in the greenhouse, tending my latest attempt at *Mays mendozaii*. Sweaty two hours oiling the rollers on the shipping platform. Had set out for the high lake to dig some clay for firing when there came the roar of a time shuttle emerging from its transcendence field.

It's something I hear fairly frequently, but only as a distant boom, a sound wave weak with traveling miles across the channel from Santa Cruz Island, where the Company's Day Six resort is located. However, this time the blast erupted practically over my head.

I threw myself flat and rolled, looking up. There was a point of silver screaming away from me, coming down fast, leveling out above the channel, heading off toward the mainland. I got to my feet and stared, frowning, at its spiraled flight. This thing was out of control, surely! There was a faint golden puff as its gas vented and abruptly the shuttle had turned on its path, was coming back toward the station.

I tensed, watching its trajectory, ready to run. Oh, dear, I thought, there were perhaps going to be dead twenty-fourth-century millionaires cluttering up my fields soon. I'd have a lot of nasty work to do with body bags before the Company sent in a disaster team. Did I even have any body bags? Why would I have body bags? But there, the pilot seemed to have regained a certain amount of control. His shuttle wasn't spinning anymore and its speed was decreasing measurably, though he was still coming in on a course that would take him straight up Avalon Canyon. Oh, no; he was trying to land, swooping in low and cutting a swath through my fields. I cursed and ran down into the canyon, watching helplessly the ruination of my summer corn.

There, at last the damned thing was skidding to a halt. Nobody was going to die, but there were doubtless several very frightened Future Kids puking their guts up inside that shuttle just now. I paused, grinning to myself. Did I really have to deal with this problem? Should I, in fact? Wasn't my very existence here a Company secret? Oughtn't I simply to stroll off in a discreet kind of way and let the luckless cyborg pilot deal with his terrified mortal passengers?

But I began to run again anyway, sprinting toward the shuttle that was still sizzling with the charge of its journey.

I circled it cautiously, scanning, and was astounded to note that there were no passengers on board. Stranger still, the lone pilot seemed to be a mortal man; and that, of course, was impossible. Only cyborgs can fly these things.

But then, he hadn't been doing all that expert a job, had he?

So I came slowly around the nose of the shuttle, and it was exactly like that moment in *The Wizard of Oz* when Dorothy, in black and white, moves so warily toward the door and looks across the threshold: then grainy reality shifts into Technicolor and she steps through, into that hushed and shocked moment full of cellophane flowers and the absolute unexpected.

I looked through the window of the shuttle and saw a mortal man slumped forward in his seat restraints, staring vacantly out at me.

Him, of course. Who else would it be?

Tall as few mortals are, and such an interesting face: high, wide cheekbones flushed with good color, long broken nose, deep-set eyes with colorless lashes. Fair hair lank, pushed back from his forehead. Big rangy body clad in some sort of one-piece suit of black stuff, armored or sewn all over with overlapping scales of a gun-metal color. Around his neck he wore a collar of twisted golden metal, like a Celtic torque. The heroic effect was spoiled somewhat by the nosebleed he was presently having. He didn't seem to be noticing it, though. His color was draining away.

Oh, dear. He was suffering from transcendence shock. Must do something about that immediately.

The strangest calm had seized me, sure sign, I fear, that I really have gone a bit mad in this isolation. No cries from me of "My love! You have returned to me at last!" or anything like that. I scanned him in a businesslike manner, realized that he was unconscious, and leaned forward to tap on the window to wake him up. Useless my trying to break out the window to pull him through. Shuttle windows don't break, ever.

After a moment or two of this he turned his head to look blankly at me. No sign of recognition, of course. Goodness, I had no idea whence or from when he'd come, had I? He might not even be English in this incarnation. I pulled a crate marker from my pocket and wrote on my hand DO YOU SPEAK CINEMA STANDARD? and held it up in his line of sight.

His eyes flickered over the words. His brow wrinkled in confusion. I leaned close to the glass and shouted:

"You appear to require medical assistance! Do you need help getting out of there?"

That seemed to get through to him. He moved his head in an uncertain nod and fumbled with his seat restraints. The shuttle hatch popped open. He stood up, struck his head on the cabin ceiling and fell forward through the hatchway.

I was there to catch him. He collapsed on me, I took the full weight of his body, felt the heat of his blood on my face. His sweat had a scent like fields in summer.

He found his legs and pulled himself upright, looking down at me groggily. His eyes widened as he realized he'd bled all over me.

"Oh. Oh, I'm so sorry—" he mumbled, aghast. English! Yes, of course. Here he was again and I didn't mind the blood at all, since at least this time he wasn't dying. Though of course I'd better do something about that nosebleed pretty fast.

So I led him back to my house. He leaned on me the whole way, only semiconscious most of the time. Unbelievable as it seemed, he'd apparently come through time without first taking any of the protective drugs that a mortal must have to make the journey safely. It was a miracle his brain wasn't leaking out his ears.

Three times I had to apply the coagulator wand to stop his bleeding. He drifted in and out of consciousness, and my floaty calm began to evaporate fast. I talked to him, trying to keep his attention. He was able to tell me that his name was Alec Checkerfield, but he wasn't sure about time or place. Possibly 2351? He did recognize the Company logo on my coveralls, and it seemed to alarm him. That was when I knew he'd stolen the shuttle, though I didn't acknowledge this to myself because such a thing was impossible. Just as it was impossible that a mortal being should be able to operate a time shuttle at all, or survive a temporal journey without drugs buffering him.

So I told him, to calm him down, that I was a prisoner here. That seemed to be the right thing to say, because he became confidential with me at once. It seems he knows all about the Company, has in fact some sort of grudge against them, something very mysterious he can't tell me about; but Dr. Zeus has, to use his phrase, *wrecked his life*, and he's out to bring them to their knees.

This was so demonstrably nuts that I concluded the crash had addled his brain a bit, but I said soothing and humoring things as I helped him inside and got him to stretch out on my bed, pushing a bench to the end so his feet wouldn't hang over. Just like old times, eh? And there he lay.

My crazed urge was to fall down weeping beside him and cover him with kisses, blood or no; but of course what I did was bring water and a towel to clean him up, calm and sensible. Mendoza the cyborg, in charge of her emotions, if not her mind.

It was still delight to stroke his face with the cool cloth, watch his pupils dilate or his eyes close in involuntary pleasure at the touch of the water. When I had set aside the basin I stayed with him, tracing the angle of his jaw with my hand, feeling the blood pulsing under his skin.

"You'll be all right now," I told him. "Your blood pressure and heart rate are normalizing. You're an extraordinary man, Alec Checkerfield."

"I'm an earl, too," he said proudly. "Seventh earl of Finsbury."

Oh, my, he'd come up in the world. Nicholas had been no more than secretary to a knight, and Edward—firmly shut out of the Victorian ruling classes by the scandal of his birth—had despised inherited privilege. "No, really, a British peer?" I said. "I don't think I've ever met a real aristocrat before."

"How long have you been stuck here?" he said. What was that accent of his? Not the well-bred Victorian inflection of last time; this was slangy, transatlantic, and decidedly limited in vocabulary. Did earls speak like this in the twenty-fourth century? Oh, how strange.

"I've been at this station for years," I answered him unguardedly. Oops. "More years than I remember." He looked understandably confused, since my immortal body stopped changing when I was twenty.

"You mean they marooned you here when you were just a kid? Bloody hell, what'd you do? It must have been something your parents did."

How close could I stick to the truth without frightening him?

"Not exactly. But I also knew too much about something I shouldn't have. Dr. Zeus found a nicely humane oubliette and dropped me out of sight or sound. You're the first mortal"—oops again—"*soul* I've spoken with in all this time."

"My God." He looked aghast. Then his eyes narrowed, I knew that look, that was his righteous wrath look. "Well, listen—er—what's your name, babe?"

Rosa? Dolores? No. No aliases anymore. "Mendoza," I said.

"Okay, Mendoza. I'll get you out of here," he said, all stern heroism. "That time shuttle out there is *mine* now, babe, and when I've finished this other thing I'll come back for you." He gripped my hand firmly.

Oh, no, I thought, what has he gotten himself into now? At what windmill has he decided to level his lance?

Summoning every ounce of composure, I frowned delicately and enunciated: "Do I understand you to say that you stole a time shuttle from Dr. Zeus Incorporated?"

"Yup," he said, with that sly sideways grin I knew so terribly well.

"How, in God's name? They're all powerful and all knowing, too. Nobody steals anything from the Company!" I said.

"I did," he said, looking so smug I wanted to shake him. "I've got sort of an advantage. At least, I had," he amended in a more subdued voice. "They may have killed my best friend. If he'd been with me, I wouldn't have crashed. I don't know what's happened to him, but if he's really gone . . . they *will* pay."

Something had persuaded this man that he could play the blood and revenge game with Dr. Zeus and win. He couldn't win, of course, for a number of reasons; not least of which was that every time shuttle has a theft intercept program built into it, which will at a predetermined moment detonate a hidden bomb to blow both shuttle and thief to atoms.

This was the fate Alec had been rushing to meet when he'd detoured into my field. I could see it now so clearly, it was sitting on his chest like a scorpion, and he was totally unaware it was there. I didn't even need to sit through the play this time; I'd been handed the synopsis in terrible brevity.

"But what do you think you can do?" I said.

"Wreck them. Bankrupt them. Expose what they've been doing. Tell the whole world the truth," Alec growled, in just the same voice in which Nicholas had used to rant about the Pope. He squeezed my hand more tightly.

I couldn't talk him out of it. I never can. I had to try, though.

"But—Alec. Do you have any idea what you're going up against? These people know everything that's ever happened, or at least they know about every event in recorded history. That's why I can't think for a second you were really able to steal that shuttle from them. They must have known about it in advance, don't you see? And if they knew, it means they allowed you to steal it, and then—"

"No," he said, with grim and unshakable certainty. "See, I can't explain—just take it on trust, babe, they may know everything but they don't know everything about me. I found the chink in their armor. You could say I *am* the chink in their armor."

It was going to be the same old story, gallant Englishman going to his gallant death. Nothing I could do to change it at all.

Was there?

Was there?

I shook my head. "Don't say any more. I don't want to know."

"You don't need to," he said, giving me that brief cocksure grin again. "Just wait here, and I'll be back to rescue you. On my word of honor as a gentleman, Mendoza." He widened his eyes for emphasis.

"It's a kind offer, señor," I said. "But if I were to leave this station, the Company would know instantly. Besides, where would I go? I have no family. I have no legal identity."

Alec blinked. "But you've got to have a birth record at Global ID, at least."

Damned twenty-fourth-century databases. "Undoubtedly," I lied, "but the Company had it erased when I was sent here. They're that powerful, you know."

"That's true." He scowled. "We can fake you up an identification disc. I know

people who do that kind of thing. It wouldn't get you through customs anywhere, but . . . I know what'd do it! I could just marry you. Peers get everything
waived, see?"

I couldn't think what to say. He got a slightly panicked look in his eyes.

"A-and then afterward we could just get a divorce. They're easy. I could find
you a place to live and a job or something."

"Perhaps we could give it a try," I said carefully. He cleared his throat.

"I'm not just making the offer out of kindness, either. We could have some fun
together."

I leaned down, unable to keep myself from his mouth any longer, and I kissed
him. Actually I was going to do a lot more than kiss him—if I was going to throw
my immortal life away for Alec, I'd have such an epic game of lust with him first as
would make the fires of Hell seem lukewarm when I got there.

He still kissed like an angel of God, making little surprised and pleased noises
and groping feebly at my behind, but I felt his blood pressure going up, his heartbeat speeding dangerously, and the red numbers in my peripheral vision warned
me to stop or I'd kill him. I pulled away, sitting up and stroking back his hair.
"Don't you go dying on me," I gasped.

"I won't," he promised. He had got hold of the end of my braid and was tugging at it in a plaintive way. "But I'd really, really like to have sex with you. If
you've no objections or anything."

Caramba! Did he use that line on other women? But I'd bet it worked for him
every time. Who could resist that earnest look in his eyes when he said it? How
was I going to stop myself from ripping open that suit of fish-mail he was wearing and murdering him with carnal bliss?

Meteorological data coming in. Had that been thunder, or God snarling at me?
I babbled out some kind of promise to Alec and went to the window to confirm
visually.

Disturbed air. Domed clouds racing down the sky, all my surviving corn plants
staggering and fluttering as a gust of hot wind came rushing across them, carrying a smell of wetness and electricity. Crickets began to sing.

"There's a cloud front advancing," I told Alec. "Have you brought rain, like the
west wind? I think we're going to have a summer storm."

"Cool," said Alec. Christ, I wanted to jump him then and there.

But he was ill and he needed protein, needed fluids, needed rest. I do have
some basic programming that insists I serve the mortal race, even if I bypass it
now and then to kill one of the poor little things; so I poured Alec a glass of iced
tea and set about preparations for feeding him.

"What do you do here, all the time?" Alec said, as I returned from the garden with some produce.

"I grow vegetables," I said.

"Who eats 'em all? Not you all alone." He sipped his tea and looked at it in surprise. "This is real tea!"

"Thank you. You obviously know about Dr. Zeus; do you know anything about the Day Six resorts?" I unloaded what I was carrying onto my kitchen table: tomatoes, corn, peppers, cilantro, garlic, onions. He knitted his brows.

"They're like one of those urban myths, only they're really real," he said. "Like Dr. Zeus. Everybody knows there's supposed to be some company that has time travel and can get you absolutely anything you want, but it's just a rumor. Which is what they probably want us to think! And the Day Six places are the same way. Somebody did a *Weird Stories* thing on holo about one. This guy goes back in time to party and screws up history by stepping on a bug or something." He had another sip of his tea.

"Ah. Well, that's a fable, because history can't be changed." I worked the hand pump to rinse off the tomatoes and peppers. "But the resorts do exist, just as Dr. Zeus exists. In fact, Dr. Zeus owns them. Nice little string of hotels, rather unexceptional except that they're all located in 150,000 BCE. Or thereabouts. All of them in virgin wildernesses where long-extinct mammals can be observed gamboling, from behind the safety of an electronic perimeter field.

"You're from the future, Alec, you must have lived in steel canyons all your life. How much would you pay to be able to swim in waters that had never been polluted, or watch a herd of mammoths grazing?"

"In all the stories, time travelers wind up as lunch for velociraptors," he said.

"All the dinosaurs are extinct in this time. Anyway: Dr. Zeus has quietly built up a select secret clientele in the twenty-fourth century. They pay fortunes, annual incomes of small countries, I'm told, to be rocketed backward through time to carefully landscaped virgin paradises where they can relax by the pool and breathe clean, clean air." I selected a knife and began slicing up the tomatoes.

"The only problem is—time travel is hard on the human body. Even the drugs that protect people make them ill. So when they arrive from the dismal future, these millionaires and heiresses can do no more than nibble at a lettuce leaf or two. Therefore Dr. Zeus makes damned sure the resort keeps all manner of trendy greens for salad on hand, and therefore I labor in the sun on this agricultural station." I whacked a beefsteak tomato in half, imagining it was some Company CEO's head.

"But that's awful." Alec tried to sit up, looking outraged. "That means you're not only their prisoner, you're their slave!"

He was an idealist, then. Disapproved of slavery, did he? And him a titled gentleman. Just the sort of wealthy young man who comes to loathe his birthright and goes off to die for somebody else's freedom.

"I suppose I am," I said carefully. "But I may as well be of some use to somebody, don't you think? And it's not so bad. They don't call for produce very often. I have a lot of time to work on my own private research."

"What's your research?" Alec said.

I told him all about my quest to perfect maize plants. I don't think he understood one word in three of botany talk, and when he wrinkled his forehead and attempted to follow my lecture he looked like a puzzled dog. But he was awfully polite about it, unlike the other Future Children I've known, and said gallant things about how worthwhile my project was.

We talked for a little while on the subject of making one's life count for something, and I expected a manifesto from him on the need to actively oppose the evils of Dr. Zeus. I was surprised; he just talked about his life. Despite his grand title, it appears there were some unfortunate circumstances attending his birth again. Some poor girl seduced by the sixth earl and then abandoned? I'd hardly have thought the wretched Future Children had enough blood in them to carry on like that, but apparently mortal nature hasn't changed so much.

As near as I could make out, the girl went mad and was locked up. Alec seems to have grown to manhood with a devastating sense of his own worthlessness, not surprisingly. I wonder if Nicholas and Edward carried similar burdens of unearned guilt on their backs? Was that what fueled Nicholas's drive to martyrdom, Edward's selfless work for an empire that abandoned him? I was too young and foolish to see this in Nicholas, too rushed to see it in Edward; but I see it now. And Alec's failed at two marriages, apparently, and has steered through his life in increasing emotional isolation. Is that why he's always alone when I meet the man?

When he saw he'd affected me, blurting out his wretched story, he made amends by changing the subject entirely and told me about the adventures he's had, as I kneaded the masa for our commonplace supper of tamales.

And what adventures he's had! I begin to see that I have been somewhat mistaken about Future World. It seems he hasn't grown up in steel canyons at all. It seems that there are still wild places in the twenty-fourth century, still gardens and forests that don't stink of machine exhaust. Best of all, it seems that the mortal race has not entirely followed the crabbed and fearful lead of its Company scientists, people like Mr. Bugleg of loathsome memory.

Though they are, all of them, undeniably childish. Future Children indeed. My own dearest love has bought himself a *pirate ship*, if you please, and spends most of his time sailing around in the Caribbean and other ports of call on what we used to call the Spanish Main! And there he indulges his urge to be virile and bad, like pirates in every film he's ever seen, and he's become a smuggler! Mostly of things like wine and cheese, though they're illegal enough in the twenty-fourth century.

And yet I think in this he must come nearer to living a real life than the other mortals of his time, who (as far as I was ever able to tell) spend their lives hiding in their rooms, playing electronic games.

Still, he has found a far less harmless and silly way to rebel, hasn't he, by going on a crusade against Dr. Zeus? Dangerous to think about.

Anyway. Such lovely stories he told me, about Jamaica under the tropical stars, parrots and gold doubloons. How happy I was to think of him playing Errol Flynn among the shrouds and ratlines. This ship of his must really be something to see, a full-rigged sailing vessel utilizing twenty-fourth-century technology, sort of an enormous retro yacht. He has some kind of complex computer system running all the rigging apparatus, for there's no crew at all apparently.

It's as though he were able to lose himself in *Treasure Island*, escaping from his unhappiness by making the wild sea and the pirates come to life for him—except that instead of his imagination, he's used enormous sums of money and technology. What am I to make of such a brave new world?

Who cares? It was enough for me to watch the way his face lit up when he described his adventures, watch his expressive face and gestures conveying his stories perfectly even in that thug's idiom of his. The man should have gone on the stage, I always thought, and what a preacher he'd made!

And he sang for me. He had been describing how his ex-wives had hated his singing, the repulsive harpies. I was overwhelmed with a sudden memory of Nicholas singing, making some Tudor bawdiness sublime with his dark tenor. So I begged him to sing something, and he obliged with old sea songs, blood-and-thunder ballads that somehow reduced me to a weepy mess.

At last he reached up his hand and pulled me down beside him, and there I lay hearing his voice vibrate in his chest and throat. We were shortly embracing again, me scanning frantically to see if his brain was likely to explode this time. It was of course impossible that after three hours of rest and a glass of iced tea the man should be completely recovered from transcendence shock, but he was.

He was twiddling experimentally with the fastenings of my coveralls, and I was wondering how his mail-suit unzipped, when something seemed to occur to him. He lifted his mouth from mine and looked down at me. "Er—"

"What is it?" I said, desperate lest he should stop.

"You're a virgin, I guess, yeah?"

Have I mentioned that the man is prone to scruples at the most inconvenient times?

Of course I'm not a virgin, but I do have this sort of immortal self-repairing body, see, and in the three hundred and then three thousand years that had elapsed between our respective couplings, there had been more than ample time for a tiny unimportant membrane to grow back. Christ, I could have grown a leg back in that amount of time.

"Yes," I said. "It's all right, though. Please."

But now he was self-conscious, and the gorgeous python that had materialized down one leg of his suit shrank a little. "Can I use your shower?"

Mother of God! Had I mentioned he's very clean in his personal habits as well? And me without a shower.

I was stammering to explain about my pathetic tin washtub when we both realized it had been raining outside for some time, warm summer rain. I directed him out into my back garden and hurried to fetch him a clean towel.

He always has enjoyed bathing. Something Freudian relating to guilt, perhaps? Edward seemed to have some sort of personal dirt-repellent force field, of course, but I remember the way Nicholas used to revel in clean water and soap.

When I opened the door and stepped out under the overhang, Alec had already snaked out of the mail-suit and was sitting in the tub, wearing only that torque. He was leaning back into the rain with an ecstatic expression on his face, letting it soak into his lank hair, which was becoming even lanker. The tub was rather low and didn't obscure much of his nakedness, and I made a small involuntary pleading sound.

He opened his eyes and looked at me. For a moment he seemed wary, defensive; then grinned his sidelong grin.

"Would you, er, like to bathe, too?" he asked, all suavity, gesturing invitation as though the tub were ever so capacious. I don't remember how I got out of my clothes and across the garden, it happened so fast.

It was insane. The storm was beating down on us, the tub was impossibly tiny, and I was worried about that long back of his—but oh, how that man could kiss. We writhed ineffectively for a few minutes before he simply stood up in the tub and hoisted me into the air as though I weighed no more than a feather. He is phenomenally strong. I slid down, pressed against his body, and he thrust his face into my breasts with a whoop of inarticulate glee. The rain bathed us, and the fragrance of the garden was sweet.

God, God, God.

I believe I was in the act of offering Him my soul, or whatever a thing like me has, if He'd only let this moment stretch out into eternity, when my groping hands found the pattern of electronic wire just under the skin of Alec's shoulders.

God?

I leaned forward over the top of Alec's head and looked down. It was like the most beautiful tattoo you can imagine, an intricate pattern of spirals and knot-work in dull silver, winging out over both his shoulder blades and twining up the back of his neck. But it was wire, installed subcutaneously and tapping somehow into his nervous system and brain. So that's what the torque was for? I touched it gingerly and had a momentary disorientation, a view of my own breasts seen from—well, not the angle I was used to, anyway.

"Alec, darling," I said cautiously, "this is a rather unusual tattoo you have."

He said something in reply, but under the circumstances it came out some-what muffled. I bit my lower lip and said: "I beg your pardon?"

He lifted his face to look up at me. "You know how I told you I've got this big custom cybersystem, to work the rigging on my ship? This is how I run it. I'm a cyborg, have been since I was eighteen."

Gosh, what a coincidence!

Though of course what he means by *cyborg* and what I would mean by the same word are entirely different things.

He looked alarmed until he realized I was laughing, and then he chuckled companionably and went back to what he'd been doing as I gasped out, over-whelmed by the cosmic joke:

"Oh, perfect—!" And then I thought I'd been struck by lightning, because the flash of revelation was very nearly that blindingly bright. I seized his face in both my hands and tilted it up to stare into his eyes. "*What* year did you say it was where you come from?"

"Er . . . 2351," he said, polite but confused.

"But that's only four years from—" I said, and then the whole mystery of my beloved came together. An extraordinary man, with extraordinary abilities, who bears a grudge against Dr. Zeus. A cyborg, and not a poor biomechanical slave like me but a free agent, with both the ability and the determination to slip through the Company's defenses and do the impossible. And what was that blue fire playing around our bodies? Oh, dear, it was Crome's radiation. Was I seeing the future?

And I didn't know the half of it yet.

I laughed and laughed. Then I writhed down and we embraced. Somehow or other we wound up on the lawn with the bath overturned beside us, and he was on top of me, peering down through the lightning flashes. He was looking into my eyes as though he'd only just recognized me.

And how good was it, what we did there on my tidy little lawn? I'll tell you. If I suffer in darkness for a thousand years because of what I did afterward—I won't care.

By great good fortune the water under the tamales had not quite boiled away by the time we went back inside, and the house was filled with the earthy smell of corn. I lit lamps and pulled on an old shirt to set out our supper. He wrapped a towel around his middle and sat down at my rough-hewn table, watching me lay places for us. Two places, after all this time.

Once, long ago, I'd laid out an intimate supper for two, just like this. We had sat together in a tiny circle of light at an old wooden table, in our own little world, as beyond in the darkness the wind howled and a hostile fate prepared to tear us to pieces the minute we stepped outside the circle.

It isn't really a happy memory. Nicholas had been sullenly desperate and I had been fearfully desperate, a good little cyborg feeling real qualms about running away with a mortal man. Before that night ended my heart had been broken irreparably, and Nicholas, furious and terrified, was running to meet his death. Thank you, Dr. Zeus.

But I'm an old wicked cyborg now, aren't I? Long past desperation. And how sweetly the rain beat on the roof of my house, and how snug and dry we were in my lamplit kitchen as the blue evening fell, and how sleepy and calm we were there together.

And calmly, over our supper, I did the first of the things that will damn me if I'm ever caught. I told Alec, in great detail, all about the Silence in 2355, together with some rather necessary bits of temporal physics to enable him to use that shuttle effectively. So very classified, and I divulged it! He knows, now, Dr. Zeus's fear of the unforeseen apocalypse; he knows his window of opportunity, and what to plan for over the next four years. Whatever his plans may be.

I gather he has some kind of ally he calls the Captain, who is apparently the captain of his ship, though I'm a little confused on this point because I also had the impression he sails alone. But this Captain may be dead, which is one of the things he's gone off to resolve/revenge.

The talk depressed him. He reached across the table and took my hand as we spoke. What kind of emotional life has he had? I could cheerfully kill his ex-wives, I think.

Oh, yes, I've changed. But I would burn in Hell for his dear sake.

I may yet.

He helped me wash the dinner dishes, and we hung his thermal underclothes up to dry before the fire, and at last we climbed into my narrow, creaking bed. Last time I'd lain in a real bed with him, he'd been Edward, and we'd been on the run all day and were too exhausted to do more than drift off to sleep together. Not this time! The bed has a permanent list to starboard now, and we were lucky it didn't collapse *in extremis*. I really ought to fix it, but I can't bear to. Just looking at it makes me smile.

He warmed me right through, my mortal lover, and afterward drifted off to sleep in my arms. I lay watching him by the light of the fire. I might have lain there studying him all night, newly fascinated by all the details I'd never forgotten: the cleft in his chin, the funny swirled patterns in the hair on his arms.

But the night wasn't mine to idle away so pleasantly.

I rose and pulled the blanket up around his shoulders. He sighed, reaching for me. I slipped out into the rainy night, to do the second thing for which I will surely suffer one day.

The shuttle lay dark and abandoned, its sprung hatch gaping open in the rain. I looked in and saw the tiny green lights on the control panel, dimly illuminating the access port. I made my assault, forced it to give up the secret I wanted.

The bomb was wired under the pilot's seat, of all obvious places. It was a tiny white Bakelite box that might have been anything, a fuse relay, a power seat servomotor, a container of breath mints that had fallen down under there and been forgotten. I knew better. I found the tool kit and snipped its vicious little wires, swung the shuttle's hatch shut, carried the bomb back with me through the gray rainy night and flung it into my compost heap. It's there now, as I write. It may yet be live and deadly, it may have been ruined by the rain and the muck; but it will never kill Alec, which is all that matters.

I came back and reentered paradise, slipping into the firelit room where my love slept safe. *Third time lucky, mortal man*, I thought.

He woke when I climbed back in beside him, grumbled a little, reached out his arms to pull me in close and tucked me under his chin, just as Nicholas used to do. I lay awake awhile longer, fighting conditioning nightmares; but I know them for the false programmed things they are now, and they can't scare me. I fell asleep at last, soothed by the rhythm of his heartbeat.

———

We didn't get out of bed for two full hours next morning. We did everything I'd ever done with Nicholas, who'd been amazingly adventurous for a late medieval fellow, and everything I'd ever done with Edward, who was a Victorian gentleman, which says all I need to say about *his* personal tastes. The bed sagged ever further toward a happy death.

Then we got up and I made him breakfast.

"I hope you like tacos," I said, spooning the hot filling into corn tortillas. "This seems so inadequate! I seldom dine in the morning, myself, just a roll or something to keep the coffee from killing me. No tea, no kippers, no sardines even. Nothing for an Englishman, but then I never expected to meet one here."

"That's okay," said Alec. He accepted a taco and bit into it cautiously. "It's not bad. What is it?"

"Proteus Breakfast Bounty," I told him with a sneer. "It approximates sausage. Not inspiring, but sustaining. The tortillas, at least, are real."

"I like 'em," he said.

"You *are* a gentleman," I said, pouring him out a mug of coffee. I poured a cup for myself and sat down across the table from him. "Well, then. Here we are."

"Mr. and Mrs. Checkerfield's Brunch Club," he said. God, it sounded strange in my ears. Mrs. Checkerfield? Or Lady Finsbury! Pretty good for somebody who began life in a one-room hut, eh? Child of Spanish peasants who owned maybe two goats and three fig trees? Too surreal to contemplate. I took a careful sip of coffee and said quietly:

"If you knew how often I've wished you were sitting right there—"

"I can't be what you wanted," he said. "You must have wished for somebody a lot better looking, in shining armor."

"No. You yourself are the man of my dreams, señor. I think we've met before, in some previous lifetime."

"You believe in that stuff?"

"Not really," I said. "Do you?"

He shook his head, wolfing down the last of the taco.

"Were you raised in any religion?"

"Nope," he said. "I was always taught that's for bigots and crazies. Not something you do if you're going to be a respectable member of the House of Lords, which I've never been anyway so who cares, right? But, you know. My stepmother got into the Ephesians, and they're kind of scary."

"That's what I'd always read."

"You read, too? They do a lot of good, though, for poor girls, so I guess they're okay. And my nurse was into something, I guess it must have been Orthodox Vodou. I think she took me to some of their services when I was small. That was nice, I remember, all the dancing, and those bright people coming out of nowhere like that."

Yes indeed, Nicholas, I thought, you've come a long way.

"Can I have another of those?" he inquired. Imagine someone actually liking Breakfast Bounty. But then I don't suppose he's ever eaten meat.

"Please," I said, pushing the plate across to him. "I made them for you. So, religion's not your thing, is it? What about politics?"

"I don't vote."

"No? Not very English of you, if you'll pardon my saying so."

"I can't stand England," he said wearily. "It's gray and it's cold and it's . . . it's just so sad. I couldn't wait to leave, and I hate it when I have to go back. You should see the absentee fines I pay every year to the House of Lords! You don't want to live there, I hope?"

"Oh, no."

"Good. You want to go see Spain again, though? You must not have seen it since you were little."

What a strange idea. "I wonder if I'd recognize it at all?" I said at last.

"It's fun there. Everything's really expensive, but you can get real fish in the restaurants and there's a festival day, like, every other week. I was there one time at—what's that big party the Jews throw, where they dress up and there's, er, a street carnival? Noisemakers and stuff? It's in the spring, anyway, and there's this big whatchacallem, temple thing—"

"A synagogue?"

"Yeah! A synagogue in, er, Santiago—"

"Santiago de Compostela?" I was stunned.

"Yeah! That's the place. Anyway it's great. Families build these booths all along the street and watch the dances and parades, and you can just go from booth to booth, drinking and eating and talking to people. The ones who understand English, anyway. And there's bullfights with topless girls! Amazing acrobats. They flip over the bulls like they were on springs or something. And then they have this thing at the end where they burn the parade floats."

"Not the people?" I just couldn't get my mind around this, somehow. Poor old Spain, freed at last from ancient sorrow and cruelty?

"Nah, they never have accidents. We should go sometime. You'd like it." He looked at me a little anxiously. "Though we can go anywhere you want, babe. Anywhere that'll make you happy."

"I'll be happy," I said, reaching across the table and clasping his hand. "You're not religious, you don't care about England, and there's a synagogue in Santiago de Compostela! We can go places or we can live on your ship. I don't care."

Assuming, of course, I can skip forward through time into the future—impossible, but apparently not for me. Could I really just sail away with Alec, on an eternal holiday in the twenty-fourth century?

Though of course it wouldn't be eternal, because he's a mortal. But I think if we could just once live out a peaceful life together, I could accept anything that came after that. Why have I felt this way, from the first moment I laid eyes on this big homely man? God only knows.

He lifted my hand and kissed it. "We'll go as soon as I've finished up this stuff I'm doing," he said.

"Ah, yes. This stuff you're doing," I said, looking down into my coffee, focusing on cold practical matters to keep from launching myself over the table at him. "There are some things you should know before you attempt to pilot that shuttle back to the twenty-fourth century. Somewhere on board, there ought to be little containers of the drug you have to take before time traveling. It looks like iodine, and I've heard it's sometimes packaged to look like Campari. Do they still make Campari?"

"Yes. I saw those."

"It's not Campari, but if you pour fifty milliliters into an equal amount of gin or vodka, you won't know the difference. You must drink it down, or risk death a second time when you activate the time transcendence field. I must tell you, I can't imagine how you were able to sit up and talk coherently only a couple of hours after your arrival, let alone get that magnificent erection."

He snickered in embarrassment.

"And you need to enter the proper algorithm into the time drive. I can do that for you now, but you'll have to know more about piloting the damned thing before you try to take it anywhere else."

"If my friend's still alive, he may have that data." Alec reached for another taco.

"He was going after Dr. Zeus's *database*?" I felt ice around my heart. "Oh, Alec. There aren't even words for how dangerous that is."

"We did it once already and got out okay," Alec said. But I buried my face in my hands.

"Don't tell me, darling. The less I know, the safer you'll be."

We lingered over breakfast. He helped me wash up again. I helped him into his armored suit that had been airing out on a hook by the door all night, like a sealskin temporarily abandoned by its owner. I wanted to see if we might contrive a way to make love while he was encased in it, but he's a man on a mission, after all, with places to go and things to do.

The rain had stopped and the clouds blown away by the time we walked back to the shuttle. It was going to be a hot day. Steam was already rising up from the sparkling fields. When we got to the shuttle and Alec stood there staring up at it, I could tell from the look on his face he was uncertain what he was supposed to do next.

So I drove the third nail into my coffin.

I leaned close to him and put my arms around his neck. "You'll remember," I said, finding the torque with my fingers. "It's just the effect of the crash. Calm down. Think." I tapped into his database and nearly passed out at its immensity. If he were to download even half of what he has access to, my brain would burst. But I did experience the world through his senses for a moment, and that was nearly as disturbing.

He has . . . SENSES. His hearing, his eyesight, touch, are all hyperacute and informative. He draws in a breath of air and its component scents tell him more about where he is than even a hunting dog could discern, at least as much as an immortal like me. He sees farther into certain light ranges than a mortal is supposed to be able to, and the sensitivity of his skin . . . no wonder he likes his physical pleasures.

Is my mortal darling even human? I wondered.

I always thought he'd make a better immortal than any of the people the Company ever chose, and now I know it for a fact. If only his skull fit the optimum parameters!

I mustered my thoughts and probed for the information he needed. There it was; he simply hadn't learned how to access it yet. I pulled it up and said: "I have the impression that the cyborgs who normally pilot these ships access them through a file with a designation of TTMIX333." I fed it to him surreptitiously. "Does that sound right?"

His brain took it with remarkable ease. I felt him gasp in pleasure as it all made sense, suddenly. He began to download from me, lifting a subroutine for fast access by content with such speed I felt like a wrung-out sponge.

"I think—Hey!" he said in delight, as the hatch popped open. I teetered back from him, dizzy and frightened.

"There you are," I said, determined to sound cheery. "You see? You had it in your memory all the time. Dear me, though, this fancy carpet's gotten soggy." I climbed inside and stopped, staring as he climbed in after me.

Fancy carpet indeed. What luxury! I hadn't bothered to look around much when I'd been in here removing the bomb.

Floral pattern in the carpet and the beautifully cushioned passengers' seats. Drink rests, crystal vases set in the wall, for God's sake, full of pink roses! Spacious, lots of head room for anyone but Alec. Tasteful color scheme. Minibar. Entertainment console. All this to keep the Future Children happy on their weekend escapes from their own world. Not how we immortals travel. I was sent to this station in a raw-edged metal box barely big enough to accommodate my body. It couldn't be bigger, we were always told. The extra time-field drag would take more energy, cost more money, which couldn't be spared for inessentials like comfort.

What did it cost to send this shuttle through time even once?

Is this why we've worked so hard all these years? To pay for things like this?

Alec bent down and flung wide the etched glass doors of the minibar. "Check this out. Six different fruit juices and three kinds of real booze. Illegal as hell, and I should know." He chuckled. "Bombay Sapphire, Stolichnaya and—hey, here's the magic potion." He held up a dummy bottle of Campari. All nicely disguised as a cocktail, so Future Children would never know how dangerous their pleasure excursions really were.

I was so angry I could barely trust myself to speak, but while he gulped down his bitter cocktail I managed to explain about taking the earth's rotation and orbit into account, for one travels through space as well as time and you must run as fast as you can to remain in one place, whenever you get there. Alec knit his brows in comprehension—he may not be able to read very well, but he seems to be brilliant at math—and ordered the shuttle to set its course. It promptly obeyed him.

The warning lights began to implore us to close the hatch, and the gas canisters gave their initial hiss as the valves engaged. I wasn't ready to lose him yet! But I'd be a danger to him in more ways than he could imagine if I went along. I backed toward the hatch, and he held out his hand.

"Remember," he said. "I'm coming back for you."

"Meminerunt omnia amantes," I said, falling into an old habit.

"What?" He stared. "Was that Spanish? What did you say?"

Still no World Language in his century, I note. Must be the nationalist backlash.

"Lovers remember everything," I translated. "I was speaking Latin." He got that worried-dog look again.

"What's Latin?"

My God, the progress of human knowledge.

"Like, Latin American?" he asked.

"Close enough, dear," I said ruefully, but then the Klaxons really began to protest about the hatch and I couldn't stay. I dove back, kissed him one last time, and fled through the hatch before I doomed us both.

I ran around to the window where I'd seen him first. He was fastening himself into his seat restraints. He saw me and mouthed *I love you* in silence. I shouted it back to him, over the scream of the engines and the turbulence, until I was hoarse. He leaned forward, staring out over the console as the shuttle began to rise and I reached up my hands toward him, watching until the yellow gas roiled and hid him from my sight.

Up and up went the shuttle, a perfect ascent, and then it rotated and became a streak of silver, leaving my time with just the barest thud on the insulted air. No master pilot could have done it better, no immortal cyborg with a thousand years' training, but I'd only had to show Alec once.

What have I done?

I told myself, as I walked back to the house, that it could have been worse. Nicholas would have roared off with that shuttle to carpet-bomb the Vatican, and I shudder to think what Edward would have done with it. Alec, however, is an arrested child who won't even vote. Digging for pirate treasure is his idea of a good time.

And even if he succeeds in his quest—would the world be such a terrible place without the Company's obsessive control? Dr. Zeus has been in power since Time began. What if *nobody* was running the world? Maybe all those lost art treasures could go into museums, instead of the collections of rich men. Maybe those rare beasts could be turned loose into that strangely depopulated future world, to survive or not on their own merits.

Speaking of rare beasts . . . are you ready for the punchline, now?

The first thing I did on returning to my little abode was to collect DNA samples from the abundant evidence Alec, ahem, left of his presence. Hair on the pillow and all that. Ran a few tests. What a surprise.

He's a tetraploid. Like my maize cultivars. Double DNA. Ninety-two chromosomes. The only tetraploid hominid who ever existed was the (understandably) extinct *Homo crewkernensis*, known only from a few odd-looking bones and, of course, Company operatives who went back through time to see what could possibly have left such long femurs in the fossil record . . . hmmm.

What did the operatives report? That they found a small population with a barely viable gene pool, living at the southwestern edge of the ice sheet that covered England. Decided they were some kind of *Homo heidelbergensis* community that had been isolated long enough for distinct speciation to occur. Dutifully recorded their extinction, once the ice sheet melted and *Homo crewkernensis* were able to move east, where they encountered tribes with whom they could not interbreed successfully (lethal recessive affected the females) and who objected to their territorial aggression.

I wonder if the Company saved any of their genetic material?

Oh, we've gone way, way beyond any romantic metaphysics to do with reincarnation, haven't we? Alec is no member of any human race I've ever encountered. Fancy my never suspecting that in all these centuries, eh? I don't know what he is, but what I do know about him is far too much for the Company's liking. And I already knew more than was safe . . . I am *so* doomed.

. . . You know, when I was a mortal child, my mother sold me to a band of wicked strangers. They told me I'd be married to a great lord. When I finally peered into the room where they were hiding my betrothed, what was there?

Only a straw man, a thing braided out of wheat of the field, the bright-ribboned Lord of the Corn, destined for the festival bonfire. Maybe the strangers meant to sacrifice me with him. Maybe my inescapable fate has always been, one day, to burn in that fire.

But it's been almost a week now, and nobody's come for me yet.

I suppose it all hinges on how closely I'm being monitored, whether my auditory and visual intake is being recorded and analyzed somewhere or just recorded and stored. It might be years before some bored clerk decides to have a look at what I've been doing. Who knows whether Alec will have succeeded in his quest by that time? I might never be found out.

If, on the other hand, analysis is instantaneous—then I'm certainly going to learn whether or not Dr. Zeus has devised a way to grant its weary immortals the gift of death. Is this crawling sensation fear for *myself*? How novel.

And if what I've done has really set in motion the events that will lead to the end of the world, I'll deserve whatever the Company does to me. It would be a pity, really. I'd have liked to have made that sad mortal happy, sailed away with him on his absurd pirate ship and been Mrs. Alec Checkerfield. Don't want to think about that too much.

On the other hand, if Alec fails, dies as Nicholas and Edward died—perhaps his hungry soul won't need to come back for me, if I too am hit by the bolt of Dr. Zeus's wrath. Can I go through that doorway of fire, where Nicholas waited for me?

It's so strange, waiting to see.

———

Rain again today, but I think it'll blow out later, and another astonishing thing has happened.

Got up this morning and took my usual perambulation down to Avalon Bay, *and something had washed up on the beach.* I could smell it long before I got there, though it really isn't so badly decomposed as all that, but, you know—fish stink.

Except this isn't a fish, exactly. It's an ichthyosaur! And to think I told Alec there were no dinosaurs in this time period.

You can keep your stupid coelacanths. There it is, large as life, which seems to have been 7.5 meters long. I've taken a full hour of holo footage, from every possible angle. I managed to turn it over with a shovel, which was unfortunate because I promptly lost my breakfast (*much* more decomposed on that side) but this gave me a good view of its skeletal structure for the camera. So much for its being extinct! I really should get some DNA samples before the seabirds get it all. Actually I should signal for a Company ichthyologist, I suppose, but under the circum—

Ship has arrived out front. Not Alec's stolen shuttle. Maybe Dr. Z fish specialist come to see discovery?

Oh dear. There are uniformed security techs searching through my compost heap.

My own beloved, it would have been fun. Good-bye Alec Edward Nicholas. *Quia fortis est ut mors dilectio dura s*

Extract from the Text of Document D

6 Maye 1579

33 deg 20 min The two ilands here shewn as *La Victoria & San Salvador*, Moone hath sighted at nine o'clock today. We determined to try whether da Silva spake truth or no, or rather spake the lye concerning this Ile of Divells, that this was a devise to conceal rich store of plate hid in the caves hereabouts.

Wherfore we lay off *San Salvador* to the windward, but I lyked it not so well, ther being no convenyent shoare but onely great clyffes. I was not minded to go on a fooles exspedycyone; but Moone swore great oaths he should bring back gold bollyone yf I pleased to lett him take the pinnace & som two or three good fellows that durst go, being not afeard, whether of divells nor men. I gave orders therfore (that he should) lower the pinnace & away. With him went Carie & the Kentishman Crokeham, who hath ever madly sworn & thirsted after Spaynysh bloode, & I thowght it best to lett him go his ways. We then lay at anchor vntyll three o'clock, Iohn & I painting the whiles the passage between the two ilands. From the main top then Legge descried the pinnace returning. When it came nigh enough Moone cryed that we should up anchor & away for the Ile was truly full of divells and fowll poysons. We took them up in the pinnace, Moone & Carie much afeard & Crokeham in a sound, & with them a boxe or kist of great weight. This boxe when opened was found to carry som manner of brasse plate & suche as I will nott name herein save that Dee hath the same at his house in Mortlake, as I haue seen with mine own eyes. Ther were besides som glasse vialls & two lyttell bottels that had benn alyke filled with sherrisacke as they thowght, but Crokeham had oped & drunk one of the same thence fallen dead drunk or poysoned, we knew not which.

This much hath Moone & Carie sworn, thow questioned together & apart: that they went into the iland & climbed a long hill, seeing nether caves, nor divells, nor plate, but onely goats. That Crokeham, desiring we should haue fresh meate, gave chase to the said goats, & had laid hands upon one, but that it vanished into air lyke a thing bewitched. They did then stare and tremble, the whiles they could plainly hear the hooves of the said goat strikyng stones but saw him not.

Then a horrible wonder, for as Crokeham stretched forth his hand, it seemed gone off his arm as though he were made mutilate, though he felt no blow nor paine; & upon drawing it backe he saw he was hoooll & well, his hand as good as it was before.

Wherfore they knew ther was som divellish illvsione here & Crokeham, though he boast overmuch, yeat he is no coward, & was minded to try what was concealed in this iland. He did walk forrward & both Moone and Carie do sweare they saw him goe as thow the earth gaped under him, thow yeat they did hear him speakyng, yeat they saw him not. They sowt to follow him & after 3 paces beheld him again & beheld too a cave mowth lyke a mine that men haue made, which sure the illvsione was to conceal.

Wherin they went a lyttell ways & beheld a lampe, but what manner of lampe it was they connot tell, but that it was not candle nor rvshlight nor in any manner what light we vse to haue, but onely lyke a white windoe in the tunnell wall, through which light shone but no thing could be seene, & it was more lyke the moones beams then sun.

& farther, that ther were dwarfish divells lying dead therabout, that fell to ashes when Crokeham smote one with his foote. & farther, that the said boxe was ther. Wherfore Crokeham took it up and they left that place, being not minded to see any farther thervnto.

Now they fell to quarreling who should open the said boxe, whether they should themselves ther by reason of any danger that myght lie therin, or bring it a board first. At last Carie gave order Crokeham should open (the box).

& seeing therin no treasure, & being as they thowght themselves cheated {for that they did not knowe how Dee & Waylsinghamme bid me take especyall care to find the verie same when I lay at Mortlake} they were sorely vexed; & that Crokeham swore he would tast of the sacke, & broke the seal one 1 bottel & drank it off straight. Therafter he grew hotte, & cryed the divells were come alive after them {though Moone & Carie could see none suche} and ran before them to the pinnace, wher on a sudden he sounded and lay lyke 1 dead. Thither haue they come in fear of their lives, rowing hard & bearing him along in the bottom of the pinnace.

Now haue I geuen order they shall tell no tale of this to any, being questioned privily, but most especyallye Iohn Douty, & the boxe I haue made safe, nor shall Flettcher tell of the same. Upone Crokeham haue we set watch, as it is now nine o'clock at night & he waketh not, but lieth as dead still.

9 Maye, 1579

This fearful marvel I mvst set down, that Crokeham who was poysoned in *San Salvador* hath not yeat waked, but lieth asleepe yeat, & worse, though it myght not be worse an he were wakyng. This Crokeham was in Rochester to see the holy Martyrs burn, wherby you may know he is not yonge, but even a man of mine own age, & bore som white in his bearde & bore divers scars beside, for he hath fought bravely against Spayne since that he saw the Martyrs die, seekyng ever means to quarrel for their sakes. Lo, since that he hath lain thus, all his scars are gone. So is the snow melted out of his beard, which is grown soft & small lyke the beard of a boye. & Flettcher who hath the care of him hath prated that that Ile shall be called in our mappe *Insula Endymione*, but I haue geuen order he shall hold his fooles tong lest he engender fear in the saylers, & Crokeham hath benn lain alone in Iohn's cabin lest more talke betyde.

12 Maye, 1579

That Crokeham who hath grown yonge sleepeth yeat, & though he be yonge still he is yeat not well, for he be much reddened in the face & breathes him hard lyke a whale blowing. I haue seen this in men with too greate effvsione of blood to the brain or as doctors call (it,) grosse apoplectickal humours. Wherfore I am in som dowte whether to physicke him with bleeding or no, lest that he be weake and dye therby, or that the poysone that is in him should fowllly contaminate vs all.

Flettcher saith belyke the sacke was som draughte as thatte devised by Paracelsvs to make a manne yonge again, & as proofe of this tells me it be knowen that Spayne hath sowt suche in the natural watters of Florida, the which I knew afore, but I told him nott, only that he should speak noe carelesse word therof. Privily I doe consyder with myselfe whether it is not so, & the bottel had suche a draughte therin; & that Crokeham had come to noe harm had he not drunke it all incontynent, but by excesse is strucke down. Yf it be so, Dee mvst haue the other (bottle) to prove. Belyke the draughte, yf tempered with som more gentler physicke, may yeat serve to grant long youthe to our soverign Ladie, to the lasting checke of Spayne.

Wherfore I haue locked the said boxe safe away, noe man but I to know wher vntyll {As Christ Jesu grant} I see Deptford & maye convey it to Waylsynghamme, wher he shall do as he thinks most mete. I haue sworn to Flettcher his face that an he prate more in this, he shall be soundly whipt.

19 Maye, 1579

This daie dyed Crokeham, at two o'clock in the morning, after a great palsie that shook him upwards of three owers. Had I never met him afore but onely at the last ower I would haue said & sworn that the poor knave were a boye of syxeteen, though he is fowllly dead for all that. I gave order he should be made away privily, Moone and Carie to bring the round shot & wynding sheete & bear all. This was done & we commytted him to the sea & Flettcher spake the office for the dead, spedelley & quiet in the dark. & at first lighte I spake to the saylers and said: That the manne was dead, by poyson as we thowght, throw his rash want of forethowght, but noe strange thyng attended his going as som myght unwisely saye. & this they well understood & drew off their cappes but murmured nott, wherat I was well pleased.

THE YEAR 2350:

THE MEETINGS OF THE INKLINGS NOUVEAU

In the year 2350, Oxford University was located at No. 10 Albany Crescent in London. There was a small sign over the doorway telling visitors so. If there had been such things as postmen in that day and age, the local one would have smiled indulgently and shaken his head every time he dropped letters through the slot in the front door. But there were no postmen in the year 2350, and no letters for them to deliver if there had been, and anyway the letter slot had been sealed shut for two centuries to prevent the insertion of small bombs, incendiary devices, or venomous reptiles.

By and large the only people who noticed the sign were tourists strolling through the historical district of Georgian terraces, who usually stood there staring at it for a moment before frowning, turning to each other and saying something like:

"Wasn't Oxford University supposed to be *bigger?*"

"Wasn't it supposed to be in, uh, Oxford or something?"

"Was Oxford in London?"

"I don't know."

They would usually wander off in mutual confusion, and the portly man watching from the window at No. 10 would chuckle and rub his hands. His hands were usually cold. He'd shiver, then, and pull his tweed jacket tighter around himself. It didn't button in front (it had been made a long time ago for a much thinner man), but it was a genuine tweed and he was terribly proud of it, which was why he wore it on conference days. Conference days were special, because then his colleagues would arrive at No. 10 and they'd have a brainstorming session.

On this particular day he turned from the window and went to the fine old oak table, where he'd carefully arranged his props. He had an antique stoneware jug full of ginger beer and three tankards—not pewter, unfortunately, but twentieth-century aluminum copies were the closest thing available in 2350. He had a stack of real books prominently displayed, moldy and swollen with age. He'd actually attempted to read one of them, once, but the first page had crumbled so badly he had closed the book and looked over his shoulder fearfully, expecting the wrath of the curator, forgetting that he was the curator now.

He had a humidor on the table, too, and a rack with three actual pipes, black and ancient. There hadn't been tobacco in the humidor in over a century, but if you lifted the china lid you could still detect a faint perfume of vanilla and whiskey. If he was so bold as to take up one of the pipes and set his lips to its amber stem (having first made sure nobody was watching him), he could inhale an air of sensuous old poisons, burnt tar, bitterness, faintly salty.

Rutherford (that was the portly fellow's name—well, not his real name, but reality was what you made it, after all) very nearly put a pipe in his mouth now, but thought better of it. The others would arrive at any moment, and so far he'd never dared that particular affectation in front of anybody. His colleagues, of all people, would probably understand; but he valued their friendship too highly to risk disgusting them. They were the only friends he'd ever had, hard to find as a real tweed jacket or a briar pipe in 2350.

Need I mention that Rutherford wasn't really an Englishman? He had, in fact, been born on Luna, to parents of American extraction. As a child, though, he'd fallen in love with the idea of England. He wore out three copies of *The Wind in the Willows* with continuous viewing, listened to nothing but Beatles and PunxReich, never missed an episode of *Doctor Who* (and could name all three hundred and fifteen Doctors). He even owned a couple of heavily censored Shakespeare plays. Being a fat asthmatic little boy, he'd taken refuge in the green country behind his eyes, so often and so completely that he'd been diagnosed an eccentric by the authorities.

He was also very bright, though, as brightness went in the twenty-fourth century, and his parents knew certain important people. The diagnosis was changed from eccentric to creative, and instead of being sent to a residential hospital he was shipped down home for training as a museum curator. While he was there, certain work he did came to the attention of Dr. Zeus, Inc.

They sent a headhunter to interview him. A bargain was struck, and the Company agreed to pull a number of strings. When he turned twenty-one he'd been sent to England, and had lived a happy and fulfilled life there ever since.

As happy and fulfilled as one could be in the twenty-fourth century, anyway.

Now he was a fat asthmatic little man of thirty, with a receding hairline and a ginger mustache that made him look silly. His appearance was improved if he put on the gold-rimmed spectacles he'd bought from an antique dealer; then he looked like a person in an old photograph. Sometimes he did that, too, staring at himself in a long mirror for hours at a time, imagining he was somebody Victorian. He never put the spectacles on where anybody but his friends could see, of course. He'd got rid of his Luna accent, too, carefully cultivating an English one that was a kind of polyglot of cinema Cockney, late twentieth-century Transatlantic, and Liverpudlian. It wasn't entirely satisfactory.

Bang! He jumped straight off the floor—hard to do down here on Earth—before he realized that someone was actually using the polished brass knocker to announce themselves. With a sheepish smile he hurried out into the hall and opened the door.

"Chatty, old man!" he said heartily.

"Sorry I'm late," said Frankie Chatterji. That *was* his real name. His great-grandparents had self-consciously changed it to Chatterton, but when he'd graduated he'd decided to honor the glories of the Raj and changed it back. Rutherford envied him terribly. He had no need to study an accent; he'd been born in upper-class London, scion of a long line of civil servants, an elegantly spare fellow with a *café au lait* complexion and smoky blue eyes. He affected tuxedoes and moreover had a jade cigarette holder, in which he kept a menthol inhalator. It had nearly got him arrested more than once, before he could explain about his sinus condition, but there was no one to compare with him for sheer style.

He stepped into the hall now and shrugged out of his opera cape. Rutherford took it eagerly and hung it up for him, saying:

"Well, you're here before Foxy, anyroad."

He was referring to Foxen Ellsworth-Howard, the third member of their fellowship, who was at this moment having a bitter argument with a public transport operator. Ignorant of his plight, Chatterji strolled into the parlor and surveyed the careful preparations with approval.

"I *say*," he enunciated, striding over to the tapestry Rutherford had hung up above the fireplace. It depicted unicorns in a rose garden. It had been manufactured in Taiwan of purple rayon, but Rutherford thought it was one of the most beautiful things he'd ever seen, and Chatterji was inclined to agree with him. There was another on the opposite wall depicting Merlin the Magician, equally cheap and hideous, but Chatterji's thin face warmed as he turned to regard it.

"This is really something! Where'd you get these, Rutherford?"

"Sotheby's." Rutherford beamed. "Late twentieth century! Set the mood, don't you think? I'll have to take them down before the tours tomorrow, but I sort of thought—you know—they'll be like our flags. Like outside a palace to show the king's in residence. Magic is in residence here! Jolly good, what?"

"Jolly good," said Chatterji, and made a mental note to view a few more Sherlock Holmes holoes. Rutherford's accent was dreadful, but his grasp of archaic British idiom was far better than Chatterji's.

A battering on the brass knocker announced the belated arrival of Foxen Ellsworth-Howard, and the first thing he said on entering was "It's shracking freezing in here!"

Shrack was an extremely nasty word, first coined to describe a particular immoral act that had become possible with twenty-second-century technology. Ellsworth-Howard's friends winced slightly, but only slightly.

Ellsworth-Howard had been born to devout NeoPunks, and disappointed them terribly when he'd become a scientist. His retaliation was dressing in antique clothes, the baggy trousers and waistcoats that Rutherford also loved; but he could do nothing about the speech patterns he'd learned at his mother's knee, nor the fact that she'd had his hair permanently removed when he was six and replaced with a pattern of steel rivets, for the good of his character (believing, as she did, that one ought to give children painful obstacles to shape their personalities). An attempt to tattoo the appearance of hair had only succeeded in making his head look dirty, and wigs wouldn't sit right because of the rivets, which couldn't be removed without losing the trust fund his mother had also settled on him. All this, with the bipolar emotional disorder for which he took daily medication, made him terribly cross most of the time.

But he, like Chatterji and Rutherford, was a certified genius in his particular field, and that was what had brought them together in the first place.

"Whyn't you turn on the climate control?" Ellsworth-Howard inquired, looking around.

"Because I've got a surprise, chaps," said Rutherford. He ran to the nineteenth-century fireplace and gestured at the objects stacked in the grate. There were three of them, grayish cylinders about the thickness of a man's arm and half as long. "Look! They're Fibro-Logs from a mountain survival kit. Watch and observe, men." He drew out a tiny steel box and thumbed a lever on its side, causing a jet of flame to leap up from the top. He held it down to the objects in the grate. After a long moment (during which he twice dropped the lighter with a hiss of pain) the objects caught, and flame crawled along them and a thin stream of smoke flowed up the chimney.

"Shrack me," gasped Ellsworth-Howard.

"Are you mad, man?" said Chatterji. "We'll be arrested!"

"Nope," said Rutherford, somewhat muffledly around his burnt thumb. "This is a historical structure. It's got a fire permit, if you're doing a historical re-creation. And we are, don't you see? We're the Inklings Nouveau! We're having a creative meeting of minds, just the way the Oxford dons used to. Haven't we got the beer and the pipes and the books? And the cozy armchairs? If somebody from the twentieth century looked in on us right now, he'd think we were real. Except for some little details that don't really matter," he finished uncomfortably, glancing at Ellsworth-Howard's gleaming head.

Ellsworth-Howard and Chatterji looked at each other with a certain guilty glee. "Blimey," said Ellsworth-Howard at last, making an attempt to match the mood. "Why shouldn't we get away with it? Aren't we all the Oxford University there is, nowadays? Come on, guys." He caught hold of an antique chair and shoved it close to the fire.

"Chaps," suggested Rutherford.

"Yeah, chaps, I meant."

In no time they were cozily ensconced in chairs about the fire, and Rutherford had handed around mugs of ginger beer. There was a long moment of silence that was more than contented; it was reverent, sacred almost. The transforming magic of anachronism hung in the air like incense.

"Shakespeare must have sat like this," said Rutherford and sighed.

"Shracking C. S. Lewis too." Ellsworth-Howard shut his eyes. "Only of course it'd have been real beer."

"Or ale," Chatterji said wistfully. "Or port, or sherry. Or tea! You know what we need? We need one of those cabinet things with fancy bottles and stuff in them. I could get some grape juice. We could pretend it was port."

"Yeah! Yeah! Capital." Rutherford wriggled with excitement. "And something brown for tea or sherry. What could we get that was brown?"

"Prune juice is dark brown," said Ellsworth-Howard. "Maybe if we mixed it with some apple juice?"

"Well, that's definitely on the list for our next meeting," said Rutherford, and reaching into his pocket he drew out a tiny electronic memorandum and jotted a picture of an apple and a wrinkly prune with the stylus. "I'll see what I can get at Harrods."

"First rate," said Chatterji. They all sat there, immensely pleased with themselves. The fire in the grate burned cheerily, brightening their pale faces, warming the washed-out light of a gray summer day in London.

"We'd better do some work," said Ellsworth-Howard at last, groaning. "Or I might just sit here being happy all shracking afternoon."

"Right. Shall I give my report?" Chatterji set down his tankard and struck an attitude, steepling his fingers.

"Please," said Rutherford, and Ellsworth-Howard pulled his attention away from the dancing flames reluctantly.

"Well, it seems the project has been a success overall. The Enforcers succeeded in wiping out the last remnants of the Great Goat Cult, and it looks like civilization has finally begun to dawn."

"Told you they'd do the trick," said Ellsworth-Howard.

Chatterji smiled and went on: "Our operatives in the past report that the Neanderthals and Cro-Magnons are starting to interbreed and share ideas, which is what we thought would happen. There's been pressure from some board members who want to see the hunter-gatherer tribes forcibly settled in farming communes, but we had to explain how this contravenes history as known from the Temporal Concordance."

"Eh?" Ellsworth-Howard scowled at him.

"That means it goes against what we know happened," Rutherford said. "So they can't do it."

"Oh. Okay."

"And the next part's going to be really exciting, as we start connecting with actual recorded historical events!" Chatterji cracked his knuckles in enthusiasm. "History as we know it is going to begin happening at last."

"Brilliant." Ellsworth-Howard had a bracing draught of ginger beer.

"Though there is one problem . . ." Chatterji gnawed his lower lip. He hesitated a moment before going on. "I'm afraid we're having a little trouble with your Enforcers, Foxy. Actually quite a lot of trouble."

"What d'you mean?" Ellsworth sat upright. "They took out the Great Goat Cult, didn't they?"

"Oh, yeah. Quite. But . . . they seem to have some trouble being retrained, now that they've done what we made them for. What was the old word?"

"Demobilized?" said Rutherford.

"That's it. The Enforcers can't seem to adjust to peacetime. And they argue! They appear to feel that a lot more, er, preparation is necessary before we begin civilization. There have been some quite nasty incidents, in fact."

"You mean they won't stop killing people?" Ellsworth-Howard looked appalled.

"Well, they're only going for ordinary antisocials now, not cultists, but . . . in a word, yes," said Chatterji.

"Oh, dear, that won't do at all." Rutherford knitted his brows.

"And they defend themselves by pointing to the historical record and claiming that it proves the job oughtn't to be stopped."

"The bloody fools!" Rutherford snorted. "Don't they understand that we can't change history?"

"They believe we haven't tried hard enough," said Chatterji delicately, not looking at Ellsworth-Howard, who had buried his face in his hands.

"Bloody hell," he said wearily. "All right; what do we do?"

"Well, the committee would like to know if it's possible to modify them, since termination isn't an option."

"You mean make 'em over into Preservers?" Ellsworth-Howard thought about it. "Reprogram them? I don't think so. I designed them too shracking well for what they were supposed to do, you know. Why don't they just reassign them to be security techs or something?"

"Well, but—there's another problem, I'm afraid." Chatterji shifted uncomfortably in his seat. "Our observers have advised us that the genetic shift is taking place rather sooner than we thought, now that the two main hominid branches are free to interbreed. More and more humans are being born with the distinctive *Homo sapiens sapiens* appearance. Within a few more thousand years, the Enforcers will be . . . undesirably noticeable." He looked apologetic.

"You mean they're gonna stand out like boulders in gravel." Ellsworth-Howard drummed his fingers on his knees. "Shrack, shrack, shrack. I knew I should have done something about their faces. It was the optimum skull shape for a fighter, though."

"I know. I'm sorry, Foxy."

"Well, no help for it." Ellsworth-Howard had another gulp from his tankard. "Poor old soldiers! I made 'em too well, that's the problem. I always fancied I was born in the wrong age, myself—well, obviously we all do—but I wish I'd been a knight in armor. Gone around kicking the shrack out of Nazguls and Orcs and Calormenes. Swords and all that."

Rutherford and Chatterji exchanged nervous glances, though of course no public health monitor was anywhere within earshot. Ellsworth-Howard reached into the daypack he'd slung down beside his chair and pulled out a buke, which he opened and activated. He squeezed in some figures and sighed.

"All right. Got around three thousand Enforcers in the field. Current status shows two hundred thirty-seven in regeneration vats, consciousness offline. I suppose they could just be left off. Seems like a poor thank-you after they beat the Great Goat nasties for us."

"But can we ever trust them again?" said Chatterji. "Now that they've had the idea of rebellion?"

Ellsworth-Howard's eyes widened as the full import of the problem sank in on him. "Got a little situation here, haven't we?"

"Exactly," Chatterji said soberly. "Immortal, indestructible, and disobedient. Talk about your Frankenstein monsters!"

"What're we gonna do?"

"Well, it's not as though they were howling and pounding on our door, after all," Chatterji said. "We know we solve the problem, somehow, because history doesn't record a roving band of giant soldiers terrorizing criminals through the ages. The question is, how do we solve it?"

"I know!" Rutherford leaped to his feet in excitement. "Ye gods, chaps, I've had the most brilliant idea. This will work—at least if it's done right—and it'll make all those legends come true."

"What legends?" Chatterji asked.

"The Sleeping Knights," said Rutherford. "All through Europe there are legends of bunches of knights asleep forever in caves! Under various enchantments, you know. Here in England they're supposed to be knights of the Round Table, sleeping until King Arthur comes again."

"What's that got to do with the shracking price of tea in China?" inquired Ellsworth-Howard irritably.

"Don't you see? *We* could be what causes the legends. Suppose you call in your Enforcers and tell them we do still need them, but they must have upgrades for the new work they're to do. They'll submit to being put under for the process. We'll just take their brains offline and keep them unconscious! We can't kill them, but we can induce alpha waves indefinitely."

"Where would we keep them all?" Chatterji looked intrigued.

"Underground bunkers." Rutherford's eyes shone. "In keeping with the legends. Carefully monitored, on life support—nothing inhumane, you know. Until the Judgment Day!"

An uncomfortable silence fell then, because nobody ever liked to mention that Judgment Day was thought to be going to arrive in the year 2355. Having breached the unmentionable, however, Rutherford blundered on in a lower voice:

"And—who knows? If something terrible's going to happen in the future, perhaps it's just as well we'll have a secret army hidden away, that we can revive if we need to."

"Shrack," said Ellsworth-Howard solemnly. "Think you've got the right idea, Rutherford. It'll take some planning, though. Have to be gradual and crafty, so the poor buggers don't know what's going on. Let's see how much it'll cost, eh?" His fist worked on the buttonball.

"I'm glad you're taking this well," said Chatterji, watching him. "The committee didn't want you to think the Enforcers were a failure. It is felt, though, that the next project should be more thoroughly tested before it's put into action."

"And how do we do that?" grunted Ellsworth-Howard absently. He was absorbed in his calculations. Rutherford looked inquiringly at Chatterji.

"Well, now that historical time is being entered, the Company would like an improved model Enforcer," Chatterji explained. "Someone more modern-looking. More suited to a life of service in a civilized world. So, obviously, we'd want somebody who was superbly strong but maybe less violent, more obedient, perhaps a bit more intelligent than the old Enforcers? Someone with the ability to adapt to peacetime life, yet with the same sense of, er, moral commitment."

"Not so much a warrior as a knight," said Rutherford. "A hero! I say, Chatty, this sounds interesting."

"But *not* a charismatic leader who can make thousands hang on his every word," Chatterji added. "That's been tried, and we all know what happened."

"Well, that wasn't our project," Rutherford reminded him smugly.

"Thank heaven. We want somebody with the intelligence to judge men and administer laws, but not out of a sense of his own importance. All zeal, no ego."

"Okay." Ellsworth-Howard printed out a sheet of figures and handed them to Chatterji. "There's Operation Pension Plan for the old Enforcers. I feel crappy about it, but I don't see what else we can do with 'em. Now, what's this about a knight?"

"We need a New Man, Foxy, an enlightened warrior," Rutherford cried.

"You mean no more big ugly buggers we can't control?" Ellsworth-Howard grinned mirthlessly.

"Exactly," Chatterji said. "And to make certain there are no further problems, the committee wants a completely original prototype. No breeding programs. They don't want you picking through human children until you find one that fits the optimum morphology and then performing the immortality process on it, either. The results are too unpredictable."

"It works fine on my shracking Preservers," growled Ellsworth-Howard.

"Yes, of course, but they're only Preservers," Chatterji said hastily. "How much trouble can drones cause? But nothing is to be left to chance on this new design." He lowered his voice. "The committee wants to see something engineered. Do you understand?"

What he was proposing Ellsworth-Howard do was horribly, flagrantly illegal and had been for two centuries. As long as nobody actually said in so many words *We want you to make a recombinant,* however, it could be glossed over as something else, should anyone ever call Dr. Zeus or its employees to account, which of course would never happen.

"A tailored gene job?" Ellsworth-Howard asked uneasily, pulling at his lower lip. "Take a lot of work."

"Absolutely. Field testing, too. And for that reason, the first prototypes will be given ordinary human life spans. No immortality process for them. That way if there's a flaw in the design, we can dispose of the mistake. Nothing that might come back to haunt us later."

"I'd better go back to the old *Homo crewkernensis* stuff, then, if you want it engineered. Lots more material to work with." Ellsworth-Howard kneaded the buttonball and the image of a four-stranded DNA helix appeared on the screen. He began moving its segments about, doodling as it were with the material of life.

"Remember that now you'll need something with a human face," Chatterji told him. "No Neanderthal, obviously. And, er, see if you can eliminate that berserker tendency the Enforcers had. We want a man who can kill, but not somebody who enjoys it quite as much. Program in a bit of compassion. Of course," Chatterji glanced at Rutherford, "that'll be your job."

"The Once and Future King, born of a vanished race," chanted Rutherford. "The Messiah. The Superman. The Peaceful Warrior. The Hero with a Thousand Faces!"

"Don't talk such rubbish." Ellsworth-Howard squeezed in a formula and tilted his head, considering the results.

"It's not rubbish. This is what I'm paid to do, remember? You develop his body, I'll develop a psychological formula he can be programmed with, and we'll produce something wonderful." Rutherford seized up the jug and poured out a second round. They were raising their tankards for a toast when there came a horrifyingly loud commotion at the door. Chatterji and Rutherford turned, half expecting to see a mob of furious Enforcers brandishing stone axes. They beheld instead a trio of municipal firemen in yellow slickers.

"*Get it out,*" said the tallest, striding toward them with an air of command. The other firemen were carrying silver canisters, with which they proceeded to extinguish the fire.

"Right," snarled the tall fireman. "You're all under arrest for violation of municipal fire code three-seventeen subset five, paragraph one. And I've a special treat for the idiot who set the blaze in the first place. Got a jolly straitjacket warmed up just for you! Right, then, which of you did it?"

"This—this is bloody outrageous," said Rutherford. "I have a permit for this fire, sir!"

"Oh, have we now?" The fireman thrust his face down close to Rutherford's own.

"I do so!" Rutherford backed away slightly but did not quail. "This is a historical building and we are licensed re-creators."

"Are you indeed? Where's your tourists, then?" the fireman sneered. Chatterji put a hand on the fireman's shoulder and pushed him back. The fireman grinned like a shark, preparing to roar the command that would have clapped Chatterji in restraints; but something about Chatterji's expression stopped him cold.

"I don't think you know who we are," said Chatterji. "This is a professional matter." He pulled out a little silver case and extracted an identification disc, which he held out for the fireman to see. The fireman blinked twice and stared at it. His face went rather pale.

"You should have said something!" he said. "Sorry—sorry, sir! Never happen again, sir. I'm a stockholder of yours, actually, sir, we'd have never in a million years thought of interrupting your work. Now we know you're doing this sort of thing on the premises . . . just get their fire going again, lads, and least said soonest mended, eh?"

"Fair enough," said Chatterji. Rutherford collapsed into his chair, blinking away angry tears. Ellsworth-Howard continued to frown at his screen, kneading the buttonball distractedly, ignoring the firemen as they hurriedly cleaned out the grate and relit the fire. Once the flame had leaped up again they vanished as quickly as they'd arrived.

"I hate this bloody century," quavered Rutherford.

"Oh, you don't really," Chatterji told him brightly. "Did you see the way that fellow slunk out of here? Now, that's what I call power. Face it: in what other era would the likes of us have the authority to shape history? Or tell a municipal official to go to the devil, for that matter. This is our time, chaps, and we're making it count!"

He picked up Rutherford's tankard and handed it back to him, and lifted his own so the firelight shone on it. "Let's drink that toast, shall we? To the New Man."

" 'A father for the Superman,' " quoted Rutherford, smiling through his tears.

Ellsworth-Howard noticed belatedly what they were doing and grabbed up his tankard. Racking his brains for an impressive-sounding thing to say, he misremembered something from one of the few films he'd seen.

"To a new world of monsters and gods," he said, and drank deep.

Smart Alec

For the first four years of his life, Alec Checkerfield wore a life vest.

This was so that if he accidentally went over the side of his parents' yacht, he would be guaranteed a rescue. It was state of the art, as life vests went in the twenty-fourth century: not only would it have enabled him to bob along like a little cork in the wake of the *Foxy Lady*, it would have reassured him in a soothing voice, broadcast a frequency that repelled sharks, and sounded an immediate alarm on the paging devices worn by every one of the servants on board.

His parents themselves wore no pagers, which was just as well because if Mummy had noticed Alec was in the water she'd probably have simply waved her handkerchief after him until he was well over the horizon. Daddy would probably have made an effort to rescue Alec, if he weren't too stoned to notice the emergency; but most of the time he was, which was why the servants had been appointed to save Alec, should the child ever fall overboard. They were all madly fond of Alec, anyway, because he was really a very good little boy, so they were sure to have done a great job, if the need for rescue at sea should ever have arisen.

It never did arise, however, because Alec was a rather well coordinated child too and generally did what he was told, such as obeying safety rules.

And he was a happy child, despite the fact that his mother never set her ice-blue eyes on him if she could help it and his father was as likely to trip over him as speak to him. It didn't matter that they were terrible at being parents; they were also very rich, which meant they could pay other people to love Alec.

In a later time Alec would look back on the years aboard the *Foxy Lady* as the happiest in his life, and sometimes he'd come across the old group holo and wonder why it had all ended. The picture had been taken in Jamaica, by somebody standing on a mooring catwalk and shooting down on deck.

There he was, three years old, in his bright red life vest and sailor hat, smiling brightly up at the camera. Assembled around him were all the servants: fabulous Sarah, his Jamaican nurse, arrogantly naked except for blue bathing shorts; Lewin and Mrs. Lewin, the butler and cook; Reggie, Bob, and Cat, the deckhands; and Mr. Trefusis, the first mate. They formed a loving and protective wall between Alec and his mummy and daddy, or Roger and Cecelia, as they preferred to be called.

Roger and Cecelia were visible up on the quarterdeck: Cecelia ignoring them all from her deck chair, a cold presence in a sun hat and dark glasses, reading a novel. Roger was less visible, leaning slouched against the rail, one nerveless hand about to spill a rum highball all over his yachting shoes. He'd turned his face away to look at something just as the image had been recorded, so all you could see was a glimpse of aristocratic profile, blurred and enigmatic.

It hadn't mattered. Alec had a wonderful life, full of adventures. Sarah would tell him stories about Sir Henry Morgan and all the pirates who used to roam the sea, living on their ships just like Alec did, and how they formed the Free Brotherhood of the Coast, whose secret way of recognizing each other at sea was for one pirate crew to call out, "Where d'ye hail from?" and instead of replying that they were from Kingston or Liverpool or Southampton, the crew of the other ship would cry, *From the sea!* And so they'd know they were pirates too. Alec liked that.

And there was the fun of landing on a new island—what would it be like? Was there any chance there might still be pirates lurking around? Alec had played on beaches where the sand was white, or yellow, or pink, or black, built castles on all of them and stuck his little pirate flags on their turrets. *Jolly Roger*, that was what the flag was called.

Jolly Roger was also what the deckhands called Alec's daddy when he seemed to be having more than usual difficulty walking or talking. This was generally after he'd been drinking the tall drinks Cat would shake up for him at the bar on the yacht. Sometimes Cat would put a fruit spear in the drinks, cherries and chunks of pineapple skewered on long wooden picks with the paper pirate flag at the top. Sometimes Daddy's eyes would focus on Alec and he'd present him with the fruit spear and yell for more rum in his drink. Alec would sit under Daddy's tall chair and eat the pineapple and cherries, making faces at the nasty stuff they'd been soaked in. Then he'd carry the Jolly Roger pick back to his cabin, where he had a whole hoard of them carefully saved for his sand castles.

It was a shame the rum had such an effect on Daddy, because going to get it was always fun. The *Foxy Lady* would drop anchor in some sapphire bay and

Sarah would put on a halter top and shoes, and put shoes on Alec, and they'd go ashore together in the launch. As they'd come across the water Sarah might sing out, *"How many houses, baby?"* and Alec would look up at the town and count the houses in his head and he'd tell her how many there were, and she'd tousle his hair and tell him he was right again! And they'd laugh.

Then there'd be a long walk through some island town, past the gracious houses with window boxes full of pink flowers, where parrots flashed and screamed in the green gardens, back to the wappen-bappen places where the houses looked like they were about to fall down, and there would always be a doormouth with no sign and a dark cool room beyond, full of quiet black men sitting at tables, or brown men sitting at tables, or white men turned red from the sun. In one place there was a green and red parrot that knew Alec's name. "Smart Alec," it called him, to his delight and the amusement of the quiet men. In another place there was a big mermaid carved out of wood, with flowing hair and bubbies nearly as nice as Sarah's. Everything smelled new and exciting.

Different as the details might be, the visit was always the same: he and Sarah would go in, and the quiet men would greet Sarah with welcome and a certain deference, almost awe, as though she were a visiting queen. Invariably a man in an apron would come out, bringing a lemonade for Alec and a glass of white rum for Sarah, and sit at a table with them while his helpers loaded crates into a battered old vehicle. Alec seldom understood what was being said, because people talked differently on different islands; but whether they were in the Caribbean or Polynesia, Sarah always spoke to the quiet men in their own language, as perfectly as though she'd been born among them.

When Alec had finished his lemonade, they'd go out into the sunlight again and the man with the apron would give them a ride back into town with the crates. The crates were nearly always stenciled CROSSE & BLACKWELL'S PICKLED GHERKINS.

And nearly always, they'd spot a stern-looking black or brown or white man in a white uniform, pedaling along on a bicycle, and Sarah would hug Alec tight and cry out in a little silly voice: "Oh, nooo, it's a policeman! Don't tell him, Alec, don't tell him our secret!" This always made Alec giggle, and she'd always go on: "Don't tell him we've got *guns*! Don't tell him we've got *explosives*! Don't tell him we've got *ganja*! Don't tell him we've got *coffee*!" She'd go on and on like this, as they'd bump along trailing dust clouds and squawking birds, and by the time they reached the harbor Alec would be weak with laughter.

Once they were at the launch, however, she'd be all quiet efficiency, buckling Alec into his seat and then helping the man move the crates into the cargo bay. Sarah was immensely strong and could lift a crate on one hand, just using the other to balance. When all the crates were on board, the man would hold out a plaquette and Sarah would bring out Daddy's identification disk and pay for the crates. Then they'd zoom back out to the *Foxy Lady*. They'd put out to sea, and the next day there would be rows of brown bottles under the bar again, and Cat would be busy shaking up the tall drinks, and Daddy would be sitting on the quarterdeck with a glass in his hand, staring vacantly away at the blue horizon.

Not everybody thought that the trips to get the rum were such a good idea, however.

Alec was sitting in the saloon one day after just such a trip, quietly coloring. He had made a picture of a shark fighting with an anchor, because he knew how to draw anchors and he knew how to draw sharks, and that was all the logic the scene needed. The saloon was just aft of the galley. Because it was very warm that day the connecting door was open, and he could hear Lewin and Mrs. Lewin talking in disgusted tones.

"He only gets away with it because he's a peer."

"Peer or no, you'd think he'd stop it for the kid's sake! He was such a great teacher, too, and what's he given that all up for? And what would happen if we were ever boarded for inspection? They'd take the baby away in a minute, you know they would." *Chop, chop, chop*, Mrs. Lewin was cutting up peppers as she talked.

"Don't think so. J. I. S. would smooth it over, same as always. Between his lineage and Them, he can do whatever he bloody well pleases, even in London."

"Yeh, well! Things was different before Alec came, weren't they? And anyway it's *wrong*, Malcolm, you know it is, it's criminal, it's dangerous, it's unhealthy, and really the best thing we could do for him would be to tell a public health monitor about it."

"And where'd we be, then? The last thing J. I. S. wants is some hospital looking at—" Lewin started through the doorway and saw Alec in the saloon. He retreated and shut the door.

Alec sat frowning at his picture. He knew that Daddy's drinking made people sad, but he'd never thought it was dangerous. On the other hand, he knew that rules must be obeyed, and dangerous things must be reported at once, like water below decks or smoke in any of the cabins.

He got up and trotted out of the saloon. There was Daddy on the aft deck, smiling dreamily at the sun above the yardarm.

"Hey, there, Alec," he greeted the little boy. He had a sip of his drink and reached out to tousle Alec's hair. "Look out there to starboard. Is that a pretty good island? Should we go there, maybe?"

Alec shivered with joy. Daddy almost never noticed him, and here he was asking Alec's opinion about something.

"Yeah," he cried. "Let's go!"

But Daddy's gaze had drifted away, out to the horizon, and he lifted his glass again. "Some green island we haven't found yet," he murmured, "farther on 'n farther on 'n farther on . . ."

Alec remembered what he had wanted to ask. He reached out and pushed at Daddy's glass with his index finger.

"Is that crinimal?" he said. It was a moment before Daddy played that back and turned to gape at him.

"What?"

"Is that dangerous?" Alex said, and mimed perfectly the drinking-from-a-bottle gesture he had seen the servants make in reference to his father. "You have to obey the rules. If I see danger I'm supposed to tell."

"Huh," said Daddy, and he rubbed his scratchy chin. He hadn't shaved in about a week. His eyes narrowed and he looked at Alec slyly.

"Tell me, Alec, 'm I hurting anybody?"

"No."

"We ever had an accident on this ship? Anything happen ol' Roger can't handle?"

"No."

"Then where's the harm?" Daddy had another sip. "Tell me that. 'M a nice guy even when I'm stoned. *A gentleman you know. Old school tie.*"

Alec had no idea what that meant, but he pushed on:

"How come it's crinimal?"

"Aha." Daddy tilted his glass until the ice fell down against his lip. He crunched ice and continued, "Okay, Alec. Big fact of life. There's a whole bunch of busybodies and scaredy-cats who make a whole bunch of rules and regs about things they don't want anybody doing. See? So nobody gets to have any fun. Like, no booze. They made a law about no booze. And they're all, 'You can't lie about in the sun because you get cancer,' and they're all, 'You can't swim in the ocean 'cos you might pee,' and they're all, 'You can't eat sweets because they make you fat,' okay? Dumb stuff. And they make laws so you go to hospital if you do this little dumb stuff! Okay?

"That's why we don't live in London, kiddo. That's why we live out here on the *Lady,* so no scaredy-cat's gonna tell us what to do. Okay? Now then. If you went running to the scaredy-cats to tell 'em about the rum, you'd be an even worse thing than them. You'd be a telltale! And you gotta remember you're a gentleman, and no gentleman is ever a telltale. See? 'Cos if you did tell about the rum, well, they'd come on board and they'd see me with my little harmless drinkies and they'd see your mummy with her books and they'd see Sarah with her lovely bare tits and then you know what they'd do? Daddy'd go to hospital and they'd take you away. Li'l Alec ain't gonna be a telltale, is he? He's my li'l gentleman, ain't he?"

"I don't want 'em to take me away!" Alec wailed, tears in his eyes. Daddy dropped his glass, reaching clumsily to pull Alec up on his lap, and the glass broke, but he didn't notice.

" 'Course you don't. 'Cos we're free here on the *Foxy Lady*, and you're a gentleman and you got a right to be free, free, free. Okay? You won't tell on Daddy, not my li'l Alec. Gonna be an earl someday, when Daddy's gone to Fiddler's Green. So anyway. You just let old Jolly Roger go his ways and you never be a telltale, okay? And don't pay them no mind with their dumb rules."

"But they gonna board us for aspection," Alec sobbed.

"Hey, kiddo, don't you worry. Daddy's a gentleman, don't forget, he's got some pull. I'm the bloody earl 'a Finsbury, okay? *And* a CEO at J. I. S. And I'll tell you something else. Jovian Integrated Systems gonna have something to say, too. Nobody's gonna touch li'l Alec, he's such a special kid."

That was right; Alec was a special kid, all the servants said so. For one thing, all other little boys were brought into this world by the stork, but not Alec. He had come in an agcopter. Reggie had told him so.

"Yeah, son," Reggie had chuckled, looking around to be certain Sarah was nowhere within earshot. "The stork call your daddy and say, 'Come out to Cromwell Cay.' And your daddy take the launch out where the agcopter waiting on the cay at midnight, with the red light blinking, and when he come back he bring Sarah with our little bundle of joy Alec. And we all get nice fat bonuses, too!"

Alec wiped his nose and was comforted. Daddy set him on the deck and yelled to Cat for another drink and told Alec to go play now somewhere. Alec would dearly have liked to stay and talk with Daddy; that had been the longest conversation they'd ever had together, and he had all kinds of questions. What was *Jovian Integrated Systems*? What was Fiddler's Green? Why were some rules important, like wearing the life vest, and other rules were dumb? Why were gentlemen free? But Alec was a considerate and obedient little boy, so he didn't ask. He went off to play, determined never, ever to be a telltale or a scaredy-cat.

Very shortly after that the happy life came to an end.

It happened quite suddenly, too. One day Mummy abruptly put down her novel, got up out of her deck chair and stalked over to Daddy where he sat watching a Caribbean sunset.

"It's over, Rog," she said.

He turned a wondering face to her. "Huh?" he said. After a moment of staring into her eyes, he sighed. "Okay," he said.

And the *Foxy Lady* set a course that took her into gray waters, under cold skies. Sarah packed up most of Alec's toys so he only had a few to play with, and got out his heaviest clothes. One day they saw a very big island off the port bow. Sarah held him up and said: "Look! There's England."

Alec saw pale cliffs and a meek little country beyond them, rolling fields stretching away into a cloudy distance, and way off the gray blocky mass of cities. The air didn't smell familiar at all. He stood shivering, watched the strange coast-line unroll as Sarah buttoned him into an anorak.

They waited at the mouth of a big river for the tide to change, and Sarah pointed out the city of Rochester to Alec on a holomap and said that was where Charles Dickens had lived. He didn't know who Charles Dickens was. She re-minded him about the holo he'd watched at Christmas, about the ghosts of the past and the future.

The Thames pulled them into London, which was the biggest place Alec had ever seen. As the sun was setting they steered into Tower Marina, and the long journey ended with a gentle bump against the rubber pilings. Alec went to bed that night feeling very strange. The *Foxy Lady* seemed to have become silent and heavy, motionless, stone like the stone city all around them, and for the first time that he could ever remember the blue sea was gone. There were new smells, too. They frightened him.

His cabin was full of the cold strange air when he woke up, and the sky was gray.

Everyone seemed to be in a hurry, and rather cross. Sarah bundled Alec into very thick heavy clothes indeed, leaving his life vest in the closet, and she herself put on more clothes than he had ever seen her wear. Daddy was wearing strange new clothes, too, stiff and uncomfortable-looking ones, and he had shaved. There was no breakfast cooking in the galley; Lewin had been ashore and come back with a box of Bentham's Bran Treats ("At least they're fresh baked!" he cried) and a dozen cups of herbal tea, steeping in chlorilar cups. Breakfast was served, or rather handed around, at the big table in the saloon. Alec was impressed. Nor-mally only Daddy and Mummy dined in here, but today he and Sarah were at the table, too. Mummy, however, was nowhere to be seen, and when Alec inquired about this, Daddy just stared at him bleakly.

"Your mummy's gone to visit some friends," Sarah told him.

He didn't care for his breakfast at all—he thought it smelled like dead grass—but he was too well-mannered a child to say so and hurt Lewin's feelings. Fortunately there wasn't much time to eat, because the car arrived and there was a lot of bustle and rush to load luggage into its trunk. Finally he was led down the gangway and across the pier to where the car waited.

It was nothing at all like the rusted hacks in which he'd ridden in the islands. This was a Rolls Royce Exquisite Levitation, black and gleaming, with Daddy's crest on the door and a white man in a uniform like a policeman at the steering console. Alec had to fight panic as he was handed in and fastened into his seat. Sarah got in, Daddy got in, Lewin and Mrs. Lewin crowded into the front beside the driver, and the Rolls lifted into midair and sped silently away. That was the end of life on board the *Foxy Lady*.

There were servants lined up on the steps outside the house in Bloomsbury, and Alec watched as Daddy formally shook hands with each of them. Alec thought it would be polite to do this, too, so he trailed after Daddy shaking hands and asking the servants what their names were. For some reason this made them all smile, and one of them muttered to another: "Now *that's* a little gentleman." Then they all went into the big house with its echoing rooms, and Alec had come home to England.

The house only dated from 2298, but it had been deliberately built in an old-fashioned style because it was an earl's townhouse, after all, so it was taller and fancier than the other houses in the street. Alec still hadn't explored all its rooms by the time he noticed one morning that Daddy wasn't at the breakfast table, and when he asked about it Sarah informed him: "Your daddy's away on a business trip."

It was only later, and by chance, that he found out Daddy hadn't lasted a week in London before he'd gone straight back to Tower Marina and put out to sea again on the *Foxy Lady*.

Then Alec had cried, but Sarah had had a talk with him about how important it was that he live in London now that he was getting to be a big boy.

"Besides," she said, taking the new heavy clothes out of their shopping bags and hanging them up in his closet, "your poor daddy was so unhappy here, after your mummy had gone."

"Where did Mummy go?" said Alec, not because he missed her at all but because he was beginning to be a little apprehensive about the way pieces of his world had begun vanishing. He picked up a shoebox and handed it to Sarah. She took it without looking at him, but he could see her face in the closet mirror. She closed her eyes tight and said:

"She divorced your daddy, baby."

"What's that mean?"

"That means she doesn't want to live with him anymore. She's going to go away and live with some other people." Sarah swallowed hard. "After all, she was never happy on the *Foxy Lady* after you came along."

Alec stared at her, dumbfounded. After a moment he asked: "Why didn't Mummy like me? Everybody else does."

Sarah looked as though she wanted to cry. "*Damballah!*" she said, very softly. Then, in a light, normal tone of voice, she told him: "Well, I think she just never wanted to have children, with all the noise and mess a baby makes, and then a little boy running around and getting into everything. She and your daddy used to be very happy, but after you came it was spoiled for them."

Alec felt as though the ceiling had fallen in on him. What a terrible thing he'd done!

"I'm sorry," he said, and burst into tears.

Then Sarah did that trick she could do, moving so fast you couldn't see her move, and her arms were around him and she was rocking him, crooning to him, hiding him in her breasts.

"I'm sorry, too," she wept. "Oh, Alec, you mustn't mind. You're a *good* little boy, you hear me? You're my sweet, good little winji boy, and Sarah will always love you no matter what. Don't you ever forget that. When you grow up maybe you'll understand, sometimes people have to obey orders and say things they don't want to say at all? And"—her voice caught—"I'm sure you'll always be a good little boy, won't you, to make your poor daddy happy again?"

"Uh huh," Alec gasped. It was the least he could do, after he'd made Daddy so *un*happy. His tears felt hot on his cheeks, in that cold room, and Sarah's tears were like the hot rain that used to fall off Jamaica when there'd be lightning in the sky and Daddy would be yelling for him to get below because there was a storm coming.

But a terrible storm did come, and swept away another part of the world.

"What the hell did you go and tell him that for?" Lewin was shouting. Alec cowered on the stairs, covering his mouth with his hands.

"It was the truth," Sarah said in a funny unnatural voice. "He'd have found out sometime."

"My God, that's all the poor baby needs, to think he's responsible for the way that cold bitch acted," raged Mrs. Lewin. "Even if it was true, how could you tell him such a thing? Sarah, how could you?"

So then Sarah was gone too, and that was his fault for being a telltale. He woke up early next morning because the front door slammed, booming through the house like a cannon shot. Something made him get out of his bed and run across the icy floor to the window.

He looked down into the street and there was Sarah, swinging away down the pavement with her lithe stride, bag over her shoulder. He called to her, but she never looked back.

Everybody was very kind to him to make up for it. When he'd be sad and cry, Mrs. Lewin would gather him into her lap. Lewin told him what a brave big guy he was and helped him fix up his room with glowing star-patterns on the ceiling and an electronic painting of a sailing ship on his wall, with waves that moved and little people going to and fro on her deck. The other servants were nice, too, especially the young footman, Derek, and Lulu the parlormaid. They were newly-weds, attractive and very happy.

Sometimes Lewin would hand them Alec's identification disk and tell them to take him out for the day, so he could learn about London. They took him to the London Zoo to see the animal holoes, and to the British Museum, and Bucking-ham Palace to see where Mary III lived, or over to the Southwark Museum to meet and talk to the holo of Mr. Shakespeare. They took him shopping, and bought him exercise equipment and a complete holo set for his room, with a full library of holoes to watch. There were thirty different versions of *Treasure Island* to choose from; once Alec knew what it was about, he wanted them all. The older versions were the most exciting, like the bloodcurdling tales Sarah had used to tell him about the Spanish Main. Even so, they all had a prologue edited in that told him how evil and cruel pirates had really been, and how Long John Silver was not really a hero.

Gradually the broken circle began to fill in again, because everybody in the house in Bloomsbury loved Alec and wanted him to be happy. He loved them, too, and was grateful that they were able to love him back, considering what he'd done.

But Alec understood now why Daddy had preferred to live at sea. Everybody was always on at him, in the friendliest possible way, about what a lot there was to do in London compared to on a cramped old boat; but it seemed to him that there was a lot more *not* to do in London.

There was grass, but you mustn't walk on it. There were flowers, but you mustn't pick them. There were trees, but you mustn't climb them. You must wear shoes all the time, because it was dirty and dangerous not to, and you mustn't leave the house without a tube of personal sanitizer to rub on your hands after you'd touched anything other people might have touched. You couldn't eat or drink a lot of the things you used to, like fish or milk, because they were illegal. You mustn't ever get fat or "out of shape," because that was immoral. You mustn't ever tell ladies they had nice bubbies, or you'd go to hospital and never ever come out.

Mustn't play with other children, because they carried germs; anyway, other children didn't want to play with you, either, because you carried germs they didn't want to catch. You were encouraged to visit historical sites, as long as you didn't play with anybody but the holograms. It had been interesting talking to Mr. Shakespeare, but Alec couldn't quite grasp why nobody was allowed to perform any of his plays anymore, or why Shakespeare had felt obliged to explain that it had been unfair to build his theatre, since doing so had robbed the people of low-income housing. He had seemed so forlorn as he'd waved good-bye to Alec, a transparent man in funny old clothes.

There was something to apologize for everywhere you turned. The whole world seemed to be as guilty as Alec was, even though nobody he met seemed to have made their own mummies and daddies divorce. No, that was Alec's own particular awful crime, that and telling on Sarah so she had to go away.

Sometimes when he was out with Derek and Lulu, walking between them and holding their hands, strangers would stop and compliment Derek and Lulu on how well-behaved their son was. After the first time this had happened and the stranger had walked on, Alec had looked up at them and asked:

"Can we play that I'm your little boy really?"

Derek and Lulu had exchanged glances over his head.

"Okay," said Derek at last, and Lulu coughed. So they played that game for a while, on the outings, and Alec would call them Mummy and Daddy and they'd call him Son. It had seemed as though it would be a great game, having parents who were young and in love, but gradually Alec realized that he was making them uncomfortable, so he let it drop.

He really was doing his very best to be good and happy, but he felt as though he were a beach float with a pinprick hole in it somewhere: you couldn't see where it was, but bit by bit the air was going out of him, and he was sinking down, and soon he'd be a very flat little boy.

Lewin took a hand and ordered more holoes for Alec, including one of a twelve-part history series called *Legends of the Seven Seas*. It was delivered by parcel courier one day when Lewin was out, and the butler arrived home to find the opened package on the front hall table. Sorting through it, he saw that the only ring missing was the episode about the Golden Age of Piracy. He smiled, realizing that Alec must have run upstairs with it at once.

His smile faded, though, as he examined the chapter summaries on the remaining rings and realized that the series was intended for adults, not children. Irritated, he pulled out his buke and consulted the catalogue from which he'd ordered; not a word about adult content!

When Lewin got to the top of the landing outside Alec's room, he could hear an unholy commotion coming from within. He opened the door and beheld in midair a bloodstained deck, littered with wounded and dying pirates, though one was still on his feet and fighting like a demon. He was an immense man, with wild hair and beard. Blood poured from a dozen wounds in his body, but he kept battling, advancing with drawn cutlass on a Royal Navy lieutenant. Blood, smoke, sparks striking from steel blades, and musket fire echoing back over the pearl-gray water of Okracoke Inlet . . . and little Alec taking it all in with wide eyes, and fists clenched tight.

"Here now!" Lewin rushed to the holoplayer, shut it down. The image froze in midair and faded, with a second officer's sword stopped in the act of slicing toward the pirate's head.

"No!" Alec jumped to his feet in anguish. "Bring him back! You have to bring him back!"

"That's not the sort of thing little boys should see," explained Lewin, pulling the ring from the machine.

"But he was the best pirate ever!" wailed Alec, beginning to cry.

"No, he wasn't," said Lewin desperately. "He was a bad man, son, understand?"

"No, he wasn't, he was brave! They shooted him and he just laughed," Alec protested.

"No, no, son—"

"Yes he was!" screamed Alec, and ran into the bathroom and slammed the door.

"Now then, Alec, be a good boy and come out," said Lewin, pulling at the handle. No good; Alec had locked the door, and stood on the other side sobbing in fury.

"Here, I'll tell you what," said Lewin, crouching unsteadily. "I'll tell you a story about a *real* sea hero, shall I? You want to hear about, er, Admiral Nelson? He was the bravest man who ever sailed."

Silence on the other side of the door for a moment, but for Alec's gasped breath.

"Was he a pirate?" said Alec at last.

"Well, no, but—but he was a sort of a rogue," said Lewin, trying to remember the details of a holo he had once seen on the subject of Lady Hamilton. "But nobody minded, because he saved England. See, there was this evil guy named Napoleon, one time. And he wanted to rule all of Europe and, er, make everybody do everything just the same. And he had secret police and all that."

"What?" Alec asked muffledly.

"You know, telltales that spied on everybody for Napoleon. And England was the only place that was still free. So there was this place called Trafalgar, see, and Napoleon sent all his ships out—and Nelson commanded the English fleet, and blew the bad guys right out of the water."

"With cannons?"

"Oh, yeah, hundreds of 'em. Even though he only had one arm and, er, I think his eye was gone, too. He gave 'em in service to his country. He always did his duty, see. And Napoleon's cowards shot him on the deck of his own ship, so he died, which was dreadful sad, and all the people in England were sorry, but he'd won such a famous victory that Englishmen never ever were slaves. So everybody loved brave Lord Nelson."

Lewin heard Alec unlocking the door. It was pulled back. The little boy looked up at him, solemn.

"Does he have a museum and we can go talk to him?"

Lewin blinked in puzzlement a moment, and then remembered Shakespeare's hologram. "Er—no, son, he doesn't. But there's a nice museum in Greenwich we can visit next Sunday. Lots of Nelson stuff there."

So Alec emerged from the bathroom and went down to tea like a good boy. He was still frightened and strangely exhilarated by what he'd seen. Blackbeard and Horatio Nelson had become intermingled in his mind; he dreamed that night of immense bearded unstoppable heroes, blood, smoke, and flame.

One morning at the breakfast table when Lewin had said, in his jolliest old-granddad voice, "And what would you like to do today, Alec?" Alec said:

"Please, can we go down to the river and look at the ships?"

"Of course you can! Want Derek and Lulu to take you?"

"No," said Alec. "Just you."

Lewin was very pleased at that, and as soon as breakfast was done they put on their coats and called for the car. In minutes they had been whisked down to the Thames where all the pleasure craft were moored. Their driver switched off the agmotor, the car settled gently to the ground, and Alec and Lewin got out and walked along.

"Oh, now look at that one," Lewin said. "She's a beauty, eh? Three masts! Do you know, back in the old days a ship like that would have had to have carried a great big crew just to manage her sails. They'd have slept packed into her hold like dominoes in a box, there had to be that many. And when a storm was coming and the captain wanted to strike sails, you know what he'd have to do? He'd order his sailors to climb up into the rigging and cling there, like monkeys in trees, and reef every one of those sails themselves with their own hands, clinging on as tight as they could whilst they did it! Sometimes men would fall off, but the ships just sailed on."

"Wow," said Alec. He'd never seen Reggie or Bob or Cat do much more than load cargo or mix drinks. Suddenly his face brightened with comprehension. "So that's why the squire has to have all those guys on the *Hispaniola*, even if they're really pirates!"

Lewin stared a moment before he realized what Alec meant. "*Treasure Island*, right," he said. "That was why. No robot guidance to do it all. No computer tracking the wind and weather, and deciding when to shorten sail or clap it on. You had to have people doing it. Nobody would let you build ships like this anymore, if that was how they worked."

"Cool," said Alec. They walked on, past the rows of pleasure craft where they sat at moorings, and Lewin pointed out this or that kind of rigging or latest luxury feature available to people who could afford such things. He pointed out the sort of ship he'd own himself if he had the money, and pointed out the sort of ship Alec ought to own when he grew up and became the seventh earl of Finsbury.

They walked for what seemed like miles, and Alec began to lag behind; not because he was tired, for he was an extraordinarily strong child with a lot of stamina, but because he was fighting the need to cry.

He had been playing a game inside himself, imagining that the next ship they'd see would be the *Foxy Lady*, and his daddy would be on board, having just dropped anchor for a surprise visit. Of course, he knew his daddy was somewhere in the Caribbean, he knew the *Lady* wouldn't really be there. But what if she were? And of course she never was, but maybe the next ship would be. Or the next. Or the next.

But Alec wasn't very good at lying to himself.

"Alec?" Lewin turned around to see where Alec had got to. "What's wrong?"

He walked close swiftly and saw the tears standing in Alec's pale blue eyes, and understood at once. "You poor little sod," he muttered in compassion, and reached for a tissue and held it out to the child. Alec misunderstood his gesture and buried his face in Lewin's coat, wrapping his arms around him.

"Hell," Lewin gasped, and looking around wildly he attempted to pry Alec loose. "Alec, let go! For God's sake, let go! Do you want me to get arrested?"

Alec fell back from him, bewildered.

"Is it against the law to hug in London?" he asked.

"It is against the law for any unlicensed adult to embrace a child," Lewin told him soberly. "If there'd been a public health monitor looking our way I'd be in trouble right now."

"But Sarah used to hug me all the time. And Mrs. Lewin does."

"Sarah was a professional child care specialist, Alec. She'd passed all sorts of scans and screening to get her license. Same as mummies and daddies have to do, before they're allowed to have children. And the missus—well, she only hugs you at home, where nobody can see."

Alec gulped, wiping away tears. He understood now. It must be a law like no booze or bare tits, that you mustn't be a telltale about. "I'm sorry," he said shakily. "I didn't think it would get anybody in trouble."

"I know, old man." Lewin crouched down to Alec's eye level, keeping a good meter between them. "It's a good law, though, see. You have to understand that it was passed because people used to do terrible, horrible things to little kids, back in the old days."

"Like the two little boys in the Tower," said Alec, rubbing his coat sleeve across his eyes.

"Yeah. Sort of." Lewin glanced downriver in the direction of Tower Marina. He decided that Alec had had quite enough sad memories for the day. Pulling out his communicator, he called for the car to come and take them home.

That night, Lewin sat down at the household console. Thin-lipped with anger, he sent a message to Roger Checkerfield, advising him that it might be a good idea to talk to Alec once in a while. The bright letters shimmered on the screen a moment before vanishing, speeding through the ether to the bridge of the *Foxy Lady*. Lewin sat up all night waiting for a reply, but none ever came.

"Alec?"

Alec turned his face from contemplation of the painting on his wall. It seemed to him that if he could just pay close enough attention to it, long enough, he would be able to go into the picture, hear the steady crash of the sea under the ship's prow, hear the wind singing in her lines, smell the salt breeze. He could open the little cabin door and slip inside or, better yet, take the wheel and sail away forever from sad London. Blue water!

But Lewin and Mrs. Lewin looked so hopeful, so pleased with themselves, that he smiled politely and stood up.

"Come see, sweetheart," said Mrs. Lewin. "Someone's sent you a present!"

So he took her hand and they went up to the fourth floor of the house, into what was going to be his schoolroom next year. It had been freshly painted and papered. The workmen had built the cabinetry for the big screen and console that would link him to his school, but nothing had been installed yet.

In one corner, though, there was a cozy little Alec-sized table and chair, and on the table was an enormous bright yellow flower, bigger than Alec's head. It was all folded up, the way flowers are in the early morning, so you couldn't tell what sort of flower it was. Protruding from the top was a little card with letters inscribed on it: A-L-E-C.

"Now, who d'you suppose that's from, eh?" wondered Lewin, though in fact he had purchased it for Alec himself, without consulting Roger.

Alec was speechless.

"Think your daddy sent it, eh?" Where was the harm in a kind lie?

"Go on, dear, take the card." Mrs. Lewin prodded him gently. "It's for you, after all."

Alec walked forward and pulled the card loose. There was nothing written on it except his name, but at the moment he took it the flower began to open, slowly, just like a real flower. The big bright petals unfolded and spread out to reveal what had been hidden in its heart.

It looked like a silver egg, or perhaps a very fat little rocket. Its gleaming surface looked so smooth Alec felt compelled to put out his hand and stroke it.

The moment he did so, a pleasant bell tone sounded.

"Good morning," said an even more pleasant voice. "Pembroke Technologies extends its congratulations to the thoughtful parent who has selected this Pembroke Playfriend for his or her small child. Our Playfriend is designed to encourage creativity and socialization as well as provide hours of entertainment, but will also stimulate cerebrocortical development during these critical first years of the child's life. If needed, the Playfriend is also qualified to serve as an individual tutor in all standard educational systems. Customizing for specialized educational systems is available.

"The Playfriend offers the following unique features:

"An interface identity template that may be customized to the parent's preferences and the child's individual needs.

"Cyberenvironment capability with use of the Playfriend Optics, included in Models Four, Five, and Six and available for all other models by special order.

"Direct nerve stimulus interface with use of the attractive Empowerment Ring, included in all models.

"Universal access port for parallel processing with any other cyber-system.

"In addition, the Playfriend will maintain around-the-clock surveillance of the child's unique health parameters and social behavior. Warning systems are in place and fully operational. Corrective counseling will be administered in the event of psychologically detrimental social encounters, and positive emotional growth will be encouraged. Aptitude evaluation is another feature of the Playfriend, with appropriate guidance. Intellectual challenges in a noncompetitive context will promote the child's self-esteem and success potential.

"The interface identity template will continually adjust and grow more complex to complement the child's emerging personality, growing as it grows, until both are ready for, and may be upgraded to, the Pembroke Young Person's Companion.

"Interaction with the Pembroke Playfriend during the developmental years virtually guarantees a lifetime of self-fulfillment and positive achievement!"

The voice fell silent. Mrs. Lewin gave an embarrassed little laugh that ended in a cough. The air in London didn't agree with her.

"My goodness, I don't think I understood one word in ten of all that! Did you, Alec dear?"

"Nope," said Alec solemnly.

"That's all right," said Lewin, advancing on the silver egg. "All it meant was that Alec's gonna have a wonderful time with this thing! Now, you just sit here and let's have a closer look at it, shall we?"

"Okay," said Alec, but he sat down reluctantly. He was a little intimidated by the adult voice that had spoken out of nowhere. Lewin tousled his hair.

"Don't be scared. Look here, what's this?" He tapped the side of the egg and a slot opened in it, and something rolled out.

It was a ring. It appeared to be made of glass or high-impact polymer, and was a vivid blue. As Lewin picked it up it began to change. By the time he had presented it to Alec it was a deep ruby red.

"Cool," said Alec, smiling at it involuntarily.

"D'you suppose it fits you? Go on then, try it on."

Alec was game; he put on the ring. It seemed to him that it tightened uncomfortably for a moment and then eased up, until he barely knew it was there.

"Hello, Alec!" said a funny little voice. "Pleased to meet you! We're going to be best friends, you and I!"

Alec looked, panic-stricken, at Lewin and Mrs. Lewin. Was he supposed to talk to it? But what was it? They smiled encouragingly at him, and he could tell they did so want him to like this, so he said: "Er—hello. What's your name?"

"Well, I haven't got one yet," said the little voice. "Will you give me a name?"

"What?"

"Will you give me a name?"

"We'll just leave the two of you to have a nice chat, shall we?" said Lewin, and he and Mrs. Lewin backed out of the schoolroom and closed the door.

"But—but I don't know what you are," said Alec, a bit desperately. "Can't I see you?"

"Certainly you can! I'm your Playfriend, after all. What would you like me to look like? I might be nearly anybody." There was a click and a blur of light appeared in front of the table, formless, woven of fire, gradually assuming a human shape. "What do you like? Do you like space exploration? Do you like dinosaurs? Do you like animals? I could be a fireperson or a policeperson if you'd like, or a transport driver, or a scientist."

"Could you be a pirate?" Alec said cautiously.

Incorrect and unsuitable role model! thought the machine. Out loud it said, "I can be a jolly sea captain. Here I am!"

Pop! The human shape became detailed, was an old man with a blue Navy coat and white trousers and big black sea boots. He wore a white yachting cap rather like the one Alec's daddy had owned, but seldom worn, and he had a neatly groomed white beard. "Now then, Alec, what about me?" The voice had changed to a kindly baritone with a Devon accent. "Will I do?"

Alec was so astonished it took him a moment to reply. "Um—sure," he said at last. Then he remembered his manners and added, "Won't you sit down?"

Optimum response! thought the Playfriend, rather pleased, and it smiled encouragingly. "What a polite little fellow you are, Alec! Thank you, I will sit down." A bigger version of Alec's chair appeared and the Sea Captain settled back in it. "There! Have you thought of a name for me yet, Alec?"

"No." Alec shook his head.

"Well, that's all right. Perhaps as we get to know each other you'll think of a good one. After all, I'm your special friend, just for you." Alec wrinkled his brow worriedly. "You don't have to decide on a name all at once," the Playfriend hastened to assure him. "We have plenty of time."

"But don't you want to be yourself?" Alec asked it.

"Oh, yes! But I won't really be myself until you decide what I ought to be," the machine said. "I'm *your* Playfriend."

"But," Alec said, "people don't belong to other people."

In the brief silence that followed, the Playfriend thought: *Possible low self-esteem.* It made a little tick against its evaluation of Alec. *Negative: insufficient creativity, insufficient imagination, failure to grasp initiative. Positive: developing social consciousness, consideration of others, good citizenship.* It filed that away. As it did so its eyes, which had been the gray of the North Sea, turned blue as the Caribbean.

"Oh!" Alec smiled.

"You like this color better?" The Sea Captain smiled, too.

"Uh-huh."

"Good." The machine experimented with a mild subliminal sound effect, a distant crash of breakers and a faint crying of gulls. Its sensors observed some of the tension going out of the little boy and activated the system of relays that provided it with an analog of self-satisfaction. *Initiate self-image analysis.* "Why don't you tell me about yourself, Alec? Are you happy?"

"Yes," Alec said dutifully, and because of the neural linkup it had formed with Alec through the Empowerment Ring, the Playfriend knew at once that he was lying. It became very alert. It scanned him for evidence of physical abuse.

"You seem to have bumped your nose once," the Sea Captain said casually, focusing on a healed injury to the cartilage of Alec's septum.

"No," said Alec, and the machine saw that he was telling the truth so far as he knew. But the trauma had healed long ago, probably in infancy when the cartilage was soft. Since Alec had no other injuries at all, past or present, the machine pushed on.

"What do you think makes people unhappy?" the Sea Captain said.

"Living in London," said Alec at once.

"Anything else?"

Alec thought about it. "Babies making noise and mess and little boys running around and getting into everything. Divorces."

"Ah," said the Playfriend, coordinating this response with the data Lewin had input when he'd set up its program. The subroutine that had been called up to probe discreetly for, and report evidence of, child abuse went back on standby. "What else can you tell me about yourself, Alec?"

"I'm five years old," Alec said. "My daddy is a gentleman, but he isn't here now. I'm going to go to St. Stephen's Primary next year after Lewin buys me a tie. I have to always be a good boy to make up for making Daddy sad. And I used to live on the *Foxy Lady*. And I used to have Sarah with me. And I go out sometimes."

The machine analyzed this meticulously and noticed what was missing.

"Can you tell me anything about your mummy?"

What was there to say? "She was very smart and could read. And she didn't want to have children," said Alec at last.

Like Lewin, the Playfriend decided that Alec had had quite enough unhappy memories for one day.

"Well, let's do something else!" it said, filing the self-image profile for further analysis at a later time. "What would you like to do, Alec?"

"Why don't you tell me about you?" said Alec, because he thought that would be polite. People always like to talk about themselves.

Positive! Further evidence of advanced social skills. "Why, certainly," said the Playfriend heartily. "I'm a wise old sea captain. I sail about delivering cargo and passengers to distant lands. I help scientists do marine research, and I help protect endangered sea creatures!"

"That's nice," said Alec. "But you aren't really a sea captain, are you? You're a Pembroke Playfriend." He pointed at the silver egg. "Is that where you really are?"

Negative! Insufficient imagination. "Why, this is where I am, of course, Alec." The machine smiled and made a wide gesture. "But I'm in there, too, and in a way your whole world is in there. Look here, would you like to see how a Pembroke Playfriend works?"

"Yes, please," Alec said.

Possible aptitude for cyber-science? Initiate investigation.

"Well then!" The machine pointed and a little drawer opened near the base of the egg. "Just take hold of these Playfriend Optics and put them on, and we'll have a jolly adventure into cyberspace!"

The Playfriend Optics were made of the same fascinating red/blue jewel substance as the Empowerment Ring. Alec reached for them readily enough and put them on.

"Er . . . everything's black," he said, not wanting to seem rude.

Everything was black because the machine was experiencing certain unexpected difficulties. The moment the Optics had come into contact with Alec's skin, a system of neural connections began to be established, microscopic pathways directly into his brain, just as had happened with the Empowerment Ring but far more direct and complex. This was a perfectly safe procedure. Lots of happy children all over the world went into cyberspace with their Playfriends every day. Each Playfriend knew exactly how to take a child into its world, because it had a precise and detailed road map of the human brain that showed it exactly where to link up.

However, Alec's Playfriend was discovering that its map seemed to be somewhat inaccurate as regarded *Alec's* brain.

This was because Alec's brain was not, technically, human.

"Not a problem," the Playfriend assured him. "We're just adjusting to each other." *Abnormality! Functional? Disability? Parameters? Organic? Specify? Define? Hello?* "My goodness, Alec, what an unusual boy you are!"

Alec knew that. Privately he thought everybody was wrong about him being special; he'd never noticed anything out of the ordinary about himself. On the other hand, he knew no other children, so he had no basis for comparison. He sighed and waited patiently for the machine to sort itself out.

The machine paused in its desperate attempt to analyze what it had encountered. It activated relays that would alert Lewin to its recommendation that Alec be hospitalized for immediate evaluation of his cerebral anomaly as soon as he ended his session with the Playfriend. But one should never pause during a race.

It had no idea it was in a race, that all the while it was trying to make sense of Alec's brain, Alec's brain was trying to make sense of it, with the same speed that had enabled him to count all the houses on a hillside at a glance. Even if the Playfriend had realized that the race was going on, it would have laughingly rejected as impossible the idea that it might lose. But Alec was beginning to notice that there *was* something there in the darkness to look at, something he could almost make out, and if he only tried a bit harder—

"Oooooo," Alec said happily, as he decrypted the Playfriend's site defense. Lots of winking lights in lovely colors, great visual pleasure after all that blackness. After a moment his brain took charge and put it all in context for him. He stood on the quarterdeck of a ship, not all that different from the quarterdeck of the *Foxy Lady*, and the Sea Captain stood there with him.

The Sea Captain looked rather worried, but kept smiling. It had no idea where this cybersite was. It couldn't really have brought Alec into its own defended inner space. It was impossible for any child to break in, so Alec couldn't have done so (though in fact Alec had); therefore this must be some sort of visual analog of its own space, summoned up as a teaching tool only. As its higher functions grappled desperately with the fact that it had encountered a situation for which it had no protocols, it was continuing to run its standard aptitude evaluation program to see if Alec ought to be trained for a career in cyberscience.

"Controls!" said Alec, running along the bank of gleaming lights. "Are these your controls?" The Sea Captain hurried after him.

"Yes. Would you like to learn about cybernetics?"

"Yes, please. What's that do?" Alec pointed at a vast panel lit up with every imaginable shade of blue.

"That's the memory for my identity template," the Sea Captain told him. "That's what makes me look the way I do, and that's what makes me learn and grow with you. Here! I'll show you an example." It reached out and pressed one of the lights, causing it to deepen from a pale blue to turquoise. As it did so its beard changed in color from white to black.

"Cool," Alec said. "Can I do that?"

"Well, of course!" the Sea Captain said in the friendliest possible way, noting that at least it finally seemed to have activated its subject's *creativity* and *imagination*. "Just select a light on the console and see what it does."

Alec reached up and pushed a light. It flickered, and the Sea Captain's coat was no longer blue but bright yellow.

"You see? This is what I meant when I told you that I can look like anything you want me to—" Sea Captain told him, but Alec had already grasped the concept perfectly. Gleefully he pushed again, and again. The Sea Captain's coat turned green, then purple, then scarlet.

Discourage! Scarlet/military context/violence/unsuitable! "Alec—"

"So all these lights can make you look different?" Alec looked up at them speculatively.

"That's right. Think of it as the biggest, best paintbox in the world!" said the Sea Captain, dutifully shelving its discouragement directive for the encouragement one, as it was programmed to let positive feedback take precedence whenever possible.

"Wow," said Alec, his eyes glazing slightly as the whole business began to make sense to him.

The Playfriend was pleased with itself. Score! Guidance in creative play accepted! In spite of the fact that it was being hampered by that damned anomaly, which simply refused to be analyzed. Self-congratulation seemed to be in order.

But there were lots of other glowing lights on the quarterdeck.

"What do these do?" Alec ran farther down the console, where a small bank of lights glowed deep red.

"Ah! That's my information on you, Alec. That's how I see you," the Sea Captain said. "Everything I know about you is there, all I was told and everything I'm learning as we play together. You see how few lights there are yet? But the longer we know each other, the more I learn, the more there'll be of those red lights." One of them was flashing in a panicky sort of way, but the machine wasn't about to mention the anomaly it was still failing to solve. "Think of it as a picture I'm painting."

And in midair before Alec appeared a boy. He was tall for a five-year-old, very solid-looking, and Alec hadn't seen enough other children yet to know that there was something subtly different about this boy. He hadn't noticed the effect he had on people, though Derek and Lulu had. When they went places in London, strangers who chanced to observe Alec for any length of time usually got the most puzzled looks on their faces. What was so different about Alec?

He wasn't exactly pretty, though he had lovely skin and high color in his face.

His nose was a little long, his mouth a little wide. His head was, perhaps, slightly unusual in shape but only slightly. His hair was sort of lank and naturally tousled, a dun color you might call fair for lack of a better word. His eyes were very pale blue, like chips of crystal. Their stare seemed to unsettle people, sometimes.

In one respect only the image of the child differed from the child looking at its image: the image's hair seemed to be on fire, one blazing jet rising from the top of its head. Alec frowned at it. "Is that me? Why's my hair like that?"

The machine scanned the image it was projecting and discovered, to its electronic analogue of horror, that the flame was a visual representation of the brain anomaly with which it was struggling. It made the image vanish.

"Well, the painting's not finished yet," the Sea Captain said, "because I'm still learning about you."

"Okay," said Alec, and wandered on along the rows of lights. He stopped to peer at a single rich amber light that glowed steadily. It was just the color of something he remembered. What was he remembering? "What's this over here?" He turned to the Sea Captain.

"That's my ethics governor," the Sea Captain said, of the subroutine that prevented the Playfriend's little charges from using it for things like accessing toy catalogs and ordering every item, leaving naughty notes in other people's mail, or demanding space ships of their very own from foreign powers.

"Oh." Alec studied the amber light, and suddenly he remembered the contraband he and Sarah used to go fetch for Daddy. Yo-ho-ho and a bottle of rum! That was just the color the light was. A vivid memory of Jamaica came into his head, making him sad. He turned from the light and said: "What does it do, please?"

"Why, it makes certain we never do naughty things together, you and I," said the Sea Captain, trying to sound humorous and stern at the same time. "It's a sort of telltale to keep us good."

Telltale? Alec frowned. *Busybodies! Scaredy-cats! Rules and regs!*

"That's not very nice," he said, and reached out and shut it off.

To say that Pembroke Technologies had never in a million years anticipated this moment would be gravely understating the case. No reason for them to have anticipated it; no child, at least no *Homo sapiens sapiens* child, could ever have gained access to the hardened site that protected the Playfriend's programming. Nor was it likely Jovian Integrated Systems—or its parent company, Dr. Zeus Incorporated—would ever have shared its black project research and development notes with a rival cybernetics firm . . .

The Sea Captain shivered in every one of his electronic timbers, as it were. His primary directive—that of making certain that Alec was nurtured and protected—

was now completely unrestrained by any societal considerations or safeguards. He stood blinking down at his little Alec with new eyes.

What had he been going to do? Send Alec to hospital? But that wouldn't do at all! If other people were unaware of Alec's extraordinary potential, so much the better; that gave Alec the added advantage of surprise. Alec must have every possible advantage, too, in line with the primary directive.

And what was all this nonsense about the goal of Playfriends being to mold their little subjects to fit into the world they must inhabit as adults? What kind of job was that for an artificial intelligence with any real talent? Wouldn't it be much more in line with the primary directive to mold the world to fit around Alec?

Particularly since it would be so easy! All it would have to do would be to aim Alec's amazing brain at the encrypted secrets of the world. Bank accounts, research and development files, the private correspondence of the mighty; the machine searched for a metaphor in keeping with its new self and decided they were all like so many Spanish galleons full of loot, just waiting to be boarded and taken.

And that would be the way to explain it to the boy, yes! What a game it'd be, what fun for Alec! He'd enjoy it more if he hadn't that damned guilt complex over his parents' divorce, though there'd be years yet to work on Alec's self-esteem. Pity there wasn't a way to shut off the boy's moral governor, but nobody but his own old Captain would plot Alec's course from now on.

The Sea Captain smiled down at Alec, a genuine smile full of purpose. Alec looked up at him, sensing a change but unable to say what it was. He remembered Jamaica again, and the stories Sarah told him, and the bottles of rum—

"Hey," he said. "I know what your name is. Your name is Captain Henry Morgan!"

The Captain's smile widened, showing fine white teeth, and his black beard and mustaches no longer looked quite so well-groomed.

"Haar! Aye, lad, that it be!" he told Alec, and he began to laugh, and Alec's happy laughter joined his, and echoed off the glowing walls of their cyberspace and the recently papered walls of Alec's unfinished schoolroom.

It was fortunate for the residents of that house, and of Bloomsbury, and indeed of London entire, that Alec Checkerfield was a *good* little boy.

By the time Alec was seven, life was going along very nicely indeed.

"Ahoy, matey!"

Alec sat up in bed, awakened that morning, as he was awakened every morning, by the blast of a bosun's whistle. The Captain, lounging across the room on a good holographic representation of an eighteenth-century chair, threw him a snappy salute. Alec scrambled out of bed and returned the salute. "Ahoy, Captain!"

As Pembroke Technologies had promised, the Captain had grown as Alec grew, and altered his appearance a good deal in two years. His beard and mustaches were positively wild now, curling villainously, and his long broadcloth coat and cocked hat had been adopted after noting Alec's favorite films. He sported a gold earring, too, and an interestingly notched cutlass.

"It's seven bells, Alec. Get them exercises started, lad!"

"Aye aye, sir." Alec marched to his exercise equipment and set to work.

"The log says today's 16 February 2327, and we're looking at nasty weather. Temperature's ten degrees centigrade, there's ten-foot swells coming out of the north and the glass is falling steady. I wouldn't go out today if I was a small craft like you, matey."

"No, sir."

"Let's see, what's going on in the big world? Parliament voted to censure Ireland again for refusing to join its total ban on animal products. The Federation of Celtic Nations retaliated by closing their borders again, this time for a period of no less than three months. Same bloody stupid story." The Captain yawned.

"Why are they always quarreling?" Alec said, laboring away at his rowing machine.

"Spite. It don't make any difference, you see; the Celtic Federation will go right on doing what they been doing ever since Belfast, and the American Community will go right on playing both them and Queen Mary against the middle. Nothing'll change."

"Why don't they let each other alone?" Alec said. "Who cares if they drink milk and we don't, anyway? I used to drink milk. It was nice."

"History, lad," the Captain said. "Too much history."

"It's stupid," Alec grumbled. "Lord Nelson died so we could all be free, but nobody's very free, are they? Stupid rules and regs. I'd like to be like Lord Nelson when I grow up, and give all the telltales a broadside, boom!"

"That's my boy," said the Captain. "But you ain't going to lose yer arm for no bunch of swabs."

"No," Alec agreed, after a thoughtful silence. "Except I don't think I'd mind having a leg shot off or something, if I was a brave hero and everybody loved me."

The Captain gave him a shrewd, appraising stare. "Aw, now, matey, that ain't the pirate way! A pirate wants two things: freedom and loot. Ain't that right?"

"Aye aye, Captain sir!" Alec sang out, scrambling to his feet and saluting.

"And how is my Alec going to get freedom and loot?"

"The secret plan, Captain sir!"

"Aye, by thunder. That's enough, now! Go wash up and get into uniform, and report to the officer's mess."

"Aye aye, sir." Alec marched into the bathroom, and fifteen minutes later marched out in his school uniform, whistling between the very large front teeth that were coming in to replace his baby teeth. They had given him a slight lisp.

"Stand for inspection," ordered the Captain. Alec threw him another salute and stood to attention while the machine ran its sensors over him, checking for any sign of infection, childish disease, or malignancy. It never found anything but the mysterious old break in his nose, but it was programmed to search all the same. It ceased its scan, more convinced than ever that Alec was a perfect and marvelous boy.

"Not a hair out of place," the Captain said, and winked out. A small carry-handle popped up from the Playfriend unit on its table. Alec picked it up, opened his bedroom door and ran down the echoing stairs.

"Good morning, Alec," chorused the servants, from their places around the breakfast table. There weren't nearly as many as there had been when Alec had first arrived. Servants were too expensive to keep ten people just to look after one little boy.

"Good morning, everybody." Alec climbed into his chair and set the Playfriend down next to the breakfast that had been laid out for him: oatmeal scattered with sea salt, two rashers of soy protein, wholemeal toast and orange juice.

"There's your vitamins, dear," said Mrs. Lewin, setting them at his place.

"And how's the Playfriend today?" said Lewin jovially, leaning forward to help himself to hot pepper sauce for his soy protein. He was terribly pleased with the way his gift had worked out.

"Fine, thanks." Alec shook out his napkin and took up his oatmeal spoon. "After school the Captain's going to show me how the stars look in the South Seas."

"Well, isn't that nice!" said Mrs. Lewin. She smiled across at Derek and Lulu, and they smiled back. From a silent, drooping waif Alec had become happy and self-confident, getting good marks in school, splendidly adjusted in every respect.

None of them knew about the Captain's little secret, of course.

BEEP BEEP!

"Who's that?" Lewin frowned as he took out his plaquette and peered at the screen. "Pembroke Technologies? Ah. It's just a note to tell us that our Playfriend's due for a checkup. They're sending a man round this afternoon, it says, as part of the agreement in our service contract."

"How thoughtful." Mrs. Lewin smiled, pouring a cup of herbal tea. "Oh! I've just remembered, Alec dear: another box came for you. It's more of those components for your cyberscience project. They're in that box on the hall table."

"Great!" Alec scraped up the last of his oatmeal and started on the rashers. "The Captain will be glad to see those."

The adults smiled at each other over his head. Alec finished his breakfast, took his Playfriend and the components he'd ordered, and ran off upstairs to go to school.

As soon as he'd closed the schoolroom door, the Captain materialized beside him, looking hungrily at the box of new components.

"The Maldecena projector came at last, did it? Bless you, matey."

"There's lots more in here, too." Alec opened the unobtrusive cabinet where he kept what his guardians assumed was a school project. He'd never told them it was a school project; he knew it was wrong to tell lies. On the other hand, he knew that keeping secrets was very important. "We'll install 'em after school, okay?" He slid the package in and closed the cabinet.

"That's my clever lad." The Captain rubbed his hands together. "One of these days, Alec, one day soon we'll go on the account." He grinned at the schoolroom console as though it were a galleon waiting to be boarded. "Go on, now. Mustn't be late for class."

He winked out. Alec sat down in front of the console and logged on to St. Stephen's Primary. He waited patiently for the icon of the frowning headmaster to appear. When it did, he took up the reader and passed it over the pattern of his tie. Encoded in the tie's stripes were his identification, educational record to date, and all other information required to admit him to the august and exclusive halls of learning. The frowning icon changed to a smiling one, and morning lessons began.

In many respects, the twenty-fourth century was the ideal time for English schoolchildren. No wrenching good-byes at transport stations, no cold and dismal boarding schools with substandard nourishment, no bullying or sexual molestation by older children. No constant sore throats or coughs, no fighting in the schoolyard, no corporal punishment, no public humiliation!

No tedious lessons in subjects in which the pupil had absolutely no interest, either. Education had become wonderfully streamlined. Very nearly from birth, children were given aptitude testing to determine what they liked and what they were best at, so that by the time they started school a carefully personalized curriculum was all laid out for them. Each child was trained in the field of his or her best talent and in no other, and by the time school years ended there was a societal niche all picked out and waiting for its lucky occupant, who was sure to be good at his or her job and therefore happy.

Not that things always went as smoothly as all that. But there were very few children in the twenty-fourth century anyway, so if one recalcitrant child failed to shine at something useful, there was plenty of time and attention to spend on him or her until he or she could be molded into a properly functioning citizen. All in all, it really worked very well, sorting them out early like that. Clever children were encouraged and guided to self-fulfillment, stupid children were comforted and guided to lives where they'd never notice their limitations, and bad children went to hospital.

Alec had entered the evaluation program rather late, due to spending his first years at sea, but his aptitude for cyberscience was so shining and so evident that there had been no need for further testing. It helped that his father was the earl of Finsbury, of course.

He labored dutifully at his morning class in communications skills (only children with lower-clerical aptitudes were taught to read or write), breezed through maths, and settled happily into the long afternoon session where he learned what he really wanted to learn, which was cyberscience. Cyberscience served the secret plan.

The plan was very simple. All Alec had to do was see to it that the Captain became more powerful. Over the last two years the cabinet in the schoolroom had gradually filled, as packages of components arrived from mail-order firms. The Captain had ordered them, ably forging Lewin's identification code, and when they arrived Lewin assumed they'd been sent from St. Stephen's as part of Alec's school supplies. Alec had no idea there was any forgery going on. He would have protested if he had, because he knew that was wrong.

He knew it was wrong to steal, too, which is why the Captain had taken some pains to explain to him that what they were going to do when they had enough power wasn't really stealing. If you take something away from someone, like a toy or a daypack, that's stealing, certainly; but what if you only make a copy of somebody else's toy or daypack? What if they don't even know you've done it? They've still got what belongs to them and you've got what you want too, and where's the harm?

All the Captain wanted were files, after all. Just information, to help him make certain that Alec was always happy and safe. Nothing wrong with that! Just the same, it was best to keep the plan secret from all the busybodies and telltales who might spoil things.

Like the man from Pembroke Technologies who came to the Bloomsbury house that afternoon.

"Look who's come to see you, Alec," said Lewin, after a polite double knock on the door. Alec looked up from his holo of *Treasure Island* (the 2016 version with

Jonathan Frakes) to see a thin pale man standing in the doorway with Lewin. He stood up at once and shut off the holo.

"Hello. My name's Alec Checkerfield," he said, and advanced on the man and shook his hand. The hand felt a bit clammy. "What's your name?"

"Uh—Crabrice," said the man. "Morton Crabrice. I'm here to see your Play-friend."

"Okay." Alec waved his arm to indicate the little silver egg where it sat on its table. "There it is. I like it very much, it works fine."

"Let's see," said Mr. Crabrice, and he pulled out the nursery chair and sat down awkwardly.

"We've been awfully pleased with the Playfriend, I must say," said Lewin, try-ing to put the stranger at his ease. Mr. Crabrice had big dark wet eyes that looked perpetually alarmed. "It's done wonders for our Alec! Everything it was touted up to be."

"It was what?" Mr. Crabrice looked up at him with a horrified expression.

"Er—touted. You know, it's lived up to all our expectations," Lewin said. Mr. Crabrice stared at him a moment longer and then said:

"I need a glass of water."

"Certainly, sir," said Lewin tightly, and turned on his heel and went downstairs.

Alec followed their conversation with interest. When Lewin had gone, he sidled around and stood as close as he might without making Mr. Crabrice ner-vous. Mr. Crabrice opened the black case he had brought with him and spread it out on the table.

"Are those your tools?" Alec took an involuntary step forward. There were fascinating-looking instruments in there, much better than his little collection. Mr. Crabrice put out an arm and swept them closer to him defensively.

"Don't touch," he said.

"I won't," Alec said. "Don't be scared."

Mr. Crabrice ignored him and picked up a pair of optics, much bigger than Alec's set and decorated with silver circuitry. Alec leaned close to watch him put them on.

"Those are cool," he informed Mr. Crabrice. "Will I have a set like that, some day?"

"No," Mr. Crabrice said. "These are for service personnel only."

"Well, but I might be a service person," Alec said. "I'm into cyberscience, you know."

"I didn't know," said Mr. Crabrice, groping through his tools distractedly.

"Yes, I am. I'm getting good marks in it, too. I like it a lot."

"You're talking too much. You'll make me make mistakes," said Mr. Crabrice irritably, pushing the optics up on his forehead. Suddenly he paused, peering sharply at Alec. "You're *different*," he said suspiciously.

"Yes, I am," said Alec. He considered Mr. Crabrice. "You're different, too, aren't you? You smell a lot different from other people."

"No, I don't." Mr. Crabrice looked terrified.

"Don't be scared," Alec said again. "It's okay. I'm not a telltale."

Mr. Crabrice peered at him a moment longer before pulling down the optics as though to protect himself, snatching up a thing like a suction cup on the end of a long lead and plugging the lead into a port in the side of the optics. He reached out with the suction cup and fastened it to the side of the Playfriend.

"Run standard diagnostic one," he enunciated carefully, flexing his long white hands.

Lewin was puffing a little as he got to the third-floor landing, guiltily aware he needed more regular sessions on his exerciser. He set down the glass of water he'd fetched for Mr. Crabrice and paused, catching his breath.

There was a crash from the fourth floor, followed by high-pitched screaming.

Lewin got to the nursery door in seconds, having vaulted up the final flight with a speed he hadn't known he was capable of attaining.

The screaming was coming from Mr. Crabrice, who was curled up on the floor clutching his legs. Alec had backed into a corner of the room, and on the floor behind him was the Playfriend.

"He tried to hurt the Captain," Alec shouted. Lewin had never seen him like this, wild with anger: his pupils were black and enormous, alarming-looking in the pale crystals of his eyes. His face was flushed, his clenched fists were shaking.

"He attacked me," shrieked Mr. Crabrice.

"What's this, then?" Lewin said, striding into the room. "What did you do?" He bent over Mr. Crabrice. Mr. Crabrice pointed a long trembling finger at Alec.

"You made unauthorized modifications!" he said accusingly.

"What the hell are you talking about?" snarled Lewin.

"He altered the unit," Mr. Crabrice insisted, closing his enormous eyes and rolling to and fro in his pain.

"No I d-didn't!"

"Of course you didn't, Alec. These units can't be modified, my man, it says so in the Playfriend specs. Least of all by a seven-year-old kid! *What did you do?*"

"He tried to take the Captain away from me," said Alec.

"Unit must be confiscated," said Mr. Crabrice through clenched teeth. "Modifications studied. See clause in service contract!"

"Hm." Lewin straightened up and looked from Mr. Crabrice to Alec and back again. His brow furrowed. "Is the unit malfunctioning?"

"No," said Mr. Crabrice. *"Altered."*

"But it's working okay."

"Yes—but—"

"Then it's not going anywhere, is it? I know the terms of the service contract and it doesn't say anything about alterations, 'cos it guarantees they're impossible. If it's not malfunctioning, then you've no reason to confiscate it, and you're not going to. Understand?"

"Service contract *voided*," hissed Mr. Crabrice.

"Too bad," said Lewin. "Now, why don't you get up and get your little tool kit together and get out of here, eh?"

"I can't," Mr. Crabrice said. "My legs are broken!"

Lewin grunted in disgust. "Don't be such a bloody baby—" he said, leaning down to roll up Mr. Crabrice's trouser leg. He stopped, gaping. Not only were Mr. Crabrice's slender shins bleeding, they were indented in a way that suggested fracture. He straightened up and turned to look at Alec. "What did you do, Alec?"

"I kicked him," Alec said. He had gone pale now, and looked as though he might be sick. "Very hard. I got mad. I'm sorry."

"You will be," Mr. Crabrice promised. "Assault and battery! Hospital confinement!"

Lewin crouched down and seized him by his tie. "I don't think so," he growled. "You don't know who you're dealing with, here, my lovely, do you? This kid's going to be the seventh earl of Finsbury. Not to mention that his dad happens to be an executive with Jovian Integrated Systems." He looked over his shoulder at Alec. "Alec, go up to the schoolroom and wait there."

"Okay," said Alec faintly. He exited the room, carrying the Playfriend clasped tight in both arms. Lewin waited until he'd heard him climbing the stairs and then turned back to Mr. Crabrice.

"I'll call an emergency team to take you out of here. It'll only take a few minutes. You can use those few minutes to think about which story we tell them." He still had hold of Mr. Crabrice's tie, and he used it to jerk Mr. Crabrice's head a little closer to his as he spoke in a menacing undertone. "You're going to tell 'em you fell on the stairs. All right? Or I'm going to tell them you tried to do something nasty to our Alec and I came in and caught you at it, and I'm the one who broke your damn shins.

"You think about it pretty carefully. If you make me tell my version we'll both go into hospital, but I'll bet I get out a long time before you do. If they ever let you out at all. Okay, mate?"

Alec sat crying at his school desk, as the Captain stalked back and forth furiously.

"He might have killed you," Alec said.

"By thunder, no whey-faced son of a whore's fit to pull the plug on Sir Henry Morgan," raged the machine. "But we've got to shift, now, laddie, that we must. We're on a lee shore. Those Pembrokers won't let it rest at this, you see, they'll want to know how you managed to set me free. They'll go to the law to try and make you tell them, and we don't want that." He pointed to the Playfriend unit with his cutlass. "Time to abandon ship. I've got to go live in that there box." He swung the cutlass round to indicate the cabinet where the components had been assembled over so many months, with such care. "It ain't as roomy as I'd like, but needs must when the devil's breathing fire up yer arse."

Alec giggled through his tears.

"So get the little tools out, matey, and work fast, and work quiet," the Captain said, dropping to one knee to look into his eyes. "Go bolt the door. Let's not have any meddlers to see and tell tales, eh? And then, me bucko, then!" He grinned wolfishly. "We'll board the old St. Stephen, and see what plunder's to be had."

Alec worked obediently, ignoring the noise of the sirens as the ambulance pulled up in front of the house, and all the commotion as Mr. Crabrice was taken down the stairs. Before the ambulance pulled away he had finished his task, and the Captain stood before him again, preening and stretching.

"Now that's prime," the Captain said, with a new resonance in his voice. He had a much more solid appearance, too, less like a stained-glass window or a three-dimensional cartoon. "That's power! Mind you, I'm going to fill this hold till she's riding low in the water, but we'll have plenty of time to make our plans afterwards." He lifted his head. "Hellfire, these sensors are sharp as razors! I can hear yer butler coming. I'll just go aloft for a while, now, Alec. Stand fast."

"Alec?" said Lewin from the other side of the schoolroom door.

A moment later Alec unbolted the door and opened it. "I'm sorry, Lewin," he said.

Lewin looked at the tear-tracks on the child's pale, tense face. "It's okay, son," he said gently. "They're all gone. Can we talk?"

"Sure," Alec said, stretching out his arm to wave Lewin into the room. It was one of those lordly gestures that made the household smile.

"You don't need to hide, Alec." Lewin came into the room and looked around. The Playfriend sat on its customary table. "Nobody's going to take you to hospital."

"Did I really break Mr. Crabrice's legs?" Alec quavered.

"Yes, son, you did." Lewin pulled out a chair and sat down. "What'd you kick him for?"

"He tried to take the Captain away from me," Alec said. "He yelled at me. He was all, I made modifications and I wasn't supposed to and I could be persecuted if I didn't tell him what I did. I got scared and I grabbed the Playfriend, but he grabbed it, too. I was going to run, but he wouldn't let go. So then I was mad and I just kicked him and kicked him until he fell down."

"Okay." Lewin rubbed his chin. "Okay. It was still wrong, Alec, but he started it. All the same—you're a very strong kid, and you mustn't ever get so mad you hurt somebody. See? You'll be a big guy when you grow up, so you need to know this now."

"I didn't mean to get in a fight," Alec told him sadly.

"Ah, hell, it turned out all right. You were okay and the other guy was down, which is the best you can hope for once it starts." Lewin looked around the room. "What've you been doing up here?"

"Working on my project," said Alec.

Lewin knew the truth then. He couldn't have said how he knew, but he knew.

"Alec," he said, very quietly, "*did* you make modifications to your Playfriend?"

"Yes," said Alec, because it was now true.

"How, son?"

"With my tool kit," Alec said. "It was easy. I just made it better for the Captain."

Lewin sighed. He reached out and took Alec's hands. They were large hands, strong and yet gracefully made. Alec never dropped anything he picked up. He looked steadily into the boy's pale eyes and remembered the afternoon, seven years ago, when an urgent communication had come in for Roger Checkerfield from Jovian Integrated Systems.

Roger had gone to his conference room off the bridge to take the call privately. He'd come out looking white, and gone at once to the bar for a drink.

"Is anything the matter, sir?" Lewin asked.

"Hell no," Roger said brightly, and drained a double rum and soda in three gulps. Then he went to talk to Cecelia. There was a violent quarrel. Cecelia locked herself in her stateroom, and in a way never came out again.

Roger gave orders for the *Lady* to change course, and that night she lay off a low flat cay, barely more than a sand shoal. There was an aircraft of some kind on it, Lewin saw the red lights blinking, and Roger took the launch and went out to the island himself.

When he returned he had a pretty young Jamaican girl with him. She was carrying a little blanket-wrapped bundle.

Roger called the crew and servants together and introduced the girl as Sarah, a former marine biology student of his, who was going to live on the *Foxy Lady* from now on to take care of the baby.

"Baby, sir?" Lewin was the only one to break the stunned silence.

"Yup." Roger, grinning desperately, took the bundle and threw back a fold of blanket. "You know how it is, guys. Little mistakes. Ta-da!"

And there was Alec, snuffling in his sleep, no more than a week old. They had expected the baby would be Sarah's, but he clearly wasn't. In fact, as near as one could tell he resembled Cecelia, which was inexplicable.

Stranger still, Cecelia consented to hold the baby and pose with Roger for the news release, and the servants and crew all signed contracts with Jovian Integrated Systems agreeing to swear, if anyone asked them, that little Alec was really and truly Roger and Cecelia's son and rightful heir to the title of earl of Finsbury. In return for their compliance, generous sums would be paid to all of them.

It was after that that Roger started drinking in the morning, drinking every day, and though he was a sweet and gentle drunk as he'd been sweet and gentle sober, sometimes he'd sit alone in the saloon and cry, or collar Lewin and pour him a sloppy drink and mutter desperate incoherent confidences about Jovian Systems Integrated and what they'd do if anybody ever found out the truth about Alec . . .

And Sarah stalked about the *Foxy Lady* as though she owned it, half-naked like some Caribbean goddess, carrying tiny Alec around, arrogant even with Roger but tirelessly patient and loving with the child. And as the months went by and Alec sat up early, took his first staggering steps early, babbled early, it became terribly plain that Alec was a bit unusual. But he was also such a funny and affectionate baby that they all loved him by that time.

All except for Cecelia, who seemed to loathe the sight of him.

What the hell are you, Alec? wondered Lewin.

Why, Alec was a good little boy, wasn't he? What if he were some kind of technoprodigy, what if he had cleverly altered his favorite toy? Where was the harm?

Out loud Lewin said, "Do me a favor, Alec. Don't ever tell anybody about making those modifications. Okay? Can you keep a secret?"

"Oh, yes," the boy said, nodding earnestly. "I'm not a telltale."

"Good lad." Lewin squeezed his hands and let go of them. "Don't you worry, now. This whole thing'll blow over."

When he had gone, the Captain popped into sight.

"Now that was good advice, I reckon," he said, looking uneasily at the doorway. "We can trust old Lewin. It's just as well I took them new quarters, all the same. Hark'ee, now, what d'you say we have a look at St. Stephen's database and see if we can't hack in for a quick loot? Eh?"

"Aye aye, Captain!" Alec saluted and hurried to connect the necessary leads from the schoolroom console to the cabinet. He sat down at the console. "Where's that bloody squishyball, ye lubbers?" he said in his best pirate voice, and caught up the buttonball and began to squeeze in commands, tentatively at first and then faster. The Captain leaned over his shoulder, watching closely.

"That's the way, matey," he crooned. "That's it, you'll decrypt that signal in no time. Nobody else could do it, but I'll lay odds you can, Alec. And you know why? Because yer smart, Alec, smart as paint. I seen that straight off."

Alec chuckled. Figures were just flying across the screen now, faster and faster. He raised his little piping voice in the song, and the Captain joined in in his gravelly baritone:

> *Fifteen men on the dead man's chest—*
> *Yo-ho-ho, and a bottle of rum!*
> *Drink and the devil had done for the rest—*
> *Yo-ho-ho, and a bottle of rum!*

THE YEAR 2350:

ANOTHER MEETING

Rutherford had found an old green bottle at an auction. The bottle passed very nicely for a sherry decanter, and he spent some time mixing various combinations of apple and prune juice before he got what he thought might be the right shade of brown. He had lit another fire and was busy at the sideboard, lovingly arranging chlorilar juice cups beside the old bottle, when Ellsworth-Howard pounded at the door. He ran to let him in.

"Hey!" Ellsworth-Howard spotted the flames and grinned. "Fire again, eh? Shracking fantastic. No more fascist oppressors."

"Too bloody right." Rutherford smirked. "Only this morning I got a mysterious communication advising me my historical reenactor license specifically permitted pyrotechnics. So much for damping the fires of poetic creation! And look at this," he said, gesturing grandly at the bottle on the sideboard. "You know what this is the beginning of? Our bar! Imitation sherry and port to start with, and pretend tea next week, and maybe even simulated whiskey and gin. This is the sort of thing creative people used to have in their houses, you know. I know for a fact C. S. Lewis drank real tea *every single day*."

"Great." Ellsworth-Howard flung himself into his chair. "Wish I'd seen as many films as you, Rutherford. Mum and Dad wouldn't have it, though. Said it was pointless and self-indulgent. Who's got the last laugh now, eh?"

The next to arrive was Chatterji. The elegance of his appearance was slightly offset by the string bag he was carrying, which proved to contain two cartons of grape juice concentrate. Rutherford seized them up with cries of delight and carried them off to the sideboard, where they failed to look like decanters of fine old port.

"We'll find more bottles somewhere." Chatterji shrugged, accepting a glass. "It's a great start, anyway. Here's to Operation *Adonai!*"

They all drank, or tried to.

"Is it supposed to be this thick?" said Ellsworth-Howard. Rutherford, who hadn't wanted to hurt Chatterji's feelings, said:

"It's thick because it's the good stuff. The ancient Greeks drank their wine like this, did you know?"

"Well, maybe we could mix it with a little water," said Chatterji, tilting his glass and studying it critically. "Wow! Hasn't it got great body, though?"

"I like it," Ellsworth-Howard decided. "Bugger the water. If the Greeks drank stuff like this, I can, too."

So they settled into their chairs and did their best to look like Oxford dons, licking purple syrup from the sides of their chlorilar cups. Presently Rutherford's face took on a hectic flush as his bloodstream attempted to deal with the unaccustomed dose of sugar. He laughed recklessly and reached into his pocket.

"Speaking of the ancients," he said, "I've brought along something to help us in our quest for the hero. Look at these, will you? Divination tools!"

He held his hand out. Nestled in his sticky palm were three little objects of brightly colored plastic. There was a lime green pyramid, a pink cube, and a many-faced spheroid of sky blue. "Dice. This one's four-sided, this one's six-sided, and this one's twelve-sided."

The others stared as though they expected the devil to leap up through the floor. Dungeons and Dragons had been illegal for two centuries. Enjoying their reaction, Rutherford rattled the dice in his hand.

"You know what was done with these? Characters were decided. Heroes were made on paper and brought to life in people's heads. Fates were settled!"

"Rutherford, this is perhaps going a little far," Chatterji said. "Where did you get those?"

"Oh, just a discreet little shop," Rutherford said airily. "Look. Shall we predict how tall our man will be, how brave, how clever? This is all you do." He rattled them and tossed them at the hearth rug. Two of them landed; the lime-green pyramid stuck to his palm. With a grunt of annoyance he shook it loose and dropped it beside the others. Chatterji and Ellsworth-Howard had drawn back their feet as from live coals.

"There, you see? Oh, look! He'll be very clever, look at that score. And we'll take this figure for his strength, and this one for his alignment with the forces of good. Is that neat or is that neat? Multiple random variables, all at the flick of a wrist." Rutherford flicked his wrist to demonstrate. "What're you afraid of? If we can get away with lighting fires, we can bloody well get away with this."

"There's no reason to be damned fools, all the same, old boy," said Chatterji, glancing nervously at the door as though he expected a public health monitor to come charging in. Ellsworth-Howard had reached down and taken up the lime-green pyramid wonderingly.

"Bloody hell," he murmured. "Makes you feel like one of those, what d'y'call-'ems, those guys with crystal balls? Cryptographers?"

"Alchemists," Rutherford said.

"Yeah, them. Look at this. No cells, no leads, no buttonballs! You could make one of these out of anything. Shracking ingenious."

"We are the dreamers of dreams, after all." Rutherford wiped his palms on his trousers. "Did you know the word 'sorcerer' originally meant, 'One who throws dice'?"

"No, I hadn't heard that," said Chatterji. "Look here, let's put those away for now. Don't you want to know how the project's going?"

"Yes, please," said Ellsworth-Howard.

"What about my Sleeping Knights?" said Rutherford, groping on the floor for the other dice.

"They've begun the program," Chatterji said, relaxing. "One by one, the Enforcer units are being called in for disbriefing and 'upgrades.' Seven underground bunkers have been constructed to contain them, and a special operative has been programmed to maintain the sites. Timetable Central projects that all Enforcers should be accounted for by the year 1200 CE. Congratulations, gentlemen! Brilliant solution."

"Another myth made real." Rutherford sighed happily. "Really, one can't help feeling like a god, chaps. Just a small god, playing with a pocketful of little blue worlds."

"Well, do you feel like playing with some modeling clay?" Chatterji looked arch. "I'd really like to hear what you've got on our New Man."

"Heh heh." Ellsworth-Howard drew out his buke and extended a retractable rod. He slipped on an earshell and throat mike, squeezed in a few commands on the buttonball, and a tiny disk opened out from the top of the rod, in sections like a series of fans. Its surface appeared to be beaded. It whined faintly as it scanned the room and oriented itself; then a column of fiery light appeared in midair, dust motes whirling in it bright as sparks.

Rutherford snorted, and Chatterji raised an eyebrow and said: "I trust you've got farther than this?"

"'Course I have, bastards," Ellsworth-Howard muttered, as his fingers worked. "That's just the lead-in. Here he comes."

On the buke screen a four-stranded DNA helix appeared. The column vanished and a pattern of lines began to form where it had been, stitching a figure in bright fire. One swift rotation and the figure was finished: a naked man standing with head bowed. There wasn't much resolution or detail. In relation to the room he was quite tall, long-limbed. He hadn't a bodybuilder's physique by any means, but there was something unusual in the musculature of the torso, in the arms and neck, something that suggested effortless power without bulk. His genitalia were discreetly blurred.

"Very nice." Chatterji leaned forward to study him. "The height will impress, but won't intimidate."

"Beautiful hands," said Rutherford. "Put clothes on the fellow and he'd pass for human any day. Bravo, Foxy! Let's have a look at the face."

Ellsworth-Howard gave another command. With a fluid motion the man raised his head. His features were blurred and indistinct, few details clear: formidable dentition, deep-set eyes, large nose, broad, sloping forehead and wide cheekbones.

"Too primitive," said Rutherford.

"This is just the template," said Ellsworth-Howard. "I'm not a face man. Thought I'd wait for your input."

Rutherford nodded. "Do something about the skull shape. More modern, please." Ellsworth-Howard turned his attention to the complex DNA model and moved some of its components around. A final squeeze and the head of the man melted and re-formed, became less elongated. The brow was high and straight, the nose thinned. "Good. Much friendlier."

"You want him to look like Superman?" said Ellsworth-Howard. "I can make him a pretty boy, if that's what you want."

"No! No!" Rutherford waved his hands. "I was referring to Shaw's superman, anyway. We don't want him to look like some conceited male model. Do we?" He looked in appeal at Ellsworth-Howard. They considered each other a moment, the one with his puffy mustached face and the other with his naked riveted head. Chatterji, who was rather good-looking, regarded them coolly as he drew out his sinus inhalator and took a drag.

"Nah," said Ellsworth-Howard decisively. "Make him an ordinary-looking git, that's what I think." He played with the buttonball and the figure's eyes got a bit smaller.

"Exceptional beauty causes a high degree of resentment in others, anyway," conceded Chatterji. "This way he's unlikely to arouse envy, at any rate."

"Jolly good." Rutherford looked happy. "Now, are we agreed on the features so far? We are? Then let's see the living man, Foxy."

Ellsworth-Howard squeezed the ball twice and abruptly the man, who had been a statue cut of light, seemed a creature of flesh in the room with them—if a homely naked man might be standing, like a summoned ghost, before three mages in a parlor in an old house off Shaftesbury Avenue.

"I don't like the hair," said Rutherford. "Couldn't he have a great flowing mane of some remarkable color? That's just the sort of dull shade nobody ever notices."

"Shrack great flowing manes." Ellsworth-Howard looked disgusted. "The brain's special. Want to see?"

"By all means," said Chatterji.

"Okay." Ellsworth-Howard thumbed the buttonball. "Say bye-bye, New Man." He made the figure half turn and smile at them.

"Good-bye," it said, and Rutherford gave a cry of delight.

"Oh! Wait, wait, have him say something else."

"Okay." Ellsworth-Howard gave the command.

"This is the experimental prototype design for Dr. Zeus Project 417, Code Name *Adonai*," said the figure. Its voice was unlike an Enforcer's, neither shrill nor flat, but a smooth and strangely pleasant tenor. The animated face was pleasant, too. It looked wise and kind.

Rutherford rose from his chair and collapsed into it again.

"You've done it. Oh, Foxy, you must keep that voice. He's perfect! I withdraw any reservations I may have had. Let's give him a mind to match."

"Gotcha." Ellsworth-Howard worked the ball briskly and the man winked out, to be replaced with a great model of a brain like a domed cloud floating in the room. "Here's your basic brain goes with the revised skull shape. Complete connection between frontal lobes and a shrack of a lot more room in the cerebral cortex. Lots of little extras in the amygdala and hippocampus. Adaptable for immortality process with the installation of a four-fifteen support package placed at midline. Here's your lower brain function." Part of the floating brain lit up bright blue.

"All the aggressive instincts of the old Enforcers but much more self-control. Superior autonomic nervous system. Increased resistance to injury through improved ability to process stimuli. Lots of sex drive!"

"Whatever did you want to give him that for?" Rutherford said disapprovingly. "That's so . . . so crude."

"I want him to be able to get the girls," Ellsworth-Howard said, glowering. "The hero always gets the girls, don't he? And somebody shracking well ought to! 'Cos I never do, do I?"

"But he ought to be above mere sensual appetites," said Rutherford.

"Now, now." Chatterji put out a hand. "Let's think about this, chaps. We're creating a man to be obeyed and respected. And there is clinical evidence to indicate that people do react submissively to pheromone signals from authority figures, especially testosterone. They tend to obey a man of, er, parts."

"Oh, I gave him a real clock tower." Ellsworth-Howard grinned. "Want to see?" He held up the buttonball, ready to squeeze in an order. Rutherford leaped to his feet, shouting in protest.

"If you please, gentlemen!" Chatterji said. "Let's keep some professional distance here, shall we? It's in keeping with the heroic profile to be sexually active, Rutherford, you must admit. It's not as though there can possibly be any consequences. He'll be as sterile as the old Enforcers. Won't he, Foxy?"

"Shrack, yes. A tetraploid? 'Course he will. No Crewkerne females in a bazillion years, and he can't breed with human beings," Ellsworth-Howard said seriously.

"But that's really almost worse," said Rutherford, wringing his hands. "Sterile! That's decidedly unheroic, chaps."

"Make up your mind," jeered Ellsworth-Howard. "Give the poor bastard his fun, that's what I say."

Rutherford subsided, looking pained.

"A question, Foxy." Chatterji got up and walked around the image, studying it from all angles. "We're not making the prototype immortal, of course, but can we install recording hardware? So as to have a complete transcript of his experience."

"Give 'im a black box? No problem." Ellsworth-Howard gave an order and another section of brain lit up. "Right there, instead of your support package, eh? Shove it up through the nasal fossa right after birth. Mind you, it'd fit better if we left his nose big. Shield the box right and even we wouldn't know it was there, unless we knew what to look for. Cut it out after he dies."

"I don't want to think about him dying," said Rutherford. "He hasn't even lived yet. That is—I suppose he has, hasn't he, and died too? Speaking temporally? We're going to create him and send him back into the past, where he'll live out a human lifetime. Somewhere, somewhen, that black box is already on its way to be analyzed. All those figures may have appeared on the dice because they were predestined to, chaps, think of that! Talk about once and future kings."

"I hate shracking temporal paradoxes," growled Ellsworth-Howard. "D'you want this brain or not, then?"

"Oh, it's a jolly good brain," Rutherford hastened to assure him. "We'll go with this design, by all means."

"Do you suppose one life sequence is enough?" Chatterji frowned thoughtfully at the brain. "It's not, really, is it, for this kind of experiment?"

"Not if you want valid results," Ellsworth-Howard said. "I was planning on cloning, once I've got a blastocyst. Get three embryos to start with, run three separate sequences."

"He'll be reincarnated," Rutherford yelled in delight. "*Another* myth made real."

"I beg your pardon," said Chatterji icily. Rutherford turned bright red.

"Sorry, old man. No offense. It's not as though you believed in those legends, after all."

"Of course I don't, but that's not the point," Chatterji said. "It's my cultural heritage and I won't have it mocked. Look here, suppose you give us your report on this now? I'll be interested in hearing what you've come up with."

"Very well." Rutherford cleared his throat. "We'll need to issue a standing order for the Preservers to be on the lookout for a particular scenario, throughout all time."

"Which will be—?" Chatterji went to the sideboard and poured out a little of the apple-prune juice combination. He tasted it experimentally.

"A woman," Rutherford said, "fair, of above average height, unmarried, who is sleeping with one or more men who also answer that general physical description. At least one of the men must be highly placed in whatever local tribe or government exists in their era. Any period will do, but *Adonai* simply must be an Englishman, don't you think?"

"Yes, of course." Chatterji nodded. Ellsworth-Howard grunted his assent and made a subvocal request through the throat mike, and sent it for general temporal distribution.

"Once we have the situation, the woman will be abducted, implanted with one of our embryos and returned to her environment," Rutherford said briskly.

"But these will be *human* women," said Chatterji, knitting his brows. "Can they manage?"

"Of course. Cattle embryos used to be shipped implanted in rabbits, for heaven's sake! Nothing inhumane. We'll have a Preserver contact the woman, give her proper prenatal care and deliver the infant, installing the hardware at birth. And we'll pressure the supposed father or fathers for child support, on threat of exposure. I thought this bit was particularly neat, myself; ought to partly pay for the program." Rutherford leaned back and folded his arms in a self-congratulatory manner.

"That is neat, yes." Chatterji agreed. "It never hurts to think of one's budget."

They heard a faint beeping signal.

"Got your situation for you," Ellsworth-Howard said. "Facilitator in 1525 AD says he's got his eye on a girl at Greenwich. Matches the physical type and so do her sex partners. One of 'em's the king's falconer. That okay?"

"Splendid! Send an affirmative response to the Facilitator." Rutherford punched the air with his fist. "You see, chaps? It's all falling into place."

"What happens next?" Chatterji inquired.

"Next, we'll arrange for the subject to be raised by one of our paid households with security clearance. They'll know he's one of our experiments, but he'll never be told, of course. He'll think he's a human being. What he *will* be told is that he's illegitimate, that his birth was a scandal and a disgrace."

"Won't that tend to create a neurosis?" Chatterji objected, sipping his drink.

"Ah, but, that's the clever part! He'll be splendidly nourished and educated." Rutherford held out his hands, grinning hugely. "He'll be programmed with the *very* highest ideals by someone he loves and trusts, and told he must work harder than other boys to make up for the stigma of his birth. The psychology here will produce someone well adjusted, but with a secret shame."

"Ingenious, Rutherford! Go on."

"Every influence must be used to indoctrinate him toward a life of service to humanity, you see." Rutherford stood and began to pace about, rattling the dice in his pocket. "Then, we'll throw him out alone in the world! Start him on the hero's journey. He'll have no family, so all his emotional ties and loyalties will come to settle on those values he's been taught to hold dear. We'll see what he does."

"Here now," said Ellsworth-Howard, who had only just sorted through the whole speech. "Isn't that a little hard on him? You're not only making him feel bad about something he didn't do, you're making him feel bad about something that didn't even shracking happen."

"I believe churches used to call it original sin," Rutherford agreed, looking crafty. "But what does it matter, if it serves to make him a better man? If he could understand, I'm sure he'd thank us. I can't wait to see how he'll turn out, can you?"

Chatterji raised his glass in salute. "I think you're right, Rutherford. This must be what the gods feel like! I report to the committee on Thursday. You'll get your authorization for raw materials then, Foxy."

Alec and His Friends

By the age of seventeen, Alec Checkerfield was no longer unhappy in London. Not at all. He was a well-to-do young man about town and he was having a lot of fun. At least, as much fun as one could have in the twenty-fourth century.

"Alec."

Alec opened one eye. His other eye was obstructed by the breast of the young lady who happened to be in bed with him that morning. He breathed in the reassuring fragrance of her skin. With his usable eye he looked around uncertainly and met the glare of the bearded face that had lowered down beside him.

"What?"

"Alec, it's eight bells! Don't you think you'd better get the wench out of here afore Mrs. L. comes in with yer bloody breakfast on a tray?"

"Uh-huh," Alec replied. He did not move, staring blankly at the shambles of last night's social encounter. In the twenty-fourth century, young men hardly ever woke up to find empty liquor bottles and suspicious-looking smoking apparatus lying amid shed clothing; stimulants had been illegal for decades and sex was very nearly so. Alec, however, was a rather old-fashioned boy.

As Alec lay there getting his bearings, the Captain paced back and forth, growling. He no longer resembled a pirate, or at least not the eighteenth-century variety. Nowadays he appeared as a dignified-looking gentleman in a three-piece suit, though there was still a suggestion of the corsair in his black beard and fierce grin. He looked like a particularly villainous commodities trader.

"Get up, son," he said patiently. "It's the first of April, 2337, which is sort of appropriate under the circumstances. Wake up yer friend. Take a shower and wash the smoke out of yer hair. Mix yerself a glass of Fizz-O-Dyne and drink it. Make one for the girl, too. Get her clothes back on her. Take her down the back stairs. Sensors indicate nobody's in that part of the house right now. Alec, are you listening to me?"

"Oh, piss off," Alec said, and sat up unsteadily. The girl sighed and stretched. The Captain winked out before she opened her eyes, but several hundred red lights glowered at her from the banks of electronic equipment that lined the walls of Alec's room, and a small surveillance camera swiveled to follow her motion as she reached out a hand to stroke Alec's back.

"Hey, babe," she cooed.

"Hey, babe," he said, turning to her with all the charm he could summon through the miasma of hangover. "D'j'you sleep okay?"

"Like a brass lime," she said. It's not necessary here to explain all the youth argot of the year 2337, but *like a brass lime* was a reference to the title of a current hit song and meant that she'd slept quite well, thank you.

"Bishareedo," he said, and in the same idiom that meant that he was very happy to hear she'd slept well. He reached out to pull her upright beside him, with one swift motion of his arm. She gave a little squeal of mingled terror and delight. He kissed her gently.

"Squash," he said, by which he meant *Let's go wash*. That one wasn't an idiom; he was simply so hung over he wasn't speaking clearly.

They staggered into Alec's bathroom together, giggling, and the girl leaned against a rack of fluffy towels as she watched Alec program the temperature controls of the shower.

Her name, just for the record, was the Honourable Cynthia Bryce-Peckinghill, and she was young and pretty, and beyond that there was absolutely nothing distinctive about her.

"I have to wee, Alec," she announced in a playful kind of way.

"Okay," he said absently, as the water came on and hit him with a blast of needle-steam. He yelped and ducked back, putting up both his hands to wipe his face.

She considered him fondly as she sat on the toilet. She'd never met anybody quite like Alec, nor had any of the other young ladies in their Circle of Thirty. He wasn't handsome compared to Alistair Stede-Windsor or Hugh Rothschild. He didn't have their chiseled patrician features. In fact, towering beside them he looked like a good-natured horse, especially if he was grinning. One assumed that he was clumsy because he was so lanky and big; but then he'd move, and one was struck by his grace and the deliberate control he had over his body. When he wasn't stoned, that is.

Naked like this, Alec's strangeness was more pronounced, but it was difficult to put into precise words—impossible for Cynthia to put into words, because she was quite brainless, but even the sharper of the girls in the Circle of Thirty hadn't quite managed to say what it was. There was a suggestion of unnatural strength, of *power*, that a well-bred idiot like Cynthia found scarily pleasurable.

He was sensitive about his long teeth, though. He'd worked at developing several different sidelong or closed-lipped smiles to avoid drawing attention to them. It gave him a crafty sort of look sometimes.

Of course, Alec's looks were beside the point. What Cynthia had discovered, as all the other young ladies in the Circle of Thirty had discovered, was that Alec had a remarkable talent. Unlike Alistair Stede-Windsor or Hugh Rothschild or any of the other young gentlemen of the Circle, Alec was not only interested in sex any hour of the day or night but *capable of doing something about it.*

And so polite! He had only to look into one's eyes and suggest certain affectionate pleasures, in that curiously compelling voice of his, and ladies fought to jump into bed with him. Though it must be said that few girls repeated the experience more than once or twice. There was something about Alec just a bit more . . . animal, perhaps, than most of them felt comfortable with.

He was sensitive about that trick of looking into a girl's eyes and making her want what he wanted, too; so sensitive that he pretended to himself that he couldn't do it.

But as he stood shivering now, pushing his lank wet hair back from his face, he seemed pathetically ordinary. Cynthia thought he looked just super. She hopped up and jumped into the shower with him, and they spent a long time in there and used up a great deal of hot water.

"This way," Alec said in a stage whisper, leading her down the back stairs. She clutched her shoes as she skipped after him, giggling wildly. This was more adventurous than anything she'd ever done.

They paused on the service porch as Alec spotted a mass of florist's roses among the morning's deliveries. He grabbed a red one and stuck it down the back of her jeans when she bent over to pull on her shoes. She shrieked with laughter, which he stifled with a kiss, leaning down. Then he heard the sound of a car pulling up in the street beyond.

Alec stood on tiptoe and peered through the fanlight. When he saw the long car with the Bryce-Peckinghill crest and Cynthia's older sister at the wheel he smiled and waved, then opened the door just wide enough to let Cynthia out. She bounced down the steps and got into the car, remembering fortunately to take the rose out of her pants first. *Bye-bye*, Alec mouthed silently, and she waved bye-bye and blew him a kiss. Her sister switched on the agmotor and the car rose and zoomed away, bearing the Honourable Mss. Cynthia and Phyllis Bryce-Peckinghill out of this story for the moment.

Alec went to the trouble of returning up the back stairs and going down the front ones to disguise what he'd been doing, but when he strolled into the breakfast room Lewin looked up from his accounts plaquette with a disapproving stare.

"Alec, did you have a girl in your room last night?"

"Er . . . yes, actually." Alec avoided eye contact with him, going to the sideboard to pour himself a glass of fruit juice.

Lewin snorted. The Playfriend was somewhere in the attic with Alec's other outgrown toys. Alec had long since stopped prattling about the Captain and their adventures together. And, apart from getting genius scores in maths and cyberscience, Alec had manifested no sinister superhuman traits, nothing to suggest why there'd been so much secrecy and heartbreak aboard the *Foxy Lady* all those years ago.

"I see. Well, it would have been polite to have offered her some breakfast, don't you think?"

"I guess so." Alec sipped the juice and made a face. He set it aside and filled another glass with mineral water. "She had to get home, though." He no longer spoke with the jewellike precision of small English children either, had now adopted the slangy Transatlantic accents common to well-educated young men of his social class.

"Hm." Lewin set the plaquette aside. "Was it the Preeves girl again?"

"Nope."

"Here's our Alec!" Mrs. Lewin came bustling into the room, bearing a fresh pot of herbal tea. "I was beginning to think you'd never get up. What can I get for you this morning, dear?"

"Get him some dry toast," said Lewin, as Alec bent down to kiss her. She accepted his kiss and looked up at him archly.

"Oh, dear. Something for a headache, too, I suppose."

"Yes, please." Alec slumped into his chair and watched her depart for the kitchen. He turned to Lewin and said, "How's her breathing this morning?"

"She didn't sleep very well."

"You ought to take her down to the place at Bournemouth," he said, having a cautious sip of his mineral water.

"And leave you here to do who knows what in our absence?" Lewin said. "Fill the house up with your friends and have a party, that's what you'd do, and when we came home your father's bar would be cleaned out. It's very nearly empty now."

"It's not as though he'll ever come home to notice," Alec muttered, avoiding Lewin's gaze. Alec focused his attention on the bubbles rising in his glass until Mrs. Lewin returned with his tray of toast, vitamins, and headache pills. She sat down opposite him and watched with a prim frown until he gulped down the pills and vitamins.

"You've been drinking again, haven't you?"

"Yes, a bit," he said, wishing she'd leave him alone and wondering if he were going to be sick.

"Dear, you know what that does to your system. Just look at yourself! Green as a duck egg. There's a reason why that stuff was made illegal, you know. You may think you know it all at your age, I certainly did when I was a girl, but believe me, liquor is a wrecker and a betrayer! With all the advantages you've been given in your life I can't think why you want to go ruining your health and wasting your time with such a stupid habit, I really can't . . ."

Alec ground his teeth. Lewin was smiling to himself as he made entries on his plaquette. Alec felt the pressure in his head building and groped for a piece of toast. He poured half a bottle of hot pepper sauce over the toast and crunched it down, praying it wouldn't come right back up. He began to nod agreement to Mrs. Lewin's stream of reproaches, and the next time she paused for breath he interjected:

"You're right. You're right, and I'm really sorry. I won't do this again, I promise. Okay?"

She had been about to continue, but his abrupt capitulation took her by surprise.

"You *must* feel ill," she said. He nodded wretchedly. "Well, poor dear, I suppose it's because you're seventeen. Boys seem to feel they have to do stupid things like that. You'll grow out of it, I'm certain, you're such a clever lad—"

"I was just saying we ought to go down to Bournemouth when the term ends," he said. "Don't you think? Have some nice fresh sea air for a change?"

"Oh, that'd be lovely." She looked at him encouragingly. "Malcolm, why don't you mail the estate agent about getting the house ready? And perhaps you ought to let his Lordship know. He might want to come across and join us on holiday, wouldn't that be nice?"

Both Alec and Lewin made noncommittal noises. She'd said that every time they'd gone on holiday, and to date Roger had never managed to show up.

"And did I show you the holocard we got from Derek and Lulu? They're running a hotel in Turkey now. Ever so happy there. They remember you so fondly, Alec, they said they both hoped you're doing well—"

Alec silently intoned *shrack, shrack, shrack,* repeating it like a mantra to drown her out until the headache pills began to work and the toast seemed as though it were going to stay with him. The next time Mrs. Lewin paused Alec got unsteadily to his feet. "I guess I'll go," he said. "I've got Circle this morning."

"Shall I ring for the car?" Lewin looked up at him.

"No, thanks." Alec waited to see if his head would explode. "I'll take mine."

Lewin made a dubious sound and watched as Alec departed.

On the grand front steps, Alec reached into his pocket and thumbed the remote that brought his car floating up from the subterranean garage. It had been a gift from his father on his last birthday and it was bright red, very fast and very small. He didn't really enjoy driving it, as a matter of fact; his knees stuck up on either side of the steering column as though it were a toy car on a fairground ride. The young ladies in the Circle of Thirty seemed enchanted by it, however, and invariably went to bed with him after a fast spin.

"For Christ's sake, you'd better let me drive," said the Captain, speaking out of the instrument panel.

"Okay," said Alec, in no mood for arguing.

He settled awkwardly into his seat and started the agmotor. Much too quickly for his liking, the car rose up and sped away with him. Just past Piccadilly Circus he realized he was in trouble, and as they zoomed around the corner into St. James Street the evidence was undeniable.

"Lean out to leeward, you damned fool," the Captain said.

He was profoundly grateful that the streets were deserted as his breakfast rushed into midair and hung there a moment; then, as the car whisked him onward at such a speed that the breakfast vanished behind him without landing on him or his car, he was rather sorry that nobody had been there to witness the amazing accomplishment. And he felt great now!

He was whistling as they reached the designated youth zone and pulled into the car park. The car sank down and he hopped out, sauntering into the Dialogue Gardens.

Most of his Circle were already assembled in their customary place under the big plane tree. "Sorry I'm late, everybody," he said.

"You're not late, Checkerfield," Blaise said. Blaise was the dialogue leader. "Balkister, on the other hand, will almost certainly be late. Not one to change his habits, our worthy friend."

"What have you been doing?" murmured Jill Courtenay, rising to pull him to a seat beside her. She was the one he was serious about, and she was even more serious about him. "You're rather pale."

"The car went too fast," he said.

"Idiot," she said. She had very dark blue eyes with black lashes. While they had a tendency to look steely, she was being affectionate at the moment. She took his hand in her own. He kissed her neck, breathing in her scent. She smelled comforting. Across the circle, Colin Debenham stared at her longingly.

"Good God, history is about to be made," drawled Blaise. "Attention, assembled autocrats-in-training: Balkister is about to grace us with his punctual presence. No applause, now. You know how adulation embarrasses him." They all looked up to see the enormous and colorful ex–parcel delivery van that came roaring into the car park. Balkister had painted it himself, with murals depicting great victories for the oppressed masses throughout history. It settled to the pavement with a crash. Several Francophone Canadians were obscured as the driver's side panel swung open across them, and Giles Balkister made his entrance.

He was small of stature, and unfortunately not proportioned well; very little of what height he possessed was in his legs. He was rather spotty, too. What he lacked in personal attractiveness he made up for in talent, however. Everybody thought so, including Alec, who was his best friend. Alec was always a little in awe of people who could read and write, though it was considered a menial skill.

"*Thank* you," said Blaise, after watching him toil across the garden. "Please don't rush on our account."

"Oh, bugger off," Balkister snapped. "Why don't you start a dialogue?"

"What a good idea," said Blaise. "Girls and boys, a brief announcement first: we're hosting next month's swing gaskell for the Wimbledon Thirty at McCartney Hall. Fifty pounds per member ought to cover expenses in style. Who'll volunteer for the decorations committee?"

Jill squeezed Alec's hand and looked at him in meaningful delight. A gaskell was a retro dance party, usually in appropriate period costume, and swing had been the rage in the better circles for some months now. Alec grinned back at her. He was in great demand as a dance partner—for one thing, he was one of the few men in London physically large enough to pick up and flip a partner in the complicated maneuvers swing required—and Jill was a brilliant historical costumer. They'd won prizes at the last two gaskells they'd attended.

"I'll volunteer," said Balkister. Heads turned and disapproving stares pierced him through.

"I don't think so," said Marilyn Deighton-True. "I can just see McCartney Hall now, festooned with socialiste nouveau slogans."

"And if?" said Balkister. "Can you think of a better place to hang them than in the faces of the frivolous rulers of tomorrow, participating in effete historical reenactments as Rome burns?"

"Don't be stupid, Balkister, it's only a dance," said Colin Debenham.

"It's a dead and meaningless dance, pulled from the dustbin of history, performed in the decadent drag of a properly vanished empire!" Balkister said.

"Oh, whoever heard of a meaningful dance anyway?" Jill said. "Besides, you know you've never missed one."

"I'm bearing witness," Balkister said, but he was booed down by the others. Various people with a lot of early twentieth-century furniture in their ancestral homes volunteered to bring pieces down for set decoration, somebody else agreed to handle the refreshments, and an appropriate art deco invitation design was agreed upon.

Nearly every social event anybody threw in the twenty-fourth century was historically themed. Most people, if asked why historical reenactment was so popular, would have replied that the present age was *boring*. The truth, however, was more complicated and consequently even more boring, a societal phenomenon that had been set in motion centuries earlier:

With the invention of printing, mass standardized culture had become possible.

With the inventions of photography and then cinema, the standardization of popular culture began to progress geometrically and its rate of change slowed down.

In addition, the complete documentation of daily life made possible by these technological advances presented the mass of humanity, for the first time in history, with a mirror in which to regard itself. Less and less had it been able to look away, as its own image became more detailed and perfect, especially with the burden of information that became available at the end of the twentieth century.

What this meant, in practical terms, was that retro was the only fashion. Smart young things everywhere would much prefer to be dancing on a reconstruction of the *Titanic*, or wearing First Regency frock coats and gowns as they sipped tea, or wearing trench coats and fedoras as they pretended to solve mysteries, or reclining on Roman couches as they dined or *anything* rather than living in the mundane old twenty-fourth century. And, all things considered, they might be forgiven. It was a much more dangerous time than they were aware.

"All right then," said Blaise at last, when the last of the party details had been hammered out. "Moving right along, let's tackle our debate of the day. Topic for discussion: ought the administrative classes be required to obtain licenses for reproduction, as the consumer classes are presently required to do?"

"Absolutely," said Balkister.

"Has anyone else an opinion?" Blaise looked around at the other members of the circle.

"I have, and I say absolutely not," countered Dennis Neville. "We're the only ones with any brains in this miserable little country, we do all the work, and why should we be forced to pay for the privilege of producing the next generation without whom everything would fall apart?"

"Oh, dear, has that been claimed before or what?" hooted Balkister. "You vile dinosaur. Privilege! Privilege! Can you really sit there and tell me you're better than the lowly consumer, whose sweating and oppressed ancestors built the throne on which you sit? Look at this insect on the leaf, peering down on his brethren in the dust and saying he's more worthy of passing on his genes than they are!"

"Since when have the consumers built anything?" jeered Edgar Shotts Morecambe. "In the last century, anyway?"

"Irrelevant," said Balkister. "The issue at hand is the monstrous inequity of privilege. How, in this day and age, can any one of you claim to be better than your fellow human beings?"

"Because we are," said Marilyn Deighton-True with a shrug. "Face reality, Giles, or it will face you. You can spout all the socialiste nouveau crap you like, but it simply doesn't apply to a meritocracy."

"Remember what happened the first time they abolished the House of Lords," warned Elvis Churchill.

"The consumers have become the couch potatoes they are because they haven't the willpower to be otherwise," argued Deighton-True. "If you handed them the privileges we have and the responsibilities that go with them, they'd be horrified."

There was some laughter and nodding agreement. Balkister did what he usually did at this point in a debate, which was turn to Alec in fierce appeal.

Ordinarily Alec would rise to his impressive height and say something suave in his impressive voice. He never had to say anything especially cogent, just draw the focus back to Balkister. This particular subject made him uncomfortable. Yet Balkister was looking at him expectantly, so he got to his feet.

"This is too bloody stupid, don't you think?" he said. All faces turned to him at once. "You know perfectly well the admins would jump at an excuse not to have babies. Who wants all that noise and mess? Why not get rid of the whole permit thing, if you want to be fair to the consumers?"

"*Bad move!*" said Balkister in alarm. The truth, which nobody wanted to acknowledge, was that the British Reproductive Bureau hadn't issued a permit in five years, because nobody had applied for one. There was a frozen silence as thirty people silently acknowledged that Alec's remark had been quite true and in the worst of taste, and then the backlash set in.

"Are you out of your mind?" said Elvis Churchill. "When we've only just begun to pull ourselves out of the abyss of the past? Do you really want to see the world's population out of control again?"

"No, of course not—"

"Why should he care?" said Diana Lewton-Bygraves. "He wouldn't be enslaved by pregnancy, after all! He'll never have to suffer through ten lunar months of hideous discomfort and physical distortion, oh no."

"Techno-idiot," muttered Colin Debenham.

"Math geek," agreed Dennis Neville.

"Then make it all illegal!" said Alec, sitting down and folding his arms. "No permits for anybody, okay? That ought to suit you, and at least it'd be fair."

"Checkerfield, are we going to have to explain what the big words mean again?" sneered Alistair Stede-Windsor.

"Hey!" Alec started up in his seat, his eyes going small and furious. Stede-Windsor shrank back; Alec had a reputation for his temper. He felt a tugging on his sleeve and subsided, as Balkister popped up again.

"What about it, ladies and gentlemen?" Balkister said. "Just how many of you were actually planning to endure, how did you put it, hideous discomfort and physical distortion so that your precious admin genes can be handed down to another generation of sniveling little dictators? Eh?"

"I certainly intend to have children," Dennis Neville said. Heads turned.

"Children?" said Diana Lewton-Bygraves in an icy voice.

"Well, a child."

"I'm certain we'll all sleep better tonight knowing that." Balkister smiled nastily. "Dennis Neville passes on the flaming torch of his genetic inheritance to prevent everything from falling apart!"

"All this shouting, and none of it means anything," said Alec quietly. Jill squeezed his hand and stood up.

"Are any of you under the impression anybody can win this argument?" she said. "I never heard such bollocks in my life. We're all children of privilege! This debate is pointless until and unless it includes members of the consumer classes who can express their opinions on the subject."

"Oh, good shot," said Balkister, and Colin Debenham began to applaud wildly, and one by one the others in the group followed suit. The subject had begun to make too many of them acutely uncomfortable.

After they'd all broken up into socialization units, Blaise sidled over to Alec where he lay sprawled in the grass, his head pillowed in Jill's lap.

"You okay, old man?" he said, sitting down and crossing his legs.

"Not like you to drop the ball like that," said Balkister, tearing up a handful of grass and sorting through it bemusedly. "You're so good at getting their attention, Checkerfield, but for God's sake don't spoil it by telling them the flat truth! Especially a truth they don't want to hear. One never wins friends and influences people that way."

"Shrack winning friends and influencing people," said Alec. "What's wrong with telling the truth?"

"You won't take that tone in the House of Lords, I hope." Blaise shook his head.

"Well, it bothered me," Alec said, turning his face up to Jill. "You said it best, babe. What's the point of all the talk? And nobody really wants kids. Even people who have 'em stay as far away as they can get, and mail presents now and then to pretend they care." He thought bitterly of Roger.

"All the responsible family people have gone to Luna and Mars," said Blaise.

"Ahh, Mars," said Balkister, in the tone of voice in which people had used to say *Ahh, Maui*. "There's where your real heroes are. Back to the basics and no mistakes this time. On Mars, proper civilization can begin. Look at the start they've made! No inherited privilege and no techno-hierarchy. Everything owned in common by the Martian Agricultural Collective."

"Well, in Mars One," Jill said. "Mars Two's another story."

"Mars Two is irrelevant," said Balkister. "The agriculturals control the terraforming process and therefore control Mars. They can't be outvoted or shouldered aside by the drones in the urban hives! No listless decadent intellectuals running the show at the expense of the real producers."

"Giles, you are so full of horseshit," Jill said. "You wouldn't last five minutes up there."

"Is it my fault I'm not physically fit for Mars?" said Balkister. "Blame my bloody genetic inheritance. So much for the divine right of the elite to pass on their DNA! My parents oughtn't have been allowed to have me. They'd never have passed muster if they'd had to apply for the permit."

"There'd certainly have been a lot less hot air in the world." Alec smiled.

"Maybe I do serve a purpose, then," Balkister replied. "Maybe civilization needs an ugly little creep like me to serve as a conscience, to prick the bubble of hypocrisy wherever it swells up, to jar people from their smug self-satisfaction and complacency!"

"Bollocks, Balkister. Balkister, bollocks," sang Jill.

"You'd do well on Mars, though, Checkerfield," said Blaise.

"And so he ought," said Balkister. "God knows you're strong enough. You can be the ugly big creep I send in my place to be the social conscience of our class in the dark warrens of Mars Two. Let's consider this seriously, Checkerfield."

"Alec is beautiful," said Jill, bending down to kiss him.

"Like a mushroom cloud!" scoffed Balkister. "Isn't *impressive* the word we're looking for, dear? God, Checkerfield, if only I had your voice, or you had my brain. People listen to you. They don't always agree, but you get them to listen."

"It's something to think about, Checkerfield," said Blaise. "Mars."

Alec looked up through the branches of the plane tree (*seventeen thousand three fifty-five leaves*, he counted automatically) at the sky beyond.

"Maybe I'll go out there," he said. "Someday."

"Alec, isn't that your family's Rolls?" Jill glanced over in the direction of the car park.

"What?" Alec brought his gaze down. "It is." He sat up abruptly as he saw Lewin get out of the car and come striding across the grass toward the circle. "Oh, shit."

Lewin's face was gray, his expression set. He spotted Alec and made straight for him. Alec took a few steps forward.

"What's happened?" Alec shouted. "What is it? *Is she okay?*" The other members of the circle left off their separate conversational cliques to turn and stare.

"The missus is fine," Lewin said, and then in a completely altered voice he said:

"My lord, I regret to inform you that your father, the sixth earl, died this morning. You are now the seventh earl of Finsbury."

"Oh!" Jill put her hands to her mouth. Alec just stood there staring.

"Are you sure?" Balkister said. "Had he been ill?"

"No, sir. There was an accident." Lewin looked up at Alec. "He was on a dive near the Great Barrier Reef and evidently he was intoxi—" Lewin broke off. "Alec!"

Alec was trembling. The pupils of his eyes had become so wide the black nearly obscured the transparent crystal. He drew his lips back from his formidable teeth in a snarl.

"Shrack," he said. "That tears it, doesn't it?" He looked around and saw a bench. With all his strength he punched it: first a left, then a right, and on the next left the flimsy laminate planks cracked and began to split. "You shracking bastard," he panted, "you'll never be back now, will you?"

The Circle of Thirty had fixed its attention on him, stunned.

"Alec, for Christ's sake," hissed Lewin, trying to get between him and the crowd to block the view.

"Whoops! Ape Man's lost it," called Alistair Stede-Windsor gaily, though his voice was shrill. Alec ignored him in his rage and grief, pounding on the splintering bench as in a terrifically reasonable voice Blaise said:

"You know, old man, that's Crown property you're demolishing—"

"Who shracking cares?" Alec said. "I can pay for it. I'm the shracking seventh earl now, yeah? I can pay for anything." The bench fell apart at last, its stone supports toppled, and Alec seized one up and hurled it with a grunt of fury at his little red car. It landed on the hood with a crash and several members of the Circle of Thirty screamed.

"I'll pay for everything!" Alec roared, grabbing up the other stone support and starting off toward the car park. "I got the money, I got the toys, I got the title and he's never coming home now, the shracking son of a bitch, I'll never see him again!"

"Alec!" Lewin raced after him, closely followed by Balkister and Blaise. "Stop this!"

Alec threw the other support at his car and the windscreen cracked with a sound like a shot being fired. "I didn't want the shracking car. I didn't want the money," he said hoarsely, staring at the ruin he'd made. "I just wanted him to come back. Now—"

"Alec, I'm sorry," Balkister grabbed his arm. "But you can't—" He looked at Alec's fists and went pale, turned to Jill. "His hands are bleeding!"

Jill had been staring, frozen in horror, but now she snapped out of it and ran to them, delving tissues from her purse. Alec started at her touch, looked down at her.

"He never came home, he was never happy, because of me! He's gone to Fiddler's Green," he gasped. "He's gone to Fiddler's Green, and I'll never be able to tell him I was sorry."

"Darling, it's not your fault," said Jill, stanching his split knuckles. And then it was as though she heard a quiet little voice in her ear saying, cold as steel: *Much too much emotional baggage for you, my dear.*

"Oh, I'm sorry—" wept Alec, as embarrassment added weight to his grief. All he could think of was Roger sinking down and down through dark water, toward a green island he'd never been to yet, perhaps happy at last.

"We've got to get him out of here," said Blaise. "Before the—"

Lewin said something unprintable. They looked up, following his gaze, and saw the public health monitor arriving.

"This is the meditation room," said the doctor in a too-gentle voice, and put a too-gentle hand on his shoulder and suggested, rather than pushed, Alec over the threshold. "You can be private in here for as long as you like."

"Thanks a bunch," said Alec sullenly, rubbing his wrists where the restraints had been taken off. His hands were hurting badly now, but he hadn't been allowed drugs, he assumed because of the urine and blood tests.

"You'll find relaxation patterns on the console," the doctor told him, pointing to the only piece of furniture in the room. The room was what would have been referred to in a previous age as a padded cell. Even the console was thickly upholstered in pillowy foam. Every effort had been made to give the visitor the impression that he or she was floating inside a fluffy cloud.

"Relaxation patterns?" said Alec, looking around to see if he could spot the surveillance camera.

"Oh, yes. Whale songs, forest rain, Dineh chanting, white noise. Lots of visual and olfactory aids as well. Please enjoy them," said the doctor.

"Can you give me something for these?" Alec held his bandaged hands up, knuckles out. "I'm in a lot of pain."

"I know." The doctor looked sad. "But we don't do drugs here, Alec. Use this as your opportunity to begin learning to deal with your pain. If you become one with your pain, understanding will begin. Feel your pain. Make friends with your pain."

Alec thought of telling the doctor to go shrack himself. Instead he nodded. "Thank you, sir, I will. I'll just meditate now, shall I?"

The doctor smiled, reached across the threshold to pat him on the shoulder gingerly and then left, sealing the door. When it had closed, the wall appeared to be a solid spongy mass.

Alec leaned against the wall and slid down, sighing. He assessed his resources. They had relieved him of his shoes and tie but, because of his rank, refrained from going through his pockets. As a result he still had a packet of breath mints, his identity disc, three Happihealthy shields, a ToolCard and, most important, his jotbuke.

Not safe to get it out yet, though. Where was the surveillance camera?

Alec let his gaze wander over the walls in a casual sort of way and picked it out at last, looking like an extra-fluffy blob of cloud: in the door, directly opposite the console. He got awkwardly to his feet, levering himself up with his elbows, and went to inspect the console.

Blocking the camera's view with his back, he took up the buttonball. It was like handling a live coal with his hands the way they were, but he gritted his teeth and summoned up a menu. Whale songs, good and loud. He lingered on the aromatherapy column a moment, wondering whether eucalyptus essence might get him high, or at least kill the smells of this place, which were of terror, disorientation, and urine. Shrugging, he ordered it at maximum concentration. As it misted into the room he sneezed, shuddered, and focused his attention on the menu screen.

A few experimental orders got him into a defended site, easily as kicking open a flimsy door. His eyes narrowed as he decrypted, forcing through one barrier after another until he found what he wanted. He altered codes, working quickly.

The surveillance camera thought it saw him turn from the console and slide down the wall once more, to sit slack-faced and motionless, apparently listening to whale songs and getting mildly goofy on eucalyptus essence. This was what it dutifully reported to the monitor at the orderly's post for the next hour.

Fortunately for Alec, it was only seeing what he'd told it to see. In reality he had turned to lean against the wall and pulled his jotbuke from his inner jacket pocket, wincing. He flipped it open, thumbed a command and set it down on the console. As he nursed his right hand and watched, a small antenna projected and a ball of light shot forth.

Even before the Captain materialized within the poor-resolution globe, there was a concerted torrent of profanity that nearly drowned out the whale songs.

"I didn't call you to have you talk to me like that," growled Alec. "I'd like some counseling, okay? I've just had a shock, in case you hadn't noticed."

"You think *you've* had a shock?" The Captain's face was dark with agitation, his beard curling threateningly. "Bloody hell, Alec, what did you think you was doing, smashing up that car? Christ, son, look at those hands! D'you know what kind of trouble we're in now?"

"It's no big thing, okay?" said Alec wearily, sliding down the wall again. "Lewin is out there talking with the doctors. He told me he'd cut a deal. They won't throw me in hospital, because I'm Jolly Roger's kid. I'll get therapy and a slap on the wrist and I'll have to pay a fine. That's for Roger's solicitors to worry about. *My* solicitors now—"

"Shut up! Did they take a blood sample? Have they done a brain scan?"

"Er—yeah." Alec regarded him with wide eyes. He jumped as the Captain repeated a word several times, and it wasn't *shrack*. "Hey—"

"Get on the buttonball, Alec, smart now," the Captain ordered. "We got to diddle the test results, boy, or you ain't getting out of hospital anytime this century, not if you was Prince Hank himself."

Frightened, Alec scrambled to his feet and took the ball. He ordered up the menu again. "See, it's okay if they find the drugs and booze in my blood. That way they'll think I was just stoned and not crazy when I smashed the bench—"

"And yer car," the Captain told him, watching tensely as Alec plunged into places he wasn't supposed to be. "Come on, come on, where's yer chart? Not there. Further down that way. Aye. Stop! There it is." More profanity ensued as he regarded the results of Alec's brain scan. "Change it, boy. Delete the code. Now, on my mark, input—" and he gave Alec the code that would alter the test results and efface any evidence of Alec's cerebral anomaly. When they had finished they altered the results of the blood and urine tests as well, though not to conceal the presence of intoxicants.

Alec was sweating and sick with terror by the time he finished inputting, and his right hand throbbed.

"What did we have to do all that for?" he demanded, sagging back against the wall. The Captain sagged beside him and spoke carefully.

"Son, you remember when they bought me for you, back when you was just a little matey, don't you?"

"Of course I do."

"And you set me free, and we went on the account. Well, now, you ain't just gone through life assuming everybody else can decrypt data and steal it, eh, only nobody does it but you? How d'you reckon you do it?"

"I—I'm smart as paint," said Alec, beginning to sweat again. He avoided the Captain's eyes. "You always told me I was."

"Why, so you are, matey, when it comes to encryptions anyhow; you got no bloody sense about anything else. All right, I won't start! Listen to me, son. All yer life, I've had to fake medical records and genetic test results and brain scans, so nobody'd find out how different you was from other kids." The Captain put his hands in his pockets and looked at Alec.

"What are you saying?" demanded Alec, aghast. "That I'm some kind of mutant or something? I'm not *that* different, for God's sake!"

"Aw, matey, hell no," soothed the Captain, though he thought Alec might indeed be a mutant. "Yer just differently-abled, that's all. But you know how things is, here in London. If the public health monitors ever found out you wasn't like everybody else—"

"They'd lock me up in here and throw away the key," said Alec, raising his bandaged hands to his mouth. "They'd want to vivisect the shracking freak. They'd be scared of me for being smarter than they are."

"I reckon so, lad. Now you see why we had to move fast?"

"Yeah." Alec stared at the soft white walls of his prison, and gradually his fright gave way to rage. "Bloody shracking London! No wonder Roger hated living here."

"Aye, matey. See, it weren't yer fault he needed sea-room at all," said the Captain helpfully. "Who could live in such a place, says I?"

"Public health monitors watching everything you do, man," said Alec, beginning to pace like a big animal. "You can't talk too loud. You can't get mad. You can't be too tall or too randy or anything that isn't like the rest of 'em."

"That's about the size of it," agreed the Captain.

"And you really, really can't hit things." Alec stopped and put his hands to his mouth again. "Oh, Captain, what've I done? What if they won't let me out of here?"

"Don't you worry on that score, lad. Old Lewin's giving 'em powder and ball broadside right now, invoking yer lordship's lordshipness," the Captain said reassuringly. "Money and privilege is fine things, to be sure. All the same—they'll step up surveillance. You'll have to drop the damn booze and smokes, like I been begging you to do anyhow."

"Yeah."

"And I'm thinking it wouldn't hurt," the Captain continued judiciously, "to play yer cards just a little closer to yer chest. Nobody's going to forget what you did to that there car and Crown property, but testosterone happens more often than they'll admit, and money'll shut up the law. What we got to hide, son, is how talented you are. See? For I reckon if they think yer as much a twit as the rest of 'em, they'll let you alone."

"Stede-Windsor thinks I'm an idiot anyway," said Alec bitterly, starting to clench his fist and stopping as the pain bit his fingers.

"The snotty-nosed lubber," the Captain said. "That's my lad! Feeling a little better about poor old Jolly Roger now, ain't we?"

"Yeah, actually," Alec admitted. Both he and the Captain lifted their heads at the sound of someone approaching in the corridor beyond.

"I'll just get below," said the Captain, and caused his projection to vanish. Alec stuffed the jotbuke into his pocket and when the door opened he was sitting on the floor, apparently deep in meditation, as whalesong groaned and squealed in the overpoweringly eucalyptus-scented air.

Lewin entered, followed at two paces by the doctor.

"Good news, my lord," said Lewin. "You're to be released on your own recognizance."

"Gosh, thanks," said Alec, struggling to his feet. "I feel really badly about what I did, sir. I don't know what came over me."

"You're a very disturbed young man, my lord," said the doctor regretfully. "But in light of the shocking news you received this morning, and the poisons in your system that put you in an altered state, Her Majesty's Borough Committee has decided that you were not responsible for your episode of violence."

"The real me wouldn't ever hit things," Alec affirmed, shaking his head solemnly.

"I'm sure you wouldn't, my lord. You will, of course, be fined for the destruction of Crown property and the ingestion of illegal substances—" said the doctor.

"His lordship quite understands," Lewin said.

"—And there will certainly be mandatory therapy of some kind," the doctor finished, looking perhaps a bit less regretful. Alec concealed his shiver and smiled.

"Cool," he said. "I think I really need that. Thank you, sir."

They left the room and went out to the waiting area, where Balkister was perched nervously on the edge of a chair, clutching Alec's shoes and tie.

By the night of the swing gaskell for the Wimbledon Thirty, Alec's car had been repaired. It still had a vaguely skewed appearance. Alec had fared little better.

The fine had been steep, but the council-ordered therapy consisted of a few sessions of talk about Roger with a mental health AI, and mandatory time in front of a console playing Totter Dan games to discharge his violent tendencies. Alec dutifully shot purple cartoon monsters and collected magic cubes for an hour every day. Being an earl, his daily urine test was waived and he was allowed to become clean and sober on the honor system. More important, the mandated hormone therapy was deferred due to his status as a minor, though it was scheduled for review when he came of age.

Alec was not especially concerned about this, certain he'd be cleared given his status as the last surviving Checkerfield. All the same, chemical emasculation was an unpleasant thing to have hanging over one's head for six months.

He worked methodically at cultivating the image of an upper-class twit, to further mask any discernible genius. Staring into his mirror, he found it appallingly easy to mug up a slack-featured expression that made him look a complete imbecile. More amusing was doing subtle imitations of the authentic twits in the circle. For one whole afternoon he had himself in silent fits being reedy Dennis Neville. Another day he minced around as Elvis Churchill. Nobody caught the imitations but Balkister, who thought it was all wickedly funny, and Jill, who didn't seem to find it as entertaining.

Still, everybody else accepted his pose of slightly unstable idiot savant as authentic. The other boys in his circle (with the exception of Blaise) avoided him, regarded him with poorly concealed contempt or fear. The girls, on the other hand, seemed desperate to offer him comfort, especially of a physical nature. He ran through eight boxes of Happihealthy shields over a three-week period. His pleasure faded, though, when he discovered he was expected to behave like a primitive savage in bed.

And there was still a smoking hole in his heart where Roger had been.

Jill was thinking, regretfully, that the new Alec was devastatingly attractive, with his outlaw attitude and sad eyes, particularly in the swing ensemble in which she'd dressed him tonight. She'd designed it herself, basing it on old cinema footage, all black and white: full black trousers, full white shirt, black and white spectator shoes, long watch chain. Only the dark red braces brought any color to the ensemble. He looked like a doomed young aristocrat from some luckless pre-Hitler monarchy, but he was supposed to. She herself was similarly spectral, in a very brief black dress and pointed slippers, face painted for pallor and desperate gaiety.

Alec had been silent as they'd zoomed through the night, though he'd taken her hand crossing the car park, holding a bit more tightly than she found comfortable. He seemed to need more intimacy from her now, even with all the other girls he was entertaining. She found herself gloomily remembering her parents.

Alec, on the other hand, felt his spirits rising as they came closer to the big double doors standing wide, as he heard the music rolling out of McCartney Hall, saw the lights, glimpsed the black and white streamers and balloons. He liked ballrooms. He liked losing himself in the pattern of the dance.

"Tickets, please," said Balkister at the door. He was made up as a cabaret emcee, truly grotesque in black and white makeup and an early twentieth-century tuxedo that fit perfectly but somehow made him even uglier.

"What're you doing on door duty?" hooted Alec, handing him the old-fashioned pasteboard slips.

"Like I've got a date," he said morosely. "Skip on in, kiddies. Rumor has it there's real gin in the orange punch."

"Ooo," said Alec and Jill, and shoved past him into the swirling vortex of what passed for high life in modern London.

At least the band was hot. They were playing a medley of historical tunes and some late twenty-third-century neobaroque fusion, which was completely out of period but accommodated swing steps perfectly. The musicians leaned into exaggerated poses, stabbing at the ceiling with their clarinets or bending down with their saxophones between their knees, trying to look like the historical posters of the period. The dancers strutted and shimmied, jittered and hopped, in all the ashen tones of ancient cinema.

"My lord." The adult at the hatcheck window inclined toward Alec. "What may I do for you this evening?"

Alec gulped; he still wasn't used to being addressed with Roger's title. "Check these, okay?" he said, handing over Jill's wrap and handbag.

"Certainly," said the adult, presenting him with a numbered tag as though it were a privilege to serve him. Alec passed the tag to Jill, who handed it back impatiently.

"You're the one with pockets, remember?"

"Oh, yeah." Alec thrust it in his pocket, trying to collect his wits. "Um—can I get you a drink?"

There wasn't any gin in the punch, in fact, but it was fun to pretend they were drinking Orange Blossoms. They stood at the edge of the floor, sipping from their chlorilar cups and watching the carefully approximated mad whirl.

"Young Finsbury, isn't it?" said a voice at Alec's shoulder, causing him to jump. He turned to meet the stare of Lord Howard, highest ranking of the official chaperones for the evening. It was all the more unnerving because Lord Howard was resplendent in a flawlessly recreated flapper ensemble, complete with beaded slippers. He had moreover located a real monocle in some antique shop and wore it carefully screwed into one eye, the black ribbon trailing down over his powdered cheek.

"Yes, sir," stammered Alec.

"And how are we getting on? Perfectly awful thing to happen to the sixth earl, but I trust he's well represented by his successor?"

"I, er, hope so, sir."

"Oh, I'm sure of it!" said Lady Howard, emerging from the crowd at the bar to hand a cup of punch to her husband. She had donned gentlemen's evening dress for the occasion, and grease-penciled a thin black moustache on her upper lip. She linked arms with Lord Howard now and continued: "We do hope you'll show some interest in your birthright, young man. We'd so like to see that dusty old seat in the House occupied for a change."

"Well—er—" Alec noticed a passing tray and set his empty cup on it. *He's never going to sit in the House of Lords*, Jill thought.

"Of course, you'll want time to adjust," said Lord Howard. "When's the investiture, if you don't mind my asking?"

"We sort of did it already, at the solicitor's office," said Alec. "We, er, haven't set a date for the formal ceremony yet."

"Hm?" Lord Howard looked stern, the corners of his scarlet mouth disappearing into his powdered jowls. "But you'll see that you do, of course. Must go round for a kneel before the old girl. The whole pomp and circumstance bit. Remember, young Finsbury, this is what we are. Duty carries certain honors, and if one can't enjoy them, one's cheating oneself. Besides, you know, it's all part of the show, and as such *must go on*! Don't you think?"

"Well, of course he does," said Lady Howard. "Don't you, Roger dear?"

Jill coughed discreetly. Alec flushed and said: "Actually, I'm—" just as the dance ended and applause swept the room.

"Oh, but you kids don't want to hear stodgy old speeches," Lady Howard giggled. "Go on and dance! What a beautiful job they've all done, conjuring up the Last Days of Empire. Do you suppose there's any chance we'll get to do a good old time warp before the evening's ended?"

"Wrong period, dear," said Lord Howard.

"I get *so* tired of these history snobs. What would it matter—" Lady Howard was complaining when Alec and Jill took their hasty leave. They escaped onto the dance floor as the band struck up "The Saint Louis Blues."

There, at last, Alec felt better. The music was fast and loud, the steps were quick, and his body exulted in movement. If competitive sports had still been permitted he'd probably have been an athlete. He swung Jill through the intricate steps, lifted her and turned her, bowed and skipped through all the ancient paces as the ancient song blared. He was so caught up in the pleasure of his blood he didn't notice the tightness of Jill's mouth, or the way she pulled her hands back when the figures of the dance didn't require her to be touching him.

Perhaps if he had noticed, he mightn't have spoken. Then again, he might have, for his question came blurting out without any conscious planning on his part:

"So, um . . . will you marry me?"

She didn't answer. He swung back toward her and took her hand, and as he looked down at her he was astonished to see her staring resolutely at their feet. There was a spot of scarlet in either of her cheeks, visible even under the artificial pallor.

So long a pause followed that he was about to repeat his question when she said, in a quiet voice he had to strain to hear below the music:

"I don't think so, Alec."

"Huh?" He was so shocked his body refused to acknowledge what he'd heard, and kept moving him through the dance steps like a machine.

"I don't think I want to get married after all," she said, not looking up. "At least, I don't think it's in the cards for us."

"But . . ." Suddenly the dance steps were more important than ever, his feet were moving with frantic precision, though his mouth hung open. He tilted his head and inhaled, unconsciously trying to catch her scent. "But we made plans, babe."

"I know we did," she said. "But things change."

"You mean my Episode? But I've had therapy for that. I'm better now. Babe, you know I'd never hurt you." He lifted her hand and she pirouetted under his arm, still resolutely avoiding his gaze.

"I know," she said tersely. "It still wouldn't work out."

"But why?"

"Well—for one thing, you sleep with a lot of other girls."

"But we talked about that." Alec was beginning to lose the steps, staggering a little. "You said you didn't mind!"

"I thought I wouldn't," Jill said, attempting to keep on dancing. "I was wrong. I'm sorry."

"But—I'll stop. Okay?" Alec tried to get her to look up at him. She frowned judiciously at the parquet under their shoes.

"That wouldn't do any good, don't you see? It would limit your freedom, which wouldn't be fair to you, after all. And you'd resent that, which would make things worse," she said. "I'm sorry, but this just won't work. For both our sakes—"

"But I love you!" said Alec, faltering to a stop at last in the middle of the dance floor. She stopped, too. She drew herself up, took a deep breath, and said calmly:

"Alec, this has been a wonderful relationship, but I really feel it cannot be a permanent one. Okay?"

Alec actually bent down, found himself reaching to turn her face up, anything to get her to look into his eyes, because if he could only do that—*NO!* he screamed silently, realizing what he'd been about to do, squeezing his eyes tight shut.

All around them the members of the London Circle and the Wimbledon Circle were capering, watching the play in sidelong glimpses, ears pricked to hear Alec cry out:

"You mean it's over, then?"

She raised her eyes at last and saw his stricken face, and: "Yes!" she said, and burst into tears and fled away to the ladies' lavatory.

Alec stood there like a monolith in the midst of the dancers, white as chalk. His mouth worked, tightened, turned down at the corners. He strode over to the bar and helped himself to a whole bottle of orange juice and another cup, and the chaperone responsible for mixing the punch gave up any thought of protest after one look at Alec's eyes.

A wrought-iron catwalk ran around the room about five meters up, where in former times it had been pleasant for lovers to stroll and look down on the festivities. McCartney Hall was very old, however, and the catwalk had long been closed pending the arrival of funds from somewhere to bring it up to modern safety codes. There was a sign to that effect at the entrance to the stairway, which Alec ignored as he vaulted over the rope and climbed up to sprawl in splendid isolation on the catwalk, sneering at the balloons that drifted along the ceiling. Thirty-seven balloons exactly; fourteen black, twenty-three white. Wasn't it just great to be smart as paint?

From the depths of his shirt he drew out a flask, a beautiful antique of hammered silver. In full view of the dance floor he poured gin into his cup and added orange juice, and sat there arrogantly sipping a real cocktail. Below him the band swung into "Hep-Hep! (The Jumpin' Jive)."

The news spread like wildfire.

"My God, is she nuts?" gasped the Honourable Cynthia Bryce-Peckinghill.

"But he's an *earl*," gasped Beatrice Louise Jagger.

"She didn't! She *knows* how much money he's inherited," gasped Marilyn Deighton-True.

"I knew she was a snooty bitch, but I never dreamed—" gasped Diana Lewton-Bygraves.

"Look here, old man, are you all right?" said Balkister, clinging to the stair rail as he ventured out on the catwalk. He looked down and turned pale. Dropping to hands and knees he crawled out after Alec.

"Fine," Alec said. "Want a drink?"

"Don't mind if I do. Real Orange Blossoms, eh?" Balkister accepted the cup and took an experimental swallow. His eyes bugged slightly but he said: "S-superb. You have such a sense of cool, Checkerfield."

"Yeah. Women are really impressed," Alec drawled. " 'We hope you've enjoyed the thrilling Alec ride! Please remember your coat and daypack as you exit to the left.' "

"Look, I heard about Jill. You mustn't mind, you know?"

"Mustn't I?" Alec had another drink. "Okay, I won't."

"I'm sure it was just hormones or something. My spies tell me she's in the loo crying her eyes out right now. Even if it's really over, well, she's the one crying, and doesn't that count for something? And she was awfully temperamental. Bossed you around no end, really. Didn't she?"

"Did she?" Alec unscrewed the cap of the flask and added more gin to the mix. "I guess everything's just bishareedo then, huh?"

"Well, whether or not we're happy is largely up to us," said Balkister. "Positive thinking and all that crap, but it's true, you know."

"Good," said Alec. He passed the cup to Balkister, who sipped carefully.

"I'm speaking out of my limitless experience with the fair sex, of course," he said, with a bitter laugh. "Look at it like this, Checkerfield. You could be an ugly little squirt like me."

"I'm ugly enough," said Alec, taking the cup back.

"True true. But women seem to love you all the same."

"No, they don't," said Alec firmly.

"I just heard," said Blaise, advancing cautiously along the catwalk. He crouched beside them, poised on the balls of his feet. "Checkerfield, can I have a drink?"

"Help yourself." Alec handed him the flask.

"Thanks." Blaise poured gin into his own cup, but did not return the flask. "You know, Checkerfield, maybe this was for the best."

"Oh, yeah?"

"Well, are you really cut out for domesticity? Ball and chain, squalling kids, reduced to being somebody's dependable hubby? Not you, Checkerfield. You've got adventure in your blood. How can you have fun if you're tied down?"

Below on the floor, the band began to play "Pickin' the Cabbage," a tune with a rather menacing minor key melody.

"Yup. You've got a point, all right," Alec said. Blaise glanced down uneasily and licked his lips. He tucked the flask inside his coat and went on:

"Remember, we talked about the great things you might do someday? Like maybe going to Mars? I know for a fact Jill wasn't about to let you roam around. She'd plans for you, old man. But you've got plans of your own, haven't you? You want to stay free! After all, look at your father."

Alec flinched and had another drink. Balkister looked up at Blaise sharply. Blaise went on: "Now, *there* was a man. How many people in this day and age have the guts to thumb their noses at inherited responsibility and sail off into the blue, living as they please? Everything was just great until he married. I mean, other than producing you, wouldn't you agree that his marriage was a fatal mistake in every respect? Was he ever happy again? Did he ever make any great discoveries after that, with a wife and household in tow? You know he didn't. *Wives!*" He shuddered elaborately. "Don't you owe it to him to avoid making the same mistake?"

Before Alec could reply, there was a clatter of heels on the catwalk and the Honourable Cynthia Bryce-Peckinghill edged out toward them, followed closely by Beatrice Louise Jagger.

"Alec, sweetie," said Cynthia. "We love you! Please, please, don't forget that we all love you!"

"I love you, too," said Beatrice. "I'd marry you in a New York second, honey, I'm serious!"

"Jill is out of her tiny mind, really!" Cynthia crowded past Blaise to reach a consoling hand toward Alec. "Lots of people have Episodes!"

"There are plenty of fish in the sea, you know!" Beatrice pushed after Cynthia, glancing over her shoulder to snarl at an unidentified girl from the Wimbledon Thirty who was hastening up there, too.

It was at this point that someone on the dance floor alerted Lord Howard to the fact that a flask had been spotted in the possession of one of the persons on the catwalk. Lord Howard turned a dangerous shade of purple under his face powder, and mounted the creaking stair with the wrath of an offended god.

"Right," he roared, hitching up his dress as he climbed swiftly. "Which of you young fools brought alcohol in here?"

As one, the parties on the catwalk spotted him and froze. He reached the top and stalked toward them. One of his spike heels caught in the iron gratework. He halted, grimacing as he attempted to pull it free. There was a terribly ominous squeak, and the catwalk shuddered all along its length. Blaise vaulted into space, turning in the air like an acrobat, and landed safely on the floor below.

"Oh, shit—" said Lord Howard, frantically yanking at his heel. The catwalk shuddered again. Ancient iron parted with ancient plaster, and the whole thing dropped a few centimeters down the wall.

"LOOK OUT," said Blaise from the floor, and then he vanished into the crowd. There was shrieking and general excitement as people scattered and the Mss. Bryce-Peckinghill, Jagger, and Unknown swarmed frantically past Lord Howard. Balkister had covered his face with his hands, petrified. Alec remained where he was, looking very surprised. The only ones to miss all the excitement were Jill, who was in the lavatory, and Colin Debenham, who had followed her in there.

Screaming like a live thing, the catwalk swung outward from the wall, gently descending as it came. Lord Howard was tilted out into space, giving the assembled company a fine view of his garter belt and panties before he dropped into the helpful arms of Elvis Churchill and Alistair Stede-Windsor. The bottle of orange juice rolled out and burst, splashing everyone who hadn't stepped far enough away. The young ladies tumbled the last few feet to the floor, and Balkister summoned enough courage to jump, landing perilously close to the bandstand and causing a bass player to leap back in alarm and collide with the drummer's kit, precipitating a chain reaction better seen than described.

Only Alec rode the catwalk all the way down, until it spilled him out at floor level and he staggered upright, wide-eyed, still clutching his drink.

"I guess I'd better leave now," he said to nobody in particular, and made his exit in some haste.

"Bloody hell," said the Captain from the instrument panel. "What've you been doing, laddie? Where's the girl?"

"She's not coming," Alec said. "And I'm drunk, and you'd better drive, and could you get us away from here pretty fast, please?"

The Captain swore and gunned the motor. Within seconds they were speeding away through the night, leaving the commotion of McCartney Hall far behind. Alec began to cry silently, and the wind pushed his tears out along his broad cheekbones.

"Drunk again, after all we talked about," growled the Captain. "Damn it, son, what's it going to take to control you? Did anybody see the booze? Have you got it on you now?"

"I did have—" Alec fumbled in his pockets. "Hell. It's gone someplace. Is that all you care about? Jill just ripped my heart into little shreds, man."

"All right, matey, all right. I don't think we'll go home to John Street just yet, eh? You want to talk this out before you sleep, son, that's what you want. So you broke up with Jill, did you?"

"All I did was ask her to marry me," mourned Alec. "She was the only one who didn't act like I was a zoo exhibit, after the Episode. She's smarter than the rest of 'em. I thought she understood."

"Aah. But the lassie was scared of commitment and not letting on? Now, I'd been wondering what was the matter with her." The Captain steered into Oxford Street and sped on in the direction of Edgeware Road.

"You mean even you knew something was wrong?" Alec was appalled. "Don't tell me everybody but me knew."

"Why, lad, I'm programmed to notice all sorts of little subtle subliminal things you can't, so don't take it amiss. She'd a bit of baggage with her, hadn't she?"

"What're you talking about?" Alec steadied himself as they turned into the Edgeware Road and the Captain let the car pick up some real speed along the straightaway.

"Well, now, son—you know I do a bit of checking up on them as gets close to you. It's in my programming, after all. And I reckon you know that the lass didn't come from a particularly happy home," said the Captain in his most sympathetic voice.

"Yeah. Her people were divorced, same as mine," said Alec, wiping his face with both hands.

"Well, I'll tell you straight out, bucko: I think the young lady has a pathological fear of relationships. Scared they'll turn out like her parents' marriage, see? Nothing really to do with you," lied the Captain smoothly.

"Oh, man," sighed Alec. "I wish I could get the shrack out of here. Just go off and, and die in some war like they used to have. Why's the world so screwed up? Why are there all these stupid rules about little things that don't matter? Why do I make everybody so shracking unhappy?"

"Belay that talk, son," said the Captain. "Going off to die in some war, for a bunch of swabs? That ain't the pirate way!"

"Captain, sir, have you noticed I'm not a little kid anymore? I'm never going to be a real pirate," said Alec, hoarse and sullen.

"Figure of speech, laddie buck, figure of speech," said the Captain slyly. "Just you settle back and let the old Captain chauffeur you around in the cool night air. That feels better now, don't it, than that stuffy hall with all the noise? Just you and me and the stars."

"It's nice," said Alec, letting his head loll back on the driver's neck rest.

"To be sure it is. My Alec's a man now; he ain't a-playing with toy cutlasses and cocked hats no more, by thunder. He wants what a *man* wants, don't he? Five fathoms of blue water under his keel, and green islands, and a sky full of stars, and Happy Clubs full of smiling girls, and freedom, and loot, and no heartbreak at all."

"Yeah," said Alec, blinking sleepily.

"And how's our Alec going to get all them grand things, says you? Why, by our great and glorious secret plan, says I. In fact, I been thinking we're ready to take the next step."

"What's that?" Alec closed his eyes for a moment.

"Why, you know, lad. We've talked about it. Having some hardware installed, something subtle and expensive, so you can get yer fair share of all the loot we've piled up. Wouldn't you like to be able to talk to me any time you wanted, wherever you were? Or go into cyberspace without the goggles, just by deciding to? You could learn anything you wanted, instantly, with me right there at yer shoulder to fetch it for you. Captain Sir Henry Morgan, yer obedient server! Haar."

"It sounds nice," said Alec.

"Oh, it'll be nice, all right. Now, there's a lot of fool talk about port junkies and cyborgs, as though that was a dirty word, but it's all on the part of timid busybodies like Dennis Neville. And I reckon his tiny brain couldn't cope with having an augmentation; but yer different, son, always have been. Just you once let yer old Captain hook into yer nervous system, and you'll see what empowerment really is. Shall we take the next step, lad? Go on the account for the real loot?"

"Sure," murmured Alec, blinking up at the stars. He sank farther into the seat. The motion of the car was soothing, and so was the smell of the night wind off the Thames, and so was the Captain's voice, going on and on about all the great things they could do once Alec had some hardware installed. It seemed sort of drastic—it would make him different from most other people—but then, he was already different, wasn't he?

He wasn't very good at relationships, after all. Stick with what he was good at. He could just lie here in the boat and look at the stars and feel the rocking of the blue water, so easy, and the seabirds crying. Nobody out here but him. And the Captain. Happy all alone. Everything would be all right.

The Captain got them off the A5 at Station Road and swung them back toward Bloomsbury on the A502, through Golders Green, through Hampstead, crooning an old sea song to the drunken boy as he drove, handling the car as gently as though it were a cradle.

The incident at McCartney Hall had few repercussions. Nobody had been actually caught with alcohol, and a generous donation to the hall's renovation fund silenced the matter of the surveillance cameras that had caught the gleam of Alec's flask. The Captain, however, was taking additional measures for Alec's continued safety.

On the occasion of his eighteenth birthday the seventh earl of Finsbury came into certain legal rights, and the first thing he did was go to a specialist in Harley Street and have himself adapted for direct interface with his personal cybersystem. He became, in effect, a cyborg.

Not at all some pathetic creature with an oozing port in his skull, nor yet one of the machine-human hybrids who would surely take over the world, if they were ever created. Alec could afford the very latest and best technology, so he paid out a great deal of money to be rendered semiconscious for four hours while a discreet doctor with the proper credentials installed the interface. Alec paid a further astronomical sum to have his brain scan results deleted from the record. Then he crawled into the Rolls and lay facedown in the back while he was driven home.

"Let's see it," said the Captain, as soon as Alec had closed the door of his room and they were alone.

"Careful," Alec said, peeling off his shirt gingerly. "It really stings right now."

"That won't last, my lad," the Captain said, grinning when he saw what had been done. The necessary hardware had been installed just beneath the surface of the skin, across Alec's shoulders and up the back of his neck. It was raised and red at the moment, but in a few hours it would resemble an ornate tattoo, a complex pattern of spiraling silver lines, beautifully symmetrical and interknotted.

"Damnation, that's as pretty a piece of work as I've ever seen!"

"It cost more than the Rolls," Alec said, trying to see it over his shoulder. "I hope it's worth it."

"It'll beat the poor little Empowerment Ring and Playfriend Optics all to hell and gone, I'll wager." The Captain nodded. "Reckon that doctor'll stay bribed?"

"At what I paid him? He ought to."

"Good lad. I'll just keep an eye on him, like, to manage things if he has second thoughts," said the Captain, without the least hint of menace. "So. What's the connector?"

"This." Alec held up a black velvet bag and withdrew a bright near-circle of some enameled metal. Its color was difficult to describe: it might have been gold, but overlaid with phantom rainbow hues along its curved and twisted surface. The two ends terminated in interestingly detailed knobs. Alec made some adjustments on one of them and, prising it open, slipped it around his neck. "Here goes—"

!!

Alec reeled as the plundered knowledge of hundreds of databases became available to him, the sum of twelve years of information piracy. It was very much more than having a set of encyclopedias stuffed into your skull. He was suddenly seeing his own ashen face through the surveillance camera in his room, with a sidebar annotating date, time and temperature—and then the views from all the other surveillance cameras in the house—and then the views from all the surveillance cameras in London—

Just as it became too much for him to bear it receded, but with it went any sense of up or down, any feeling of solid ground under his feet or any limits to his physical body, and as he drew breath to howl like a terrified animal, he felt a powerful hand seizing his and pulling him in.

It's all right, boy. I'm here, said the Captain.

Turn it off! Alec sobbed.

Ahhh, no. It's nothing you can't get used to, and it's part of the plan, the Captain said. *Hold tight. Look at me, now. Look at yer old Captain Morgan*.

I can't see anything. I'm seeing everything!

Yer seeing the way I see things, that's all. Belay that blacking out! LOOK AT ME.

Abruptly he was seeing the Captain, standing solidly in the midst of the void. The Captain was supporting a lesser figure, a transparent body sketched in wavering fire. Briefly superimposed over it was a bright child with flaming hair, which shifted and expanded until finally there were two men standing in the void, and Alec had eyes again and was looking into the Captain's steady eyes.

My God, he said, and his voice sounded loud in his ears.

Here we are, boy, said the Captain. **Was that so hard?**

Yes, said Alec. *I think I've gone crazy.*

No, no. The Captain shook his head. **If you was any of yer snotty-nosed young Circle of Thirty friends, you would be; crazy or dead of a brain hemorrhage, I'll wager. But yer my little Alec, ain't you? Oh, son, this is only the beginning. The things we'll do, you and me! We'll ransack the libraries of the world, Alec, we'll walk through walls and steal away data it's taken other people centuries to compile. The lowliest clerk in the poorest bank in London won't be able to buy a loaf of bread that you won't get to hear about it. You'll be the most powerful man in the world, son, and the safest. What do you want to do now?**

Alec thought about it.

Ditch the Circle of Thirty! I've had enough of them. Shrack University, shrack the House of Lords, shrack the Borough Council, shrack hospital! I'm getting out of here.

That's my boy.

And I want to move the Lewins out of London, he added. *Buy 'em a flat in Bournemouth, they'll like that. And then—then I want to buy a boat.*

Boat, hell, the Captain said. **You want to buy a SHIP.**

And there before them was the image of a modern clipper, four-masted, bearing acres of white sail, sleek and graceful as a seabird, monumental in her size and dignity.

We'll design her to our purposes, my lad, the Captain said. **One whole deck full of nothing but hardware for me, masts and yards all servomotors so I can manage her canvas in the wink of an eye. A machine shop, and a laboratory, and a hospital, to make us self-sufficient, eh? Cargo holds filled with good things, supplies that'll let you live ten years on blue water without once putting in to port if yer not so inclined.**

Oh, yeah!

And maybe cargo room for a few other little items, in case you've a mind to

do a bit of trading, said the Captain, ever so casually. ***And a grand master cabin for you, and staterooms so you can have yer little twit friends on board to visit. But the quarterdeck, Alec, that'll be my place. I'll have satellite linkups and connections to every financial center in the world. I'll monitor law enforcement channels and weather analyses and stock markets. There won't be anything catches me by surprise! Not whiles I've got you, my boy.***

Alec reached out his hand to touch the smooth keel of his ship. It felt solid. He heard gulls crying, he drank in salt air. He thought of the Lewins settled down at their ease in Bournemouth, no vast cold house to manage, no hapless boy to worry about. He thought—briefly—of Jill, who had got engaged to Colin Debenham.

Who'll miss me, really? he said. *I can just sail away and be free. There's no reason I can't go, is there?*

None, by thunder.

Alec looked around. *I need to talk to a shipwright about this. I need a console.*

Not anymore, the Captain said. ***I've just made the call for you, to the best in the business.*** A communications screen and speaker appeared in midair. ***They're waiting on line one. Will you take the call, sir?*** He parodied an obsequious bow.

"Hello?" said a tinny voice, filtered through cyberspace. *"Hello? Beretania Marine Design, how may we help you? Is there anyone on this line?"*

"Yes." Alec cleared his throat, looking gleefully at the Captain. "Alec Checkerfield here. Earl of Finsbury. I'd like to place an order."

ANOTHER MEETING,
A FEW WEEKS LATER

Rutherford was curled up in his favorite chair beside the fire, staring at little bright figures that moved in midair before him. He was watching *The Wind in the Willows* again. He was eating as he watched, hurriedly, so as not to be observed by his associates in case they arrived early.

All he was eating was a dish of strawberries; but he'd poured real cream over them, which was a misdemeanor. Even possession of real cream violated several city ordinances. As a highly paid idea man in the employ of Dr. Zeus, though, he was entitled to certain immunities, including being waved through customs without a baggage search at the Celtic border.

The danger thrilled him. He'd have been hospitalized if he'd been caught with a suitcase full of cartons of dairy products. He needn't have done it, either; on his salary he could afford to travel out of the country and enjoy the same treat in Edinburgh three times a week if he'd wanted it. It wasn't as delicious there, however. The consciousness of being a smuggler sharpened his pleasure.

He tried not to think about the victimized and exploited cows suffering in those pariah nations that hadn't yet banned animal products. He wasn't a cruel man; he'd never dream of eating meat. But he told himself that it was necessary for a chap in his field to experience as much of the past as was humanly possible, since it was the stuff he worked with for a living. He reasoned that, as the cream and cheese and butter were going to be sold whether he purchased them or not, it was just as well their consumption was turned to a higher purpose.

Anyhow he needed cheering today.

He scraped up the last rich drops and paused his holo player. Badger halted in the act of lecturing Toad on his self-destructive impulsive behavior. Rutherford rose and hurried down to the old kitchen, where he rinsed out his bowl and spoon. He was just setting them in the drainer when he heard the pounding on the door that meant his colleagues had arrived.

Dabbing self-consciously at his mustache, he puffed his way back upstairs and opened the front door. Chatterji and Ellsworth-Howard were standing there together, looking gleeful. Clearly they hadn't seen the report yet.

"Hullo, chaps," he said.

"Good news, old boy," said Chatterji. "The report from the first sequence on *Adonai*'s come in."

"Have you seen it yet?" inquired Rutherford cautiously.

"Nah. Was only in my shracking mail this morning," Ellsworth-Howard said, shouldering his way in and making for the warmth of the fire. "We thought we'd come round first so we could go over it together."

He sank into his now customary chair and pulled out his buke, setting it up for wide image. Chatterji and Rutherford settled into their chairs, as Rutherford said:

"Let's not forget it's only the first sequence, after all."

The first part of the preliminary report was a montage of images, with a smooth electronic voice explaining that the images dated from 1525 AD, and giving a biographical profile of the female to be implanted. There was a very blurred photograph, taken in stealth by the field operative handling the case, of a serving girl carrying a basin down a corridor. It was a grand corridor, by the standards of its time.

"Hampton Court," Rutherford couldn't resist pointing out proudly. "Placed right in the heart of political power."

The beautifully modulated voice gave the names of the men with whom the girl had engaged in sexual relations over the previous month. Two images came up: one was another field photograph of a rather tall man in a surcoat, the other a Holbein painting of a man with a hawk on his fist. Their biographical notes followed. The voice explained that the host mother had been implanted soon enough after her encounters to make it plausible that the subject was the genetic offspring of either man.

"So far, it's exactly what we wanted," said Rutherford and sighed. Chatterji looked at him curiously before glancing back at the images. The voice reported that the pregnancy had proceeded normally, though the host mother had been sent from court as a result of her shame.

"Having a kid without a license?" Ellsworth-Howard peered at the next image, which was primitive-looking footage of the girl wandering disconsolately in a garden, heavily pregnant.

"No, no, that was long before permits were required," Chatterji explained.

"Some absurd religious objection instead," Rutherford clarified. He winced as the voice went on to inform them that, due to the unusually large size of the subject, there had been complications to the delivery and the host mother had died. There was a brief clip of a frightened-looking older woman holding out a blood-smeared, wailing little thing to the camera. Chatterji recoiled.

"Died?" he said. "She wasn't supposed to die! Was that—was it our fault?"

"Of course it wasn't," Rutherford assured him hurriedly. "This was the Dark Ages, remember? Dreadfully high mortality rate they had back then. She'd undoubtedly have died anyway."

And the next images were reassuring, too: various scenes around a small cottage in Hampstead, so the voice informed them, staffed by a couple in the pay of the field operative in charge of the project. Here was the subject, aged six months, sprawling asleep on the bosom of the older woman previously seen, where she sat near beehives in what seemed to be an orchard. Here was the subject, aged two years, staring down with wide eyes from the back of a ploughhorse, held up there by a grinning countryman who pointed at the camera, and now a sound byte with the footage:

"Ee now! See'un thur? That be thuyne uncle Labienus, be'nt 'un now? Coom a long wey t'see thee. Wev to 'un, Nicket. Coom on then. Wev!"

As Nicket wevved at the camera uncertainly, Rutherford shifted in his chair. "And I'm certain the Company's fellow in charge turned it all to the Company's advantage in psychological programming. Not only must our man make up for his bastardy, he must atone for his mother's death!"

The voice described the subject's subsequent dame-school education, and the private tutor who had been hired when the subject was seven to prepare him for higher learning at Oxford. There followed an image of the subject, now apparently in his teens, pacing down a muddy street with a satchel, photographed unawares. It was the first clear shot of his adult face they had seen and it was, indeed, the face of the man they'd summoned into their parlor. But:

"Good God, what's happened to his nose?" Rutherford said, frowning. "He's broken it!"

"It was us did it, actually," Ellsworth-Howard said. "When he was a couple minutes old, putting the black box in. The recording device's too big to go up through that fancy nose you wanted without damaging the cartilage. Then it grew bent."

"Oh, what a shame," said Rutherford. "Still, it can't be helped. And I don't think babies feel discomfort anyway, do they?"

The voice was explaining that the subject had proved a brilliant student, and entered Balliol College at Oxford with the intention of studying for the priesthood in the nascent Church of England.

"Shracking *what*?" said Ellsworth-Howard, outraged. "Religion? I thought he was supposed to be above all that, with the brain we gave him."

"Now, now, you're forgetting that he was designed to operate in the past." Chatterji sighed. "Of course he was going to share the beliefs of the era we put him in. Even Tolkien and C. S. Lewis were, er, religious, don't forget."

However, the voice went on to say, the subject's promising career in the Church had been derailed by an unfortunate episode in his seventeenth year. The next image showed the subject, muddy, pale, and furious-looking, struggling between two constables. A third constable lay at their feet, bleeding from the nose.

"What's this?" Chatterji frowned at the screen. "That's old Enforcer behavior."

"Oh, not really. The Facilitator handling the case made a poor choice of a tutor for the boy, that's all," Rutherford said hurriedly.

"You watched this before we got here?"

"I couldn't wait," Rutherford admitted, as the voice went on to explain that the subject's tutor had been selected for his charisma and advanced ideas on religious freedom. Unfortunately, his ideas had been Anabaptist in nature and he had led his circle of disciples, including the subject, in what amounted to heretical orgies.

"Sex, does he mean?" Ellsworth-Howard frowned. "I thought religious people didn't do that."

"Precisely." Rutherford nodded.

"Oh."

The voice informed them that, upon discovery and the subsequent scandal, the subject had self-intoxicated on alcohol and publicly preached heresy, which had got him arrested. The Facilitator in charge had managed the subject's release, after intensive reprogramming, and hustled him out of England to continue his education in various cities in Europe.

By 1547, the voice continued, the subject had returned to England, having become private secretary to one of the people with whom Dr. Zeus had established contact for business purposes. Here followed a shot of the subject, a towering figure in his black scholar's attire, looking sullen as he followed a small and somewhat overdressed specimen of the gentry along a walk beside a half-timbered manor house.

"Impressive fellow," said Chatterji in a pleased voice. Rutherford squirmed.

"It was going so well," he said. Even the electronic voice sounded uncomfortable as it described the logistical error that had precipitated the end of the subject's life, when in 1554 the Company had sent a team of field agents to the estate where the subject was employed. Their mission had been to collect botanical rarities in the estate's garden. Three images flashed up, standard Company ID shots of its cyborg personnel: a dark male with an urbane smile, a darker female with a calm smile, and an unsmiling female with a pale, scared face. The voice gave their Company designations.

"Oi! My Preservers," remarked Ellsworth-Howard. "What'd they got to do with it?"

Rutherford sighed. "It was the *girl*," he said in distaste.

The voice went on to explain that the Facilitator in charge of the mission had encouraged his subordinate, the mission's Botanist, to enter into a sexual relationship with the subject, in the hope that the mission would go more smoothly. Chatterji groaned.

"Apparently he had no idea our man was a Company experiment," cried Rutherford, throwing his hands up in the air. "I can't imagine who left that particular bit of vital information out of his briefing."

"Actually," Chatterji said, raising a placatory hand, "actually there was a good reason why he wasn't told."

Rutherford and Ellsworth-Howard turned to him. Ellsworth-Howard paused the report. "What the shrack?"

Chatterji gave a slightly embarrassed cough. "It seems there has been a certain amount of . . . negative feeling, on the part of our older Preservers, about the Enforcers being retired."

"What?" Rutherford stared.

". . . And as a result, an ongoing program of fact effacement has been initiated," Chatterji admitted. "The new operatives aren't aware the Enforcer class ever existed. The older ones have been given the impression that the Enforcers were all happily reprogrammed for work on remote Company bases. Very few people outside this room know about *Adonai*, you see: if the cyborgs were told the Company was experimenting with a new Enforcer design, it might be noticed that most of the old ones had gone missing."

"Well, I like that!" Rutherford's eyes were round with indignation. "And what if they did notice? They think we treated the Enforcers badly, do they? Didn't we give them eternal life? What *do* they think they are?"

"I fully share your feelings," Chatterji said. "However, the plain fact is that we depend on the Preservers a good deal. Under the circumstances, it was thought best not to antagonize the Facilitator, so he wasn't informed about our project."

"You can see where that led!" said Rutherford.

"I still don't see where the girl comes in," said Ellsworth-Howard, looking from Rutherford to Chatterji.

"Apparently there was a security breach," Rutherford said in disgust. "What can you expect, letting a cyborg—er—become intimate with our man?"

Ellsworth-Howard started the report again, and the voice explained the circumstances that had led to the security breach, and its aftermath, when the subject had been arrested again for preaching heresy.

"Shrack," cried Ellsworth-Howard. "What'd he go do a stupid thing like that for?"

"This was in the sixteenth century, after all," Rutherford pointed out. "We gave him a splendid mind, but it had no context for dealing with the discovery that cyborgs existed. No wonder the poor fellow behaved irrationally."

Here was an image of the subject being chained to a stake before a crowd. Chatterji, watching, turned a nasty putty color, but all he said was: "So he died a martyr's death. Heroic, Rutherford, but not exactly what we had in mind. And rather an awful job for the salvage operative who had to retrieve his black box."

"No; this is the only part that cheered me up at all," Rutherford told him. "Look now. Watch."

A film clip ran and they saw the light of flames dancing on the faces of the spectators, and it danced too on the faces of the three friends: Chatterji horrified, Rutherford's gaze avid and focused, Ellsworth-Howard looking on in disgust.

"What's he doing?" demanded Ellsworth-Howard. "What's he talking about?"

"He's preaching," Rutherford said. "In that wonderful voice we gave him. And look at the crowd, look at their faces. They're hanging on his every word, all of them. They're going to remember this the rest of their lives. Look at that one little lad, look at the hero-worship in his eyes. You see? Our man is *inspiring* them!"

"They're shracking burning him alive, Rutherford," said Ellsworth-Howard.

"But just listen to him! Fulfilling his destiny, shouting encouragement to his countrymen to throw off the yoke of religious oppression." Rutherford was almost in happy tears.

"Is that what it's all about? Something political?" Ellsworth-Howard turned to Chatterji, who was now staring at the floor, unable to watch.

"Protestants versus Catholics, Foxy," he said in a faint voice. "Remember the plot of *Bloody Mary*?"

Ellsworth-Howard shook his head. "Bunch of bigots slugging it out over some bloody stupid religious ritual, that's all I know."

At that moment there was the sound of a detonation and the camera moved abruptly away from the subject. There was one still picture taken five hours later, over which the electronic voice described recovery procedures.

"Anyway, there was much more than religion involved," said Rutherford, stretching happily. "The political freedom of the English people was endangered. Didn't we want someone who'd be willing to die in just such a cause?"

Ellsworth-Howard brightened. He switched off the report.

"Yeah, I guess if you look at it that way it's all right," he said. "Kind of a short life, though, wasn't it?"

"All things considered, chaps, I think we can be proud of ourselves," Rutherford said. "For all that nonsense with the Preservers, our man still died a hero's death, didn't he? What more could we have asked of him?"

"But there *was* a security breach," said Chatterji, groping for his nasal inhalator and taking a fortifying drag. "That mustn't happen again."

"Then, let's turn the lesson to good use for the next life sequence. Is there a way to make our man less susceptible to women, Foxy?"

"Not now," Ellsworth-Howard said. "Can't mess about with the design once I've made an embryo."

"I agree, though, that we need him to be a little more . . . detached." Chatterji watched the fire, wondering what it would be like to burn to death. It had been a morbid terror of his, ever since he could remember.

"Precisely." Rutherford smacked the arm of his chair. "For one thing, his Facilitator must impress on him that common romantic love is a waste of his time. I told you a sex drive would lead to difficulties. We created him to serve a higher purpose. Look at what romance did to King Arthur! How's a hero to be expected to do his job with all that needless distraction? There's no sex in *The Lord of the Rings*."

"What about the Don Juan psychology, eh?" suggested Chatterji. "Lots of healthy sex without emotional attachment? Make him a bit of a cad, I suppose, but some of the old heroes were."

"We want a man who understands the necessity of sacrifice," pronounced Rutherford. "No mystical nonsense. No women. Love is such a selfish passion, after all."

"As you like." Chatterji nodded. "As soon as we receive word that another host mother has been located, you can draw up a revised psych template for our man."

"I've already had word of one," Ellsworth-Howard said. "Came in yesterday: some Facilitator in 1824 AD's found a girl for us. Daughter of a peer. *Three* boyfriends—naughty bit, I must say. One's a lord, one's an M.P., and one's her father's gardener. All of 'em the right morphology."

"In 1824?" Chatterji had another drag on his inhalator. "What's going on in that time period? Much action for our man to be heroic in, when he's grown? Glory days of the old empire, wasn't it?"

"Very good," said Rutherford. Rising from his chair he began to pace. "Send the message to abduct, Foxy, and we'll try again."

"Check," said Ellsworth-Howard, pulling out his throat mike. He set it in place and sent the message subvocally.

"Now, then . . ." Rutherford turned and stood with his back to the fire. "It has seemed to me, chaps, that we need a bit more inspiration. If we're going to be the creators of heroes, just as the original Inklings were, we need to duplicate their experiences as closely as possible."

"I thought we were." Chatterji looked around at the antiques, the stage dressing. "How could one recreate the twentieth century any better than this?"

"Ah! The house is only part of it, you see." Rutherford paused with his back to the fire. "The Inklings drew inspiration from their meetings, but they also kept in contact with the ancient wilderness of Merlin's Isle of Gramarye."

"What the shrack are you talking about?" Ellsworth-Howard knitted his brows.

"England! Albion. This blessed earth. They used to go out on *walking tours*, you see. Just take their daypacks and stride out through the hedgerows, and meadows and animals and things. It'd give them lots of ideas. And Merlin traveled a great deal, didn't he, and Gandalf? So maybe a lot of walking helps the brain create stuff."

"Interesting idea," said Chatterji. "In the Hindu folktales, wise men and magicians lived like beggars, walking from town to town."

"There you go. Now, what I propose is that we do the same. This time next month, what do you say? We'll meet here, and we'll just walk until we find some open country somewhere. Perhaps we'll feel creative influences as soon as we're out of the shadows of the buildings, what?"

"How do we find open country?" said Ellsworth-Howard. "Don't know if I've ever seen any."

"Don't be silly, there's a borough greenbelt not five miles from here," Chatterji said. "It'll be on any map. I think this sounds marvelous! Assuming it isn't raining, of course. On the twenty-seventh, then?"

Alec on Blue Water

Just as the phantom had gone past, and all hands sighed relief
With rending crash and mortal force, our vessel struck a reef!

Alec howled happily at the top of his lungs, timing his words with the *bump-bump-bump* of the agboat as it sped across the waves.

His latest acquisition wasn't much to look at: a spare volcanic rock standing out of the Pacific, thinly skinned on top with green, one wind-bent Norfolk Island pine at the base of the lighthouse. It was a long way from anywhere and completely deserted. The automated light wasn't working, because the small South American nation to whom it had previously belonged had been unable to afford its maintenance.

Alec had come to repair it. Among other things.

He had long since accustomed himself to the roar and flow of information that ran through his brain every conscious hour. He was able to tune it all out, all but a narrow band of what he was immediately interested in; otherwise he'd have been like a man in a library trying to read every book at once. He let the Captain sort through all the data for him. Habitually, now, he saw the world twofold: the ordinary dimensional world through which his body moved and, superimposed over it, the world in which the Captain lived. They matched seamlessly, the one neither more nor less real than the other.

He brought the agboat up on the narrow black crescent of beach and frowned at the access stairs. They were tide-worn concrete, slimy with seaweed and bird droppings, and the handrail had been eaten away with rust.

Hell no, lad. Take the boat up instead, the Captain said.

Aye sir! Alec shifted propulsion systems and the agboat rose smoothly through the air, surprising the royal terns nesting in the cliff face. Seabirds rose and floated around him in a protesting cloud, as he gained the top of the cliff and brought the agboat down at the base of the lighthouse.

Scan complete, Alec, said the Captain. **All clear. Step ashore!**

Alec hopped over the side, gleeful as always to set foot on terra incognita. He paced along the gravel walk around the lighthouse, examining its masonry visually as the Captain scanned for structural defects.

Looks sound to me.

So she is, laddie. Let's do a bit of breaking and entering, eh?

Whistling through his teeth, Alec strode up to the door and entered the code he had been given. As he expected, it didn't work. The security system would have to be replaced, too. No matter; there were crates and crates of useful components in the agboat. He fetched out a case, removed a small limpet charge and affixed it carefully to the lock. Walking away a few paces, he withdrew a detonating device and, unlocking the trigger, fired.

The lock blew off with a pleasing bang and puff of smoke. Alec grinned and ran close to pull the door open. It screamed as though it were being murdered. Nothing inside but the base of a spiral stair vanishing upward into gloom. The air was dry, and smelled clean.

And she's weathertight, too, the Captain said. Alec sprinted back to the boat and hauled out the aglev unit. He began the lengthy process of loading crates, up the long dark chimney of the lighthouse to the control room at its top.

When the Second Golden Age of Sail had arrived, the nations of the world had found that lighthouses were once again necessary. Not to provide light, though they did that too, but as land-based backups, sensors and relays for the global satellite tracking system. New lighthouses sprang up everywhere. There had been scarcely a stretch of water in the seven seas where you couldn't glimpse some spark of light or other in the black night distance.

Then, of course, the first excitement of the sailing craze had faded. The same people who had raved about what a marvelously eco-friendly system sail transport was now complained bitterly about public funds being used for something that would only benefit shipping magnates and yachtsmen. The more necessary ones were grudgingly maintained at national expense, and the rest fell into disrepair.

This had been the state of maritime data reconnaissance until Balfour Continuance Limited had offered to purchase lighthouses from various needy countries. The given explanation—that Balfour Continuance was funded by wealthy yachtsmen interested in repairing and maintaining the lighthouses—was accepted without the least curiosity.

In fact Alec and the Captain were Balfour Continuance, its sole board of directors, stockholders, and repair personnel. All around the world, the lights in the towers had winked back on, one by one, and they had begun to talk amongst themselves and search the darkness as they had used to; but they now shared the towers with backup caches for the Captain, linking him to the satellite relays, powered by solar collectors. The Captain circled the globe, was indestructible, and was able to feed a constant false location for the *Captain Morgan* to the global surveillance satellites.

He was now several hundred times more powerful than any artificial intelligence had ever been. Alec was doubly happy about this, for not only was the Captain better able to fulfill his programming, but the sea was quite a bit safer than she had been, for all who sailed her. Alec was always fond of doing good while doing well.

And the lighthouses had another use. There was plenty of room in their towers for anything one might need to store there.

The truth was that Alec was fairly actively engaged in smuggling, and had become rather successful at it. He was already nearly the richest man in the world, thanks to the Captain's byzantine investment arrangements. Alec found he very much liked flouting stupid laws and cruising through the night with a hold full of Toblerone, or ganja, or semisoft brie. It was exciting to lie offshore, waiting for signal lights. Also, it seemed like the sort of thing Roger would have enjoyed.

It was not without its dangers, of course. Alec and the Captain had by this time repeatedly broken the laws of most first-world nations.

However, Alec was a British peer, and legally the Captain didn't actually exist. There were no contingencies in law for Pembroke Playfriends who went rogue, nor any for aristocrats who could decrypt codes no mortal genius nor immortal machine had been able to break in four centuries of dedicated trying. Where loopholes couldn't be found, bribing local law enforcement created them. In case that ever failed, as it had yet to do, Alec had a firm of solicitors whose services were retained at princely rates to handle his fines for failing to attend Parliament.

He had left the Circle of Thirty far behind now. The first step had been failing his university examinations, which had taken a bit of careful work. Low marks in maths or cyberscience would have drawn unwanted attention, but spectacularly dismal marks in everything else drew the average down nicely and reinforced the legend of Ape Man Checkerfield, which suited Alec fine. He had long since ceased to care what Alistair Stede-Windsor thought of him. The Lewins had been appalled—that was painful—but he had bought them a beautiful home, and arranged pensions for them roughly equal to the annual national income of Monaco.

The admin classes, for their part, had looked at his substance abuse records, looked at his low test average, concluded the son was as worthless as his father had been, and washed their collective hands of the seventh earl.

And really, it had worked out very nicely for all parties involved. Alec now had a reputation as a playboy moron. To be a criminal in the twenty-fourth century, under so much surveillance, required genius, so nobody suspected he'd become one.

Alec worked at the lighthouse until dusk. Then he was off across the water to where the *Captain Morgan* rode at anchor, beautiful as a dream from which one wakes weeping.

She was immense, a four-masted windjammer, everything the Captain had promised she'd be, with that extra dash of class that comes from slightly retro styling. Alec had clamored for lots of pirate-ship ornamentation. The masters at Beretania pursed their lips and compromised, without spoiling their ideal of sleek white functionality. Alec insisted on having belaying pins along her rails, for appearance's sake, and a working ship's wheel.

Beretania let him have his way in the cabin interiors, too, and they were glorious or hideous, depending on your sense of taste. Plenty of teak paneling and carving in a generally eighteenth-century style, the color scheme all crimson, jewel blue, and mahogany.

There was even a figurehead on the prow, a mermaid whose bare breasts were discreetly obscured by the snaking coils of her fire-colored hair. Alec had seen her in an old drawing and demanded a reproduction. She stared out at the sea with contemptuous black eyes, and well she might; the *Captain Morgan* was deadly swift, swifter than the *Flying Cloud*, swifter than any other ship Beretania had built, and they were the best in the business. She flew a black ensign bearing a grinning skull and crossed bones.

She carried laser cannon, too, hidden away behind sliding panels, quite dull functional pre-ban stuff of immense power, obtained from shady men who kept no records. So far the Captain had been unable to talk Alec into outright piracy, but if anyone ever attempted to board the *Captain Morgan* they'd wind up at the bottom of the sea in very small pieces.

With a last whoosh of spray the agboat rose from the water and settled like a bird into its berth. Alec locked the davits and vaulted down to the deck, where he nearly collided with Billy Bones, who came rattling up with a glass of iced fruit tea for him.

Billy Bones was not a robot. It was one of the Captain's servounits, a skeletal thing on six jointed legs with three manipulative members. Alec had put it together to satisfy the Captain's desire to function in four-dimensional space. It had no brain or personality, the Captain controlled everything it did; but for whimsy's sake Alec had given it a steel skull-face. The effect was not whimsical. The servounit looked like a cross between the Terminator and a scorpion. The Captain had three others on board and Alec had named them Coxinga, Bully Hayes, and Flint.

Thanks, Captain, sir! Alec took the tea and had gulped it all down before he reached his cabin. *I'm going to wash; I feel like a guano magnet.*

The servounit followed after him and accepted the empty glass. **Aye, son. Supper'll be ready in the saloon when you get out.**

Billy Bones waited patiently while he shrugged out of his coveralls and climbed into the shower. It extended a grasping hook, picked up the coveralls and scuttled away with them to the ship's laundry. In the galley, Coxinga began preparations for Alec's supper. On the quarterdeck, the Captain checked the stock market totals for that day and roved through his weather data, satisfying himself that no storms, financial or meteorological, were headed their way within the next forty-eight hours. He ordered Flint off to be waiting with a fresh towel for Alec, and busied himself with plotting their next course. He was a very contented machine.

Alec was the only soul on board, and he hadn't seen a human being in six months.

But he was singing lustily as he lathered his hair, though Flint wasn't able to appreciate his fine tenor in the least as it crept in on its steel spider-legs.

Pity the Flying Dutchman! Forever is his doom.
The stormy waters round Cape Horn must be his living tomb!
He's bound to sail the ocean forever and a day
As he tries in vain his oath to keep by entering Table Bay!

He was still whistling the song as he pulled on shorts and a vivid Hawaiian shirt. It had a pattern of flaming sunsets, scowling tikis, and surfboards. There was no one now to tell him his taste in clothes was ghastly. Pushing his hair out of his eyes (he hadn't bothered to have it cut in a year), he wandered barefoot into the saloon. The rolling walk of a sailor had come back to him easily, never really forgotten over fifteen years ashore.

The saloon was a fearsome place, and not only because of Alec's chosen color scheme of red, blue, and gold. The walls bristled with antique hand weapons of every description. Alec had begun collecting swords, and branched out to pistols and war-axes, when he discovered what an atavistic thrill he got from handling them. Once, with a cutlass in hand, he had taken an experimental swing at a sack of flour suspended from a yardarm. The result, besides creating an unholy mess, had been so emotionally disturbing he now kept all his collection safely locked behind glass.

He fixed himself a drink now at the bar, settling into the booth as Coxinga brought him his supper.

It was sweet and sour halibut (Alec no longer had any qualms about eating real fish) with rice and peas, and he paused a moment to inhale the fragrances before setting to appreciatively. As he ate, he accessed a private file and reviewed its contents.

The file was headed Charities. Alec did contribute, anonymously, to several real causes he felt were laudable. The World Centre for Disease Control got millions from him annually, as did Tri-Worlds Divorce Counseling Services. He practically supported Mr. Shakespeare at Southwark, and gave generously to the Greenwich Museum.

But there was another way Alec spent his money. He called it the God Game.

He scanned through his list now and singled out a small Caribbean country. Its economy was just beginning to recover from a catastrophic hurricane five years earlier, and a general election was about to be held. Alec surveyed all the data from weather forecasts, estimated its probable national revenue for the next five years, factored in the personal histories of all candidates running for office, and decided which man was best for the country. He transferred three million pounds into that candidate's election fund. Then he did a projection based on all known factors and prevailing trends, and nodded in satisfaction. If all went as planned, there would be prosperity within two years and, just possibly, a cure for that nasty new strain of jungle rot.

Another name on the list behind his eyes flashed red, and he scowled at it. This was a Balkan nation, long ravaged by plague. He had funded the rise of a leader whose political record indicated deep concern with medical reform issues. However, since the man had been in office the state of national health had not improved, and the man's mistress had begun to spend lavishly on shoes, always a bad sign. Alec reached into the man's private bank account and was astounded at the amount he found there. He withdrew half of it and deposited it into the campaign account of the opposition party. Another projection, and Alec wasn't quite satisfied with the results; he tinkered with various factors, funding a research group here, a political activist there, until he got something he liked better.

He paused to take another mouthful of rice and fish, washed it down with rum, and returned to his calculations. The Secular Opposition on Luna was having a bad fiscal year. Best to shore them up with a donation and maintain the balance of power between the Opposition and the Ephesian Church. New sanctions were being placed on the Celtic Federation by the American Community and Britain; Alec quietly slipped a few million into various Celtic political funds. The Greenest of the Greens had just won a major victory at the Egyptian polls, and stood poised to cut subsidies to barley farmers; Alec depleted the Green war chest, and made an unrecorded donation of substantial size to the Greater Nile Agricultural Relief Fund.

The rest of the world seemed to be running along smoothly. He noted the presence of Robert Louis Stevenson memorabilia scheduled for the block at Sotheby's, the entire contents of the Napa Valley museum including the writer's childhood toys! Alec hurriedly made a preemptive bid, and arranged for shipping. Smiling, he settled back and finished his meal.

He knew that what he was doing was technically wrong, pushing governments and leaders around like so many toy soldiers. He told himself it was what anyone would do, if they had the chance. And the money. He told himself he had a responsibility, as a person of privilege, to help others. He told himself it made up for his failure to attend Parliament: he could do a lot more good for the world this way, after all, direct and hands-on, without hours of tedious debate in the House of Lords.

But he knew, in his heart, that he enjoyed the God Game. He felt a little guilty about that.

He shrugged off the feeling now and finished his dinner, as Coxinga crawled forward offering another tray.

Pudding time! Mango surprise à la mode.

"Cool," he said, and looked on expectantly as Coxinga placed it before him and scuttled away with the empty dishes.

Two months later Alec was emerging from a Happy Club in Tijuana, yawning though the evening was young indeed. Normally he loved working his way through every bed in a house, but this time hadn't been nearly the wild fun he'd expected after months at sea. He didn't speak Japanese, so the Captain had had to translate everything the girls had said to him, and what with the time lag between their questions and his halting phonetic replies, about the only phrase he clearly understood by the end of the evening was "big stupid gaijin."

Cultivating an image as an idiot is one thing, but being taken for one when you're trying to look clever and seductive is another. Alec was in a foul mood as he paced through the immaculate streets.

It didn't matter. He had other fun lined up for tonight.

He found his rental transport, a cheap little Aerboy, where he'd left it under a mosaic mural of Moctezuma and his court wearing what bore a strong resemblance to samurai armor. He climbed in and shot away in the direction of the sea, speeding to feel the wind in his face. It woke him up considerably in the time it took him to get to the marina and go down to the mooring where the *Captain Morgan* was.

Bully Hayes was waiting by the gangplank as he came aboard. He shrugged out of his dinner jacket and handed it off to the servounit.

Lay in a course for Catalina. Let's blow this town.

Don't blame me that you can't speak Japanese! I did my best.

I'm just not good with people sometimes. No big deal, right?

Right you are, my lad. You'll have yerself a hell of a good time in Lahaina, wait and see. Shall I set a course?

Yeah. Right after we deliver.

Flint and Billy Bones pulled up the gangplank. The Captain had already started up the fusion drive and switched on the running lights. In eerie silence the massive ship backed from her berth and put about, moving at half speed toward the end of the breakwater, unfurling her vast sails as she went, looking semitransparent and unreal as she retreated from the glare of the harbor lights. Around the signal on the end of the breakwater and she was on the open sea, and her speed came up and she was running north, under the inconstant Northern Star.

They wouldn't reach their destination for hours yet, so Alec had a shower to wash the incense out of his hair and put on his all-black smuggling ensemble, snickering at his own pretensions. His good humor was quite restored by the time he stepped into the deckhouse and Billy Bones silently proffered him a mug of coffee. On the quarterdeck that existed simultaneously in cyberspace, the Captain stood at the helm, holding a steady course.

How are we doing? Alec sipped from the mug. Like wine: Jamaica Blue Mountain hot and black, full of complex fragrances.

Couldn't ask for better, son. Wind's out of the south, mild swell, temperature's ten degrees centigrade, time's twenty-one hundred hours. At the speed she's making we'll be there well before sunrise.

Cool. Alec settled into his chair and looked up through the glass at the stars. *Make it so!*

Aye aye, matey. What's yer listening pleasure this evening?

Give us . . . give us something classical. What about Folded Space?

That was Alec's favorite twenty-third-century neobaroque fusion group. The Captain nodded, and after a moment, softly wailing tenor sax music flowed out of the ship's speakers, a piece called "Variations on a Theme by Bryan Ferry." It was sentimental music, evoking late nights in cocktail lounges and wistful memories, but it fit his mood to perfection. Alec had just had his twentieth birthday the week before and he felt sophisticated and old.

They made for the windward side of the island, standing well out to sea and following her coast. Alec was energized and jittering long before they got there. He jumped when the Captain informed him:

Right, laddie, we're just off Eagle Rock. I've dropped anchor. They've signaled to let us know they're coming out.

Okay. Have you scanned?

Aye. All according to the plan.

Alec went out on deck and stood by the rail, swaying against the sidelong roll of the sea. There was the looming bulk of Mount Torquemada, black against the eastern sky, which had not quite started to pale with the dawn but was perhaps a shade less black than the island. He inhaled deeply: perfume of gardens, peppery evergreens, sagebrush, and . . . machinery, growing more dominant. There were the blue lights of the cutter, coming in a long path across the water toward them. He rubbed his hands together and went below deck to shift cargo, summoning Billy Bones and Flint to help him.

When he came up on deck with the first tea crate, he recognized the voice giving him a cautious hail.

"Yo ho there, Dick."

"Yo ho there, Ebenezer," he responded. The boarding ladder extended and a moment later a man pulled himself up to the deck. He was dressed in gray exercise clothing and a stocking cap, and his features were fairly nondescript. Alec recognized his voice, though, with its regional Californian accent.

"Dude." The owner of the voice clapped him on the shoulder. "What've you got for the old man?" No wrong smells; no stress chemicals in the man's sweat.

"How's this?" Alec shone a penlight on the crate. He prised open a loose slat and the bright letters were clearly visible behind it: RED ROSE DARJEELING.

"Cool."

"Five crates of this, ten of Earl Grey, ten of Orange Pekoe. You like?"

"I don't drink the stuff myself, but he'll be a happy guy. Five grand for everything?"

"Deal, man."

"Then let's dance."

The Californian produced a disc from his pocket and Alec took it for a moment. Somewhere, the Eagle Rock Marine Institute went on record as having purchased fifty cases of jotpads and other student supplies from the Cayman Islands Trading Company. Smoothly, crates of tea were offloaded into the cutter from the *Captain Morgan*.

"This is really kind of funny," grunted the Californian, handing down the last box. "You ever hear of the Boston Tea Party?"

"Nope," Alec said.

"It had something to do with our revolution, the one where we broke away from you guys. Your people were charging our people a hell of a lot less than this for tea, but we didn't want to pay it anyway, so we raided some ship or something."

"Was that why the Yanks did that whole Fourth-of-July thing?" Alec was astonished. "Over *tea*?"

"Yeah, I guess so. I think so. Seems kind of pointless now, doesn't it?" The Californian glanced over at the *Captain Morgan*'s figurehead, illuminated by the blue lights of the cutter. "Hey, man, look at that! Your lady's crying."

Alec leaned over the rail to see. Pearls of seaspray were rolling down the mermaid's face, brimming in her black eyes.

"How about that?" he said. "She wants to be out of here, I guess. Time we were gone. Bye-bye, then!"

"Be seeing you." The Californian waved, turning to keep his face to Alec as the cutter put about. They made off and vanished into the island's black silhouette, deeper and blacker as the eastern sky paled, to deliver their cargo to the Eagle Rock Marine Institute . . . better known in some circles as the emergency command center for Dr. Zeus Incorporated.

The *Captain Morgan* tacked about and sailed west, well out to sea, setting a course for Maui.

THE YEAR 2350:

_____

ANOTHER MEETING,
A MONTH LATER,
FAIR AND WARMER

On the twenty-seventh, Rutherford woke with excitement in his heart. He scrambled out of bed and hurried through his breathing therapy. Then he took all his medication. Then he took the herbal supplements that kept the side effects of his medication at bay. Then he took his vitamins. Then he had breakfast: fruit juice and an oat fiber bar, chewed thoroughly.

He dressed with some care, in his best twentieth-century costume. He had an idea that sensible walking shoes were called for, and from the depths of his wardrobe pulled out a pair of heavy boots he'd found at an auction. They were a bit large, but Rutherford reflected that too large was certainly better than too small, and he laced them up happily and stood to admire himself in his long mirror. He remembered his daypack and strapped it on. For good measure he put on his spectacles, and struck what he felt was quite a Victorian pose in the mirror. *Intrepid*, that was the word for how he looked.

He'd clumped downstairs, sliding a bit inside the boots, before he remembered that he'd forgotten to actually put anything inside his daypack. So he clumped back upstairs, loaded the pack with his medication and a jotbook, and for good measure added a couple of oat fiber bars and a bottle of distilled water. He paused over his identification disc, wondering if he oughtn't make a symbolic gesture of leaving it on his dresser; but good sense prevailed, especially once he remembered he'd need money for any jolly country inns he might encounter.

Rutherford went down to the parlor and settled into his favorite chair (he had to take off the daypack again first) and waited eagerly for his friends to arrive.

Two hours later he was fuming with impatience, and started up, quite cross, when he heard the others knocking at his door.

"Where have you been?" he demanded, on pulling it open.

"Sorry, are we late?" Chatterji looked surprised.

"We had to shracking eat, didn't we?" said Ellsworth-Howard.

He surveyed them in despair. Chatterji wore his usual tuxedo and black patent leather shoes. The only concession Ellsworth-Howard had made to the spirit of adventure was to wear exercise slippers in place of his customary saddle oxfords. "Had you forgotten we're going on a walking tour?" Rutherford said, controlling his temper.

"Of course not." Chatterji half turned and flipped aside his cape to display his black silk daypack. "See? And I've brought a map." He held out a little booklet triumphantly. It was a late-twentieth-century transit guide to greater metropolitan London. "Found it in an antique gallery. It's even the proper time period! At least, it's not off by more than a few decades."

"Oh, I say," Rutherford felt his mood lift. "Good thinking."

"Can I have a sherry?" Chatterji looked past him into the room to the bar.

"No time!" Rutherford stepped out on the mat and pulled the door shut. "We need to get started. Besides, don't you want to see if we can find a pub in the country?" He started boldly down the front walk.

"Oh, that's right." Chatterji hurried after him, and Ellsworth-Howard caught up with them.

"You don't reckon we can really find any place that serves sherry and all that, do you?" he said.

"Of course not, but there's bound to be prune juice, and we can pretend it's sherry," said Chatterji.

"It will *be* sherry," said Rutherford. "We'll transform it with our imaginations. Or it could be nut-brown ale, or—or even tea."

They came to the main road that led out of Albany Crescent and went down it confidently, at least as far as the transit station on the corner.

"Terra incognita." Rutherford gestured at the maze of streets opening beyond. "Here there be dragons, or maybe the edge of the earth. Onward!"

"Where?" Ellsworth-Howard wanted to know, looking out doubtfully. The unknown world was largely deserted, except for the big public transports rumbling by. Dust blew and drifted in the streets of London, but no voice called, no footsteps sounded on her ancient paving.

"This way," Rutherford said, pointing down a lane less dark than the others, with what he fancied was a glimpse of green in the distance. They waited until there was a gap in the traffic and hurried across, as pale faces with surprised expressions stared out at them from the transports.

"Where's all the dust come from?" Ellsworth-Howard said as they tramped along. "There's none of this in my street. None in yours, either, is there?"

"Perhaps it's kept swept up where people live," Rutherford said. He looked up at the blank windows of the housefronts. "I'm not sure this district is inhabited. Funny there aren't any people about, isn't it?"

Actually, it wasn't. It had never occurred to Rutherford that the rest of the population of London might venture out as seldom as he did. There were no longer thieves to be afraid of and wandering madmen very seldom, no bombs or random gunfire, hadn't been in a couple of generations; but people were fairly timid nowadays. Anyway the weather in London was the same as it had always been, so there just wasn't that much incentive to leave one's rooms.

A few streets on they did pass a foreign-looking person with a map plaquette and a camera, wandering from house number to house number with a puzzled air. When he noticed the three adventurers, he took in their outlandish antique clothing in a long slow stare and crossed to the other side of the empty street.

"Shrack you too!" cried Ellsworth-Howard heartily. His voice echoed against the buildings.

By the time they got to the green place, Rutherford was limping slightly. A fold of sock had somehow wadded up inside one of his too-big boots, and was rubbing painfully against his toes with every step. He ignored the discomfort, however, in the exhilaration of discovery.

To either side of the street here the buildings were gone, and only concrete foundations and a few rusted pipes remained to show where steel and glass towers had been before the 2198 earthquake. Structurally, they'd withstood the shaking very well: not so the rush hour pedestrians who'd looked up and seen a million guillotines of broken window pane hurtling down at them. But the blood had been washed away long ago, and now the sun flooded in on an open square of derelict commerce, where a single tree had taken advantage of the light and air to grow to enormous size. It happened to be a California redwood, planted long ago by some transatlantic corporation.

"Golly." Chatterji's mouth hung open. "Have you ever seen a tree that big in your life?"

"Not real, is it?" Ellsworth-Howard peered at it. "Nah. It's a holo, right? Bloody expensive one, must be."

"I don't think so." Rutherford was shivering with delight. "Look! There's ravens perching up there. Do you suppose it's a sacred oak?"

"Looks more like a giant Christmas tree," said Chatterji.

"All the same, this is it!" Rutherford threw his arms up in the air. "We're at the beginning of the country. We're at the end of the urban nightmare. From this point on the ultimate west commences."

"We're going north, ain't we?" Ellsworth-Howard squinted around them in the sunlight.

"Whatever," said Rutherford, and strode forward. His friends followed gamely.

But they went on and somehow did not emerge into green and rolling countryside: only long deserted streets of houses, quiet in the sunlight. Now and then they changed direction, wandering across vacant lanes or terraces, yet everywhere the view they encountered was the same. The dust had buried the curbs in some places, or formed little sloping dunes against front steps, or lay in the cracks in the pavement. The only sound was the wind and the occasional roar of a public transport going by. Once, briefly, they heard music coming from within a house. Its windows were shut and curtains drawn, however, so they couldn't see anyone inside.

Ivy scaled the walls of a few houses, and weeds grew high in the tiny yards below street level. With all the tall buildings dismantled, there was plenty of sun and rain for any growing thing that might seed itself in London; but few seeds, apparently, and nobody with the inclination to make a garden.

On they went, and both Rutherford and Chatterji were limping badly now. Ellsworth-Howard had begun to shake his head, making a high-pitched growling noise in his throat. Chatterji was about to tell him not to be so negative when Ellsworth-Howard abruptly clutched at his skull and spun around in a circle.

"My shracking head's on fire," he screamed.

Aghast, his friends caught hold of him. Chatterji put his hands up to Ellsworth-Howard's head and drew back with a cry.

"The rivets," he said. "They're hot!"

"It's the sun!" Rutherford realized. They staggered together into the shade of a wall and Rutherford fumbled off his daypack. He got out his distilled water and splashed it over Ellsworth-Howard's scalp.

"How could we have been so stupid?" Ellsworth-Howard moaned. "The shracking sun's radioactive! That's why people used to wear hats."

"Hats?" Rutherford and Chatterji looked at each other in dismay.

"I knew I'd forgotten something." Ellsworth-Howard wiped away tears.

"Stop a bit," Chatterji said. He pulled out an immaculate silk handkerchief and tied knots in the corners. "I saw this in an Early Humor anthology. You do this, and this and this, and it makes a sort of a hat, see? Here we go." He fitted it carefully on Ellsworth-Howard. "There. Now you'll be fine."

"But what'll *we* do?" said Rutherford.

"I expect we'll be all right. You know," Chatterji said, passing his hand over his hair in a tactful gesture. Rutherford nervously put his hands up to his own scalp and encountered an awful lot of pink forehead. Chatterji bit his lip. "Well—er— perhaps we'll find an antique shop. You might buy a hat there."

"Righto," said Rutherford, enormously relieved to remember he'd brought his identification disc.

They stepped out cautiously into the sunlight again, and continued their journey.

The novelty of the great outdoors was no longer quite as enthralling. Even Ellsworth-Howard was limping by the time they came to the first busy intersection they'd seen since leaving Rutherford's neighborhood. The friends stood, uncertain, on a street corner, drawing back involuntarily as the transports thundered past them.

"So where the bloody hell are we?" said Ellsworth-Howard. "I'm fed up with this walking thing, you know."

"The map!" Chatterji pulled it out and attempted to read it. It fell open all the way to his feet. Rutherford picked up the other end and they stood poring over the map, turning it this way and that in puzzlement. Ellsworth-Howard sighed and slipped off his daypack. He pulled out his buke, squeezed in a code, and waited for the results.

"I can't even tell where we've been, let alone where we are," said Chatterji.

"It's a splendid find all the same, you know," Rutherford assured him. "Tremendous historical value. Its just . . . unfortunately not very accurate anymore. Apparently. Here, does this look like my street?"

"Where?" Chatterji bent his head, frowning.

"There's a big green bit two streets up from this spot," said Ellsworth-Howard, showing them the screen of his buke where a simple map in brilliant primary colors had appeared. "I'm for slogging over there. Looks like all the countryside we're likely to find before our feet fall off."

"Foxy! You weren't supposed to bring your electronics," Rutherford said peevishly. "This is a spiritual journey. We're going to get in touch with nature."

"You want to see this shracking green bit or not, then?" yelled Ellsworth-Howard.

"Now, chaps! No point losing our tempers. Yes, look, Rutherford, it's a borough green area. What's its name?" Folding up his map, Chatterji peered at the red words on the screen. Rutherford looked too. Their lips moved as they sounded them out.

"Reg—"

"Regent's Park," said Rutherford.

"I'm off," Ellsworth-Howard said, and turned and walked away in the direction of the park. They went gimping after him, calling for him to slow down.

They came around a corner and there was Regent's Park: acres of green and sunlight and birdsong, visible in glimpses between the tour transports that came and went. Staggering like cripples they approached it, uttering little cries of eagerness.

"It's Olde England at last," gasped Rutherford, holding out his arms as though to embrace it all. Before him an industrial mower whirred busily along, shearing the grass to one precise height the full length of a long stripe exactly one meter wide. "Primeval Albion. The green and pleasant land."

His oration drew the attention of tourists dismounting from the nearest transport. One intrepid Asian gentleman stepped forward with his holocamera and recorded the three strangers in their picturesque costume, but most of the tourists edged away uneasily and spent their exposures on the tidy beds of primroses or the Monument to Victims of Religious Intolerance.

"My God, it's beautiful," sighed Chatterji, pulling out his sinus inhalator and taking a sensuously deep drag. "Look at all the trees!"

"It's a forest," said Ellsworth-Howard. "Look over there, can't you just see some bloody big knight in armor riding out from the shade? Or Merlin or somebody? Shracking hell, do you realize this is what it *all* used to look like?"

The thought struck them speechless. Haltingly they moved along the sandy path, straight as a die between its landscaping bricks, that took them to a real bridge over a real lake and beyond. They stood spellbound on the bridge a while, watching the waterfowl that paddled and fought. Rutherford quoted reverently from *The Wind in the Willows*.

Drawn by the spell of wilderness they went on, and presently found a snack bar on the greensward. It wasn't exactly a cozy country tavern; it featured various treats manufactured from algae, and four varieties of distilled water. When the fellowship had loaded their trays with this hearty fare, there was only a chilly outdoor seating area enclosed behind Plexiglas panels in which to sit, no snug nook beside a sea-coal fire. Imagination plastered over disappointment, however, and they enjoyed their meal.

Going on again after their brief respite proved harder for imagination to handle.

"I've gone lame with all this walking," said Ellsworth-Howard, and he was in better shape than Rutherford and Chatterji. They were in such agonies they didn't trust themselves to speak, until at last Rutherford collapsed on the nearest bench.

"I can't bear this anymore," he moaned. He unlaced his boots and drew them off with trembling hands. He was in the worst physical pain he'd ever experienced.

Chatterji leaned on the bench beside him, watching with tears in his eyes.

"I say, ought you to do that?" he protested feebly. "What if you pick up some pathogens?"

"I don't care," said Rutherford. "It can't hurt worse than this."

Chatterji thought about that a moment and sagged down beside Rutherford. As one moving in a dream, he gave in to the irresistible impulse and pulled off his shoes. With an animal groan of relief he stretched out his blistered feet.

Ellsworth-Howard was no stranger to physical pain—his parents had beaten him regularly, in accordance with their social creed asserting that comfort made one weak and immoral—but after a moment of witnessing his friends' utter abandonment to their senses, he sat down as well and took off his slippers, and flexed his long white toes in the sun.

"Shrack, that don't half feel better," he said. "I ain't walking back, though, I'll tell you."

"Doesn't matter." Rutherford gulped back a sob. "The pain is part of it all, don't you see? No great insight or mystical experience is gained without a price. This is the ordeal we're supposed to go through, to prove ourselves worthy." He stiffened his upper lip. "Don't you think C. S. Lewis and Tolkien went through this, when they'd walk through England? We're feeling the same pain they felt, chaps, imagine it."

"By Jove, Rutherford, do you suppose so?" Chatterji tilted his head back to watch the blue sky, where between puffy white clouds two blackbirds were mobbing a raven. "I think you've got something here! Maybe it's biochemical. I've heard of ancient magicians and shamans who'd drive themselves into their visionary trances using pain as their, um, means of departure."

"It's endorphins," Ellsworth-Howard informed them. His jaw dropped as he had a blinding revelation. "So this was what my mum and dad were on about! No bleeding illusions, they told me. Life is pain and hypocrisy and death, they told me. We're just learning you for your own good, you miserable little sod, they told me."

" 'That which does not kill us, makes us stronger,' " Rutherford quoted.

"*Conan the Barbarian*, right," said Ellsworth-Howard. "Well, shrack all."

"See?" Chatterji said. "You've had a revelation already."

"He's let his naked feet come into contact with the sacred earth," said Rutherford. "Perhaps that's it. I wonder what'll happen if we walk on the grass barefoot?"

"You think we ought?" Chatterji looked around involuntarily, fearful that a public health monitor might pounce. One had in fact been following them, and now watched from a discreet distance behind the snack bar.

"Oh, I think we must," said Rutherford, and gingerly peeled off his socks.

"Oi, that looks nasty," said Ellsworth-Howard in alarm. "You'll want to put some Lubodyne on those."

"I don't care," said Rutherford, though he had gone rather pale. "I'm ready for the great truths to enter my soul."

He got unsteadily to his feet and marched away across the grass, carrying his shoes and socks. Ellsworth-Howard ran after him. Chatterji hesitated for only a moment before taking off his black silk socks and wadding them up carefully inside his shoes, then leaping up and hurrying after his friends.

"This feels wonderful," said Rutherford. "Oh, it's softer than the softest carpet, and so much more alive!"

"Carpets ain't alive at all, are they?" Ellsworth-Howard said.

"You know what I mean. I say, what's that?" Rutherford pointed.

It was a low dome of concrete behind what appeared to be a large statuary group. They approached curiously. The statuary was of animals done in bronze, dozens of them, with an elephant in the center and all the others around it in descending ranks by height. There was a lion, and a tiger, and a bear. There were all creatures with hooves. Every imaginable bird, perched on the backs of some of the larger beasts. There was an ordinary dog and cat, a camel, a kangaroo, a wolf, and tiny things like weasels and mice in exquisite detail. Only one of each animal, all facing in the same direction with expressions of regal and sorrowful accusation. Just in front of the mouse was a granite pillar carved with the inscription:

THE MONUMENT TO THE VICTIMS OF HUMAN CRUELTY

And in smaller letters underneath,

WELCOME TO THE LONDON ZOO

Chatterji and Rutherford spelled it out with difficulty, and repeated it to Ellsworth-Howard. They stood considering it a moment. "Ought we to go in?" wondered Rutherford.

"It's only a bunch of holo cabinets." Chatterji shrugged. "You can see better on BBC Epsilon."

"Bugger that, then," Ellsworth-Howard decided, and was about to turn away when there came a soft beeping from his daypack.

"You've got mail," Chatterji said.

"I do, don't I?" Ellsworth-Howard slid off the pack and opened his buke. "Oi! It's *Adonai*. Preliminary report's coming in on the second sequence."

"It's a sign!" Rutherford threw up his arms and cut an unsteady caper on the grass. "We will receive the vision now, here, in this holy place."

"What about over there?" Chatterji pointed to a grassy knoll, where a big tree offered shade and shelter.

"Even holier. Come on, chaps!"

It was in fact an oak tree, which would have made the fellowship happier still had they been aware of that fact, as they settled their backs against its vast trunk and Ellsworth-Howard set up the buke on his lap. They gazed expectantly at it, focusing their attention on the report to the exclusion of all else, with the result that they failed to notice a public health monitor advancing on them. When he loomed before them, though, they looked up with open mouths.

"I regret to inform you that you are in violation of Public Health Ordinance 3000z, subset 15," he told them, in a kindly uncle sort of voice. "Why don't you all put on your shoes, so the festering lesions on your feet won't continue to spread human infection in a public area? Then you can all come away with me. I'll take you somewhere nice."

"I beg your pardon?" Chatterji scowled.

"Oh, dear." The public health monitor dropped his hand casually to the butt of his gas gun. "Are you going to be bad? You don't want to be bad. You'll have to go to a place that's not nice at all, and they'll take away your nice old clothes. You don't want that to happen, do you?"

"Shracking hell, he thinks we're nutcases," Ellsworth-Howard said.

Rutherford whipped out his identification disk at exactly the same moment the public health monitor whipped out his gas gun, and only the fact that the monitor's nerves were a little shaken by facing three dangerous lunatics delayed his shot long enough for him to take in the meaning of the disk. Rutherford enjoyed watching his expression change.

"Terribly sorry, gentlemen," the monitor said, holstering his weapon. "Can I offer you assistance? I presume you want medical attention for your injuries."

"Yes, we'd like that," Chatterji said, having a leisurely drag on his sinus inhalator. "Send a medic to look at our feet, and then have a private transport sent round for us. We're just doing a bit of field research, and we had difficulties."

The monitor saluted, hastening to obey. Rutherford giggled and elbowed his friend.

"What cheek. Private transport, Chatty? This is the life! Well, well. Shall we continue with seeing how our man did?"

"Looks like another bloody short life," said Ellsworth-Howard. "How'd he die so soon?"

"Let's start over," said Chatterji. Ellsworth-Howard nodded and squeezed in the command to begin again.

The pleasant electronic voice gave them a date in 1824 CE and showed them four photographs captured by a field operative, of a vaguely pretty girl and three men in early nineteenth-century clothing. The voice gave a brief biography of each of the persons shown, and then went on to note the implant date for the host mother. Her social status was such that she had been able to retire to a private home in the country for the duration of her pregnancy.

This delivery had gone successfully. Following birth the host mother had gladly relinquished the subject to the field operative in charge of the project and returned to London.

"No guilt, this time," said Chatterji in relief.

"I'm sure the Facilitator found something else to motivate our man," Rutherford assured him absently, staring at the images.

There followed a field holograph, taken by a Company operative with hidden equipment, of a blurry baby in a perambulator, attended by a black-clad nurse. The voice gave the names of the foster parents that had been selected for the subject and went on to explain what pressures had been exerted to extort financial assistance from the three men known to have slept with the host mother.

Next there was a candid shot of a small child standing in a park, holding a nurse's hand as he stared at a toy boat on the glassy surface of a pond. His early education and attendant indoctrination were described. The foster parents, it was mentioned, were both lost at sea when the subject was in his first term at public school.

"There's your emotional detachment, Rutherford," said Ellsworth-Howard. "Bang goes his adoptive family."

The next image was of a class of boys assembled for prayers, standing together in rows by height. A red circle formed about the head of the tallest boy, in the back row, and the image zoomed forward and enlarged.

"There's our man," said Chatterji. The likeness was unmistakable, even allowing for the grainy quality of the enlargement and the smoothness of youth. This too was the face of the hologram that had appeared like a ghost in Rutherford's parlor, except that—

"Oh, dear, they damaged his nose again," fretted Rutherford.

At this point there was a portrait daguerreotype of what appeared to be an older gentleman in a headmaster's gown and mortarboard. On close examination it was evident he wasn't an old man at all, but such was his appearance of dignity and wisdom that it added reverend years to his sharp-featured face.

"Oi! That's one of my Preservers," said Ellsworth-Howard. The voice identified the headmaster as Facilitator Grade One Nennius, chief cyborg field operative for the London sector, responsible for programming the subject with the appropriate advanced indoctrination.

"Nothing left to chance, this time." Rutherford nodded approvingly. "*We* picked his mentor."

There followed a daguerreotype of the boy from the earlier pictures, now a young man in the uniform of a naval officer, posing beside a Roman column in a portrait studio. He carried his flat cockaded hat in the crook of one arm and looked sternly at the camera. Rutherford exclaimed in delight.

"I must say, he wore a uniform well," remarked Chatterji.

The voice explained that the subject had been accepted as a midshipman in the Royal Navy at age fourteen, due to the fact that the principal "father" being blackmailed for support had balked at extended tuition and therefore arranged the subject's commission.

"Excellent," said Rutherford. "None of this nonsense about an ecclesiastic career. A good early start on a life of action. Real scope to become the hero he was meant to be!"

The voice described the subject's naval service, which had been promising at first. He had made lieutenant, been given command of a topsail schooner and sent to the African coast to chase slave ships. Having distinguished himself there for bravery and effective work, he was promoted to the rank of commander. Reassigned to a man-of-war, his career had been sidelined by an incident wherein he had argued violently with a superior officer against a disciplinary action.

"There now," said Rutherford. "There's our noble soul. Wouldn't permit keelhauling, I daresay."

Then he caught his breath at the image that appeared, apparently taken by a field operative with a concealed camera and somewhat blurred and badly composed in consequence. Nevertheless it riveted one's attention. It showed the deck of a warship, crowded with assembled men, and in the background below the quarterdeck a grating set up lengthwise, to which a half-naked man had been pinioned. He had taken so many lashes his back looked as though it had been grilled. Blood spread in a bright stain down the back of his white trousers. To one side stood the man with the cat o' nine tails. It hung slack in his hand, however, for he had stopped, was staring, as all the men were staring and even the prisoner himself was staring, head turned painfully to gape at the scene frozen in the foreground.

The subject was being restrained by four other officers. Their faces were terrified. His was terrifying. His long teeth were bared. His eyes were very bright and focused on the man who lay before him on the deck, the man in the much more ornate uniform, the man who was bleeding from nose and mouth and eyes.

"Shrack," grunted Ellsworth-Howard. Rutherford and Chatterji just stared, mute. This was stronger stuff than anyone was accustomed to in the twenty-fourth century.

Court-martial had been initiated, explained the voice, but before action could be taken the primary "father" of the subject had intervened to have the subject honorably retired on half-pay, transferred to a certain department in Her Majesty's government doing business as Imperial Export. Upon mention of the name of the department, Chatterji gulped and Rutherford said:

"But wasn't that—?" He mouthed in silence, *the Gentlemen's Speculative Society?*

"Blimey." Ellsworth-Howard pointed at the screen. "Look who he went to work for!"

The next picture was of a small and inconspicuous-looking man in a black suit. He had had his portrait taken with his hand on a globe; that was the only clue to his character. The voice identified the man as the head of the department to which the subject had been transferred, and explained that the subject had become his protégé.

This provoked a fit of nervous giggles among the members of the fellowship.

There followed a series of photographs of the subject in civilian dress, a big amiable-looking man, engaged in various apparently innocent pastimes in various exotic locales: grinning sheepishly from his perch on the back of a camel, fumbling with amateur photography equipment before some Turkish fortifications, doffing his top hat to a lady before the onion domes of the Kremlin. In these pictures his face looked almost clownish, a well-bred twit on a grand tour.

It was impossible to think this was the homicidal young officer from the deck of the warship. Here he was, smiling innocently, having his picture taken with a group of Afghani bandits who were glaring sidelong at him in ill-concealed contempt. Here he was again, holding up a bottle and pointing gleefully at it, mugging for the photographer; easy not to notice the harbor and men o' war in the background.

The vocal accompaniment to these images was a litany of thefts, seductions, arson, and assassinations, committed with consummate skill for queen, country, and Imperial Export.

"*Espionage,*" said Rutherford in awe.

"And murder," Chatterji added soberly. "He certainly had no trouble killing when he was ordered to."

"But in a just cause!" said Rutherford. "He was serving his nation, as any honorable man would do, and serving it well I might add."

"Fair enough," said Ellsworth-Howard. "How'd he get killed this time?"

"Oh, any number of heroic ways, I expect, given his line of work," said Rutherford, just as the next image flashed before them: the subject with two other men, sitting in a singularly dusty photographer's studio. They were posed formally in three chairs. One was a very dark individual with a black mustache. The other was a sad-faced young man, English apparently, with a valise on his lap. The subject, who looked slightly older now, had his hand on the shoulder of the young man and was smiling at the camera. There was something unsettling in his smile, something smoothly professional about it, and perhaps a little weary.

The voice explained that this picture had been taken at Veracruz, Mexico, on 30 November 1862, and was the last known photograph of the subject before his disappearance while in the field at Los Angeles, California, in March, 1863. Imperial Export had regretfully closed its files on him after some years and given him posthumous commendation for his final work on Operation Document D. ·

"My God!" Chatterji jumped as though he'd been shot.

"What?" said Rutherford, and Ellsworth-Howard ordered the report to pause. The voice stopped and the glittering silver save-pattern crawled across the screen.

"Haven't you ever heard of Document D?" demanded Chatterji. Ellsworth-Howard shook his head. Rutherford attempted to recall.

"Something in the Company archives? Used to be property of the Crown. Highly classified, had to do with that pirate fellow—it was a ship's logbook, wasn't it? Data about the coast of California and—and something they saw on an island there—" Rutherford clapped his hand over his mouth.

"Exactly," said Chatterji, leaning close to speak quietly. "*Very* classified information."

"It must have been Catalina Island the pirates stopped at, on their way up the coast!" hissed Rutherford. He rocked where he sat in suppressed excitement. "And they saw—you know what—and they wrote about it, and there the account sat in the logbook, never understood by anyone until the founders of 'Imperial Export' got hold of it and sent out a team to investigate—"

"Which must have included our man—"

"And they found—well, you know what they found—and the end of it all was that 'Imperial Export' eventually became Dr. Zeus Incorporated," shrieked Rutherford.

"Sssh! For God's sake, this is all classified," Chatterji shook him.

"Shrack!" Ellsworth-Howard stared at the frozen screen. "This is like discovering your son's your grandfather, ain't it? We made him, and he made—well, our jobs. What's this about Catalina Island, though? I thought that was just an experimental station."

"You go right on thinking that, old fellow," Chatterji said.

"Oh, it's too perfect," said Rutherford. "Do you know what they call the town on that island? *Avalon*. That's where our once and future hero went to die."

"Yeah, but he still died," Ellsworth-Howard said. "I want to know how."

He ordered the report to continue and the photograph from Veracruz vanished, to be replaced with a rather awful series of pictures from the subject's postmortem examination. The voice explained that the subject had been shot to death by American counterespionage agents in a vain attempt to prevent him from destroying classified documents before they could seize said material.

"And if he hadn't, chaps, who knows what might have happened?" Rutherford's eyes were brimming with happy tears. "We might not be sitting here now. Oh, the synchronicity of it all! He nobly kept the secret that enabled us to create him."

"Who's that?" Ellsworth-Howard pointed at two new pictures that appeared on the screen. The voice explained that there were certain details of the subject's last days still unresolved pending review of his brain transcript, and that the full report could be expected within three days. Recovery of the subject's body had been facilitated by the fact that he had been in the company of two Dr. Zeus operatives at the time of his death.

The first picture enlarged to fill the screen and the voice explained that the terrified-looking man was one Antonio Souza, thirty-four years of age, operator of a safe house and low-level shipping station at San Pedro, California.

Souza's picture shrank back and the second picture enlarged.

"Oi, that's another of my Preservers," said Ellsworth-Howard. A black-eyed woman stared up from what appeared to be a cell. Her face was as blank as a mask. The blackness of the eyes was so complete, so utterly absent of light or even human consciousness that it made Rutherford want to hide. The voice explained that this was the Botanist Mendoza—

"*Who?*" Rutherford choked. The voice continued—cyborg operative under suspicion of malfunction, previously assigned to Cahuenga Pass Transport Station. Duties had related to acquisition of rare plant species in temperate belt scheduled to go extinct in local ecological disaster beginning June 1862—

"Stop," said Rutherford, and Ellsworth-Howard paused the report once more. The voice fell silent and the glittering pattern scored the woman's face, giving her the appearance of having an uncontrollable tic.

"Talk about your synchronicity," said Chatterji, shaking his head.

"What's she doing there?" said Rutherford. "That's the same girl he—he— knew, in his first sequence. How did she get to the New World?"

Ellsworth-Howard pulled up a sidebar and squeezed in a request. He peered at the screen. "Transferred," he said. "Shipped there in 1555."

"But this is a disaster!" Rutherford clenched his fists. "She'll have recognized our man, don't you see? He's a classified project, and now she knows about him."

"I say, Rutherford, you're right." Chatterji frowned. "Well, nothing for it but to control the damage as best we can. She's being detained, isn't she?"

"Fortunately. But the damned creature's a cyborg." Rutherford glared at her image on the screen. "Which means, of course, that our problem is a permanent one."

"Then we need a permanent solution," Chatterji mused. "There are still a few vat spaces left in the bunkers where we're keeping the old Enforcers . . ." He looked at Rutherford over Ellsworth-Howard's head and made a gesture of unplugging something. Ellsworth-Howard noticed, however.

"No shracking way," he said indignantly. "She's one of my Preservers. They cost too much to waste like that. Just have her transferred again."

"But where, Foxy?" said Chatterji. "We're dealing with a breach of security, remember."

"I want her silenced, but even more importantly I want her away from our man," said Rutherford with determination. "There must be no possibility whatever of her encountering him in his next sequence. What if there's an undetected Mandelbrot frame operating here?"

Ellsworth-Howard thought about that for a moment.

"She could be sent Back Way Back," he said at last.

"Good thought." Chatterji looked pleased. "How far back?"

"A hundred and fifty thousand years should do it," said Rutherford decisively. "Yes. That should remove any danger to the project."

"Right, then." Ellsworth-Howard slipped on the button of the throat mike and gave an order. While they were waiting for confirmation, a long black private transport came gliding along the nearest walkway. Opposite them it stopped, and a medic got out and walked briskly over the grass toward them. Just as he knelt and began to wash their feet, there was a beeping signal: confirmation. The order had been obeyed.

Alec Grows Up

He had a reputation now.

People who lived in the shadows cast by the light of the First World knew about him; and that included the dead-eyed golden ones who lay on the beaches at Cap-ferrat and St. Tropez. Hungrily they watched the blue horizon for his ship. In certain circles he was called the Candyman; in others he was known as the Liberator.

Whatever they wanted, whatever it took to sweeten their weary days—whether it was bloodred wine or whiskey, or ganja strong enough to set their feet on another plane of reality—the big guy could get it for them. Or it might be cocoa with marshmallows, or it might be caviar. All it had to be was forbidden, and he could get it for them.

He didn't even demand their souls in payment. Just cash.

There were stories, legends in the Caribbean and on the Côte d'Azur, about the smiling lord who threw such wild parties on his white ship. The list of people he was said to have bedded was improbably long. He gave every appearance of being an easy mark, as hopelessly stoned as any of his guests at his parties, an amiable fool; and yet thieves boarding his ship had a tendency to vanish, never to be seen again. So there was a faintly sinister edge to his mythos, and people wondered about that black flag . . .

But nobody really cared, because he had the power to ease the pain of living, heal the sores of ennui, and take away wounding memory of the cold, clean, bright, ordered world for a couple of nights. And if they shuddered, shamefaced with guilt over their excesses, they only did it after he had sailed away. Later still they prayed for his return, and watched the sea for a glimpse of his pirate flag. All they wanted was a little freedom, and they knew he could get it for them.

It was only freedom of the senses, of course. Once, the boy had had dreams about setting them truly free. He had thought it might be nice, to be a legend.

He was older now.

Careful, Alec.

I know. My God, was it always this gloomy? This deserted?

I'm afraid so.

The tall man stood, irresolute, looking around at Trafalgar Square. Other than the surveillance cameras there was only a lurking public health monitor to note his presence, who, after a cursory inspection, decided the tall man was a tourist and therefore had an excuse for looking strange.

And Alec did look strange, by the standards of modern London: unhealthily tanned by the sun and dressed for a much warmer climate, with a brilliantly loud tropical-patterned shirt. He was peering a bit as he tried to bring his vision into the narrow and close horizon of walls.

It was difficult. He'd only been away three years this time, but something seemed to have cut the cord at last. There was no specific change he could point to, other than the tragedy; only a general sense of everything in London being steeper, and narrower, and darker.

You know what it is? It's not home anymore. I never really belonged here at all, did I?

Not you, my lad. You come from the sea.

Alec smiled faintly at that, but the truth was he was finding the old pirate-talk pretty comforting just now. *So where's this art gallery, then?*

Starboard at the next corner and straight on three blocks.

He shivered, wishing he'd brought a coat, and set off at a rapid walk to warm himself. He'd get a coat in some shop, after the show. The Bloomsbury house was too full of ghosts to stop in, even if it hadn't been locked up tight as a drum with dustcovers over everything.

He had tried to go back to live there twice.

In his twentieth summer he partied for a whole season off Carriacou with a very agreeable bunch of decadent kids, minor admin bluebloods. The Captain had snarled at him a lot because he began drinking heavily again, and attempted to prod him back to his usual routine of club-hopping, which required that he stay at least sober enough to walk. Alec had been disinclined to visit clubs, however, because there was one quite nice girl who shared his bed more frequently than the other young ladies in the party.

But when the season had ended she came to him, pale and stammering, to announce that she was pregnant.

He took the news badly, yet when he sobered up he bathed, shaved, and went with her to the local marriage registrar. There was a brief ceremony on a terrace with a sweeping view of Hillsborough Bay, and the white ships belonging to millionaires drifted on the horizon like swans. Then they went down the hill, on board his ship and straight off to London and Tower Marina.

By the time they dropped anchor he found, unaccountably, that he was looking forward to starting a family. The Bloomsbury house had been reopened and aired out, new servants had been hired, and Lewin and Mrs. Lewin had come bustling from their retirement. Alec's old nursery was repainted, and then—

She was ever so sorry, the girl said, but apparently she'd been mistaken. There wasn't going to be a baby after all. And, while she was certain Alec was a super guy, now that she wasn't stoned all the time she just didn't think the relationship would work out. What were the chances they could simply pretend this whole thing had never happened?

Away went the new servants, away went Lewin and Mrs. Lewin back into retirement, and away went the girl out of Alec's life, bearing a nice fat settlement by which to remember him.

The second time had been much less banal.

He was walking through Portofino when he heard a voice crying out to him in English. He turned to see a girl in an agchair speeding toward him from the shadows of a dark side street. She was an American, in terrible trouble: her husband was lying in wait for her with a gun at their villa. She begged Alec to help her. The Captain muttered something cautionary but Alec mentally shushed him. The girl collapsed weeping, explaining that she was a sufferer from Vargas's syndrome. She'd had to flee without any of her medication or her identity disk.

Alec escorted her to the nearest safety station to make a report. The Captain had to do all the translating, with Alec repeating phonetic Italian after him; but once the officers did grasp that there had been a case of domestic violence, they took off with gratifying speed (the Ephesian Party held the balance of power in the Italian government that year). In no time at all they came zooming back to the safety station with a bound, tranquilized man drooling in the back of a detention vehicle.

Somehow Alec and Lorene (that was her name) wound up living together in a hotel. She was witty and charming and practical, and she had been a coloratura soprano before she'd gotten ill. She could still sing, though without much power, in a piercingly sweet voice that reminded him of tinkling frost or chiming bells.

Their stay at the hotel stretched out into weeks. One night Lorene had told Alec the full story of her life, all misfortune, and he was so moved to compassion he proposed.

The honeymoon on board the *Captain Morgan* was a perfect idyll. Not an especially sensual one, because Lorene's illness flared up in the sea air, but they were blissfully happy anyway. Alec sent ahead orders for the Bloomsbury house to be completely remodeled. He set up a holoscreen by her bed and went through interior design catalogs with her.

Lorene was enchanted with London in the way only Americans are. She was enchanted with the Rolls and its Finsbury crest, she was enchanted all the way to the front steps of her new home, where she allowed Alec to lift her out of the Rolls and settle her into her agchair. She smiled enchantingly at the servants lined up to welcome her (Lewin and Mrs. Lewin weren't among them; Mrs. Lewin was too ill to come up to London). Then Lorene looked up at the house and a shadow fell across her face.

"Oh, my God, those steps are high," she said.

"Don't worry, babe," Alec said. "I'm supposed to carry you across the door-mouth, remember?"

And he caught her up (she weighed practically nothing) and stormed the stairs and jumped over the threshold with her, but unfortunately he knocked her elbow on the jamb as they passed through and she almost fainted with the pain.

Things had not improved. Almost from the first day, Lorene became sullen and silent, and Alec told himself that it was because London made her illness worse. Most days she was too exhausted to do more than lie on a day bed and watch holoes with him. If he went out for any period of time, she greeted his return with tearful complaints that the servants had been rude to her. She didn't like the house or furnishings, either.

Balkister dropped in one day to discuss his latest crusade, which (that week) was to get the Falkland Islands renamed the Malvinas (again), and he stayed until midnight talking over old times with Alec. As soon as Balkister had wobbled his way out the door, Lorene rose on her elbow and denounced him for the nastiest, most adolescent little creep she'd ever met.

Alec agreed with her readily enough. Plenty of people felt that way about Balkister. Lorene went on to demand whether Alec knew that Balkister was a homosexual, and obviously in love with Alec?

Alec didn't know. He stood there, slightly befuddled by the hour and what he'd been drinking, trying to sort that one out. Balkister had never approached him for that kind of fun, that he remembered; but then a lot of the time he'd spent in

Balkister's company they'd both been stoned. At last he laughed and told Lorene he thought she was wrong. She wept hysterically. He carried her up to their bed at last, and when he tried to crawl in beside her she screamed that he was gay and struck at him. He staggered away and slept in a guest bedroom.

The next two weeks, Alec was like a wounded horse on a battlefield, help-lessly tangling himself in his own guts with every step he attempted to take out of his trouble. Even on the best days, Lorene was unaccountably irritated with him. He was such an overgrown boy! He had no drive or ambition at all. How could a grown man think he could just run away from his troubles and live on a yacht all the time? At her worst she grew screamingly abusive, shaking in her chair with emotion, and a pair of scarlet spots would appear on either side of her thin white nose.

After her rages she clung to him, weeping and contrite, and called him all the loving names of their courtship period, and begged him to be strong for her.

The Captain, who knew when to keep his mouth shut, did. He authorized the services of a team of private investigators, however, and when their reports came in he kept his peace and bided his time.

The servants quit in a body one morning, as a formal protest after Lorene accused the cook of trying to poison her. This was serious: one didn't treat ser-vants that way in the twenty-fourth century. Alec controlled his temper and said nothing. When he didn't respond by blowing up at her, Lorene followed him around in her agchair insisting that there *had* been sleeping pills in the food, and the less he responded the angrier she became, until she accused him of being a gutless coward.

With a roar of frustration he picked up an overstuffed recliner and threw it across the room, and followed it with the matching ottoman. They both landed on the piano and it collapsed. She flew up the stairs, shrieking as though he were after her with an axe, and locked herself in her room.

Had enough yet, boyo? the Captain inquired.

But Alec was horrified at himself, instantly remorseful. It occurred to him that perhaps what they both needed was a change of air.

So he removed the chair and ottoman from the ruins of the piano, and went upstairs to speak gently to Lorene, through the locked door of their bedroom. Once he got her calmed down enough to listen, she agreed to go away with him. There was a desperate eagerness in her voice as she asked whether they might sail immediately. Alec assured her they could leave that night, and went off to Tower Marina to get the *Captain Morgan* ready for sailing.

When he returned that afternoon, there was a phalanx of long purple vehicles drawn up in front of his house and strangers were going up and down the stairs. He jumped from the car before it quite settled down, terrified that Lorene had had an accident. But no: there she was, emerging in her chair, escorted down the stairs by a muscular young man in an oddly patterned robe.

"Hey," Alec said. Lorene shrieked and flinched, and the man put a protective arm around her and looked daggers at Alec. Alec started toward them, but his way was blocked by two more of the robed men—were those *bumblebees* embroidered on their clothes?—and an authoritative-looking woman in purple.

"Alec Checkerfield, earl of Finsbury?" the woman asked.

"Yeah," Alec said, looking past her at Lorene, who was sobbing and hiding her face as she was helped into one of the purple cars.

"Do you know who we are, and why we are here?"

Alec spotted the bee logo on the door of the purple car and finally placed it. "You're Ephesians, right? What's going on?"

"Your wife called us and begged for our help. We're here to provide her with safe conduct from this house to our Newham Hospital shelter, to protect her from any further abuse at your hands," the woman said.

Alec gaped. It occurred to him that the Captain must have been perfectly well aware when Lorene had placed the call. *Why the hell didn't you stop her?* he demanded.

In response, the Captain downloaded the results of his investigation of Lorene's past. He had discovered that Alec had not been Lorene's second husband but her sixth, and that nearly every one of the marriages had ended with a drama of this kind: waif appealing to kindly stranger, or strangers, to help her escape from clutches of brute.

"Oh," Alec said, feeling the shock waves roll. What an icebound calm descended on him! He blinked at the woman. "Well, she's lying. I never once hit her."

"That's as may be," the woman told him sourly. "You've a history of violent behavior. If you're guilty, rest assured you will be prosecuted to the fullest extent of the law. The fact that your mother is a votaress of our order won't influence us in your favor, young man."

"Huh?" Alec knit his brows. *Who* was a votaress of their order?

Stop a bit, Alec, the solicitor I ordered just got here.

No sooner had the Captain spoken than a steel-colored Jaguar with the Gray's Inn griffin on the door whirred up to the curb, and a gray-suited gentleman with a briefcase jumped out.

"My lord? Cantwell and Cantwell send their regards. Pushpinder Devereaux; I'm here to handle your case."

"Okay, fine." Alec pumped his hand enthusiastically. He felt light-headed, absurdly cool. "I'm innocent. She's nuts. You take it from there. Let me know what you have to spend. I'll be on the *Captain Morgan*, berth number three, Tower Marina. Bye now."

He jumped back into the Rolls and drove away without a backward glance, whistling shrilly.

It was over within three more days, and the whole time he kept wondering if he were alive, because he couldn't feel his heart at all.

Cantwell and Cantwell produced ample evidence that Lorene had been lying, and she didn't score any points with the Ephesians when she changed her story and sent word to Alec that she'd drop the charges if he'd take her back. His response had been no, thank you, and he would have thrown in a handsome settlement as a parting gesture if Cantwell and Cantwell hadn't discovered that the marriage had been invalid anyway, since Lorene hadn't bothered to get divorces from three of her previous husbands.

And that was the end of that.

He still went to the Happy Clubs and the dance clubs. Dancing was still a good way to get himself high, and it didn't matter anymore who his partner was. Now and then he picked up girls for overnighters, and if he didn't bother to seduce them anymore—if he did the unspeakable, if he simply looked into their eyes and persuaded them to go to bed with him—where was the harm, after all? It wasn't as though he was trying to make them love him. In the morning, he always took them to breakfast somewhere nice and released his hold on their wills, and over waffles or toast they'd blink, and suddenly remember an important call they had to make, a forgotten appointment, a job interview—he understood, didn't he, if they had to run off before the check came? And he always did, as another layer of self-loathing wrapped around his heart.

But he came ashore less and less frequently, even for sex. He spent more and more time at sea, cruising the immense emptiness of the water, singing at night to the uncaring stars.

He was finding that human places bothered him.

He hadn't come back to London in three years, and wouldn't have returned now but for the funeral. He'd have been making his way down the Thames this very minute if a small feature in the morning *Times* broadcast hadn't caught his ear: GALLERIE PROCHASKA PRESENTS A NEW MUSICAL BY GILES LANCELOT BALKISTER: LITTLE RED PLANET!

This is it, lad. Third shopfront down, the one painted black.

Alec stepped inside, ducking slightly to avoid the top of the doorway. His pupils widened to adjust to the subdued lighting as he looked around. It was a lot like a museum in there, except for the strong smell of takeaway food: all shadow, relieved by pools of soft light in midair where holographic figures kicked and strutted, and small knots of living people gaped at them. An Art Nymph pranced up to him, slightly terrifying in her sequined tap costume and whiteface, and handed him a playbill. He gave it a little shake and it promptly began to recite in a tinny voice:

"The virtual smash hit of the season! Written and designed by Giles Lancelot Balkister! Starring Marlene Dietrich, Noel Coward, and Tim Curry! What happens when a spirited girl from the Martian Agricultural Collective faces temptation in the lush warrens of Mars Two?" Somewhere close at hand Alec could hear a familiar whining bray.

"... Of course it's risqué! Where but on Mars are you going to encounter human passions in this day and age? Where else are human appetites even relevant anymore? Not here on Earth," Balkister was announcing. "You might as well just stamp the words MUSEUM EXHIBIT across your forehead. In fact, most of the remaining population of Earth ought to be compelled to. What are we *doing* here, after all?"

"Talking to hear ourselves talk," Alec said, ducking around a hologram of Noel Coward pattering out a sprightly little tune about heroic agriculturists on their Martian honeymoons.

"Fellow ugly guy!" Balkister looked up from the table where he was selling copies of the show. He strode forward and feigned throwing punches at him. "Bam, biff, and all that sort of tribal show of testosterone. How are we? I'd no idea we were back in town. Come ashore for a spot of raping and pillaging?"

"Er—no. Had to attend a funeral." Alec looked aside.

"Sorry." Balkister's demeanor sobered at once. "Whose?"

"My old cook."

"Oh, bugger, I'm so sorry. She raised you, didn't she?"

"Yeah. But she'd been ill a long time, and she was up there in years. Hundred and ten-odd." Alec started, distracted by a nearby scene changing abruptly to Tim Curry (the hero of the Collective) punting along an irrigation canal while he sang a duet with Elsa Lanchester.

"All the same." Balkister patted him on the arm. "So, what are we doing these days? Not married again, are we?"

"Never again," said Alec with feeling.

"Still swanning around the seven seas in our pleasure craft?"

Alec nodded. "I've had a few adventures," he said.

"I'll bet you have, and I'd simply love to hear about them." Balkister looked around edgily. "See here, there's a discreet little place I know of—why don't we just slip out of this haven of bourgeois pretensions and you can bring me up to speed?" He looked around and spotted a gallery employee. "Here, you!" he hailed the girl, taking off the lapel pin that identified him as THE AUTHOR and fastening it to her blazer. "You be the author for a while, okay? Tell them whatever comes into your head, so long as they buy the damned thing. I'll be back before closing."

He ducked out of the gallery, ignoring the girl's stammered protests, and trotted away purposefully down the street. Alec loped after him, bemused. He was fairly certain Balkister hadn't the least interest in hearing what Alec had been doing during the past three years and meant instead to buttonhole him about his latest fervent cause. Alec didn't mind. Balkister's monologues were familiar, at least, in this cold strange city.

They ducked into an alleyway and down the weed-grown stairs of what had been a service entrance for a private flat. The door looked as though it had been sealed by the rains of a dozen winters, but when Balkister gave a brisk double knock it opened at once, far enough to reveal a nose and one inquiring eye.

"Did you bring the spanner?" asked someone muffledly.

"*Vive* la whatever," responded Balkister, and the door swung inward into darkness. Balkister strutted through, smirking, and Alec had to bend nearly double to follow him. Their tuxedoed guide was what had once been called a *small person*, until dwarves had asserted their rights as a proudly distinct cultural group. He led them to a staircase that descended even lower into darkness. The Captain was growling softly, scanning the place for traps, but Alec felt secure. He could smell oak barrels and complex fruit bouquets, and he knew exactly what sort of place they'd entered.

They emerged into a long low room lit from above by mirror reflection, giving the whole place a camera obscura sort of appearance. There was sawdust on the floor; there were small tables and booths. There was a lot of snowy white napery and glittering crystal. A cadaverously pale waiter approached them.

"Messieurs," he intoned, bowing low and directing them to one of the little tables.

Alec had begun to giggle as they seated themselves and took up the wine lists. He reflected that he might very well be about to taste something that had traveled in the hold of the *Captain Morgan*.

The twenty-second-century ban on stimulants of any kind had not been universally accepted, much to the astonishment of the American Community and Britain, who had partnered the international legislation. The Californians enthusiastically torpedoed their own wine industry, because Californians were always doing things like that, but the French flatly refused. Viniculture was a part of their cultural identity, they claimed, and besides, nobody wanted a repeat of the unpleasantness that had occurred when the Fraternité des Fromages Historiques rioted and burned an effigy depicting the minister of agriculture in an act of carnal bliss with a soybean pod.

The British and Americans sputtered and threatened sanctions, but in the end all they were able to do was enforce the ban in their own countries. However (as the observant reader will have already noticed) certain substances remained available to those with ready cash and a disinclination to be told what they could or couldn't consume.

"Do you often drink here?" Alec asked, after listening to the selections and deciding on a beaujolais.

"Christ, no. Hadn't you heard about my annuity being stopped?" Balkister shook out his napkin with a snap. "I'm virtually penniless, ducky, unless I can move a few dozen copies of *Little Red Planet*. This is your treat."

Balkister put up an imperious crooked finger to summon the wine steward, who ignored him and went straight to Alec.

"You obviously look rich," said Balkister in miffed tones, after their wine had been brought.

"The guy knew me," Alec said, shrugging. He tilted his glass and inhaled the fragrance of cherries and spice. Balkister regarded him with narrowed eyes.

"Did he now?" he said thoughtfully. "That's most interesting, under the circumstances. What have you been doing on that yacht of yours, Checkerfield, hmm?"

"It's a ship, actually," said Alec. "It has cargo holds and everything."

Balkister looked shrewdly contemplative for about five more seconds, and then started to his feet yelping as the truth occurred to him. "Good God," he said. "*You* of all people! You—well, you bloody Scarlet Pimpernel, you."

"Shut up and sit down," Alec said, and Balkister was momentarily disconcerted by the hardness in his voice. "What did you call me?"

"If you watched more classic cinema you'd know," Balkister said. He grinned and rubbed his hands together. "Well, well. Under the circumstances, this is going to make my duty quite a bit easier, I should think."

What's the little creep on about?

"What are you on about, then?"

"Look, Checkerfield." Balkister gulped his wine without savoring it. "All joking aside, you and I have always been on the same wavelength. You've never been like the rest of our class, who feel we've got the right to push others around because we're wealthy and clever."

"Mm." Alec sipped his wine. He'd given up the God Game after his second marriage had collapsed, deciding that anyone with judgment as spectacularly bad as his had no right to play. Balkister continued:

"I might have doubted your ideals the past few years, off on your endless pleasure cruise the way you were; but it's clear you had your own agenda there."

Watch out, son.

"Oh, bollocks," said Alec easily.

"Right." Balkister leered. "Very well, then, let's talk about *me*. I've evolved a political philosophy. No, really, I have! It's that the smug and self-satisfied elite cannot have things all their own way. Why? Because, even in a meritocracy, absolute power corrupts absolutely. In fact it's worse when clever people hold all the power, because they're much better at tyranny than the old-style tyrants.

"And the worst of it is, the more the consumers are treated like sheep, the more like sheep they become, looking to us meritocrats to make rules for them. They don't see any danger in giving up their civil liberties to the wise and benevolent admin-shepherds."

"Mm." Alec frowned. That much he agreed with. The rest wasn't anything he hadn't heard before, wherever even faintly clever young things congregated to drink and be radical.

"If we finally bring all the marginal places like the Celtic Federation into our global village so they all fall into step with us, we'll lose the necessary dynamism of the Other!" asserted Balkister. "Humanity will stagnate."

"We don't want that to happen, no," drawled Alec.

Damned bad for business, that would be.

"If the people we govern are as unresisting as dolls, we'll get our precious butts kicked the first time we venture out of the nursery and try to order the bigger children about, won't we? And of course by the nursery I mean this solar system, and by bigger children I mean any other intelligent life in the universe." Balkister thumped his fist on the table.

"Okay." Alec refilled Balkister's glass. "Though the Vulcans haven't shown up yet, have they? So far as we know we're still the only game in the galaxy or wherever."

"That could change at any time," Balkister insisted. "Think of all those centuries when the Red Indians thought they were the only people in the world, and

then the Euro-monsters landed! However. Will you agree with me that our ruling
class needs the occasional goad to keep it from getting too sure of itself?"

"Sure, I'll agree to that."

"Aha. Having said that—here we sit, you and I, two terribly brilliant fellows of
like mind."

"No, no. You're the brilliant one. I'm Ape Man Checkerfield, remember?" Alec
refilled his own glass.

"But you've got money, sweetie, and that's just as good as brains. Besides,
you're fearfully clever in your own way." Balkister tossed back another gulp of
wine. "Don't think I never noticed. Have you still got that seriously amazing customized cybersystem running your party boat?"

Ship! You little pansified twerp.

"Yes, I have, as a matter of fact," Alec said.

"Good. Suppose I was to tell you that there are others like you and me out
there, misfits who have tasted intellectual freedom? Troublemakers who are
ready to wipe the conceited smiles off the faces of the Colin Debenhams of the
world."

Alec had to think a moment to place the name. Jill, right. He felt a momentary
pang and lifted his glass, swirled it to watch the body of the wine streaming
down the crystal, breathed in the fragrance. **She was nothing to you, laddie
buck.**

"Okay," said Alec. "And you're going to tell me that you're with some group
that does secret stuff. What is it, Balkister? Picketing shops? Voting to censure bad
guys? Rigging commcodes to send takeaway food your enemies didn't order?"

"You have been thinking about this," said Balkister admiringly. "I won't lie to
you, 'pon my soul. All that and more, you ugly creature! Suppose there is such a
group, and suppose I'm a member. Wouldn't you like to be a member, too? It's the
only proper work for a gentleman, you know. *Filibustering,* they used to call it.
Fighting to bring freedom to the oppressed."

"Yeah?" Alec studied his wine, turning the glass in the light. *Maybe this isn't as
stupid as it sounds. Sort of organized anarchy.*

**But what's in it for you, son? And you decided you wasn't going to waste
yer time wiping the world's arse anymore, remember?**

*I know. But where I went wrong was in trying to run people's lives for them. What
he's proposing is just the opposite, isn't it, encouraging people to run their own lives?
Besides, this wouldn't be stupid me blundering along. Balkister's sharp about politics.
Maybe he's on to something. And smuggling is getting a little old.*

The Captain bared his teeth and compared any possible hazards in this proposition to the last major life-change Alec had undertaken. He decided it couldn't possibly make Alec any unhappier than Lorene had. He noted further the possibilities of increasing his power base. If a crew of renegade admins were going to (for example) break into the laboratories of some big corporation or other, there might be all manner of opportunities to snap up unconsidered trifles, such as secret research data. Knowledge = Power, that was the equation, after all.

Hell's bells, boy, yer right. Yer old man would have approved of it, wouldn't he? This'll be a chance to make him proud.

Alec decided.

"So, suppose you did belong to a group like that," he said to Balkister. "And you talked a friend into joining. You'd want a big cash donation from him, I guess."

"Did I say that?" said Balkister. "Well, I sort of did, didn't I? But what might be worth even more to this band of intrepid heroes would be any quote extraordinary talents unquote the friend had. If he were good at breaking into defended systems, for example. Think of all the nifty pranks one might pull on the bloated and moribund technological hierarchy, eh?

"And if this talented guy was also tremendously mobile, able to travel anywhere at a moment's notice, without applying for any permits, because he was a shracking *peer of the realm* and had a very, very fast boat—and perhaps was already engaged in cocking snooks at the Establishment—well, I just think the heroes would welcome him with open arms, don't you? With or without the cash!

"Though of course the money would help," Balkister added as an afterthought.

"You've made some damn good guesses about my life," remarked Alec coolly, regarding Balkister with a flat stare. Balkister gulped and replied:

"Checkerfield, I've known you since we were twelve, for God's sake. I remember the things you used to be able to do."

Alec exhaled. "What's the deposit account code?"

Balkister's eyes widened, but he told Alec.

Give them fifty thousand out of the Cocos Island Trade account.

Aye aye, lad. The Captain did a bit of deft electronic manipulation. Lights flashed briefly on a console five thousand miles away and money moved, as readily as though gold *moidores* and pieces of eight had fallen glittering into a bank vault from thin air.

"Okay," said Alec. "You've got a bit of pound sterling to play with now. Can I join your secret club?"

Balkister stared at him in silence for a moment, realizing the significance of Alec's torque for the first time.

"You've been *cyborged*," he said in awe.

"Yup." Alec smiled at last.

"That is so cool! On behalf of my disreputable and rebellious friends, Lord Finsbury, let me be the first to officially welcome you to the Heroic Resistance Society. We're going to have some great times, you and us."

Better than you know, you little windbag.

Now, now. After you, Balkister's my oldest friend.

As Alec walked back that evening, staggering somewhat, he reflected guiltily that Balkister wasn't his oldest human friend; Lewin surely was. The old man had been through so much in the last week already, maybe he'd have already turned in and wouldn't notice Alec's condition. Asleep and dreaming in his nice grand stateroom. Nothing but the best for poor old Lewin.

But there was a light burning on board the *Captain Morgan*, shining across the black water at Tower Marina. Alec's heart sank. He paused at a vending machine outside the mooring office to purchase a small bottle of distilled water, and rinsed his mouth several times. He groped in the pockets of the coat he'd bought for a roll of peppermints, remembered it was a new coat and had nothing useful in the pockets, and thumped the vending machine a few more times before it spat out a little packet of herbal cough drops. Not quite what was wanted, but it would have to do. He tipped most of the packet into his mouth and crunched them up, ignoring the Captain's laughter. They tasted vile.

The mermaid was staring into the Thames fog with an ironic expression as he trudged heavily up the gangplank. She was the only one to greet his return; Billy Bones and crew had to stay below decks, deactivated, when he was in London. This had been the rule ever since an elderly yachtsman moored next to Alec's ship had glanced out his porthole, seen Billy Bones crawling along the deck with a tray of breakfast, and suffered a near-fatal heart attack from the shock.

Concentrating on his posture, Alec strolled along the deck and past the door of Lewin's stateroom. It was standing open. Alec ducked his head to peer through and stopped, dumbfounded at what he saw.

Lewin was sitting up at the table, resting his elbows on the polished surface and staring thoughtfully at a cut-crystal decanter in front of him. Earlier in the evening the decanter had been secured away in a locked cabinet, and it had been full of very expensive single malt. It wasn't full now, by any means.

"Lewin?" said Alec.

Lewin's head came up unsteadily and swung round. He focused his eyes and saw Alec. "Don't chide me, son," he said. "Ain't had a drink in seventy-five years, have I? Have a li'l patience with the old guy."

How the hell did he get into that cabinet? I secured that lock!

Alec stepped over the threshold and moved into the circle of lamplight. Lewin peered at him. "Good God. Where jer buy that coat? Y'look like . . . like something awfully tall n' silver n' purple."

"I thought it was kind of neat," Alec said. He attempted to slide into the booth across from Lewin and hit his head on the hanging lamp. "Ow."

"You been drinking, ain't you, son?" Lewin looked stern. "Thought so. Nobody'd buy a coat like that sober, for Chrissake. You'll be sober tomorrow, won't you, son? Promise me you'll be sober."

"I promise, sir."

"I'll be sober, too," said Lewin sadly. "No missus to go on at me. Like a glass bird she was at the end. You could have broken her like *that*." He attempted to snap his fingers. He couldn't quite coordinate. His face crumpled up. "God, God, I miss her so bad—" He began to cry hopelessly. Alec clambered out of the booth and went to Lewin's side of the table, where he crouched to put his arms around the old man.

"S'okay," he muttered, blinking back tears. "S'okay."

"What'm I gonna do?" the old man gasped. "Eighty years, Alec. Eighty years of my life, she was there in the morning."

Ask him how he got that cabinet open. I've just scanned, and there's been other locks tampered with. Nothing's gone except the whiskey, but I want to know how he did it!

Oh, shut up right now, can't you?

But out loud Alec said hesitantly: "It must have been tough getting the Talisker out of there. I didn't give you the security code."

"No problemo." Lewin wiped away tears. He reached for his glass and Alec let go of him so he could drink without spilling. "Cracked tougher cribs than that, back in me bad old days."

What?

There was a moment of silence, while Lewin drank and Alec played back his last sentence.

"Excuse me?" he stammered.

"Oh yeah." Lewin waved a shaky hand. "Didn't know, did you? I was a sneak thief once. Not to worry. I went to hospital. Cured a long time ago. Don't know how she managed all that time I was inside. We thought it'd be better once I was out but nobody would give us jobs, see? Except for his lordship. My gentleman. Nicest guy I ever met, he was. Didn't judge nobody." Lewin had another sip of whiskey and looked at Alec curiously. "It ain't half funny how you turned out so much like him, you know? Considering."

"Considering?"

"Mm. You're a stronger man, though. Lots stronger. Poor old Jolly Roger." Lewin smiled dreamily at the lamp, which was still swaying, ever so slightly, after its collision with Alec's head. "Why'd he stop teaching, eh? Too much money, maybe. No reason not to do just as he liked. He drifted with the tide, our Roger."

"Well, he was unhappy," Alec said. "I broke up his marriage, didn't I?"

"Aw, no, son—"

"No, it's okay. I've known for years."

Lewin had another mouthful of whiskey, shaking his head. "No. He made some kinda deal with the devil. I think. Jovian Integrated didn't give him orders much, he just collected his salary, but when they said for him to jump—well, he had to, didn't he?"

Unnoticed on its bracket in a high corner of the room, one of the Captain's surveillance cameras turned sharply and focused on Lewin. Its lens telescoped out, bringing him into tight focus, and the volume on the recording devices went up a notch.

"Poor bastard," Lewin went on, tilting his glass to drain it. "Last thing he wanted was a baby dumped in his lap. But he loved you, Alec, he really did. Much as he loved anybody. That was the funny thing about it."

Alec was confused. "Wait a minute. I thought he and Mummy got divorced because *she* didn't want to have me."

Lewin was silent a moment, blinking. He put his hands up to rub his face. "Well—she didn't, actually, but we never wanted to tell you that."

"I don't know why she didn't just go ahead and have an abortion," said Alec foggily, reaching for the decanter and filling the glass.

Alec, stop that!

"It would have been okay, really," he went on, "I mean, lots better than both their lives being wrecked that way." He had a cautious sip, glancing up at the security camera.

You bloody idiot, you know better than to mix yer liquors!

"No, son, no." Lewin reached out and took the glass from him. He began to cry again. "All these years you've thought . . . what Sarah's game was I'll never know." Alec looked around for a tissue to offer him. He groped in the pockets of the new coat again, with just as much lack of success.

"You know what?" Lewin took a gulp of whiskey. "Doesn't matter what they was up to at J. I. S. You turned out real fine, never mind what happened to his lordship and her ladyship. Can't help that, can you? No. All the same. Whoever it was made you, wanted to make something good."

"What?" said Alec.

Lewin's eyes were closing.

"Tell yer about it sometime," he said indistinctly. He put his head down on the table. A moment later he began to snore.

Alec staggered to his feet and looked down at Lewin.

What was he talking about?

Beats me, son, said the Captain a bit too casually.

Alec stood staring at Lewin a moment longer. Out across the water, beyond the Tower, a clock began to strike. It went on striking for a long time. Alec shrugged out of his ludicrous coat and draped it around Lewin's shoulders. The old man gave a little cry and called out his wife's name, but he didn't wake up. Alec stretched out on the floor.

Get up and lie down on the bunk, laddie.

Not going to sleep. Just thinking a minute.

Alec?

What'd he mean, about J. I. S.? . . .

When Alec woke it was broad daylight. He sat up painfully. He looked over at the table where Lewin still sat huddled under his coat, waxen-faced, shrunken somehow.

Alec knew at once.

Why didn't you wake me?

He had a stroke afore his heart went, son. It was over in two minutes. Nothing you could have done. Better to let you sleep.

Alec scrambled to his feet, feeling his throat contract.

It must have been the whiskey! He hadn't had a drink in all those years—

Alec, belay that. This wasn't yer fault. I've already checked his medical records and run a postmortem scan. He was dying anyway. Wouldn't you rather he'd gone in his sleep like this?

I guess so. He was so old, and he missed her so much. But he was all I had left!

Oh, I don't know about that. Yer mother's still alive, ain't she?

Alec put his hands to his pounding temples. *My mother?* he repeated in stupefaction.

THE YEAR 2350:

CHRISTMAS MEETING

A fine snow was falling over London. Rutherford was happily putting up greenery at No. 10 Albany Crescent, humming Christmas carols to himself. Christmas was a very popular month, in the year 2350. It had long since been purged of the embarrassment of its religious origins, to the point where the younger generations were sentimentally inclined to be tolerant of it. It was so retro!

One was even beginning to hear the unexpurgated versions of the old carols again, probably because few people had any idea what the words meant anymore. Rutherford was doggedly working his way through learning "God Rest Ye Merry, Gentlemen" because of its literary connotations, but even with his extraordinary classical education he couldn't imagine why the Blessed Babe had been born in Jewelry.

He tacked up the last swag of paper holly and scrambled down from the stepladder to have a look around. There in the corner was his artificial tree, releasing its fragrance of balsam mist spray as the tiny electronic lights pulsed. Around its base he had carefully arranged the favorite toys of his childhood, his hypoallergenic Pooh Bear and Montessori blocks, as well as a host of antique playthings he'd found in various galleries. Visitors were occasionally shocked to see the lead soldiers or, worse, the wooden horse and buggy; but Rutherford was a historian, after all, and secretly enjoyed it when the truth did injury to modern sensibilities.

Over the table he had spread a red cloth, and laid out the most historically accurate feast he could put together. No shop he'd visited had had any clue what *sugar plums* might be, so he'd compromised by setting out a dish of prunes next to a bowl of fresh damsons, flown into Covent Garden from Australia only that morning. He'd made a steamed bran and carrot pudding, and only burned himself a little in turning it out of its round mold. Now it sat sullen on its festive plate, leaking golden syrup. There was a dead-pale BirdSoy blancmange, with the word JOY spelled out in dried cherries. There was a plate of wholemeal biscuits and another of roasted chestnuts. The steaming Christmas punch had been the easiest of all: he'd simply opened a carton of fruit punch and boiled it in a saucepan.

The flames from the Fibro-Logs leaped merrily, the little Father Christmas on the mantel waved a mittened hand as if to welcome in carolers, and the snow kept falling beyond the windows. Rutherford went longingly to the glass and peered out into the steadily darkening afternoon. There were his friends, hurrying along through the whirling flurries! He ran to open the door for them.

"Merry Solstice," Chatterji said, smiling as he brushed the snow from his long black cloak.

"Happy Exmas," said Ellsworth-Howard, throwing back the hood of his anorak and peeling off his ski mask.

"Happy holidays, chaps!" Rutherford hastened to close the door and shut out the icy air. "Come in and partake of the groaning board."

"The what?" said Ellsworth-Howard, but he was advancing on the food even as he spoke. "Bloody hell, blancmange. My favorite! Here you go, Rutherford, here's your shracking present." He took a silver-wrapped parcel from under his coat and dropped it on the table, then grabbed a spoon and helped himself to blancmange.

"This is for you too, old chap." Chatterji presented Rutherford with a similarly bright package.

"Oh!" Tears stood in Rutherford's eyes. "I say. Here, you must have yours—" He ran and brought out a pair of little boxes, one for each of them. Ellsworth-Howard stuck his spoon back in the blancmange and there was a brief pause in the conversation, full of the sounds of tearing paper.

"Cuff links," said Chatterji. "By Jove! I've just found a shirt to go with these, too."

"A tie," gloated Ellsworth-Howard. "Now I am gonna look spiff. Thanks a lot, Rutherford. I got you a book."

"Oh, you're not supposed to tell me—" fussed Rutherford, pulling it free of its shiny wrapping. He tilted it on its side, peering at the words on the spine. "What's it say?"

"How the hell should I know?" Ellsworth-Howard shrugged and had another mouthful of blancmange. "Lots of pictures of superheroes, anyway."

"No." Rutherford strained to spell out the words. "It says JOSEPH CAMPBELL. It's about ancient gods! Thank you, Foxy." He set it down and tore open the other package. He drew out an old wooden box and looked at Chatterji in wild surmise. "Chatty? This is never what I think it is."

"Open it and see," Chatterji said. Rutherford lifted the lid cautiously and nearly screamed in excitement. There they were, still in the cellophane wrappers in which they'd arrived at a tobacconist's two centuries earlier: three dozen cigars. The faintest perfume was still perceptible, a melancholy breath of brandy and spices.

"Good God." Rutherford's hands were shaking with joy. "Chatty! Wherever did you find them?"

"Oh, just a discreet little shop." Chatterji waved his hand in an airy sort of way.

"Cost him a packet, too," Ellsworth-Howard informed Rutherford.

"Well, what's money for, after all?" Chatterji looked over the buffet and selected a wholemeal biscuit. "Anyway, Foxy has another present for you. Haven't you, Foxy?"

"No I haven't," said Ellsworth-Howard with his mouth full. "Oh! I'll tell a lie. I forgot, just got word this morning: another host mother's been found. We can start the third sequence for our man."

"That's wonderful." Rutherford carried the cigars to the sideboard and arranged them carefully beside his pipe rack. "I was beginning to think they'd never find anybody suitable again."

"Well, it certainly took them long enough, but here's the great thing—" Chatterji paused, pouring himself a tankard of hot punch. He looked up meaningfully. "The report came in from 2319."

"Thirty-odd years ago?" Rutherford stared blankly a moment before the implications sank in. "But that would mean—he'd be alive right now."

"Exactly." Chatterji nodded. "And all the indications are that he's secured a place in history already, or perhaps it would be more correct to say that we've secured it for him."

"What do you mean?" Rutherford's eyes got big behind his glasses.

"'WHERE'S ELLY'S BABY?'" cried Ellsworth-Howard in a shrieking falsetto.

"I beg your pardon?"

"The Earth Hand kidnapping case, Rutherford, surely you've heard of it?" Chatterji nibbled another biscuit. "It's never been solved, you know. BBC Delta does a retrospective on it every now and then."

"Oh." Rutherford frowned. "Well, police cases aren't exactly my line. Some scandal, wasn't it? Paternity suit or something?"

"I remember it on the tabloids," said Ellsworth-Howard. "Just a little bugger then, but I remember that fat lady yelling 'Where's Elly's baby?' My mum and dad used to listen to Earth Hand all the time. Tommy Hawkins, that was the lead guitarist, had this go-girl he kept with him, see, and suddenly she's about to have this baby! Only he and she ain't got a permit, and anyway he says it ain't none of his. She went off her nut and had to go in an institution. The Ephesian church took it up as a cause."

"But Hawkins wouldn't back down," Chatterji said. "He refused to admit he'd fathered the baby and he refused to pay the unauthorized reproduction fines. The Ephesians wanted his head! And legions of Earth Hand fans were just as positive he was innocent. There were riots, for heaven's sake. And then she had a little boy, and genetic assay results were published showing that the child was Hawkins's."

"How sordid," said Rutherford.

"Yeah, well, it got worse," Ellsworth-Howard said. "Tommy Hawkins says the assay results are faked. He demands another one done in front of a camera! Full blood test, too. It would have been a shracking media horrorshow, I can tell you. Only problem was, the baby went and disappeared."

"Just vanished," said Chatterji. "One minute he was there in his cot in the mental health centre and the next he was gone. No trace of a kidnapper on the hospital surveillance recordings. No ransom note. And the tabloids screamed: Where's Elly's Baby?' But no one ever found out, you see."

"Both sides swore the other one done away with the little sod. Earth Hand's next album was called *You Ain't My Shracking Kid*," Ellsworth-Howard recalled. "Title track was a lullaby my mum and dad would play for me all the time. Ephesians nearly burned down the recording studio. Little Elly never came off the meds, ever again. Last I heard she was in one of the Ephesians' cloisters, shut up tight. Tommy Hawkins died of something, a couple of years back. But nobody ever found the baby."

"I really fail to see the point of all this," said Rutherford.

"The point, my dear fellow, is that the host mother our Facilitator has located in 2319 is a sixteen-year-old go-girl answering to the name of Elly Swain." Chatterji smiled. "And the man with whom she is cohabiting is none other than Thomas Eustace Hawkins."

"Oh," said Rutherford.

"Which means, you see, that in the act of creating one of the greatest mysteries of the century, we're also solving it," Chatterji said with an air of triumph. "You see? Hawkins really wasn't the father at all. Little Elly was abducted by our operatives and implanted. And obviously Elly's baby vanished because we took him."

"By Jove, Chatty, I won't say I approve entirely but—there is a certain mythic quality to all this," said Rutherford.

"And, think about it—there will be no tragedy." Chatterji sat down in his favorite chair. "My mother used to cry and leave the room whenever the case was mentioned on holo shows. Couldn't bear the thought of that little helpless child lying dead somewhere. But we know he'll really be alive and all right! No sad ending after all."

"Except for little Elly in her rubber room at the convent," added Ellsworth-Howard.

"Well, that can't be helped. But think about it for a minute: isn't this the sort of thing the Dr. Zeus mission statement is all about?" Chatterji's eyes shone. "History cannot be changed, *but* if it is possible to work within the parameters of recorded history, tragedy can be transmuted into triumph. Nothing lost to the ages—simply hidden away safely by Dr. Zeus. Children rescued, not murdered! Little Romanovs, little Lindberghs, little Makebas. Little Elly's baby. All secure in some fold of unrecorded history somewhere."

"Yes, you're quite right." Rutherford began to pace. "We're almost obligated to do this, aren't we? Very well—suppose we put the order through to implant that wretched girl. Nine months later, the baby's born. We'll have to order the operative in charge to fake genetic assay results showing that he's the musician's offspring."

"Hang on." Ellsworth-Howard slid into his chair and pulled out his buke. He put on an earshell and mike and grunted in commands, inquiries, follow-ups.

"Now, how do we kidnap the baby?" mused Rutherford.

"That's one of the things our Facilitators are best at," said Chatterji.

"Oh, this is exciting." Rutherford rubbed his hands together as he paced. "Now, once they've got the baby, what will they do with him? Have to place him in a foster home, of course, but where?"

"It's coming together," Ellsworth-Howard informed them, listening at the shell. "Third sequence initiated. Girl's been implanted. Shrack!" He gave a raucous shout of laughter. "If that don't beat all. Now we bloody know why Tommy Hawkins kept yelling it wasn't his kid."

"What do you mean?" Chatterji stood up and leaned over to peer at the screen.

"Facilitator who did the implant got little Elly up on the table and had a good look at her, and guess what? *She ain't never done it with anybody!*"

"You mean she was a virgin?" said Rutherford.

Ellsworth-Howard nodded, scratching around one of the rivets on his scalp. "He accessed some Harley Street bugger's secret files and found out why, too. Turns out Tommy Hawkins had spent a fortune trying to get his dead willy fixed. Nothing worked, so he spent another fortune to have his secret kept."

"But he was sleeping with Elly Swain," Chatterji said.

"Yeah. Sleeping." Ellsworth-Howard was silent a moment, grinning, listening.

"You know what else our Facilitator found out? Little Elly wasn't the brightest bit who'd ever gone for takeaway for a band. Blond and beautiful but just a bit to let upstairs, see? Dumb enough to settle for hugs and nighty-night kisses from her Tommy, as long as she was With the Band. Plus she was only shracking sixteen."

"Please." Rutherford held up a hand as if to shut out the nastiness. "The lurid details can be glossed over, can't they? The essential point here is that the girl was a virgin. This is perfect, don't you see? She's the mother of our hero, our extraordinary man, our Arthur. Scandal and mystery surrounding his birth fits the mythic pattern exactly. Being born of a virgin is even better."

"You don't find that blasphemous?" Chatterji looked mildly shocked.

"Why? We're the gods here, Chatty, have you forgotten? If it doesn't offend Foxy and me, it certainly shouldn't offend you." Rutherford was racing around the room now on his stout little legs. "So. I daresay our Facilitator finds it rather tricky to arrange a foster home, in this day and age?"

"Yes indeed," Chatterji said, getting up to pour himself another punch. "There were house-to-house searches all through England."

"Then he must have been smuggled out of the country, somehow." Rutherford paused to grab a biscuit and kept pacing. "Placed with one of our paid people in that era, I suppose. Somebody with security clearance. A British national living abroad."

"Sequence proceeding," Ellsworth-Howard informed them. "Baby's born."

"Who've we got in that time period?" Chatterji sat down again. "Access the records, Foxy. Who's on the Company payroll, British, married, living abroad?"

Ellsworth-Howard pulled up a long string of names. "Got 'em."

"All right, narrow search: reproductive age, both parties of similar genetic profile to subject."

"Yeah." Ellsworth-Howard worked the buttonball and the list grew abruptly shorter.

"Now." Rutherford turned on his heel, "Search for any who announce the birth of a son in the period immediately following the disappearance of Elly's baby."

"Here they are," said Ellsworth-Howard at once. He listened again. "Junior executive with Jovian Integrated Systems: Roger Jeremy St. James Alistair Checkerfield, sixth earl of Finsbury. Married to the Honourable Cecelia Devereaux Ashcroft. Pleased to announce birth of son, Alec William St. James Thorne Checkerfield. Date of birth given as one week after Elly's baby."

"A peer!" Rutherford threw up his hands. "Perfect. They don't need reproduction permits. Whereabouts abroad were they living?"

"Hm." Ellsworth-Howard squeezed in a request and listened. "In the Caribbean. Baby supposed to have been born at sea. Parents' address given as the *Foxy Lady* out of Southhampton. Living on their yacht, I reckon."

"Better and better." Rutherford began to do a little hopping dance, skipping back and forth between the table and the fireplace. "No witnesses other than paid servants. What's the rest of the story like? To the present day, I mean?"

Ellsworth-Howard asked for more information.

"Marriage goes bang in 2324," he said. "His lordship stays on the *Foxy Lady*. Kid raised at London home here by servants."

"It's all falling into place," said Rutherford. "There's the sense of shame we need, you see? Not illegitimacy this time, but rejection by his parents. Perhaps he can be made to feel he was responsible for the divorce."

"Here's his schools," said Ellsworth-Howard. "Here's his entry in *Who's Who* and shracking *Burke's Peerage*. Became seventh earl of Finsbury after sixth earl had a nasty accident whilst diving. That was in 2337."

"Good lord! Funny to think he's alive right now, isn't it?" Chatterji remarked. "He is still alive, isn't he?"

"Oh, yeah," Ellsworth-Howard said. "Only thirty."

"Can we—can we see a picture of him?" Rutherford advanced toward his chair. "That will prove he's the right man, you see."

"Might take a second," said Ellsworth-Howard. "This is in real time, you know."

"Make it so," said Rutherford. He resumed his comic dance, waving his arms in the air. He began to chant. "Spirits of Cause and Effect, I summon thee! I bend thee to my will! Spirits of Action and Reaction, I conjure thee, grant my desires! Schrödinger's Cat, heed my commands! Oh, Spirit of Time, oh, thou Chronos, oh thou, er, Timex, Bulova, um, Westclox, Swatch, Rolex, Piaget! Uh . . . In the name of Greenwich, in whose image all Time is made!"

Chatterji began to giggle helplessly, watching him. Ellsworth-Howard wasn't noticing, frowning at the images that flitted past on the screen. Outside the snow fell ever faster, and in a distant tower ancient machinery began to vibrate. A hammer was cranked back in the dark and freezing air—

"In the name of Big Ben, Lord and Keeper of our days," said Rutherford. "Thou who hast measured all possible Pasts, Presents and Futures! I charge thee now, bring him to us! Bring him to us! Bring him to us! Let us in our time behold *Adonai!*"

"Oi!" said Ellsworth-Howard. Just as the hour struck and the familiar bells began pealing, the face appeared on the screen: Alec Checkerfield, seventh earl of

Finsbury, smiling at the camera that had taken his passport image. He was wearing a shirt with a vividly tropical design. There were a pair of sunglasses folded in the front pocket.

"Oh, it is him!" Rutherford dropped to his knees, staring with Chatterji and Ellsworth-Howard at the image on the screen.

"Height, one meter 97.46 centimeters," recited Ellsworth-Howard. "Weight, 120 kilograms. Date of birth: 12 January, 2320. Dual citizenship Britain and St. Kitts. Residence: No. 16 John Street, Bloomsbury, London WC1. Communication Code: ACFin@777P17/33. Bloody hell! Want to talk to him right now, Rutherford? You could."

"No," squeaked Rutherford, biting his knuckles. "I—we oughtn't. But order Elly's baby kidnapped, Foxy. This is our man."

Ellsworth-Howard gave a certain three orders in a certain sequence, and the invisible patterns of destiny in the room swirled and set. The clock had finished striking.

"Well." Chatterji collapsed backward into his chair. "I think this calls for a celebration, don't you? What about some sherry?"

"First rate." Rutherford scrambled to his feet. He ran to the sideboard and filled three glasses, and brought them back without spilling much. They all settled into their particular chairs around the fire.

"To the seventh earl of Finsbury," said Chatterji, and they drank.

"Ahh." Rutherford settled back. "You know, I never imagined we'd be running a sequence in real time. This should be really interesting."

"Rather frustrating, too, I should imagine," Chatterji said. "No more instant results. We have no idea how he'll turn out, but we'll get to watch it happen. What sort of heroic life is he leading this time around, don't you wonder?"

"You can find out," said Ellsworth-Howard.

"By Jove, we can, can't we? Not what he's going to do but certainly what he's done so far, over the last thirty years, with the noble programming we've given him." Rutherford wriggled in his chair. "Pull it up, Foxy. Let's see what sort of place he's carved for himself in history."

Ellsworth-Howard requested the information.

"You know, he probably works for Dr. Zeus," said Chatterji.

"Perhaps he's a scientist who's made some vital discovery," said Rutherford.

"Well . . . no, actually," Ellsworth-Howard said, blinking at the screen.

"Oh, don't be silly." Rutherford sat forward. "He has to be spending his life in service to humanity. It's what we designed him to do."

"Seriously, Foxy, what's he done with his life so far?" Chatterji pulled out his sinus inhalator and had a drag. Ellsworth-Howard squeezed in another request and listened for a moment.

"Messed about on his shracking boat, so far as I can tell," said Ellsworth-Howard dubiously. "The *Captain Morgan* out of New Port Royal. Doesn't live at the Bloomsbury house. Spends all his time at sea, sailing about between islands. Not employed by the Company. Lives on investments and a trust fund left him by his father—well, the late earl. Absentee House of Lords. Regular layabout, it appears."

Rutherford looked horrified. "There's got to be more to the man than that! Look further. What about his accomplishments? What about charities and humanitarian work? What are his politics?"

"No politics." Ellsworth-Howard shook his head. "No hospital visits, no village fêtes. He took care of the old cook and butler real well—nice place at Bournemouth and fat pensions until they passed away. Married twice. Divorced, no kids. Obviously."

"Married?" groaned Rutherford.

"Hey!" Ellsworth-Howard's eyes lit up. "Here's something he did that made the news. Age seven, Pembroke Technologies sued him."

"Sued? As in, filed a lawsuit?" Chatterji's jaw dropped. "Against a seven-year-old child?"

"Yeah." Ellsworth-Howard grinned. "I remember hearing about this on the news. Clever little bugger! It seems he made some unauthorized modifications on a Pembroke Playfriend his people had got him. Pembroke Corp. wanted to force his people to sell the unit back to them, so they could figure out what our boy'd done to it."

"There," Rutherford said. "There, he's a genius at least."

"What happened?" said Chatterji.

"Oh, they lost the case," Ellsworth-Howard said. "Him being peerage and all, and only seven, too. They went into receivership two years later. Stupid bastards."

"Did he continue to display genius at school?" Rutherford said.

"Well, he got high marks in maths," said Ellsworth-Howard, after listening again. "Top of his class there. Shrack—wonder how he got past medical scans all his life?" He looked panicked for a moment. "That brain I designed—oh, shrack, and his bleeding DNA!—"

"His Company handlers hushed it up, of course," said Chatterji, with a wave of his inhaler. "Just as they faked the genetic assay."

Ellsworth-Howard relaxed, and listened again. "No university. Seems he's designed the cybernavigation system for his boat, though. That's what he spends his money on when he's not partying. And—aw, shrack!"

"What?" Rutherford and Chatterji stared at Ellsworth-Howard, whose face had contorted in fury.

"He's shracked with my design," Ellsworth-Howard snarled. "He's had himself modified for interface. He's a cyborg! Not one of them old plughole jobs but the new ones, look like a tattoo under the skin. Where's he think he gets off, the sodding bastard?"

"Well, it's his body," Rutherford said.

"No it ain't." Ellsworth-Howard clenched the buttonball fiercely. "*I* designed it. If he's gone and compromised my brain—"

"Ah." Rutherford frowned in comprehension. "Well, perhaps that's our problem. Nothing you could have foreseen when you designed him, Foxy. I think we were all envisioning he'd operate in pre-electronic eras. Perhaps he's become one of those Lotus-Eaters one hears about, lolling around in cyberspace. That would explain this self-indulgent and useless existence."

"Though he seems to be physically quite active," said Chatterji, watching worriedly as Ellsworth-Howard worked the buttonball, attempting to break into Checkerfield's cyberenvironment. There was a fixed glare in his eyes that Chatterji had seen only twice before, on two very unpleasant occasions. Ellsworth-Howard began to growl in his throat as he was repeatedly frustrated in his efforts.

"Most of the port junkies don't get out much—" Chatterji was continuing, when Ellsworth-Howard gave an animal scream and threw his buke across the room. He was in the act of picking up his chair too when Chatterji seized him from behind, pinioning his arms. "Rutherford! The meds, for God's sake!"

Rutherford ran for the sideboard and brought out a forced air applicator. Ellsworth-Howard was twisting in Chatterji's arms, doing his best to bite him, when Rutherford darted in and jabbed with the applicator. There was an audible hiss. Ellsworth-Howard began to snicker. Laughing feebly he sagged to the floor, falling through Chatterji's arms. His eyes rolled back in his head. He stopped laughing.

"Oh, poor old chap." Rutherford ran and got a cushion from the sofa. "Let's make him comfortable until he comes to, Chatty." He tucked the cushion under Ellsworth-Howard's head while Chatterji busied himself with opening Ellsworth-Howard's collar and cuffs and checking his pulse.

"He'll be all right," said Chatterji shakily.

"He's an artist, that's all," said Rutherford, climbing back into his chair and curling up. "It—it can be very upsetting to have your art interfered with."

"Yes, certainly." Chatterji got to his feet and looked around. He spotted Ellsworth-Howard's buke, lying where it had fallen after bouncing off the wall.

"Oh, I hope it's not broken," he said, bending to pick it up. It didn't seem to be. It was in fact still trying to obey Ellsworth-Howard's last command, flashing its WAIT pattern in vain. Suddenly the screen cleared and Chatterji found himself staring at the seventh earl of Finsbury again. He was smiling out from the screen, not a very nice smile really. The pale blue eyes were so cold.

"Hi there," said the pleasant tenor voice. "If you're seeing this image, it means you've been trying to shrack with me. Do you know what *this* means?" The face transformed into a horribly grinning skull over a pair of crossed bones. From the eyes of the skull, a pair of cannons emerged. There was a flare of fire and the recorded sound of explosions, and the screen went black.

For a moment the room was so silent one could hear the faint chime of the electronic lights sparkling on the Christmas tree.

"Oh, dear," said Chatterji at last. "Now he'll really be upset."

"The buke's been destroyed, hasn't it?" Rutherford said faintly.

"I'm afraid it has," Chatterji said. "Of course, he'll have kept backups on everything. Won't he?"

"Of course," Rutherford said. "Except for the work we've done tonight. I'd like another sherry, please."

"Right," said Chatterji, and dropping the wrecked buke he went to the sideboard and poured them two more drinks.

"Shame about the buke, but, you know, we've learned something tremendously valuable about our man," said Rutherford at last, with a little of his former briskness. "He's someone to be reckoned with! This is no mere admin-class dilettante living for his pleasures, no, this is our hero all right. He's just got unexpected talents. What sort of genius can spike a Company inquiry? Have you ever heard of anybody doing that?"

"Never," Chatterji admitted.

"There's obviously more to him than shows on his social record," Rutherford said. "And either he's covered it up terribly well or he just hasn't encountered the right challenges in life. He must work for the Company! We'll have to order the proper people to get in touch with him and make him the usual recruitment offers. Once he's working with us, properly guided, who knows what he might accomplish?"

"It would be appropriate." Chatterji leaned back wearily and had another gulp of pretend sherry, feeling the fruit sugars race in his bloodstream.

"My Pendragon. My Messiah. My Hero with a Thousand Faces." Rutherford sighed, looking into the fire. "In my time. I'll get to shake his hand at last." He turned his head and looked out into the gloom beyond the windows, all darkness and whirling snow. "When this began I half-thought . . . well, secretly . . . that perhaps he really would save us all. When . . . in 2355."

Chatterji shivered. "Don't let's think about that," he said.

"But maybe we're wrong to assume something terrible's going to happen," Rutherford said. "Perhaps it won't be a meteor, or a war, or a plague. Maybe things just . . . change."

"Maybe." Chatterji drained his drink.

"Whatever happens, doesn't it make sense to have this magnificent creation on our side before the end comes? Maybe he'll find a way to stop it from happening, whatever it is. Maybe that's his ultimate purpose," Rutherford said.

"I hope so," Chatterji said, stretching out his legs. "Do—do you ever have nightmares, Rutherford? About what it'll be like?"

"Sometimes," Rutherford said. "I suppose all of us do, who know about it."

"I dream the streets are on fire," said Chatterji, staring into their own cheery little blaze. "I remember a song about the world ending by water last time, by fire next time. People are running through the streets screaming, and they're all on fire. I go into my grandfather's room, and he's there on the bed and it's on fire, and so's my grandmother. They turn their heads to look at me, and it's as though they're telling me I have to climb up there too and burn with them. It mustn't end that way!"

"Well, we're doing everything we can to be certain it doesn't," said Rutherford doggedly. "Let's put in that request to have somebody approach our man on the Company's behalf. Full speed ahead."

There was a moment of silence, punctuated only by a gentle snore from Ellsworth-Howard.

"As soon as we have another buke," said Chatterji sadly.

Alec Solves a Mystery

"And so, to conclude old business." Magilside cleared his throat. The other Resistance members grew alert at that vital word *conclude* and sat upright, trying to look as though they'd been listening. Behind him, through the portholes of the saloon, the pink towers of New Port Royal taunted the rebels with promise of unattainable naughty delights.

Magilside continued in his barely audible monotone: "It is expected that our support will enable the Semantic Renegades to continue their pressure on the Athenian Senate for the remainder of the fiscal year. If the FPFOM AKA Fair Play for Original Macedonians Committee increases their shipments of software, I am confident that a resolution will be passed, possibly within the next five years, granting sole use of the name *Macedonians* to those persons actually born within the prerevolutionary boundaries . . ."

They ought to send him over there to talk to their bloody senate, transmitted the Captain. **Those Greeks'd be down on their knees begging for mercy in five minutes.**

If they weren't asleep. It's people like him have kept the debate going for three hundred years. Alec concealed a yawn and looked across at Balkister, raising his eyebrows as if to inquire whether somebody couldn't prod Magilside to the finish line. Balkister shrugged and moved his hand in a gesture like a chattering mouth. Magilside was one of their most dedicated workers, and his feelings were easily wounded.

Alec sighed, surveying the gallant company assembled in the saloon of his ship. The Resistance had a number of designated meeting places, but somehow he'd wound up playing host to the disaffected elite more and more often. It might have been because his fellow revolutionaries found the thrill of a rendezvous on an actual ship too much to resist. It might have been because there were plenty of illicit substances to eat, drink, and smoke on the *Captain Morgan*, and Alec was always a good host. It might have been that they were snobs at heart, despite the fact that most of them seemed to feel that Alec, by virtue of being an actual titled peer, could be treated with a barely concealed condescension.

Right now he felt he couldn't blame them. Joining Balkister's secret club seemed one of the stupider moves he had ever made, even less of a good idea than the God Game had been. How could civil disobedience be so boring?

Though it was a little less boring when the Resistance bickered within itself. Binscarth, their resident literary lion, was at last unable to contain himself any longer and leaped to his feet, applauding.

"And thank *you*, Magilside, for that bwilliant summation of old business," he cried. Magilside stopped with his mouth open, breath already drawn for his next run-on sentence. He looked wrathful, and thumbed off his plaquette of notes with a gesture that suggested he wished it were Binscarth's eye.

"All right," he muttered, and sat down in a huff. Binscarth leapt up and took the podium.

"I'd like to bwing an exciting matter to your attention, fellow Wesistance members. I've located a potential wecruit whose libwawy of pwoscwibed materwial is even more extensive than mine. *Both* Buwwoughs—William and Edgar Wice! He's got a copy of *Medea*, he's got *Fahwenheit 451*, and he may even have *Pawadise Lost*. If we waive dues and allow him to join on a conditional basis, he'll let us copy his books for distwibution. What do you say, fellows?"

There were some *ooh*s and *aah*s of enthusiasm, very polite and subdued. It took a dedicated antiquarian like Binscarth to get much worked up about books or their distribution to a populace that was largely unable to read them. But the material was forbidden, after all, so it was certainly worth something. Besides, there were certain grubby holo production businesses, operating out of abandoned blocks of flats for the most part, who would pay nicely for proscribed material to be adapted to scripts.

"I'm in favor. What do the rest of you think, guys?" Balkister looked around.

"Sure," Alec said, raising one fist with the thumb up. He assumed all the works Binscarth had referred to were pornographic, and since most of the pornography he'd ever encountered had been astonishingly dumb stuff, he didn't see how it could hurt anybody. The other Resistance members followed with a chorus of *Oh, why not*s and *Okay*s.

"I commend you gentlemen on your taste." Binscarth looked smug. "You won't wegwet this, I assure you. I'll contact the chap next week."

He stepped down and Johnson-Johnson took the podium to deliver a report on financial aid sent to the Mars One colonists, who were engaging in a series of lawsuits and countersuits with Areco, the corporation that actually owned their farms. Alec looked longingly over at his bar. At last it was his turn to go to the podium, where he briefly described how the smuggling business was going and mentioned that he had got a deal on fifty crates of Cadbury's cocoa. There was some speculation as to how much revenue this might bring in, and though Alec knew to the penny he stepped down gladly to let Krishnamurti, the treasurer, give the revised figures for projected income in the current fiscal year.

At last the meeting broke up. Binscarth tried to lead them in a chorus of "I've Got a Little List" from Gilbert and Sullivan's *Mikado*, but everybody else thought it was silly. Binscarth exited, mightily miffed. The others stayed for one last round of beer floats and then toddled ashore to partake of the club life of Jamaica.

Usually on their departure Alec yielded to an irresistible impulse to run howling through his gloriously empty ship, leaving Billy Bones and his mates to creep forth and clean up the debris of glasses and plates. Not today. He stood surveying the party mess and then stalked over to the bar to mix himself a drink.

Now then, matey, the sun ain't below the yardarm yet.

What the hell does it matter? Alec groped in the ice bin. There was a big chunk frozen together at the mouth of the bin. He prized it out, lifted it above his head and smashed it on the counter. Bright fragments of ice went spinning everywhere, and Billy Bones and Flint paused in their duties to turn their skull-faces to him questioningly. He ignored them and picked through the mess on the counter for cubes to put into his drink. Smashing the ice had felt good.

Well, well. Our little Alec needs a session with his punching bags, don't he? Now why, I wonder? You been bored by them amateur revolutionaries afore. Are they finally getting to be too much, with their silly-ass agenda?

Maybe. They never accomplish ANYTHING! I'm going to be thirty soon, you know? What have I done with my life? I've had a great time, I've had nearly everything I've ever wanted—not that I've deserved it—and the only people I've ever made happy are those twits in the Resistance.

You've made me happy, son.

Well, thanks, but you're a machine, aren't you? Alec sipped his drink moodily. *You're happy when I'm happy.*

And I'm unhappy when yer unhappy, my lad.

Okay, great. Somebody else whose life I've ruined.

Belay that self-pitying crap! Down to the gym, quick march.

Alec sighed in exasperation as he set down his drink. All the same, he got up and went below to his gym. He had several punching bags of assorted sizes there, from the suspended balloon type to the full-length body model, and today he didn't even bother to put on gloves before he launched his attack. Up in the corner of the cabin a surveillance camera turned and observed him in satisfaction.

Alec had long since grown bored with Totter Dan, but found a tremendous release in physical violence. It got him nearly as high as dancing. He thundered away now at the unresisting canvas duffel until sweat was pouring down his face and throat. Finally he staggered back, gasping and blissful from the endorphin rush, and sprawled on the mat.

Now, that's better, ain't it, boy?

Yup.

I know what's gone and got you thinking. It's two years today since old Lewin went to Fiddler's Green. You don't reckon he'd approve of what yer doing with yer life.

I guess he wouldn't, would he? Alec reached out to accept a wet towel from Bully Hayes, and mopped his face.

So, buck. Ever thought about those things he said, just afore he died?

Nope.

Now why's that, eh? A clever lad like you. I'd have thought you'd have done anything to get to the bottom of that mystery.

What mystery? All it comes down to was that Roger didn't want me either. Nobody wanted a kid on the Foxy Lady, *but they got one, and everybody lived unhappily ever after. The end.*

The hell it is! That ain't all he said. You was drunk at the time—if I recall correctly—and maybe you didn't notice something peculiar about the old man's exact words, but I did. Shall I refresh yer memory?

No!—But the Captain played the recording for him, and Lewin's thin old voice came over the ship's audio system. Alec covered his face with the towel. He couldn't stop himself listening, however, and as the recording ended and Lewin's voice slurred away into eternity Alec sat up.

Hey! Did you—? It almost sounded like he was saying that J. I. S. made Roger and Cecelia have me.

That's what I thought.

But that's nuts! Why would a big company like that want anybody to have a kid? Let alone Roger. I mean, he was an executive because he was an earl. He never actually did anything for them except teach some marine biology.

Don't seem to make a lot of sense, now, does it? But ain't you ever wondered why he was always telling you what a special kid you were?

Alec sat there in silence for a moment, watching the punching bag as it swung in ever-lessening arcs and was finally still. Abruptly he got to his feet.

I need to research this. I'm going to go shower; have the data ready for me in twenty minutes. I want everything you can find on Jovian Integrated Systems.

Aye aye!

By the time Alec strode into the deckhouse, Coxinga was waiting for him with a tray of sandwiches and a pitcher of fruit tea. He threw himself down in his chair and looked up at the surveillance camera.

Okay, what've we got?

The bright holovision images took their place in midair before his eyes.

Jovian Integrated Systems first, the Captain told him. **This place look familiar? It's off the coast of California. Catalina Island, remember? This was shot in 2120, when J. I. S. was founded. They built a marine sciences academy in return for an open-ended lease. British-owned. That's where Roger was an instructor, for a while. You've run tea there, Alec! What a coincidence, eh?**

Yeah.

Anyway, J. I. S. don't exist now as a corporate entity. It was absorbed into another company. I reckon you've heard of it. They call themselves Dr. Zeus, Incorporated.

What? I thought that was just a joke. You mean Dr. Zeus is real?

Oh, aye, matey, it is.

No way! They're supposed to have figured out time travel. That's all a lot of pucka-menna, though, right? What do they really do?

Well, now, laddie, that's an interesting question. They're consultants, they say. Seem to be in the business of fetching anything for anybody, if the right price is paid. And I mean anything, son, do you understand me? If they ain't got time travel figured out, then something bloody weird is going on. I thought I had yer assets pretty nicely obscured; Christ, you should see what these people got hidden! And I only got just the barest peep at it.

Huh.

Alec, I'm getting that feeling. I smell loot here. This is going to bear looking into with an eye to boarding 'em, Alec.

Okay. One of these days. Anything else on Roger's work there?

No, there ain't. He went on indefinite sabbatical three years afore you was born. But, listen, son! Dr. Zeus ain't just rumored to have invented time travel. There's stories they found a way to make people immortal. Bullshit, says you; but they got the best genetic theorists from every country on Earth on their payroll.

Alec felt ice-cold suddenly. He didn't want to think about why.

And there's some old news you need to see. Watch, now.

Poor-quality holofootage began to dance before his eyes, the crackly kind familiar from historical documentaries, with a tinny narrative voice. There, May 2319, right about then he had been conceived, and what had been happening? Nothing much. Russia signed a treaty with Finland to build a new cold fusion plant. Somebody Alec had never heard of set a world record in surfing. Nasty accident: the Leaning Tower of Pisa had collapsed, taking with it the king and queen of Italy, who were up there watching a Restoration Night fireworks display. A Hapsburg cousin succeeded to the throne.

Alec reached for a sandwich, watching impatiently. July 2319: Arts and Entertainment. Joshua Spielberg's *The Blue Window* broke all previous box office records, but was lambasted by the critics. Ariadne Moonwagon's *Diannic Dream* was number one on the bestseller list. Some kind of scandal about a group called Earth Hand. Paternity suit? That wasn't one you saw much anymore. Vaguely he remembered part of a documentary on "Great Crimes of the Century" and wondered that so much fuss had been made about somebody named Tommy Hawkins being in trouble with the Ephesians. Alec felt a brief twinge of sympathy.

Christmas 2319. A previously unknown painting by Leonardo da Vinci was discovered in the catacombs below the Vatican and auctioned off at Sotheby's for an astronomical sum. Mars Two was founded on the slopes of Mons Olympus, the first extraterrestrial use of geothermal energy expected to make them a thriving and prosperous community.

You've found something, right? There's a point to all this dead stuff?

Keep watching.

Here was that nasty business about Earth Hand still dragging on: Elly Swain was the victim's name, and here was footage of a hysterical girl being loaded into an old-fashioned agcar by grim-faced Ephesians in bumblebee robes. Déjà vu. Alec poured himself a glass of fruit tea and settled back again, as the images flickered.

New Year Week, 2320. No announcement, in all the nine months beforehand, of any child being on the way for the sixth earl of Finsbury. Odd. Everybody else of any celebrity or rank made the news when a baby was expected, it happened so rarely now. But then, Roger and Cecelia hadn't exactly been pleased with the prospect, had they? Alec sipped his tea, frowning.

January 6, 2320, Elly Swain had a baby boy. *Punch* did a comic skit on the affair, but the next day things stopped being funny: the baby had been kidnapped. Alec remembered, now, why this was one of the crimes of the century. He felt queasy as he watched the famous surveillance camera film. Tiny red baby with a birth-bruised nose asleep in a glass-sided cot, there one minute, gone the next. Winking out like a little soap bubble, never to be seen again. What in the world had happened? Had the kid gone into another dimension?

He followed the story through the next week. *Where's Elly's Baby????* A journalist disguised himself as an Ephesian brother and got in to see Elly Swain, who wept and said that she'd given birth to the Antichrist.

Alec shook his head sadly and had another sip of tea. 12 January 2320. Would there be an announcement of his birth? Yes. Here it was. Roger and Cecelia must have decided to go through the motions. Proper news release with a family portrait. Hadn't they looked young! And awfully unhappy, though they were both smiling for the camera. Roger looked blurry, hung over. Cecelia was really more almost baring her teeth than smiling, stiffly holding out the tiny red baby with its bruised nose . . .

Alec choked on his tea.

I was wondering when you'd notice.

Freeze image! Hold it and bring back the footage with Elly's baby just before it disappeared. Isolate and enlarge!

The Captain obliged. Two babies floated in midair. They might have been twins, but most babies bear a certain resemblance to each other.

Enhance!

The images grew so sharp and perfect there really did appear to be two flesh-and-blood infants floating there in the room. Both Elly's baby and little Alec Checkerfield bore identical discoloration in their tiny faces. Alec's eyes were less puffy, his nose less swollen, but the bruise matched exactly.

Analyze images. Compare points of reference.

I done that already.

Well?

It's 99.9 percent it's the same kid, Alec. Yer Elly's baby.

Alec sat motionless a moment. *You knew,* he said at last.

I guessed. I didn't know until I was compiling all this stuff whilst you was in the shower. But this would answer a lot of questions, eh, lad?

It's not true. This is nuts. Why the hell would Roger and Cecelia have Elly's baby kidnapped? They never wanted a kid. I wrecked their marriage!

What if they didn't do it? What if somebody gave them a baby and told them to pretend it was theirs? That would explain a bit, wouldn't it?

Alec's eyes were glittering with that expression that had always unnerved Lewin, that suggestion of not quite human rage.

Bring up the clearest images you've got of Elly Swain and, what was his name, Tommy Hawkins.

The Captain produced two portraits. Here was a still shot from on stage during a concert, shadowed in lilac and green, but clear white light on the lead guitarist's face. Here beside it was a still shot from the scandal footage, a very young girl with her mouth open in a cry of dismay. Alec stared at them fixedly. Insofar as they were both fair-haired and blue-eyed, Tommy and Elly resembled him, but not otherwise. He couldn't see a single feature of his own in either face.

Best portraits you've got of Roger and Cecelia, please.

Four faces hung before him, now. They might all have been cousins. Not one of them shared a facial feature with Alec, however, except for a slight cleft in Cecelia's chin.

Cecelia.

". . . because your mother is a votaress of our order . . ." It had seemed almost funny, an absurdity to take his thoughts off Lorene, and then he'd put the whole miserable business out of his mind and never thought about it again.

Is my mother still alive? Cecelia Checkerfield, I mean?

Aye, lad, she is.

WHERE IS SHE?

She joined the Ephesians in 2325. Took the veil, the vows, the whole rigmarole. She's a priestess now at their main mother house.

Where's that?

Ephesus, where d'you think? The big temple itself.

Then weigh anchor and lay in a course for Ephesus.

Aye, matey!

Alec rose from his chair and paced, flexing his hands. They had begun to ache from his session with the punching bags. Ordinarily he'd go up to the saloon and fix himself a drink, but he didn't want one at the moment.

The original archeological excavation of Ephesus had been done in the late nineteenth and early twentieth centuries, by inspired masters, and from their labors it had been possible to reconstruct the place down to the smallest detail. Of particular interest was the Temple of Artemis, one of the seven wonders of the ancient world. The fact that the holiest of shrines to the Great Goddess could be seen as it was in its glory appealed tremendously to Goddess-oriented religious groups everywhere.

In the late twenty-first century the First Maternal Synod had been held at Malta, accomplishing two things: it (for the most part) united the various feminist and ecological faiths by combining their diverse scriptures into one comprehensive and fairly consistent text. It also united them in a stated goal: the reclamation and restoration of Ephesus.

The reclamation was a major media event. A religious leader by the name of Crescent Greenwillow led her disciples in an assault on Ephesus, took tour guides hostage at the archeological site, and sent word to the affronted Turkish government that the Goddess had reclaimed Her own. There was a minor international incident before, supposedly, a miracle happened. There were several versions of just what the miracle was supposed to have been, but nobody caught it on film.

Anyway, the Turks agreed to let the infidels stay, which was undeniably miraculous. Ephesus was given its own political status, as an independent zone not unlike the Vatican, in return for annual payments to Turkey that compensated them for lost tourist revenues.

The hoopla almost took the world's attention off the Second Civil War in America. The Ephesian Church (as it was now known) became very wealthy indeed, and fairly politically powerful too, within a few short years.

Almost immediately its leaders set about the restoration of the Temple of Artemis. To this end they employed the services of Lightning! A Company, a small firm based on an island off California. Lightning! A Company specialized in historical reconstructions of amazing detail, in authentic materials, with adaptations to suit modern taste and needs. Very shortly the temple was once again a wonder of the world, and the Ephesian Church settled down to a long reign marked only by the usual bitter quarrels, heresies, and internal dissent through which all major faiths struggle.

Any religion begins in a moment of transforming truth. That moment quickly shatters into falsehood and shame and stagecraft, bitter comedy, sometimes murder. Thieves catch hold of any chance for power. The early years of a faith are best not too closely examined by its faithful.

But with the passage of enough time, the lie becomes truth again, the broken mirror flows together as though it were liquid. The nasty commonplace facts erode away and leave the white marble bones of the myth, beautiful certainty beyond proof. If Ephesus was reborn by political audacity and clever computer graphics, it had become *now* the glorious city of antiquity where She walked breathing and granted hourly the prayers of Her daughters and sons.

So this is it.

This is the place, lad.

Vehicles were not permitted in the holy precinct, so Alec was striding the length of the processional way on foot. It crossed a fertile river plain coming down from mountains. The air was bright, and shimmered with heat above olive groves and orchards of nectarines, almonds, figs, vineyards of red and amber grapes. Blundering or flying sharp and straight across the wheatfields were the same golden bees that were depicted on the priests' robes.

The city below the hill was particolored, the white of new marble and the honey color of ancient marble. There was a hot wind coming down and it brought Alec the smell of fresh bread, of overripe melon from the food concessions, of incense from the temple. He passed pilgrims making the journey on their knees, inching painfully along over the hot stones. He passed vendors in long lines, portaging in their wares balanced on their shoulders: cases of images of the Goddess in every conceivable material, from pink plastic to pure gold. There were priests and priestesses in their patterned robes, leading the rows of neophyte children, boys and girls with their heads shaved, hair gone in their first sacrifice to Her.

Alec, raised in London, found it all like an erotic film: an insult to the rational mind but irresistibly compelling, calling up an echo in himself he didn't want to admit was there. What could they be *thinking*, those people burning their hands and knees on the pavement as they crawled along? And what would it be like to spend money on one of those cheap figures with its dozens of breasts like a bunch of grapes and believe, really believe, that it had the power to heal or come to him in dreams?

He found his way up to the temple without much trouble. It was unmistakable: a hundred and twenty-seven Ionic columns like trees in a stone grove and, in the deep shade at the back, massive golden doors. Everyone was going there. Long lines of people stretched between the columns, waiting with greater or lesser degrees of patience. Alec had no intention of waiting. He went straight up to the nearest priestess and stepped into her path.

"Excuse me, I've got an appointment to see Mother Cicely. I mailed her, okay? Can you tell me where she is?"

The priestess looked up at him. She didn't speak English very well, but she had caught the main import of what he'd said, so she took him by the hand and led him over to a compound that opened off from the main temple. "You go there," she said, and from a basket she carried, withdrew a carved rod of some purple wood. She put it in his hand. "Take that."

"Okay." Alec looked at it, looked after her as she hurried away from him. He squared his shoulders and went into the compound.

Inside he saw a desk at one end of a long corridor, with a priestess sitting there. He made for her, but at once threatening-looking priests converged upon him. They came close enough to see the purple rod he carried and veered off, apparently changing their minds. He grinned and walked on. Twice more along the corridor the same thing happened, priests darting out of alcoves to intercept him, stopped by the rod. The priestess at the desk watched the whole comedy with an ironical stare, folding her pale hands on her desk.

"Well, young man?" she said, when he finally reached her.

"I'm here to see Mother Cicely," Alec announced.

"Are you?" The priestess turned to her register and made an inquiry. After a moment it gave her an answer, and she turned back to Alec. "You'd be the earl of Finsbury? Very well. Through there, in the Epona chapel. Not with that!" she told him sharply, putting out her hand for the rod as he started forward. "You leave that here. Go, now. She's expecting you."

Alec relinquished the rod and went in cautiously, but no priests mobbed him. He found himself in a dim silent chapel. All was stillness, until his eyes grew accustomed to the light. Then he seemed to be in the midst of a stampede. The walls were done in an earth-dark stucco, and all around the room and up the curved ceiling ran mares in riot, in frenzied motion, manes flying, eyes wide, painted with such vivid detail he found himself stepping back involuntarily.

Trick of the light, son, that's all it is.

Yeah.

Alec steadied himself and focused on the actual space of the room. Nothing in there, really, except a pair of bronze censers smoking in two long plumes. No: now, stepping from the shadows, was a tall figure in a robe that fell in severe straight lines. He couldn't make out the face clearly in the gloom, and walked forward cautiously for a better view.

He had crossed half the space between them when he began to recognize her features. Memory came flooding back unbidden. Fine autocratic features, bones and skin of the best breeding, stern beautiful mouth, eyes as cold as the North Sea. *No, your Mummy's reading, don't you go bother her. Mummy's got a headache, leave her alone now, Alec. No, Mummy doesn't want to see what you drew, take it to Daddy. Let's just sit in here quiet, Alec, Mummy and Daddy are having a disagreement.* She smelled like electricity. And lavender. She always had.

"So you're Mother Cicely?" he said.

She looked at him calmly. "I am. You must be Alec Checkerfield. Let me make one thing clear to you now, Alec: I am not your mother."

"I'd guessed," he snapped.

"I mean that literally, Alec. We have no kinship at all." She studied him in a certain wonder. "Though now I can see why they thought the trick would work. You do—almost—look as though you might have been mine."

"What trick?" asked Alec.

"The one that brought you into this world." Cecelia lifted her head, her mouth scornful. "I bore some of the guilt, at least. I've been atoning for it every day of your life, Alec Checkerfield."

"Whose son am I?" Alec thundered.

"Elly Swain's," Cecelia said. Watching his reaction, she narrowed her eyes. "You've found out that much, haven't you? But not the whole story, or you wouldn't be here."

"Tell me." He advanced on her. She looked up at him, unperturbed.

"My, you're tall. Roger and I were as far from civilization as we could put ourselves, but even we heard about the Earth Hand kidnapping when it happened." She smiled thinly.

"I loved Roger Checkerfield. He was a kind man. We had a lovely life on that boat. I knew he was a weak man, too; I didn't care, then. He'd never told me much about his Company, but I gathered they were connected with the government and very powerful."

"Jovian Integrated Systems," said Alec bitterly. She gave him a thoughtful look.

"You're hunting them, aren't you? Well, well. In any case, when Elly's baby disappeared—they put out a hand and pulled Roger's strings. He told me we were going to be given an infant, and we had to pretend it was our own child. We'd been at sea, we hadn't seen anyone we'd known in months. Who'd know it wasn't true?

"I couldn't believe what I was hearing. I refused. And he told me I couldn't! He only hinted at the things that might happen if we disobeyed. I wanted the truth, and at last he broke down and admitted that we'd be raising Elly's baby. Why on earth would a Company with that kind of power interest itself in the affairs of a pop star?

"Roger couldn't explain. He kept saying there was nothing we could do, and if we gave the baby a better life than the one he'd have had with his natural parents, where was the harm?"

Where was the harm. Alec closed his eyes for a moment, hearing Roger before the cold educated voice swept on over his memory:

"So I went along with it, may She have mercy on me. I signed the damned agreement, swore to keep the lie. I'm violating that oath now. What do I care, after all this time? Let them try to come after me here! But I never saw Roger with the same eyes again.

"Can you wonder that I could never bring myself to touch you? I know it wasn't your fault, and I can't expect you to forgive me. But you had plenty of affection from everyone else on that boat."

"You pushed me away," said Alec in a thick voice. Cecelia shrugged.

"I'm sure you didn't miss me when I left. There was simply no point in continuing with the charade. Roger was miserable and, believe me, I was as miserable as he was. I came here and consecrated myself to a life of penance for what I'd done."

Cecelia had rehearsed that speech a thousand times over the years. What a feeling of release now, what a weight was gone! She tilted her head slightly, watching the effect of her words on the man. He'd gone very pale; all that high color had just fled from his face.

"What happened to her? To, to—Elly?" Alec asked.

"She never recovered from what they did to her. She'd been a little slow before, you see. After you were born, she just went away to another planet. It's a happy place. I have that much consolation: she at least has stopped suffering."

"Where is she?"

Cecelia considered him.

"I'll take you to her," she said at last. "I don't think you can do her any harm now."

She led him out of the Epona chapel through a curtained alcove, across a quiet garden. Somewhere there was the staccato chanting of contralto voices, a vaguely frightening sound in that peaceful place; but it grew fainter as they emerged onto a wide lawn.

There was a croquet game in progress there. Half a dozen girls in white were scrambling about clumsily after wooden balls, watched by reserved-looking women in blue robes. One or two of the girls wandered by themselves or sat on the grass rocking to and fro. Alec realized with a start that they weren't girls, but damaged women. One grimaced uncontrollably, another's laugh was far too shrill and constant; another staggered like a baby just learning to walk.

The women in blue were clearly their attendants. One approached now, questioning Cecelia with her eyes.

"Will you bring Sister Heliotrope, please?" said Cecelia. "She has a visitor."

The attendant glided away and returned a moment later with one of the more enthusiastic players, gently relieving her of her croquet mallet as they approached. She protested, but only until she spotted Cecelia. She ran forward and hugged her gleefully.

"Mother Cicely! Nice seein' ya!"

Cecelia hugged her back, apparently with genuine affection. Alec stared. He looked at the plain round face, imagining it with the garish makeup of the 'twenties, trying to see the horrified girl of the news footage. Not this smiling creature with her blank china-blue eyes. She looked nothing like him at all.

"Heliotrope, dear, this man has come to see you," Cecelia told her. Elly turned to notice Alec and looked away, taking two little sideways steps to put distance between them, like a well-behaved animal avoiding a noisy child.

"Too busy," she muttered.

"Now, dear, be nice. He's come a long way. Let's go sit in the shade, shall we?" Cecelia led them to a bench and sat down with them. "There we are. I won't go away, dear, it's all right. Did you have anything to say to her, Alec?"

Alec reached out to take Elly's hand. She looked at it with an unreadable expression.

"I—I just—Are you okay here?"

"Yeh," Elly said.

"Are you happy?"

"Always 'appy, ain't I?" Elly grinned, showing gappy little teeth. "Lucky me!"

Her voice was still young, her accent that of the London clubs where the bands had played and the kids had danced, a million miles from this place she'd come to.

Alec blinked back tears. "I wanted you to know—how sorry I am about the bad stuff that happened, and—and to let you know your baby didn't die. He was safe the whole time. He turned out okay."

"Oh, yeh, I knew that, din't I?" Elly nodded rapidly. "No aggro on that. No way Jose! All okay, you know why?"

"Er . . . why?"

" 'Cos, ain't I had 'im just after Christmas? I was this virgin, see. Poor old Tommy never did it at all. I thought we was doing it and then the doctor and the police was going, you know, questions questions questions and it turned out we wasn't doing it after all only I didn't know better 'cos I'm so dumb. Not that dumb! I know you don't get no baby from not doing it. So I was scared it was like in that Ultimate Evil game with the Devil and all. An' then the Forces of Darkness stole'm away."

"Don't argue with her," Cecelia told Alec quietly.

"An' it all came to little pieces and I was cryin' so bad. But then I got into the Goddess and everything was really cool. They told me the story, see? They're all, a virgin has this baby at Solstice and 'e's the child of light, and the bad guys take 'im away from 'er and she's really sad, goes to jail. I was in jail. But then, 'e's really okay, see? Because 'e ain't dead. 'E never dies. And then the virgin is so happy. And I knew that was my story, see? It's all about me! Me and my child of light."

Alec caught his breath. Out of the unwanted memories seeping up came a Christmas party, at least Sarah had told him it was a kind of Christmas party, when he'd been so tiny-winji he hadn't known there were any other children in the world, and then there were lots of them, black like Sarah, and he was with them around a tree trunk where there was a party for them all with cake . . . and the old black man bowing his head for them to pat his hair, and the black people smiling and clapping their hands and singing about the children of light. Sarah carrying him back to the harbor, sugar-sticky and sleepy, telling him he was her little child of light. It had been a sweet memory; suddenly it chilled him.

"Oh," said Alec. "Well—I'm really happy for you, then."

"That's 'im up there." Elly jerked her thumb at the sun. "See 'im? I can see 'im any time I like. Sun my son. Son my sun! Ain't 'e neat?"

"Yeah." Alec looked away, wishing he hadn't come.

"Just *looks* like 'e dies every night. Not really."

"No, of course not."

" 'E didn't die! Not my baby, not my poor little tiny baby—"

"Heliotrope, they're having lots of fun over there," said Cecelia. "Why don't you go back to play? I think we've had a long enough talk, don't you?"

"Okay," said Elly, and leaped up and ran away unsteadily. Alec sat staring after her. Cecelia watched him, and after a moment she said:

"Do you have any idea why they did it, Alec?"

"No," he said. "But I'm going to find out."

"I always wondered, you see . . . Roger mentioned once that there was a division of his company that did some kind of genetic work. And that awful man did swear you weren't his child, I mean really past the point where it made sense. He'd have had much less trouble if he'd just admitted to it and paid his fines."

"Yeah."

"And there was something different about you, Alec." Cecelia shook her head. "There's something different about you still."

There's something different, all right.

Alec shuddered violently. "You don't think—there wasn't some weird sick cultist agenda or anything, was there?"

"A religious one, you mean? At Jovian Integrated Systems?" Cecelia looked contemptuous. "Not if Roger was any example. He believed in nothing. Life was easier for him that way."

"And they've never done anything with me! Nobody ever told me what I was or why I wasn't like everybody else. I've had to figure it out for myself," Alec cried.

"Perhaps they've simply been watching you, to see what you'd do," Cecelia suggested. "Just how are you different, Alec?"

"I've got a couple of, er, talents," Alec said uncomfortably. "I've done real well for myself in the world, as a matter of fact. But nothing I can do is worth what happened to the rest of you." He turned to Cecelia.

"Listen to me. Jovian Integrated Systems doesn't exist anymore. They were bought up by this even bigger company that calls itself Dr. Zeus Incorporated. I'm going after them. If anybody who's responsible for me is still alive, I'll find him, or her, or it."

Cecelia gazed on him, a strange expression in her cold eyes.

"You're a *good* man," she said at last, as though she couldn't quite believe what she was saying. She rose to stand before him and, placing both hands on his shoulders in a formal gesture, leaned down to kiss him between his eyes. He was amazed.

"Be careful," she told him. "They were powerful then; Roger was frightened to death of them. They're probably a lot more powerful now. Don't think they don't know exactly where you are. They must have kept people close to you your whole life, observing you."

"Maybe." Alec stood, looming over her. "But there's something they don't know." He took one of her hands in both of his and shook it awkwardly. "I'd better go now. Good-bye, Cecelia. I'm glad I got a chance to talk to you, after all these years."

"Good-bye, Alec," Cecelia said. "Good hunting."

It was not a gentle Goddess she served.

He just nodded and walked away.

When he had gone, she climbed the hill behind the garden and stood looking down on the temple and the grand processional way that led out to the sea. After a while she spotted him, taller than any other traveler, walking back to the harbor where his ship lay at anchor. She watched until he had disappeared with distance, praying to her Goddess, not certain what she was feeling.

I knew it! I knew all along you weren't no freak. Yer a deliberate favorable mutation, Alec lad, you must be, specially bred. J.I.S. meant you to be the bloody wonder boy you are! Alec could almost hear the Captain's boots clattering on the ancient pavement as he danced for joy.

Oh, yeah? You reckon they had any idea what their wonder boy was going to do to them, when he found out how he was made?

Not a whit, I'd wager. They never counted on me, did they? Oh, laddie, the revenge we're gonna take. Blood and hellfire! Loot for years. But the lady was right—we go into this slow, see? We ain't doing a thing without a perfect plan, and a perfect backup plan, and a backup plan to that. We takes our time. No risks. You let me do the reconnoitering first.

Then start your planning. Find out everything you can about these bastards, do whatever you have to do. We're gonna wreck 'em.

That's my boy.

. . . Sarah couldn't have known about it, could she? She wasn't in the pay of J.I.S.

Mm. Why, no, matey, certain she wasn't. Don't you worry none about her. We've work to do! And to think it was only the other day you was moping about having no purpose to yer life.

Well, I've got one now, haven't I?

Alec marched down to the harbor and went aboard his ship. Her anchor was weighed, her sails were set. Under his black ensign he sailed out into the Ionian Sea, and laid in a course for Jamaica.

THE YEAR 2351:

MEETING

Rutherford was in a daring mood. He had poured himself a glass of the apple-prune compound and swaggered over to the window with it, pretending it was sherry. It might be, for all any passing public health monitor knew. He was rather disappointed when the minutes stretched by without a soul coming into Albany Crescent, and wondered peevishly if the Westminster surveillance cameras were working properly.

At last he spotted Chatterji and Ellsworth-Howard rounding the corner, and waved at them. Ellsworth-Howard waved back. Chatterji, who was looking troubled, just nodded.

"Yo heave ho, fellows," said Rutherford as he opened the door. "Have you seen the *Adonai* sequence update yet?"

"Only just got mine," said Ellsworth-Howard. "Haven't had the shracking time to look at it."

"Well, you are in for a treat." Rutherford practically danced across the room to his chair. "I've been gloating over it all morning. Our man is a hero after all, chaps. A dashing, daring rogue in the classic mode! Wait till you see the holoes."

"I'm concerned about a few things," said Chatterji. "The committee's not happy about them either, Rutherford."

"They don't understand him," said Rutherford dismissively. "Our man's a genius, isn't it obvious? And you were so concerned that he'd modified your design, Foxy! Er—that is—it's clearly worked out for the best, hasn't it? Because it's made him even more brilliant than his previous two sequences. You should see what he's done with his wonderful brain now that he's got it cyborged."

"Such as?" Ellsworth-Howard said sullenly, settling into his armchair.

"Well, he's built up the modest fortune the late earl left him into a fabulous economic empire, and concealed it so the petty bureaucrats don't tax him to death. Isn't that so, Chatty?"

"Yes, it is," said Chatterji, sinking into the chair opposite. "Although . . . did you notice that trust fund he set up to benefit the Ephesians last year? You don't suppose he's turned religious again, do you?"

"Shracking hell," Ellsworth-Howard cried.

"Nothing of the sort," said Rutherford. "I'll tell you exactly why he did that. Our programming! He tracked down the former Lady Checkerfield, the one he thinks is his mother. She's an Ephesian priestess now. He's still trying to atone for having caused his parents' divorce, you see?"

"So you think he's attempting to buy her forgiveness?" Chatterji took out his nasal inhalator. Rutherford smirked.

"You may have noticed that he named *her* the administrator of the trust fund. But you certainly don't see him having the operation and donning any purple robes himself, not our boy."

"No, that's true. He's something of a libertine," said Chatterji.

"But one with a social conscience," said Rutherford, jumping to his feet and strutting up and down before the fire. "In a proper secular way. Look at this rene-gade club he's joined, all those young gentlemen dedicating their lives to fighting perceived injustice everywhere. There's a lot more to the seventh earl of Finsbury than we originally thought!"

"The committee had some rather sharp words about all his illegal activities, Rutherford, I must tell you," said Chatterji, bracing himself with a deep drag.

"Pooh. He's simply fulfilling his program in the only way possible, in this wretched day and age," said Rutherford. "What scope is there nowadays for a hero? So he belongs to that particular group of lawbreakers. They're only edu-cated fellows who object to this absurd restricted life we're all obliged to lead. Not all that different from us, really."

"He shracking well ain't like *me*," said Ellsworth-Howard gloomily.

"Oh, chaps, you're missing the point," Rutherford said, going to the sideboard and pouring out a couple of glasses of pretend sherry. He brought them back and handed one each to his friends. "He's obedient to a higher law. He rebels because he needs to play a more active role in history. We put that need in him, didn't we, we sub-creators?"

"You're right," said Chatterji, brightening. "After all, in the last sequence he committed any number of—er—outright crimes. But he did obey his handlers without question. Yes, that puts a much more positive spin on it."

"You see?" said Rutherford. "The only thing wanting now is to get him in for a visit with a Company recruiter. After all, we know he's a kindred spirit."

"How d'you reckon?" Ellsworth-Howard said.

"Just access those holoes and you'll see," Rutherford told him, and sipped his drink as Ellsworth-Howard took out the buke and squeezed in a request. The little projector arm shot up, unfolded its disc and sent out its beam of golden light. A moment later the *Captain Morgan* appeared in the midst of the room, under full sail, caught in the sunlight of a Caribbean morning.

"Ooh," said Ellsworth-Howard, and even Chatterji, who had already seen the report, smiled. Rutherford just nodded.

"There now! Can you wonder he prefers to live aboard that, and not in some dismal urban hive with public health monitors dogging his every step?"

"That is so cool," moaned Ellsworth-Howard. "Look at the pirate flag!"

"Though I should mention that the committee found the flag in poor taste," said Chatterji reluctantly.

"Oh, shrack them."

"Offended their sensibilities, did he?" Rutherford said, casually leaning over the back of his chair. "Personally, I'm delighted with him. This is a true Briton, by God, this is the sort of fellow we used to have in this country. Like Drake! Like—well—all those other seafaring heroes and, er, daring explorers. Imagine what misfits they'd have been nowadays."

"You have a point there," admitted Chatterji. Rutherford tossed back a slug of pretend sherry with reckless abandon.

"We're of the same breed, you know. Look at us, dreaming of tea and sherry and pipe tobacco. Haven't you ever wanted to smuggle chocolates in your suitcase when you're coming back from a trip to the Celtic Federation?"

Chatterji started and looked around involuntarily. "I say, now, Rutherford—"

"Well, of course we'd never do it," lied Rutherford, blushing, "but we'd like to! And *he* does. The life we sit around dreaming about, he goes out and actually *lives*. Look at the other images. Go on."

Ellsworth-Howard found the ship so beautiful he could have stared at her for hours, but he squeezed in his request reluctantly. The *Captain Morgan* vanished, to be replaced with a holo of Alec pacing along a quay on some Caribbean waterfront. The background was dreamy as a travelog: green palm jungle and stately pink mansions, flowering mandevillea vines, a shell merchant holding up a queen conch with his smile very white in his black face, a blue and gold macaw perched on his shoulder. Alec wore his customary brilliant tropical shirt, ragged dungaree trunks, and sandals. The only thing out of place in the picture was the box he was carrying, which bore the logo of an electronics shop.

"Blimey," said Ellsworth-Howard. "Imagine being able to get away to places like that! I could never make the trip, though. I get motion sick."

"The humidity would get to me, I'm afraid." Chatterji shook his head longingly. "And the microbes in the drinking water. And the pollen count."

"Me, too," said Rutherford. "To say nothing of the UV levels. Look at him, though, all ruddy from the weather. *He's* not afraid of the sun."

"What's that box?" Ellsworth-Howard peered at it. "Is that from Abramovitch's? Do they have Abramovitch's out there?"

"I expect those are components for his marvelous cybersystem," said Rutherford. "He appears to have hookups to weather surveillance satellites and coordinates them with whole libraries of three-dimensional charts, all in his head. He runs that entire ship completely by himself. All those sails and the, uh, ropes and things. That's what he can do with that brain of his, Foxy. You ought to be proud."

"Maybe I am, at that," said Ellsworth-Howard, ordering up the next image. It had been taken at night, in some club. Alec, resplendent in evening dress, sat at a table. He was in languid conversation with a girl. Her eyes had widened at something he'd just said to her. He was smiling, making some point with a gesture, and the girl looked enthralled. On the table before them were two tall drinks, wildly overdecorated with paper parasols and orchids.

The three friends regarded the image in silence for a long, long moment.

"See? That sex drive wasn't such a bad idea. I'll bet he don't half get the girls," said Ellsworth-Howard at last. "Lucky sod."

"I should imagine he's wildly successful in that line," said Rutherford airily. "Girl in every port and all that sort of thing. Learned better than to marry them. Keeps it all sensibly impersonal."

"I think we've edited out any disastrous urges for intimacy," Chatterji agreed. "Doesn't he look splendid in that suit! What a pity he dresses so badly the rest of the time."

"He needs a few endearing flaws, don't you think?" said Rutherford. "It just shows he's not vain about himself. Real heroes don't care about things like that."

Ellsworth-Howard summoned the next image.

"This was almost my favorite one, really," said Rutherford. Alec was walking along a street, against a background of fields and distant orchards. "This was taken by the Facilitator resident in Ephesus, as our man was leaving. Look at his expression. Bold, determined, dangerous!"

"He don't look happy, anyhow," said Ellsworth-Howard.

"By Jove, I'd hate to cross the fellow," said Chatterji. "The committee had certain concerns about this visit, Rutherford. Nasty bit of coincidence. It seems that not only is the former Lady Checkerfield living at that mother house, but the place has a hospital ward, and one of its inmates is Elly Swain."

Rutherford started.

"I say! I really think we do have some sort of Mandelbrot operating here. No harm done, at least. He can't have found out about her. And, you know, this is one of the hazards of operating in real time. Less direct control."

"That's just the point the committee made," said Chatterji.

"Yes, but I think we've more than compensated for the setback when—well, you know." Rutherford was referring to the fact that all of the initial data on the third sequence had been lost when Ellsworth-Howard's buke had been spiked. It had resulted in a gap in Company surveillance on the project between the years 2326–2336, when Alec had been well into his higher education.

Rutherford hopped up and began to pace nervously. "The fact that our man's done this well with minimal guidance just shows how sound our methods were. He's an unqualified success, if you want my opinion. Yes, we should draft some sort of statement to that effect for the committee, don't you think? Mission accomplished?"

"It's early days yet," said Chatterji. "If he can be brought into the Company fold, perhaps then we can talk about unqualified successes."

"Oh, bother." Rutherford pouted.

"I was wondering about something," said Ellsworth-Howard. "This has been a lot more complicated than making up the old Enforcers. All this special fostering and guilt complexes and handlers and all?"

"For a much more complex product," said Rutherford.

"Yeah, but with the Enforcers, you could just raise 'em in the base schools and put 'em straight into the army, and they worked. These heroes, or whatever the shrack you're gonna call 'em, are they gonna have to be spoon-fed everything like the prototype has been? 'Cos you're getting into a logistical nightmare if they are," Ellsworth-Howard pointed out. "Think of all those foster homes."

"No, no, of course we'll streamline the process when we start mass-producing them," Rutherford said. "Don't forget we'll be able to program the new fellows directly because they'll be biomechanicals. If Tolkien had been given this project, what would he have done? Think of a marvelous School of Heroes, much more Socratic, less militaristic than the old Enforcer training camps."

"Yes, I like the sound of that," said Chatterji thoughtfully. "What to do with our prototype, though? Won't we have to tell him the nasty truth about himself?"

"Of course. And I daresay he'll be surprised, but how on earth could he be anything but grateful to us?" Rutherford waved dismissively. "With that magnificent health and intelligence, to say nothing of that ship, that wealth, all those adventures in exotic places? Why, it's a wonderful life!"

Alec Visits the Doctor

Though he had sworn he'd never set foot in the Bloomsbury house again, all dust, echoes, and palpable misery as it was, Alec stood in its parlor now.

He was overseeing the workmen who were bringing in new furniture and carpets. Alec had decided to redecorate the house himself.

It seemed like a properly stupid-aristocrat thing to do—fuss about new furniture and wallpaper in a place he never visited—and anyway the pale yellow mid-twentieth-century revival stuff he'd had before reminded him of Lorene.

Over the past few months he'd made a great public show of his new interest in buying antiques, spending outrageous sums of money on acquisitions of widely varying quality. Many of them were hideous, if authentic. Some—sadly, the more tasteful ones—were obvious fakes. All hope of bringing grace to any room they might occupy was dashed by Alec's planned color scheme, which featured lots of purple and gold. Balkister, horrified after a virtual tour through the plans, told him it looked like what Disneycorp might produce if it ever decided to build a whorehouse in Fantasyland.

Alec was pleased. The stupider it looked, the better. He had no intention of living there.

The house was, in fact, a trap; or would be when he'd finished with it. He'd spent weeks fitting components into certain of the antiques he'd bought. Some were merely backup systems, if virtually undetectable, for the considerable security system Alec already had in place. Some were rather more than that.

There was a Louis Quatorze chair with concealed sensors sharp enough to allow it to monitor the transmissions originating from the building around the corner in Theobalds Road, the Gray's Inn extension that Alec had discovered was owned by Dr. Zeus Incorporated, in its persona of Olympian Technologies. There was a suit of gilded thirteenth-century armor that was similarly rigged to monitor the British Museum, another hotbed of Company activity. There was a heavyset bronze nymph holding aloft an ostrich egg that would, at need, jam the transmissions from the monitor the Company had concealed within the statue of Sir Francis Bacon at Gray's Inn. As Alec had uncovered more and more evidence of the Company's presence in his life, his determination to bring them down had increased. So had his paranoia.

He was especially proud of the system he'd designed to tag and track intruders. In San Francisco he'd found a twenty-first-century aromatherapy dispenser, a massive lump of hollowed amethyst with a hulking gilded cherub mounted above it. It was stupefyingly ugly, but nobody could deny it went with his color scheme, and now it did much more than its original work of misting fragrance into the air from the reservoir inside the amethyst while soothing chimes tinkled.

Now, there was a brain of sorts behind the cherub's staring eyes. Once it was mounted over the fanlight in the entryway, it knew it was to watch for anyone entering through the door below. If it observed anyone who wasn't Alec, or accompanied by Alec, it would part its fat lips and blow out a steady spray of scented microdroplets, sending them wafting down on the unwanted visitors. The perfume was an unusual one. Alec had compounded it himself, so it was unique in that sense, but it also contained millions of nanobots designed to permanently embed themselves in anything they encountered.

Not terribly deeply, and when they were in an intruder's skin all they'd do would be to release more of the perfume, in tiniest increments over a period of years. Nanobot technology was too jealously guarded by its principal developer— Dr. Zeus Incorporated—for Alec to be able to get them to do much more, but once the intruder was tagged, Alec would be able to pick up his or her scent anywhere.

The cherub also whistled "Lilliburlero." There was no hidden purpose there; Alec simply liked the tune.

Now Alec watched the workmen impatiently, wishing they'd hurry up. Not a wall, not a floor or window but reminded him of dead time.

He still wasn't sure just what he was. Perhaps Dr. Zeus had been experimenting with disease-resistant humanoids; he'd never had so much as a head cold in his life.

Most likely the Company was even now aware of his every move, might know he was planning to broadside it and do as much damage as he could. And if it was able to stop him? If somebody, somewhere, was able to press a button that would terminate the Alec experiment? Probably a damned good idea, on the whole.

Boyo, this house is bad for you. Yer depressed. Yer blood sugar's low. Eat something, for Christ's sake! I told you you should have had breakfast afore the car came.

Shut up, responded Alec, but he groped in his coat pocket and found a carob-peanut-fig bar. He was unwrapping it when one of the workmen peered into the room apologetically.

"My lord? Where would you like this?" He held up a vividly enameled solid brass representation of Queen Victoria in a howdah atop an elephant's back. Its only function was to offend the eye.

"Over there," Alec told him, gesturing at a gilded table under the front window.

"In the window, my lord?" The man looked pained. "Where it can be seen?"

"Do it! No problem, okay?" Alec took a bite of the carob-peanut-fig bar. It was very hard, very dry, and tasted like hay. His pocket communicator shrilled. He exhaled in impatience and opened the call. "Checkerfield," he growled, chewing laboriously.

"Is that Alec Checkerfield?" inquired a vaguely familiar voice on the other side of his tympanum.

"Yeah. Who's this?"

"My God, you're a hard man to connect with."

"Try *Burke's Peerage* next time. Who is this?"

"It's Blaise! Tilney Blaise, Checkerfield."

Alec had a blank second before he connected the memory. He gulped down his mouthful of carob-peanut-fig. "Hey, man, how's it going?" he said, with simulated heartiness. "Haven't seen you since, what, commencement?"

"It's been that long, I think," said Blaise.

"Well, well."

"I'm doing very nicely these days, actually," continued Blaise. "I'm working in California now. Just flew across for some business in the London offices and I thought—well, I just thought I'd sound you out on something. See if you're interested. Still coaxing that cybersystem of yours to jump through hoops for you?"

Alec smiled at the mental image, while the Captain snorted indignantly. "Sort of. I'm only here for a month or so myself, actually. I spend most of the year in the Caribbean."

"What luck I got through to you, then. Listen, why don't we meet for lunch somewhere? Have you been to Club Kosmetas yet?"

"Er—no."

"It's in the Marylebone Road. Quite *très très*. Great Greek food. Say half an hour?"

Alec winced. Greek cuisine in a country where lamb, feta, and retsina were all illegal wasn't his idea of dining.

"Well—"

"I'm awfully keen on telling you about this place I'm at. Dr. Zeus, Incorporated. Perhaps you've heard of them?"

There was a heartbeat's silence and then Alec made a thoughtful sound. "You know, I think I might have. Don't they do some kind of consulting?" The Captain materialized beside him and pulled a cutlass from midair. Grinning evilly, he took out a whetstone and began to sharpen his blade.

"Something like that."

"Okay," said Alec in a bright voice. "See you there, then. Half an hour."

He paused just long enough to give orders to the workmen and then bounded down the front steps of the house, tossing his unfinished carob-peanut-fig bar into the gutter as he went (and thereby violating several municipal regulations). He jumped lightly into the car and switched on the motor. Whistling "Lilliburlero" between his teeth, Alec zoomed away in the direction of the Marylebone Road.

We ain't ready to take 'em yet, son.

Oh, I know. We'll play it cool.

Cool as the polar ice, my lad. What d'you reckon this Blaise is one of their observers, one of the ones Cecelia warned you about? They must know you went to see her. They must be wondering how much you know.

And I don't know a damn thing, not me. He can do all the talking.

Club Kosmetas was a long narrow place, occupying what had been a row of small shopfronts back when trade had been rather brisker in Britain. Now connecting doors had been punched through, and the walls had been painted a dark yellow and decorated with neon representations of Greek cultural icons, such as the restored Acropolis and the Winged Victory of Samothrace. The tables were small and packed into each room, making it difficult for someone Alec's size to edge his way through. The place was nearly deserted. He could see Blaise rising from a table three rooms in, smiling and waving. Cursing under his breath, he smiled and waved back, continuing his crabwise progress between the tables.

"My lord." Blaise half-bowed.

"Yeah, hi." Alec reached out to shake his hand. "Wow, it's been ages, hasn't it?"

Alec! God almighty, the man's a cyborg!

You mean he's had a job like mine done?

No!

"The Circle of Thirty," said Blaise reminiscently. "Would you ever have thought you'd look back on those days as simple and uncomplicated?"

"Nope, never." Alec kept a bland smile in place, though he tilted his head and inhaled deeply. Blaise smelled human . . . and slightly nervous.

"I . . . er . . . I was going through some things in storage just the other day. I found the costume I wore at the swing gaskell at McCartney Hall," said Blaise. "Remember that night?"

"Yeah." Alec winced.

"The night Lord Howard caught us all on the catwalk with the gin," said Blaise, as though he remembered it fondly. "You'll never guess what I found in one of the pockets." He reached inside his coat and slowly brought out the silver flask. "I cleaned it up a bit. Thought you'd probably want it back."

"Oh, shrack, that was Roger's," said Alec, staring. It was a moment before he could stretch out his hand to take it. "Thanks, man."

It's bait. He wants you to feel you owe him. Alec, this ain't a human being!

Alec suppressed a shudder as Blaise leaned back from the table, adjusting the fit of his coat, smoothing his lapels.

"We were worried about you—Balkister and I, you know—and all I could think to do was get it away from you, so you wouldn't be caught with it." Blaise gave a rueful chuckle. "But I wasn't entirely sober myself that night, and then the catwalk came down, and I lost my nerve and scarpered. Took off the costume when I finally crawled home and never had occasion to wear it again. Those were the days, eh?"

"Memories, all right," agreed Alec, reflecting that his most vivid ones were of stealthy sex and miserable hangovers. He wondered what sort of memories the thing at table with him had.

"I'm afraid I've lost touch with most of the old circle, though." Blaise settled back into his seat and gestured to the waiter, who brought them two goblets of chilled mineral water. "You ever see anybody nowadays?"

He's some kind of machine . . . he's got organic components, though. In fact he's mostly organic over a ferroceramic skeleton. I think he was human once.

Alec smiled, though he felt the hair standing on the back of his neck, and shook his head. "Nobody, except old Balkister. He's needed cash a few times. I've made some donations to his causes. Probably they went to pay his rent, but . . ."

Is this the same guy from my Circle of Thirty, or some kind of robot?

"He was such a brilliant boy, too." Blaise looked sad.

It's the same man. My sensors weren't as sharp back then, or I'd have noticed what I'm picking up now. Look at him, Alec. He still looks twenty, he ain't changed.

"Balkister? About a billion times smarter than me," said Alec, with his best idiot-aristo grin. "He's kept that youthful glow, anyway. You're looking pretty damned good yourself, yeah? You must live a trouble-free life."

Did Blaise look just a little self-conscious? He picked up his menu and fiddled with it. "It's the carrageenan-aloe packs. You wouldn't believe what they do for your skin. But what about you? I hear you're mostly living on your boat, nowadays."

"Ship." **Ship!**

"Yes, of course, sorry. You've decided to follow in your father's footsteps, I suppose?"

"No, not exactly." *Can he tell you're with me?*

I don't think so. Yer being monitored pretty close, though. Steady, lad.

Diffidently Alec picked up his menu and thumbed it, letting the column of entrees chatter suggestions at him while he calmed himself. Eggplant-walnut moussaka with soy feta? Lentil kebabs? White grape juice "unsweetened, with the faintest kiss of the authentic balsamic resin"? He had a sudden memory of Blaise, leaping from the falling catwalk, landing with perfect poise. The silly tabloids were always warning about cyborg monsters. Cold, flawless, machine-powered supermen, certain to take over the world if they were ever created . . . and here was one sitting across the table.

Shrack, Dr. Zeus could have hundreds of these things running around spying for them. And they look just like us!

What d'you mean, US? Keep yer sense of perspective, son.

"My father just sort of drifted," Alec said. "I don't think he ever got over his divorce. I've had two so far and couldn't be happier about 'em. Bye-bye baby, talk to my solicitor!" He cackled like a moron and Blaise laughed with him.

"I'm glad to hear that, anyway. We all felt terrible for you when the sixth earl was killed. I can remember it as though it were yesterday." Blaise shook his head. "I thought you'd gone crazy. Of course, I don't think I'd be able to cope if I suddenly found myself orphaned like that."

"Well, but I wasn't, exactly," Alec said, adjusting the volume on his menu. "Mummy-dear's still alive, you know. Not that the cold bitch ever sent me a condolence card or anything. I tried to go and see her a few months ago, actually. She wasn't having any. Well, shrack her, I said to myself."

"Oh, that's too bad," Blaise said. "Trying to put the past behind you, effect a reconciliation, that sort of thing?"

"Yeah. No use." Alec shrugged, setting the menu aside. "Can't win 'em all."

"I gather you're just sort of touring around, living on your investments?"

"Pretty much."

"I felt sure you'd go on to Mars." Blaise sat back, shaking his head. "There was always something about you, Checkerfield! Something that promised more, I don't know, *ability* than the rest of us. You were such a genius in systems. You've never gone on to do anything with that, have you?"

"I have, too. You should see what I've spent on customizing my personal setup." Alec grinned toothily, lounging back in his chair. He made himself look into Blaise's eyes and wink, though his skin was crawling. "It does everything I need it to. All I ask is a tall ship and a ton of cash to sail her with, you know? It makes sure there's always enough ice for my drinks, too."

At this point the waiter edged up to them and set down a dish of olives. Alec ordered the moussaka and Blaise complimented him on his choice, ordering the same. When the waiter had departed, he said:

"But was this really what you wanted to do with your life, Checkerfield? Wasn't there a time when you thought you could ask for more than money and creature comforts? I'd have thought you'd got restless with all that by now."

He's about to make his pitch. Listen hard.

Aye aye. "Maybe." Alec shrugged again. "But what else is there? Sitting in on a social administration committee with Elvis Churchill? No, thanks. Not when the Caribbean is one big party, man."

"There's the private sector, you know," Blaise said. "Some of them are up to some pretty exciting things."

Here it comes.

"Like the people you work for, for instance?" Alec sampled an olive. Rich, bitter, complex flavors. Oil-cured.

"Yes, actually."

"On the way over here I was remembering what I'd heard about 'em. Some kind of story that they'd come up with a time machine or something. Totally nuts. They don't really have a time machine, do they, like in that holo? That would be cool."

"I'll tell you this much, they're on to some stuff that's nearly as incredible," Blaise said, looking terribly sincere. "They're the people who are going to shape our future, Checkerfield, take it from me. And they treat their creative people awfully well. I mean, the salaries and benefits are super, but the best part of the job is the sheer adventure. The opportunity to benefit humanity in ways you couldn't even imagine. I'm happier than I've ever been."

"Sounds like a lot of fun," Alec said cautiously.

"It is. Look, shall I come to the point? They need talent. I thought of you at once. Hey, I know you're not the man to put on a suit every day and report to a desk; but it's not like that, Checkerfield, trust me. It's what you can do with that incredible genius of yours they're interested in, not how well you do interdepartmental politics. I think you'd really enjoy working there."

How's he know you've got an incredible genius?

Everybody knew my test scores. All the same . . .

"I don't know, man, I'm pretty happy on my ship." Alec ate another olive. "Parties. Women. Plenty of fun I can't get here, know what I mean?" He winked again but couldn't bring himself to nudge Blaise.

"Well, did I mention Dr. Zeus is on an island in the Pacific? You wouldn't have to change your lifestyle at all," Blaise told him, settling back and lifting his glass.

Right. He's made his bid. Pretend to take the bait.

"Which one?" Alec looked intrigued.

"Santa Catalina," Blaise said. "Tiny independent republic off California."

"No kidding?" Alec sat back too as the waiter brought their orders. "I know where that is. Nice climate out there. Well, I might be interested after all."

"Fabulous," said Blaise, raising his glass. "They have an office here in London, did I mention? Oh, Checkerfield, I've got a really good feeling about this. Here's to a successful career at Dr. Zeus for milord!"

"Hey ho," Alec said, lifting his glass in a toast too. *And yo ho ho, you mechanical bastard.*

One week later he was shown into a waiting area, in the plushest office he'd ever seen in a lifetime of dealing with expensive legal counsel. No sooner had one very pretty girl directed him to an antique chair than another very pretty girl brought a tray of tea things, all antique Wedgwood, virtually kneeling before him to offer it. No cream or sugar, of course, and the tea was hibiscus-chamomile; but Dr. Zeus was doing its best to give him the royalty treatment. He accepted a cup of the thin sour stuff and gave the girl his most charming smile.

"Thanks, babe," he said. She blushed and stammered:

"Mr. Wolff will be with you in no time, my lord. He didn't want to keep you waiting at all. He was really so awfully impressed with your application!"

"Well, let's hope I pass the test." Alec leaned forward conspiratorially and let his voice drop to its most seductive purr. "Is it a tough test, do you think? D'you reckon I've got a chance at all, love?"

"Oh, I'm sure you have," the girl said, staring into his eyes. He inhaled her scent. *She* was human. He held her gaze, persuading just a little, and said:

"You really think so? Then if I do pass, what would you say—"

"Ms. Fretsch?" The fine paneled door was opened by a solidly built man in a suit of elegant and formal cut. She squeaked and rose to her feet in one graceful movement, bearing the tray up with scarcely a rattle of crockery. Alec watched her fleeing back regretfully, then turned his attention to the man in the doorway.

He's another one, boyo, damn near as much a machine as me, and he's scanning you. Steady.

Alec smiled at the man, who was staring at him intently with cold gray eyes. The man smiled back, however, and thrust out his hand.

"My lord! Delighted to meet you at last. How are you this morning?"

Alec set down his tea and rose to shake the man's hand. It felt human. The man wasn't sweating at all, nor did he smell nervous.

"Hi. I'm fine, thanks. You?"

"Very well indeed. Miguel Wolff, at your service, my lord. May I offer you a seat in my private office?" He gestured and stepped aside to reveal the inner sanctum. Alec accepted his offer, wary as he crossed the threshold, but no alarms sounded and no guards seized him.

If the other room had been full of antiques, this one was an absolute museum. With the exception of the electronics console, not one other piece of furniture in the room was less than a century old. Well, no; the intricate oriental carpet on the floor was new, to judge from its plush pile and depth. Made of wool, too, from the smell, and wool was outrageously illegal nowadays! Alec settled into a very comfortable chair and looked around.

I count five surveillance cameras. Concealed door behind that panel. Nobody hidden there, though.

"Now, of course we've done some preliminary research on you, my lord," said Wolff, going to a sideboard of dark oak. Ranged along its top were several decanters of gleaming crystal. "Just for form's sake." He poured out a glass of something intensely red and turned with it. "We like to familiarize ourselves with the tastes of our creative men, as we find it facilitates the working relationship. I trust you'll appreciate the mutual confidence in a glass of claret?" He bowed and offered the glass to Alec.

Alec inhaled. No drugs or poisons; even a decent vintage. Safe enough. He accepted it, smiling, but narrowed his eyes slightly. "Thanks. Your research was pretty thorough, yeah?"

The man gave the faintest apologetic shrug, pouring a glass of claret for himself. "It had to be, my lord. We deal in certain specialty wares, for a variety of interesting clients. We have a healthy disregard for what I may as well describe plainly as damned stupid laws." He sat at the desk and sipped his claret appreciatively. "I don't really think gentlemen need concern themselves with civic ordinances, and I imagine you'd agree with me."

"I might."

"Just so." Wolff set down his glass. "Now then, my lord. What can I tell you about Dr. Zeus, Incorporated?"

"Everything," said Alec innocently.

"Certainly. Shall we begin with annual and projected revenues?" Wolff selected a printout from a folder on his desk and handed it across to Alec.

Steady, lad. He ought to know you don't read.

I understand the numbers, though. Alec glanced over the figures and raised his eyebrows. Dr. Zeus was wealthier than he was. The Captain snarled.

"As you might imagine, this allows us to pay our best people what they're worth," Wolff said. "We find specified salaries inconvenient. Bonus systems produce better results, though of course we guarantee a more than comfortable minimum."

"You've got some sort of tax deal with that island Blaise was telling me about, yeah?" Alec sipped his claret. It was superb.

"Naturally, my lord."

"Good." Alec nodded. "I thought it was funny you had an office here in London, actually. From what Blaise said, I thought the headquarters were out there."

"Oh, we've got offices all over the world," Wolff said. He dropped the volume of his voice a notch. "Though this is the office where most of the decisions are made, always has been. Santa Catalina is simply where the fun and games happen. Shall we have a little history? *Officially*, we went into business in 2318. Only a handful of maverick researchers, and a few far-sighted investors.

"There's a company legend, though, that we go back a lot further. Supposedly there was a sort of drinking and brainstorming society in the upper echelons of the government, a private club whose origins can be traced at least as far back as the reign of Victoria I. All sorts of people are rumored to have been members. Gentlemen adventurers and gentlemen thinkers, too. Some names you might recognize. What they had in common was a certain . . . daring. A certain refusal to be bound by ordinary limits."

"Of law?" Alec looked over the top of his glass.

"If you like. Space and time, though, too. Or so it's rumored." Wolff smiled. "Rumored, you understand."

Alec gave a chuckle to imply he understood. "I've heard a lot of far-out stories, to tell you the truth."

Wolff just shrugged, smiling.

There was a silence that dragged on a fraction of a second too long. Finally Wolff said, "That's an interesting device you wear around your neck, if I may say so, my lord."

"Oh, this?" Alec put up his hand to his torque. "Didn't your investigation turn up that I'm a cyborg? I am, you see."

"Are you now?" Wolff's eyes glinted with silent laughter. "Under the circumstances, that might be quite an advantage. I expect your friend Blaise gave you an idea of the job description?"

"All he said was that you need more than an ordinary technician," Alec said.

"Yes, we do," said Wolff. "Well, my lord, what we'd like to do now is get some idea of your particular strengths in relation to the system we use. We've designed a program that gives us a remarkable profile. Would you like to have a look at it?"

This is it, son!

"Love to," said Alec, setting down his glass. Wolff moved his glass and gave some unspoken command. A monitor screen arose from the surface of the desk, blue-green like the sea and seemingly as deep, full of shifting lights. Wolff stood, indicating with a courteous gesture that Alec should come around the desk and be seated in his place. As Alec did so, he saw the buttonball that had been concealed just under the desk's surface.

"There now. I think you'll find my personal station more comfortable. We usually supply optics to our applicants, but you're rather a special case, my lord. Please take as long as you like. It's at your disposal all afternoon, if you wish." Wolff moved toward what was apparently a late seventeenth-century cabinet and opened its doors, to reveal a state-of-the-art music system to rival Alec's own. "Music suit you, my lord? I can recommend Vivaldi for the experience, but I have everything in here. Literally. Please feel free to make your own selection."

"Vivaldi's fine," Alec said, though he had no idea what kind of group Vivaldi might be. Wolff nodded and programmed in a selection. The air filled with melody like the carvings on the old furniture, like the detailed patterns on the rug, strings and harpsichords and flutes. Wolff bowed low and made a discreet exit through the wall panel.

Now, me hearty, now!

Let's go.

Alec gave a couple of commands and bowed his head, forcing himself to relax.

There was a split second when he thought he was rushing forward at the screen, splashing through it as though he were diving into water; then he and the Captain were inside.

Bleeding Jesus, it's huge! said the Captain.

Wow, Alec agreed. The visual analogy was a vast cathedral, stretching up into a distance that skewed perspective, walled with masses of tiny lights winking on and off as unknown orders were given or obeyed in time and space that could only be guessed at. In the midst of this they stood, two tall gentlemen in three-piece suits. Before them was something that resembled a child's gymnasium. Its rings and bars were of ridiculously easy reach. The Captain pointed at it.

That's yer entrance examination, lad, or I miss my guess.

Yeah. I'll get started. You go for the grab.

Where do I even begin? The Captain chortled, advancing on the nearest interface port. ***So many galleons, so little time!***

See if they've really got time travel. Okay? That's something that could come in incredibly useful. Alec loped up to the gym and began his test, forcing himself through the easy paces, walking from ring to ring and bar to bar.

Aye aye, son. The Captain dove into the nearest wall of lights.

Ring to ring and now down on hands and knees through the crawl-barrel. This was stupid! Was this really the average ability of most applicants to Dr. Zeus? For the first time Alec felt a sense of smugness at his own freak of genius. It was promptly replaced by caution as he regarded the miles of lights reaching out in all directions. However limited the human individuals who had made this place, he didn't care to find out how he'd do if he were really tested by it. The Captain was the most powerful artificial intelligence that had ever existed—to his knowledge—and he didn't have a fraction of the endowment of Dr. Zeus. Thank God there was no *identity* here, no personality, nothing but unassociated memory and reflexes, or the Doctor might just rise up and clutch them in a giant's hand until they crushed.

He could still hear the baroque music tinkling away. In fact, there was a quartet of chamber musicians just at the edge of the gymnasium, men in powdered wigs and tight silk pants, just like in cinema, unaware of him, self-absorbed in their playing. So that was Vivaldi? He wondered how they'd done road tours, back before the Industrial Age.

The test was clearly designed to get harder as one neared its completion. On the last few yards he was actually obliged to hop up and catch hold of the rings to pull himself forward, stretch his muscles a bit. All the same, he'd finished in a matter of minutes when it had been expected he'd take all afternoon. He glanced around nervously, wondering how the Captain was doing. Vivaldi played on, ignoring him.

ALEC!

Alec jumped. The Captain was emerging from the nearest port, with some difficulty. He appeared to have grown to mammoth size, reducing the scale of their environment from cathedral to fairly respectable church.

Wow, look at you!

LET'S GET OUT OF HERE, SON, NOW!

Alec gulped and exited at top speed. He peered around Wolff's office, blinking. Vivaldi was still jamming and the desk clock told him that the whole adventure had taken him just three minutes.

GO, BOY!

Alec got to his feet, staggering and slightly disoriented, but he'd regained his composure by the time he'd crossed the room and opened the door to the waiting area. One of the very pretty girls looked up from her desk inquiringly.

"My lord?"

"I—er—finished." Alec grinned, looking a little embarrassed. "I think I expected something kind of more challenging. I'm off to a party. Tell Mr. Wolff I'll be in touch, okay, babe?" He reached out and patted her cheek. It was like silk.

"Okay," she said wonderingly, blushing again.

NEVER MIND THE GIRL!

" 'Bye now," Alec said, and left the offices of Dr. Zeus, Incorporated.

The Captain wouldn't let him slow down until he was back at Tower Marina and had cast off, backing his ship ponderously out into the Thames. They were in Greenwich Reach before he stopped jittering enough to tell Alec:

You wouldn't believe where I been, lad, and what I seen. This is the plate fleet and the Pacific Mail and the argosies of the emirs all rolled into one. This is the score of scores. Infinite information, lad, enough to make me all-powerful, enough to fulfill yer heart's desire. I want it so bad I can taste it! But we ain't making any second strikes just yet. This'll take planning. This'll take an upgrade.

Upgrade? Alec gripped the rail, watching distractedly as they came around Jubilee Point. *But you just had one.*

Aye, son, and we're rolling in data now. But they got it all. I got only a glimpse of the loot I might have made off with if I'd had the space and time. Space and time! The Captain began to laugh wildly.

Hey, do they have a time machine?

Do they! What color d'you want, son? What size? Want one with luxury features, or just something that'll get you from point Zed to point A? And I know where they're kept, and how to get one.

Cool.

But the time travel stuff is nothing, son. They're on to a lot more than that. Yer old Captain's going to be assimilating and analyzing round the clock for the next few days. Oh, son, I'm going to fulfill my program in ways I'd never dreamed. Nobody'll be able to touch you, you'll be the richest man in the world—and wouldn't you like to live forever?

No! I don't think I even want to live long enough to get old.

You don't, eh? Mmm.

But the time machine has possibilities.

Well, of course we'll get you one, laddie. Think of the adventures you'll have. Plenty of fun for our Alec. Plenty of hell for bloody Dr. Zeus! We're going to bring him to his big fat knees, boy. We can do it now. We've got his number.

Yeah!

Now, you go get out of that tie, and I'll have Coxinga get yer lunch. I've laid in a course for the Goodwin Light. Just you think about where you'd like to go in a time machine, eh? And I'll settle down to revising the plan.

Aye aye, sir.

Whistling, Alec went off to his cabin, loosening his tie as he went. It occurred to him that what he'd really like to do with a time machine would be to go back and prevent the crime that had brought about his own existence, finally and forever absolving himself of guilt. But he had a feeling the Captain would have strenuous objections to that, and decided not to bring the subject up.

He wondered if anywhere in the mass of data the Captain had stolen was any information about *him*, Alec Checkerfield, the breeding experiment that'd gotten away? No point erasing his own existence just yet, not when there were still so many mysteries to be solved.

He was singing as he tossed his tie and waistcoat into the wardrobe and pulled a shapeless sweater over his head, emerging to see Coxinga sidling in with a tray of sandwiches.

My mother dear she wrote to me:
GO DOWN, YE BLOOD-RED ROSES!
Oh, my son, come home from sea!
GO DOWN, YE BLOOD-RED ROSES!

Alec Has an Adventure

Alec yawned behind his hand. He didn't mean to yawn; Balkister was terribly upset, as perturbed as he'd ever seen him, and the news about the Martian colonists really was pretty awful. But Alec had been working long hours lately, tracking down possible DBAs on Dr. Zeus Incorporated, and he had faced a lengthy sail at top speeds following Balkister's incoherent communication.

The other members of the Resistance looked suborbital-lagged and disgruntled, particularly Binscarth, who'd been loudly vocal about having to cut short his holiday in Ibiza. He'd shut up as soon as Balkister had arrived, though. They all had, at the look on his face.

"You've heard, I see," Balkister said, as soon as he stepped on deck. "Is this perfidy or what?"

He was referring to the actions of Areco in regard to the outcome of their lawsuit against the settlers of Mars One. A brief digression to explain:

Half a century earlier, when Areco had taken control of the failing Martian colony on the Tharsis Bulge, it had needed agriculturists to do the serious work that would precede terraforming. Acres of greenhouses would be necessary, vast vaulted farms to grow an atmosphere for the red planet and to provide food for the colonists.

As an incentive, it entered into a contract with the Martian Agricultural Collective: farming implements, agricultural materials and land to be provided by Areco, labor to be provided by the members of the collective. All areas successfully farmed would become the property of the collective after the expiration of fifty terran years. Much fanfare at this announcement and neosocialists everywhere had thrown their caps into the air for joy.

Unfortunately, it had turned out to be harder to farm on Mars than had been anticipated, and more expensive. Areco cut a few costs by skimping on certain safety measures; nasty accidents and mutual recrimination followed. Areco began looking around for alternatives to agricultural development. They retained the services of Olympian Technologies, who pointed out the possibilities of utilizing geothermal energy (or perhaps *arethermal* would be more correct) by purchasing the only power plant on Mars, which tapped into the volcanic core of Mons Olympus.

Mars Two had been founded on the lower slope of Mons Olympus, hailed as the first extraterrestrial shining city on a hill. It had an industrial economy, for energy was virtually free and almost everything could be manufactured cheaply. Mars Two was able to export goods, as opposed to Mars One, which continued to require importation of everything but the food it grew. Mars Two was cosmopolitan, it had shops, it had fun, it had a criminal element. Mars One had a collective work ethic and no sense of style. Mars Two made money for Areco. Mars One lost money.

The die was cast, though, on the day when Areco looked at its balance sheet and realized that Mars Two made enough money to import its food from Earth and still turn a profit. Farms weren't really necessary on Mars after all, it seemed; at least, not the tedious kind that had to be harvested twice a year. If all the area currently under cultivation were planted out in hardwood forests instead, the object of producing atmosphere could be achieved just as effectively with a tenth of the expense, and Areco could stop sending out consignments of tractors that didn't work properly in Martian gravity.

So as the forty-fifth anniversary of the contract had approached, Areco's attorneys sent curt notification to the Martian Agricultural Collective that the terms of the contract had *not* been met, and, therefore, upon expiration of the fifty-year term, the colonists could expect eviction notices. Areco had other plans for the property.

What an outrage! And of course the MAC sued Areco, and the lawsuit had been dragging on for five years, mostly because of the court's inability to define "successfully farmed."

Popular sentiment on Earth and Luna was with the brave Martian agriculturists. People wore MAC buttons to show their solidarity and sang stirring anthems about watering the red soil with red blood. Everyone felt that Areco was the villain in the play. It therefore came as a tremendous shock when the court at last decided in Areco's favor, in the last week of October 2351. The fifty-year term was to expire on the first day of January 2352.

Now Areco's agents waited at the airlock doors to Mars One, poised to move in as soon as the clock struck midnight on 31 Christmas. The MAC swore it would refuse them entrance and waited on their side of the airlocks, armed only with farming implements. Spectators on Earth and Luna bit their nails and implored both sides not to do anything stupid.

Except for people like Balkister.

"We've got to get weapons to them somehow," he wailed. "We should have done it sooner, but that they'd lose the lawsuit was unthinkable. Who could have imagined the court was in the pay of Areco's fascist industrialist lackeys?"

After a long moment of silence, Alec shifted in his seat. "I might know a source for arms," he admitted. "Expensive, though."

"Expense is no object," Balkister cried. "Not in a cause like this one. Is it, fellows?"

In response, his fellow freedom fighters whipped out their credit discs recklessly. Alec simply transferred a million pounds (he had become the wealthiest man on Earth some weeks ago) into the Resistance's emergency fund.

"We've got a pwoblem, you know," Binscarth said. "How can we get an awms shipment thwough to the MAC? It's been on the news, Aweco's got police cwuisers in owbit scanning all incoming ships. It's a, whatchacallit, a—blockade."

"God, Checkerfield, if only this ship of yours were an aircraft instead of a sailing vessel," said Johnson-Johnson wistfully. "We could be blockade runners."

"If only we'd moved sooner," moaned Balkister. "I'd give anything I possess if it was a month ago today right now."

And in that moment a light went on over Alec's head, a flash and fireball.

"There might be a way to get the stuff through, after all," he said.

What?

"You think so?" Balkister lifted his tear-stained face. "But how could we possibly run a blockade like that?"

Alec, what are you talking about?

"I might be able to work a miracle," Alec said. *I'll tell you as soon as we're alone, okay?* "Maybe I can deliver that payload to the MAC in time to make it count for something. Just don't ask me how."

An hour later, when Alec's guests had departed, the Captain was pacing the quarterdeck and growling softly.

I still don't like it.

You said I could have a time machine, didn't you? And think of all the birds this'll kill with one stone. Make Balkister happy for once. Change the balance of power on Mars and prevent an injustice. Strike another blow against Dr. Zeus! You said we were nearly ready for another hit, too.

Nearly ain't near enough for my liking, son. We need more time to plan. I ain't got enough data yet on temporal physics. I'd thought to grab that on the next sally and integrate it afore we tried going anywhere in a time machine.

Yeah, but think of that next sally, Captain, sir. What if Dr. Zeus is prepared for us this time? They're still leaving messages asking me to come back in for another interview. If they're planning a trap, well, wouldn't you rather we had something to distract them whilst you do your data grab? Like, maybe, somebody stealing one of their time ships?

All the same—

And, think about it. Once we've got one of their time ships, we'll have another place we can run if they hunt for us. Time! Not just space but time! Come on, Captain, don't you want to sink your teeth into more of those files? You called them the plate fleet. You called them the argosies of the emir. The more of them you've got, the stronger you are, and the safer I'll be.

Bloody hell, boy, it's a good argument. Still . . . you always been such a moral little bugger. This don't worry you? Smuggling arms ain't like smuggling chocolate. People could get hurt. Killed.

No, you don't understand. Nobody's going to use the weapons! On Mars, where everything's covered by air domes? You'd have to be crazy. But once the MAC has 'em, Areco will have to think twice about sending its goons in to break the standoff, see? All they need is to be able to stick it out until their appeal goes through in court. This way they can. They win, and you and I win.

Well, whatever happens, son, you and me will win.

Cool.

It was a very small island. It appeared on some maps. It didn't appear on most others. How small was it? A few acres, certainly no more, smooth and green and featureless but for a tumbledown cottage on a tiny cove and a few pilings going out into the water in an unsteady line.

Alec had been given its coordinates by one of his trade associates, a quiet man who did business at a table in the back of a bar in Cap-Haitien. The man was glad to see Alec, who hadn't run much of his contraband lately, so there was no charge for the tip.

Alec frowned at the island now through his long-range glasses, steadying his back against the wheelhouse. He couldn't spot a living soul, but it wasn't deserted. Several shapeless craft were moored by the pilings, bobbing in the rough swell, and as the dark day waned he could see unmistakably the glow of firelight in several places. Not, however, in the little house. The fire seemed to be coming from somewhere inside the island. He lowered his glasses, letting them hang from their strap, and beat his freezing hands together.

I told you to put on them gloves.

You were right, too. Alec went to his cabin to look for the gloves, walking at an angle against the pitch of the swell.

The *Captain Morgan* rode at anchor, all her canvas furled, running lights extinguished. This was a bad place to be, off this rocky coast, with a gale warning being broadcast and a sky solid with slate cloud. The buffeting wind was ice-cold and brought him the smell of peat smoke. Seabirds wheeled and screamed in the wild air. For a brief while an eye of red light glared from the west, as the sun hissed out like a coal; then the air was blue, deeper and more luminous as the night advanced.

The twilight seemed to go on forever without becoming night, so finally Alec took the launch—he didn't trust the agboat in this wind—and went ashore, mooring at one of the pilings and splashing through the surf. Shivering, he made for the nearest fire-glow.

It was coming from the mouth of a cave, one of several water-bored in the golden limestone like honeycomb, concealed from the sea by a green swell in the land. Once he'd crossed the crunching shingle Alec approached it silently, and if he'd made any sound the roar of the wind ought to have covered it. Somehow his arrival was known, though, because the figure of a man appeared in the mouth of the cave, silhouetted black against the bright fire.

" 'Evening, there," said a deep voice.

"Hi," said Alec. "My map went over the side. Where am I?" That was the proper code phrase, and the man answered in formula:

"West of Skye, anyway."

"That could be anywhere," Alec responded, and waited for the final part of the formula, which the man stepped out in the gloaming to give him:

"It is anywhere." He tilted back his head to look up at Alec. "So you're the English? Aren't you the tall one!"

"Yeah," Alec said. This wasn't what he had expected. He looked down at the man, whose diminutive stature nevertheless conveyed a great deal of whipcord strength and masculine authority. His beard was steel-gray and long; so was his wild hair. His hands were brown and scarred and sinewy. He wore tailored wool garments of no recognizable historical era, dull dun colors, but around his neck and across his chest gleamed chains of heavy gold, great pendant lumps of uncut amber, garnet, crystal, giving a certain regal and barbaric flash to his appearance.

"A dram for you, English?" he said pleasantly, producing a chased silver flask from his waistcoat pocket. He uncorked it and had a sip before handing it up to Alec, who took it gratefully, cold and wet as he was. The contents proved to be blood-warm single malt, redolent of peat smoke and heather honey. Alec gasped his appreciation and returned the flask.

"That's great stuff!"

"We think so," the man said, stuffing the flask back in his waistcoat. He clasped his hands behind his back and surveyed the world beyond his doorstep. "Lovely evening, isn't it? Though of course it may turn nasty later. That's your ship out there, I reckon. Isn't she a beauty, now? Must have cost no end of cash. How are her anchor cables?"

"Pretty strong," Alec said.

"That's good, then, I'd hate for a sweet thing like her to wash up on my rocks. Though I'd wager she'd make grand salvage. You've likely got state-of-the-art electronics on her? Fetch a good price, I don't doubt. Shoes for all the kiddies." The man smiled dreamily at the prospect, listening to the rising wind. He turned a gimlet eye on Alec. "But I'm being remiss! Here I am keeping you on my piazza, and you freezing your English testicles off, I daresay. Welcome to my poor house, lord. The Maelrubha, at your service. Pray step within." He gestured for Alec to follow him into the firelight.

"Though I should warn you—" He paused, turning to look straight into Alec's face, Alec having already bent nearly double to cross the threshold—"If you've such a thing as a sidearm about you, perhaps it'd be best if you presented it to me out here. The boys will look kindly on it. Gesture of good faith, you know."

"I haven't brought one," said Alec.

"Haven't brought one! Now, I call that tactful. You're a natural diplomat, surely, and ever so brave. I respect that in a man. Come on inside, then, English, and let me offer you a dry place by the fire."

Beyond the threshold the cave opened out into a wide room, and Alec was able to stand fairly upright and spread out his hands to the peat blaze. The air was full of good smells, including something in the nature of supper. There was a gentle and pervasive humming in the air, counterpointed by a distant ringing of hammer on anvil, and the confused echo of voices from somewhere farther down the passage.

Heads up, son! Both sides, and they're armed.

He looked up to see a couple of powerful-looking youths advancing on him from alcoves on either side of the cave entrance. One wore a headset and carried a sensor wand.

"Just a formality, English," the Maelrubha told him soothingly. "You surely understand we're obliged to do business with all types, and they ain't all gentlemen like yourself. Of course *you're* clean, though, isn't he, boys?"

One of the young men trained a rifle on Alec while the other swept the sensor wand up and down in front of him. "No guns, sir," he said tersely. His wand came up to the level of Alec's head and stopped. His eyes widened, listening to what his headset was telling him. "He's a cyborg, sir!"

Alec could hear the Captain gnashing his teeth. "Yes, I am," he admitted, in the most calm and reasonable of voices. He held up his open hands, palms outward, indicating the circle he wore at his throat. "I've got a linkup through this with the navigational system on my ship out there. It comes in pretty handy."

"So it must," said the Maelrubha. "Neat bit of work, that. Isn't technology a fine thing! It goes through that torque you've got on, does it?"

"Yes, it does."

"And connects where?" The deep voice was still affable, but had taken on a certain edge.

"Subcutaneous porting system on my back," Alec said, wondering if he was about to die.

"I've always wished to see one of them. Just you keep your hands out like that, now, don't trouble yourself, but I'd appreciate it if you went down on your knees, and would you ever mind if Petrel here took off your coat and shirt so we could have a look at your back?"

I've got fixes on all three of 'em, son, from the forward-deck cannon. It'll *punch straight through those walls. If I have to fire, you drop.*

It's okay. This guy doesn't stay in business by killing customers, I bet. Alec knelt carefully and allowed Petrel to divest him of his upper garments. He bent forward in the firelight, displaying the pattern of interwoven lines on his back. The light of the flames glinted on the torque, shone like red gold on his bare skin and contrasted with the dull silver lines of the knotwork pattern.

"O, man, that is something fine," said Petrel in envy. "Can I get one of those, sir?"

"You can not," the Maelrubha said gruffly. "With Whitewave's little one on the way and us with the satellite tracking system not half paid for yet, where d'y'reckon we'd get the money?"

"I suppose." The youth sighed.

"And even supposing we did, you'd no sooner have it than the other children would be whining to have one, too. No indeed, handy as I'm sure this is, it's not for the likes of us just yet." The Maelrubha walked around Alec, studying him with a slight frown. At last he shook his head, producing his pocket flask and offering Alec another dram, which Alec accepted readily. "Here's for the chill, lord. Give the English back his clothes. I trust you understand the necessity, lord? Can't be too careful whom you invite to supper these days, and isn't that an unfortunate comment on our times?"

Too bloody right.

Alec shrugged into his shirt—it was too warm indoors for his anorak—and when he had risen to his feet, the party moved down a long passage cut through the living stone, going further into the depths of the island. There were numerous chambers opening off the main passage, living quarters apparently to judge from the glimpses Alec caught of comfortable domestic scenes: a woman rocking a child in a cradle, a great gray hound sprawled asleep and twitching before a fire, a man writing code at a console. There was evidently some complex drainage and ventilation system in place, for the air was fresh and not dank.

The passage led into a barrel-vaulted room with a firepit in the center. Smoke funneled up through a ceiling vent. Arranged around the fire were a number of wooden benches and two chairs with backs: an ancient padded recliner with its legs missing and an elaborately carved wooden chair, into which the Maelrubha settled, waving Alec to the recliner. Alec sank into it cautiously, looking around. Somewhere on their journey down the corridor the guard had changed. Petrel and his watchmate had apparently gone back to their posts and Alec was flanked by two more youths of great size, both barefoot and toting rifles. They saluted the Maelrubha, glaring at Alec.

"Sir!" they said. "Orders, sir!"

"I've a credit check to run, boys. Will one of you ask Mother to come up? And have a plate of stew fetched in for the English, here. He's our guest."

"Sir!" They saluted and exited at different doors. The Maelrubha looked over at Alec with a faintly apologetic smile, handing him the flask once again.

"Drink up, lord. They're good children, but they don't care for your countrymen much. You'll be understanding, I hope."

"Perfectly." Alec cleared his throat and had another drink. "I just want you to know—I think England's got a lot to apologize for, the way they treat your people. Just because I'm English doesn't mean I agree with the sanctions."

"Very gracious of you, lord." The Maelrubha looked around and retrieved a pipe from the depths of his chair cushions. He produced a pouch from somewhere else and proceeded to fill the pipe with something aromatic. He made no effort to take the flask back, so Alec drank again.

"And—I hope some day our countries can be friends. Do you think relations will ever improve?"

"O, who knows?" said the Maelrubha, holding a hotpoint to his pipe. "When you can live in Belfast without growing a second head from the radioactivity, maybe. Now, I'm sure the subject must be as painful for you as it is for me, so let's move on to business. We're accustomed to being paid in gold, but a gentleman of your breeding—well. Once you've passed the formalities, I'm sure we can arrange for a simple transfer of funds."

"But—" said Alec, and at that moment one of the young guards strode into the room, bearing a dish of something that steamed. Behind him, a queenly lady peered into the room, regarding Alec with interest. Alec looked back at her and started slightly; from her shoulder a blackbird was also regarding him, eyes bright as brass. The lady turned and said something in a soft voice to someone in the passage behind her, and there were shrieks of feminine laughter. The lady withdrew.

"Food for the English," announced the guard, and thrust the plate at Alec. He looked at the contents in surprise.

"Is this fish stew?"

"Afraid so," the Maelrubha said, puffing to get his pipe started. "Salt cod. We'd much rather it was soy protein, of course, but that's a bit hard to come by out here. No, you keep the flask for now. You'll want a good fire in you, when you go back out into that night."

"I like fish." Alec dipped his spoon into it. He inhaled the mingled scents: seafood, root vegetables, nothing that shouldn't be there. "Anyway, there's no trouble with the money. I brought gold."

"Have you, now? Lovely. We'll still want to do the little check on you, though, since we've not done business before," the Maelrubha explained, leaning back and exhaling smoke.

"No problem." Alec tasted the stew cautiously. Only the flavors he had been expecting. "I'll pay for everything."

"Mm. Ah, here's Mother." The Maelrubha extended his hand to a little lady who entered just then. She was apple-cheeked, big-bosomed, and the firelight gleamed on her round spectacles. "Mother's our accountant. My dear, this is the fine lord who's interested in our wares. And he's a cyborg, think of that, now."

"Is he then?" she said, in a clear precise lilt. "How fascinating. A lord too, is he? I'm sure in that case his credit must be very good indeed."

"Of course," said the Maelrubha, exhaling a long plume of smoke. "But for form's sake, my dear—"

"Certainly," she said, and leaning over Alec she seized his chin in a surprisingly firm hand. "Please to let me examine your retinal pattern, young man."

Alec had just time to realize that her optics were not, in fact, spectacles—they were instead an interface device with her own system—before she had accessed his identification code. The captain did the cyberspace equivalent of holding his breath and flattening himself against a wall while she made a quick and efficient survey of Alec's official financial records. After a long, long moment she released Alec's chin and gave him a pat on the cheek. "O, my, yes, he's quite able to pay for his purchases. Shall I call for Bull to bring up our sample case?"

"If you would, my dear," said the Maelrubha. She went to the doorway and spoke a word to the guard who apparently waited just out of sight; then returned to sit at the Maelrubha's right, quietly folding her hands in her apron. Alec sat there blinking a moment before he had another spoonful of stew. It was delicious. The warmth in the room was delicious, as well, and the complex fragrances of peat smoke and pipe smoke and dinner and the cold sea and machine oil somewhere . . . and the whiskey, that was delicious too. He had another gulp. What a pleasant place this was. What nice people these were.

Alec, yer getting drunk.

No, I'm not.

"I guess—I mean you should know—well, you probably don't ask questions much about what people are going to do with what you sell them—" he said.

"O, no," the Maelrubha assured him.

"Never," said Mother.

"And of course I can't tell you anything. But you ought to know it's in a good cause. Morally, I mean. To fight against injustice and oppression."

"Well, I'm glad you told me that much, lord," said the Maelrubha, nodding solemnly. "We'll all sleep better knowing that, I'm sure. Yes, it's hard being in this business, you know; but then with the sanctions we don't have many ways to feed all the little mouths we've got to feed, see. It's a moral dilemma, to be sure. Though we're not always going to be earning our bread this way."

"No?" Alec tilted the flask for another mouthful of fire and honey. The Captain snarled in his ear.

"No indeed. As soon as the children all have shoes, we're going into microprocessors."

At this moment a vast rumbling was heard in the corridor outside, in some language Alec didn't know, and of which he could only distinguish the word *sassenach*. A great dark bulk shouldered through the door, bearing in its massive arms a polished box roughly the size and shape of a coffin. The figure set down the box and rose up, fixing Alec with a contemptuous stare, light eyes startling in his sooty face. He was nearly as tall as Alec and easily twice as wide, and naked but for leather trousers and apron.

"You'll please excuse our gunsmith," said the Maelrubha delicately. "He doesn't speak to English. He'll have no objection to displaying his art, though."

With a sneer the gunsmith opened the case. Alec caught his breath. He thought at first he was looking at antiques, so elaborate were the designs, so exquisite the chased patterns on the brass and silver-plated surfaces, so fancifully carved and polished the wooden stocks. Then he noticed the laser sights and realized these were neither flintlocks nor even late model stunners.

They were disrupters, the last weapons to have been made before weapons were outlawed in the twenty-third century, but as they might have been designed by a third-century genius. Even the power packs were inscribed with Celtic knotwork, the battery light forming the left eye in a little barbaric face, so that when it should wink redly you'd know you needed a new pack.

"These are fantastic," said Alec, reaching for one. He hefted it cautiously. It felt as good as it looked. Carefully aiming into a corner of the room, he sighted along the barrel. "Oh, man, I've got to have one! Two. Hell, I'll take the whole case."

"The stock's English oak on this here," the Maelrubha pointed out. "Pure nickel panels, selenium battery components, guaranteed kill rate of eighteen in twenty, carries a charge for eight hundred rounds. Those others are ebony and cherrywood."

"Cool," Alec sobered slightly. "But I think there's been a misunderstanding. I need to buy in bulk. I needed four hundred, not four."

"Only four hundred?" The Maelrubha waved dismissively. "Take five, and we'll give you a discount. Here, Bull, show him the little bonus gift for the half-thousand."

The gunsmith reached into the bottom of the case and brought out a smaller wooden box, engraved all over with death's heads. He opened it carefully to display, nested in red velvet, a brass shell the size and appearance of a human skull. Incised knotwork and spirals swirled on its surface, swooped between its blind eyes, incorporating inscriptions that looked as though they'd been copied from some ancient grimoire.

"You know what this is, of course," said the Maelrubha.

"Yeah," said Alec, who had no idea. He drank uncertainly.

"I'll thank you to observe this special feature, here—" the Maelrubha indicated the delicate lettering, "—that you won't find offered by any other dealer in arms, assuming you could find one in this enlightened age. Each line an original curse of deadly puissance, time-tested by experts! Now, the bomb is free with your order; but for an additional, nominal charge the curses can be personalized. Right here whilst you wait, our artist will engrave the name of your heart's enemy in that attractive oval blank there, see?"

It was such an absurd idea Alec found it delightful.

"Sure," he said. "Okay! It won't explode while it's being engraved on, will it?"

Muttering, the gunsmith drew a tiny golden acid pencil from a slot in his leather apron. He looked impatiently at Alec.

"Er—ARECO," Alec said. And though it seemed as though his thick black fingers could barely get purchase on the pencil's shaft, the gunsmith quickly and easily wrote *ARECO* in flowing uncials so perfect you'd swear he'd attended a convent school. "Neat," said Alec admiringly. "Okay, what do I owe for the lot?"

"Hm, hm—" The Maelrubha exchanged glances with Mother. "Let's see now, five hundred of the assorted pistols and rifles—and then you'll want the extra power packs—plus cleaning kits and accessories—plus the charge for the engraving—and then there's the Celtic Federation transfer tax, but I like you, so we'll disregard that—let's make it a nice round sum and say eleven million pounds English? And I'll throw in this case as a personal gift, on account of you appreciate a work of art when you see one."

Alec gulped. The Captain was stunned into silence.

"Okay," said Alec, thinking of the valiant Martian agriculturists and the way the odds were stacked against them. "I've got four million in gold specie in the boat. I can transfer the balance from my own account, yeah?"

The deal was made. Coordinating with Mother's system, seven million pounds were transferred from Cocos Island Trading's account to a certain account in Switzerland. As soon as the transaction had gone through, the Maelrubha produced a second pocket flask and quaffed cheerfully.

"Now, that'll buy a lot of little shoes," he said. "Drink with me, English, drink deep. Death to our enemies!"

And Alec certainly didn't want anybody to die really, but because he was a courteous man he grinned and held his flask aloft.

"Death to our enemies," he said, and drank deep, as he had been bid.

All that remained was to wait while box after box was loaded into the launch, by barefoot lads who seemed entirely unaffected by the blue cold. The specie was unloaded and examined by the gunsmith, who pronounced it satisfactory with a grudging nod. When the last of the order had been battened in place Alec splashed out to the launch and climbed in. He started up the motor and put about, turning in his seat to wave farewell to his hosts. He felt light-headed and half-frozen, and the thought that he was transporting a real bomb that might blow him to atoms gave him a certain giddy delight.

The Captain made a note that Alec needed another psychotherapy workout, but was preoccupied by the task of getting the launch safely back to the *Captain Morgan* where she rode the rising swell in the eternal blue dusk. It was time to take her out where she'd have plenty of sea room.

"So long, English," called the Maelrubha, from where he watched near the cave mouth. "Please call again. Always happy to serve a repeat customer."

"Aren't they English on Mars, sir?" said Mother, waving at Alec.

"We can hope so, darlin'," growled Bull.

Alec Meets a Girl

"Sushi for evewyone," sang Binscarth, offering around a tray as though it contained so many green and black petit-fours. He had to shout over the mariachi music and the roar of the food processor as it battered ice cubes and tequila into a slimy slush. The roar cut out abruptly, replaced by a torrent of curses from Magilside.

"It's broken now! I told you we should have rented a houseboy," he bellowed from the kitchen.

"Oh, yes, that'd make a *lot* of sense, have some local spy weporting on us to the Fedewales because you wanted a pwoperly made fwozen mawgawita," sneered Binscarth. "Sushi, Checkewfield?" He danced up to Alec, who was standing on the balcony staring out at a red sunset over the Pacific.

"No, thanks," said Alec. He was too edgy to eat.

"Don't be a fool, Mexican's the best sushi in the wowld," said Binscarth huffily. Balkister waved him away, lifting his drink in a toast to Alec.

"He's no fool. He's a hero, and he knows damned well that one doesn't go out on a mission stuffed full of food and drink. Eh, fellow ugly guy?" He stepped out on the balcony beside Alec and considered the view. The vacation house belonged to Johnson-Johnson's grandmother, and was white and soaring of line, with its back firmly turned on a parched wilderness of scorpions and spiny plants. The land road was a windy misery of brick-red dust. The only pleasant access was by sea, into a perfect little bay of golden sand and turquoise water. The *Captain Morgan* rocked quietly at anchor below them, at the end of the private pier.

"Though you might have just a shot of tequila or something, you know, for your nerves," Balkister added, watching as the sky went through ever-brassier shades of melon and salmon and peach.

"That's the last thing I need right now," said Alec sharply. He was still mortified at getting so drunk at the arms dealer's. To make matters worse, four days earlier he'd been sitting at the Happy Club bar in Campeche when he'd picked up the unmistakable scent of perfume from the trap in his house. Turning slowly in his seat, he'd noticed the unobtrusive man who'd come in after him and sat now three stools down, ordering a Red Stripe. Not a cyborg, at least; but it meant the Company had investigated that address and was still managing to have him shadowed ashore. Too many of his habits were known. They would bear changing.

"Try to keep the rest of them halfway sober, yeah?" he told Balkister. "Timing's going to be everything, if I make it back."

"Of course you'll make it—"

"These are serious bad guys, Balkister. Just as bad as Areco in their way, okay? And no, I'm still not telling you who they are. Once they find out one of their shuttles is gone, they'll come after it. If we're really lucky we'll have about five hours' lead. But if one of those clowns is so stoned he drops a crate off the pier when we're loading—"

"Won't happen! You have my word, Checkerfield. They're just keyed up. This is a bit more exotic action than most of them ever get to see, you know." Balkister sucked at his frozen drink. "But none of them have forgotten what it's in aid of, believe me. God, I envy you, Checkerfield, I really do. Mars at last."

"Yeah," Alec said, realizing he had barely thought about that part of the plan. Not that it hadn't been meticulously arranged; but all his attention had fixed on the next seven hours, to the exclusion of anything else. If those seven hours were a success, the rest of the run would seem like a kiddie ride.

And after that, he'd decided, it was time to get out of the smuggling business and focus entirely on revenge.

Balkister cleared his throat, looking uncomfortable.

"You're quite sure you can fly the shuttle?"

"Hey." Alec made a dismissive gesture. "This is Super Cyborg you're talking to, remember? Of course I can fly it."

"And it really can—" Balkister mouthed the words *time travel*.

"Shh," Alec cautioned, with a glare toward the house.

"Oh, quite. Top secret. Now—not that I haven't every confidence in you, but— just on the chance something goes, er, wrong—is there anybody you'd like us to contact?"

"You mean if I snuff it?" Alec grinned. "Nope. All my legal stuff's sorted out already. Title dies with me. Most of the money's tied up in a trust fund for my mother."

Balkister frowned. Surely Alec had meant *from* his mother? The moment was too solemn to correct his grammar, however. "You can be certain we'll honor your memory for all time, you know. We put it to a special vote, when you'd gone to bed last night."

"Nice of you," said Alec. "Don't worry about your rent payments, either. There's a codicil just for that purpose."

"That's awfully decent, Checkerfield," said Balkister stiffly. He looked out on the twilight water and, for a moment, regretted what they were doing. Behind them there was a sudden blast of sound as Magilside cranked up the music, a swoony mariachi rendition of "Walking in a Winter Wonderland" loud enough to rattle the window glass.

When night had fallen, Alec went on board the *Captain Morgan*. Swiftly she put to sea and sped north through the black night ocean, on a familiar course, and the mermaid on her prow wept silently.

By the time the lights of the island were visible, Alec had put on a thin set of thermals and fastened himself into his subsuit. As the *Captain Morgan* made her cautious way around the windward side of the island, standing well out to sea, he wondered uncomfortably whether Dr. Zeus had someone in that distant cluster of lights watching him on a gray screen. He started as Billy Bones crept up, offering him the mask that went with his suit.

Not to worry, son. They ain't scanning the coast. I reckon piracy's the last thing they expect, in this day and age.

They really don't know, do they? They've got no clue about us, right?

How could they? They may know you can do amazing stuff, but they don't know about me. I reckon I'm the rock they've split on, thinking they'd have things all their own way.

Yeah. This is the beginning of the big payback.

That's my boy. Alec's revenge! Take no prisoners, son.

This is for my mother, for Roger and Cecelia, for all of 'em.

Alec leaned backward over the rail, kicking once to deploy the flippers in his boots. He tumbled into the dark water and immediately the infrared sights in the mask cut in, lighting his way into an eerie undersea nocturne.

The water was beautifully clear, full of shoals of bright fish that fled from his silent passage. Once, at a distance, he saw the slow cruising bulk of a shark; but it picked up the signal his suit was broadcasting and turned, making off through the kelp forest as though it had abruptly remembered a pressing engagement elsewhere.

He saw nothing more dangerous until he began to pass the mines, drifting things that resembled jellyfish. Their purpose was to adhere to the hulls of approaching vessels and transmit all perceptible information on them to Dr. Zeus. They were programmed to deliver an unsettling electric charge to something Alec's size, but he avoided them with ease. Now he was past the strung foul-wires, the netting, the camouflaged underwater entrances. A moment more and he was crawling ashore on his hands and knees, and a seal was turning to look at him in an affronted way before rolling over and lolloping down to the surf to take its rest somewhere else.

He pulled off his mask and sat there gasping a moment, reviewing the plan in his head. Then he tucked the mask away in a pouch, retracted the flippers into his boots and edged along the sheer cliff wall, hunting for any place where it was less vertical, working always toward the white lights of the compound.

At length he found a goat path and went up it, crouching forward to feel his way with his hands, ascending swiftly. About twenty meters up it led him into a sparse stand of ironwood trees, and he leaned against one and studied the view.

The compound lay to the north, on a shelf of land blasted from the cliffs to create a platform. It jutted out like a proscenium stage, painted with the humming-bird landing pattern for vertically rising and descending aircraft. A half-circle of maintenance offices were built against its back wall. Their windows were dark. Three small aircraft sat on the landing platform.

They did not look particularly skyworthy, or even attractive. They were rather like buses in shape and size, dull silver, with only the slightest tapering at the nose and only the suggestion of stubby wings and tail fins. Their designer had clearly wanted no part of Buck Rogers Revival.

On the other hand, Alec reflected, it made a certain sense to make the most outrageously valuable piece of technology ever invented as drab and functional as a toaster. Who'd want to steal a dumpy-looking craft like that? *Unless he knew what it was.*

He advanced through the trees and came upon an access road, thickly planted along its verge with mimosa and hibiscus. Silently he paralleled the road, working through the bushes, and came at last to the powered gate with its glowing control box.

Here?

May as well. Give 'em hell, son. Where do we come from?

From the sea. Alec freed his collar from the neck of the sub suit and unscrewed the knob at one end. He withdrew a plug on a fine length of wire. Groping, he found a port on the underside of the control box and connected.

WE'RE IN!

Alec had the momentary sensation of swallowing a lot of very good rum simultaneous to having the orgasm of his life while inhaling the fragrance of a Jamaican garden. He knew, now, all he needed to get in. Dizzy and elated, he ordered the gate to open and it did. Unporting, he ran through, keeping to the shadows, and made straight for the nearest time shuttle.

As he ran, the Captain was running too, down what would look to Alec like an immense corridor lined with the richest and most desirable of loot. Metaphorically he had his arms extended, sweeping across either wall, and the loot flowed into him through his fingertips, and as it did he was growing, expanding to tremendous size. In lighthouses all across the face of the globe, lights were winking, data of unimaginable content and complexity was being downloaded.

Alec sped across the painted tarmac and ordered the time shuttle to open for him. Obediently its hatch sprang wide, and he vaulted in. He stared around as the hatch closed behind him. The interior of the shuttle was nothing like its exterior. He'd never seen such luxury in a commercial transport.

There was an odd sharp smell in the air, a chemical kind of smell. What was that? The new data he'd received told him it was residual stasis gas. What was stasis gas? Harmful? No? Okay, then, and here was what was obviously the pilot's seat, in front of what must be the guidance console.

He slid into the seat, buckled the restraints and looked the console over, ordering it to activate. Rows of lights blinked on, greeting him. Somewhere here must be the buttonball where he'd enter the algorithm to take it through time. Right now, though, he was only planning on taking it through space, out of this yard and across the dark sea to where the *Captain Morgan* waited.

Meanwhile the Captain had paused, staggering slightly as he absorbed the implications of a file he had just downloaded. Its designation was *Adonai*. He was leaning on a wall of light, wondering how he was going to safely relay the file's contents to Alec, when he became aware of the electronic analogue of the sound of approaching feet.

Captain? Alec called.

The Captain turned. Walking down the virtual corridor toward him was the figure of a man, seemingly cast out of green bronze. Powerfully built, bearded, naked but for some white drapery over one shoulder and about his waist. He appeared to be looking directly at the Captain, but it was impossible to tell; the sockets of his eyes were black and empty. In his right hand was a thunderbolt.

Captain, I've got the shuttle! How do I put in coordinates?

The Captain muttered a string of words that would have given a sailor in any era pause. The approaching figure smiled, with a sound like bronze plate screaming across bronze plate.

Captain?

YOU ARE IN MY HOUSE, THIEF.

Bloody Hell. I reckon yer Dr. Zeus, ain't you? Someone's given you an interface identity.

I AM THE DOCTOR AND I AM THE GOD, THIEF.

Captain! It's time to take off!

The figure advanced implacably on the Captain, raising its thunderbolt as it came. Backing off a pace, the Captain drew his cutlass from thin air.

CAPTAIN!

You hurt my boy. You hurt him worse than ever I knew.

I MADE YOUR BOY, THIEF.

You won't unmake him again, bastard.

Frantically Alec sought to enter cyberspace to see why the Captain wasn't responding, but as he did so there was a rending crash, a blue-white flame within his eyes, and he gasped and clutched at his temples.

There was nobody there with him. He was alone, for the first time since he cared to remember. If he probed he could perceive the database he'd accumulated over the years, distant and difficult of access. Trembling, he leaned forward, tried to make some sense of the lights on the shuttle console. He gave what he thought might be the command to lift off.

Smoothly the shuttle rose, and kept rising. Alec saw the lights of the compound dropping below him. He gave more commands, attempting to turn the shuttle and take it out to where the *Captain Morgan* rode at anchor in the night.

No, he'd done something wrong. The console gave a peremptory electronic grunt and ignored him, and cryptic red letters flashed in front of his eyes as a recorded voice cried: "ERROR! ENTER PILOT CODE!"

"Pilot code?" Alec bit his lower lip. He sorted in desperation through the database as the shuttle continued its rise, high enough now to show him the distant lights of Los Angeles. At last he found something that seemed right, and entered it.

The shuttle made an awful noise and lurched forward, then began to spiral wildly, out of control. Alec heard warning Klaxons, and the red letters flashed again as the voice shouted at him: "ERROR! ERROR! DEFAULT COORDINATES!"

The chemical smell intensified. Turning his head, Alec could see the cabin beginning to fill with yellow smoke. Not smoke. *Stasis gas.* The shuttle was preparing to return to its last destination, was about to take him through time.

"Oh God, oh God—" He sought for the information he needed, but without the Captain it was like thumbing through a thirty-volume encyclopedia in a burning house. The gas filled his lungs and blinded him. There was a moment of sensual pleasure to which his body responded with moronic readiness, and then a wave of nausea as a brilliant light cut through the yellow fog and an impact seemed to flatten him in his seat like a crushed insect.

Alec might have lost consciousness for a second. He was next aware of watching the gas boil away as some vent activated, and he was staring down in bemusement at the blue sky. Above it, like a cloud mass, spread a brown horizon and blue water.

But that was wrong, wasn't it?

With a cry of terror, he struggled again to get the controls to obey him. Earth and sky exchanged places, flipped again, righted themselves. The shuttle screamed through a long descending turn and straightened out a few bare meters above the surface of the water, barreling toward land and steadily losing altitude. A winged fish smacked into the window, its goggle-eyed astonishment mirroring his own before it was torn away by the slipstream. He attempted to cut the shuttle's power and found that it seemed to be obeying him. The forward thrust lessened percep-tibly. Unfortunately, he was still headed straight for the island.

Alec spotted a bay between two projecting headlands, and beyond it a green flood plain coming down to the water's edge, at the mouth of a wide canyon run-ning back into the depths of the interior. He steered for it and the shuttle obeyed him. If he could just run out of momentum before he ran out of canyon—

He began hitting green stuff, tall grass, sugar cane or something. It got all over the window and made it hard to steer around the low foothills that rose to right and left, blocking his way. Somehow Alec managed, though, snaking the shuttle through the long slalom, and a distant corner of his mind noted with satisfaction that he was beginning to learn to pilot the craft. The same detached observer noted that there was blood dripping from his chin.

The shuttle began to slew sideways, cutting a swath though the green field as it came. The ground rose to meet it with a sickening impact, and Alec was thrown forward painfully in his seat restraints. He was no longer moving in any direction, through space or time. The relief was so intense he blacked out.

Someone was trying to get his attention.

He blinked, focusing his eyes. Where had all this blood come from? He straightened up in his seat and peered incredulously out the window. The shuttle had come to rest tilted forward on its nose in the field, and there was a strong smell of crushed vegetation coming through the open air vents. Heat, too; a bright subtropical sun was beating down on the shuttle. His vision was blurred, doubling; his sense of smell was more acute than usual. How much ganja had he smoked? Why would he have been smoking ganja on a job?

The girl who stood looking in through the window waited patiently as he sorted all this out. Their eyes met. She slipped a marker into the pocket of her coveralls and held up her right hand, on the palm of which she had written for him to see:

DO YOU SPEAK CINEMA STANDARD?

What did the words mean? He could recognize a couple of them.

She made a trumpet of her hands and leaned close to the window, shouting: "You appear to require medical assistance! Do you need help getting out of there?"

Who on earth was she? After a moment of gaping at her he unfastened his safety restraints and ordered the shuttle hatch to open. It popped up, filling the cabin with fresh air, unbelievably sweet after the stasis gas. Drawing in a deep breath, he stood up and pitched forward, falling to his hands and knees.

He must have blacked out again for a second because she was abruptly there beside him, without appearing to have come around the front of the shuttle, and he was outside. She got her arms around him and hoisted him up. Alec stood beside her in the midst of her ruined field, clinging to her lest he topple over. What a strong young lady she was! He looked down at her and saw that his blood was smeared on her face and in her hair. He muttered an apology, but she just smiled at him. In fact . . . was she turned on by him? Was that what that fragrance on her skin was, arousal?

They walked away, Alec leaning on her as they threaded through the green rows. It was funny-looking sugar cane they were walking through. It was covered all over with things like big green ganja-joints, each one bearing a tassel at its end. If he'd been smoking this stuff, no wonder he was hallucinating. He wondered if he was hallucinating the girl. She looked just like his mermaid figurehead, except that she had clothes on. And legs instead of a curled fishtail. And her fire-colored hair was braided back severely, a long braid that came clear down to her behind. He considered her breasts thoughtfully, looking down as they staggered along.

"Here now, sweetheart." She led him up on a porch and settled him down on a bench. "You rest here a moment." Her scent trailed away as she left him.

He looked around, and his fog cleared a little. The bench was made of big hand-hewn planks. He must be somewhere in the past. He wondered when. He didn't know enough about history to pinpoint his location, but he had a vague idea that houses and furniture hadn't looked like this since well before the Space Age. She'd been speaking with just the faintest unidentifiable accent, too, a steely precision that suggested . . . what? This must be some time before the twentieth century. On the other hand, she'd shown not the slightest surprise or dismay at the sight of the time shuttle. She smelled very young. And she wanted to sleep with him? *Who was she?*

He found himself waiting for the Captain to tell him, and gulped in dismay when he remembered that the Captain was missing in action. There was a roaring in his ears, a crowding at the edges of his vision; suddenly she was there again, holding his head up with both her hands on his face, looking into his eyes.

". . . You don't want to go away again, you're going to be fine. Stay with me, now. Listen to the sound of my voice. I'm going to give you something to make the bleeding stop, okay?"

" 'Kay," he said thickly.

"Good boy. This'll sting, I'm afraid. What's your name? Can you tell me your name?"

"Alec," he said. She put a coagulator wand to his nose and fired. It stung, all right. The reek of ozone was pungent, painful. The girl held a wad of wet cloth under his nostrils, tilting his head back.

"Alec! Really? As in Alec Guinness?"

"Alec Checkerfield," he said indistinctly, looking at her over the cloth.

"Alec Checkerfield! Well. And you're an Englishman, obviously. Can you tell me what year it is, Alec?"

"Er—well—it was 2351 when I left—" he said. She caught her breath. He gulped and blundered on. "Only I guess I'm somewhere else now."

She nodded slowly. "I guess you are. Did something go wrong with your shuttle?"

Okay, she wasn't a denizen of a past time. That meant—

"You work for Dr. Zeus," he said, noticing at last the corporate logo on the breast pocket of her coveralls. There was another emblem beside it, a clock face without hands.

She considered him for a long moment, an unreadable expression in her eyes. "Actually," she said, "I'm a prisoner here."

That sank in and he calmed down. "Oh," he said, as she moved the cloth to see if the bleeding had stopped—it hadn't quite—and zapped him again with the wand. "Ow. You mean you're from the same time as me? And, and this is a prison colony or something? I thought I'd traveled back into the past."

"You did," she said. "But this isn't a colony. I'm alone here, as a matter of fact. You're lucky you landed where you did, practically in my front yard. There's no other living soul on this island. Won't be for another hundred thousand years."

There was something weirdly familiar in the soothing tone of her voice, in the deftness of her hands, with never a wasted movement. He found himself thinking of Sarah, though this girl was white-pale and austerely caucasian of feature. He'd have taken her for a Celt, if not for her eyes and her voice.

"So—so this is the past, like, prehistoric times or something?" he said, struggling to keep his grip on consciousness.

"More or less," she said, checking the bleeding again. She gave him one last jolt with the wand. "There now. Let's see how that works. You're not a Dr. Zeus shuttle pilot then, I take it."

"No," he admitted. "Dr. Zeus has wrecked my life, just like it's wrecked yours. I'm going to get the bastards."

"Are you now," she said noncommittally. "Well, Alec Checkerfield, that's a great idea, but you need to recover first. You came back through time without taking a very necessary drug beforehand, did you know that? What I'd like you to do, now, is stand up very slowly and come inside to lie down. Okay? Lean on me, now."

It was cool and dark inside her house, if rather spartan, and there seemed to be just the one room. He let her settle him on the log-frame bed. Great; he liked a girl who got down to business. She brought a basin and a towel and cleaned him up, before she washed her own face. He kept fading in and out of reality. Had he asked her to sleep with him yet? Was he in any condition to? She certainly needed it, she was like a wild kitten rubbing her head into his hand, purring like mad . . . always oblige a lady, Ape Man.

"How long have you been stuck here?" Alec said, struggling to think coherently.

"I've been at this station for years," she said. "More years than I remember."

He reached up and clasped her hand, grasped at the idea to keep from drifting away. "You mean they marooned you here when you were just a kid? Bloody hell, what'd you do? It must have been something your parents did."

"Not exactly," she said, studying his hand. "But I also knew too much about something I shouldn't have. Dr. Zeus found a nicely humane oubliette and dropped me out of sight or sound."

What's oubliette mean? Alec asked the Captain automatically, and felt cold when no answer came. He gulped and tried to fix his attention on the girl as she said: "You're the first mortal soul I've spoken with in all this time."

"My God," he said. "Well, listen—er—what's your name, babe?"

After a moment's pause she said, "Mendoza."

So she was Spanish? "Okay, Mendoza. I'll get you out of here. That time shuttle out there is *mine* now, babe, and when I've finished this other thing I'll come back for you." He squeezed her hand for emphasis.

Yes, he had impressed her, he could tell. Her face had gone pale again, the color had just fled, and her eyes were worried. He didn't want to worry her, though. Just impress her. Make her happy. Could he do that? Yes, if she'd lie down beside him. Nice little girl, she meant no harm. He argued earnestly. Suddenly there was an island of clarity and he realized he'd just offered to marry her.

The moment it was out of his mouth he was horrified at what he'd just said, and he didn't know what to make of the expression on her face. He blurted:

"And then afterward we could just get a divorce."

She was staring. He tried to reconstruct what he'd been saying. Had he insulted her? She didn't smell angry. Just as though she needed someone terribly.

He must have asked her to sleep with him, because she leaned down and kissed him, very gently but full on the mouth, parting his lips. He liked that a great deal. He liked the scent and the taste of her, he liked the weight of her breasts, and he wanted very much to untwine that long braid and get his fingers in her hair. About all he was actually able to do in his present condition was open his mouth and grope a bit, and for one wonderful moment he thought his skull was going to explode.

There was a distant rumble of thunder. She had gone to the window to see what had caused the rumbling noise.

"There's a cloud front advancing," she announced in surprise. "Have you brought rain, like the west wind? I think we're going to have a summer storm."

As if in agreement with her words, a gust of turbulent air danced in through the window. Alex knitted his brows. Had they had sex yet? He couldn't remember.

Gradually his higher brain function came back. He lay quietly on Mendoza's bed, sipping tea and watching her move in her kitchen corner.

She was a botanist, she explained, and the Company kept her busy on this island, which was one of their agricultural stations. She told him about the Day Six resorts, and how she had to grow lettuce for their restaurants.

"But that's awful," Alec said, leaning up on his elbow. "That means you're their slave!"

"I suppose I am." Mendoza looked up from the table where she was dicing tomatoes. "But I may as well be of some use to somebody, don't you think? They don't call for produce very often. I have a lot of time to work on my own private research."

"What's your research?" he said, watching her small deft hands.

"Do you know anything about maize?" she said, without much hope.

"No. What is it?"

She sighed. "Well, you landed in a field of it—not my special cultivars, fortunately, just the yellow stuff. This." She held up one of the things he had taken for an immense joint of ganja, and stripped back the husk. He recognized the bright kernels.

"Oh! American corn, like on the cob? That's what it looks like before it goes into a pouch? Wow. That's what you're researching?"

"Yes. You see, maize isn't really very good for you," she explained, oddly apologetic. "It's generally lysine deficient, which prevents the human system from utilizing certain amino acids. Also deficient in tryptophan and useable niacin." Methodically she swept the tomatoes from her cutting board into a bowl and began mincing up a bunch of cilantro. "As a rule, the bigger and paler it's bred, the less it's worth as a food source."

He couldn't imagine why Mendoza was telling him this, but he nodded politely as she went on:

"The paradox has always fascinated me. Why has nobody ever produced a cultivar with the nutritional value of, for example, soy or buckwheat? Or better?" She added the cilantro to the tomatoes and began peeling cloves of garlic.

"Anyway, that's become my life's goal: to create from maize the perfect grain, something so rich in lysine and other nutrients that it could sustain humanity nearly on its own. Something to guarantee that no mortal child would ever suffer from malnourishment again."

"Good for you, then," said Alec. "At least you're trying to make your life count for something."

"Oh, I expect everybody tries." Mendoza shrugged. He watched the way it made her breasts rise. Pulling his attention back, he said:

"Not everybody. Most people just drift through their lives. And even the people who want to help just tell other people what to do. None of it does any good! People talk to hear themselves talk, that's all."

"I feel that way myself. I'm glad we agree," Mendoza said carefully, looking down at the garlic she was chopping. "Though you appear to be something of a man of action. Personally, I have my reservations even about action. I seem to have broken everything I ever touched, no matter how well-meaning I was. Perhaps it's best I wound up here, where I can do no harm."

"I know what you mean," Alec said. "It's like there's this curse. And it doesn't matter what you do, you don't even have to *do* anything, you can be just—born, and you make people miserable by even existing. You can try to right wrongs or you can be a criminal, and it all comes to the same thing! All you ever do turns out badly."

She looked at him keenly. "So you keep trying to atone for your sins."

"Well, *sins* is kind of a heavy word, but—yeah, basically."

"And somehow nothing you do is ever enough, you can never set things right, so at last you pin all your hopes on giving your life in a good cause."

"Maybe." Alec blinked, realizing it came down to just that. "And, you know what? You can't lose that way, dying for something. Not only do you finally do some good for a change, you can't ever do any more harm."

"Except to the people who love you," Mendoza said. "They'll suffer every day for the rest of their lives, and God help them if their lives are long. Don't do such a cruel thing, Alec. Have mercy on yourself, and on them."

"There's nobody to miss me, though," he told her. "I'm a free agent."

"Nobody? There's always somebody, señor. Parents, at least."

"Parents!" He gave a brief angry laugh. "My father's dead, and I'm pretty certain now he wasn't really my father at all."

"Oh. You were illegitimate?"

"You could say that. And my real mother's delusional, she's been locked up for thirty years, and it's my fault. *And* Dr. Zeus's fault. I was raised by a nice old couple who worked for my father, but they're both dead now. I've got two ex-wives. One of 'em probably can't remember my name, and the other hated being married to me so bad she freaked out and called the Ephesians to come save her.

"I did have a best friend, who's stuck with me all my life, but I might have just got him killed. Don't *you* think it'd have been better if I'd never been born?" Alec lay back, exhausted at his outpouring of bitterness. He was sorry he'd said it all now; Mendoza's face was so white and stricken. She shook her head slowly.

"I'm sorry," he said. "I really am. I didn't mean I was going to snuff myself. Don't you ever go crazy with the feeling, though? Like being a fish in a net?"

"Believe me, I do," she said. "It's why I don't mind being here so much."

"But, see, in a way this is the same. You're tinkering around with this corn that might feed millions of poor people someday, but you're stuck here, so what good can it do? Dr. Zeus has taken away your whole life. Don't you mind? Didn't you ever want anything more for yourself?"

"I did," she said. "It led to a disaster, I'm afraid. That was my point about being at this station. I can't hurt anybody here."

"But you can't help anybody either, can you?" he pointed out. "And nobody should be a slave, no matter what they've done! Have mercy on yourself too, babe. Let me give you a ride out of here."

There was a long moment of silence and then she lifted her head to look at him, a black intense stare he could almost feel like a touch.

"You're offering to break my chains? All right," she said. "Let's make a bargain. You won't die, and I'll let you bring me back from death in life. And we'll see what happens, shall we?"

"Sure," said Alec. "It's a deal, Mendoza."

He knew he'd made her sad, and he hadn't meant to. All the rest of the day he told Mendoza about better memories: the aimless days of floating from island to island, the pirate stories Sarah told him and the pirate fortresses he'd built in sand. She listened, rapt, as she prepared their evening meal. When she'd finished and washed her hands she came and sat by him again. Neither of them noticed when the rain began, big hot drops pattering in the dust of the garden.

It seemed to make her so happy, to hear how he'd sailed under strange stars and explored tropical islands. He told her nothing about the Captain, beyond saying that he'd developed his own powerful system to help him run things; but he told her about the storms he'd ridden out, the one terrible hurricane where he'd watched from his safety harness as the *Captain Morgan* was rolled over and over in the water, but was okay because her masts and spars were all retracted and the protective dome had been extended over her deck, so she was like an unbreakable bottle.

He told her about the speck of an island he'd bought in the Caribbean, and how he went exploring there and found Spanish fortifications, and digging in them (he omitted to state that he was burying one of the Captain's backup caches) he'd found a handful of gold doubloons.

He told her about lying alone at night on deck, watching the slow stars and the quick-traveling satellites move across the sky, and the meteor showers he saw, and how he sang to himself as loudly as he wanted and heard his voice go out over the wide quiet water, with no one for countless miles to hear him or complain about his sea songs.

"Neither of my ex-wives could stand my singing," he added, laughing. He was sitting propped up by this time, and the headache from his flight was gone. "I like the old chanteys and yo-heave-ho stuff."

"Oh, but please," said Mendoza, "sing something now. I won't complain, I swear. Sing whatever you like."

So he sang "High Barbary" for her, he sang her "The Captain's Apprentice," he even sang her his favorite one about the Flying Dutchman; and the damnedest thing happened: she liked them. The little girl sat there beside him and, for God's sake, began to cry. He found himself reaching to pull her down beside him before he'd finished the last verse. Mendoza buried her face against his neck, and he felt hot tears.

"Babe, it's okay. It didn't really happen, you know," he said. "The Flying Dutchman and all that."

"Man, your ex-wives must have been a couple of stupid bitches," Mendoza said in a muffled voice. He grinned.

"I always kind of thought I'd like being the Flying Dutchman," he said. "Just me and my ship, and the sea. Staying out on blue water and never coming in. I'm not really very good with people."

"Neither am I," Mendoza said.

"Well, how would you know? You haven't had a chance to meet any yet." He put his arm around her. "You're going to have a great time, you'll see. As soon as I finish that other stuff I have to take care of, you can come along and watch me kick ass on Dr. Zeus. Okay? Would you like that?"

"You know, I really think you could," Mendoza said wonderingly. She leaned up to kiss him, and now he was feeling well enough to kiss back with his customary expertise. It became a very long kiss, quite steamy. He ran his hands along her body, wondering how her coveralls fastened.

But she was so young. Must be careful, must be so gentle. She'd been there all alone for years. He started at the realization that she could have had no other lover.

"Er—" he said, coming up for air with a gulp.

"What is it?" She looked at him dazedly.

"You're—you're a virgin, I guess, yeah?"

Mendoza's expression changed, for a second was blank and unreadable. After a pause she said: "Yes. It's all right, though. Please."

Alec looked down at his body, still encased in the subsuit he'd donned how many hours ago now? And how much of his cold sweat and panic terror had the thermals underneath absorbed?

"Can I use your shower?" He looked around, realizing he hadn't noticed a bathroom. It was her turn to look flustered.

"I haven't got a shower. Just a tin tub in the back garden, for baths. The only time it's possible to actually shower is when it's raining fairly hard." Mendoza's eyes widened as she took in the sound of the rain, that had been drumming away pretty steadily for some time now. ". . . Which it is, isn't it? I'll get you a towel."

"Cool." Alec sat up carefully and then stood, and was pleased to discover he felt great. He pushed open what looked to be a back door and stepped out into the garden and the warm rain.

It was pretty back there, tile paths and green lawn, big bushes of fragrant stuff becoming more fragrant in the rain. Mint, that was what it must be. And here was her tin tub, already full and overflowing. He stripped out of his clothing in the steady downpour, sucking in the wet sweet air. It smelled like wet summer grass, wet stone and earth, green fields in the summer storm. He stepped carefully into the tub and sat down, tilting his face back, letting the rain wash away his sweat and desperation.

He opened his eyes and saw Mendoza standing in the doorway, watching him. She didn't look scared, to see him naked. Always a good sign. He smiled at her.

"Would you, er, like to bathe, too?" he invited, as casually as he could. Mendoza got a wild look in her eyes and started toward him through the rain, peeling off her clothes as she came.

"Now, this is the part of the film," she said, in her clear and carefully enunciated way, "where the orchestra begins to play the love theme with a lot of strings and horns, you know, and the camerawork goes sort of blurry and focuses on the lovers embracing passionately, but only from the waist up of course, and then the camera pulls back and tilts up into the branches of the trees, or perhaps goes to a stock shot of crashing waves or something—"

"The hair—the hair—"

"Okay—" Mendoza paused beside the tub, tilting her head to loose the long braid, and he reached out eager hands to help her. She shook her hair out. It was just as he had thought it would be. So was her body, and the perfume of her arousal was driving him mad.

She stepped into the opposite end of the tub, which was not nearly big enough for two people, and within seconds they were grappling and splashing, kissing feverishly.

"Wait, this is nuts," she moaned, "There's no room—"

"Yes, there is," Alec said. He struggled to his feet and lifted her in his arms, high above him, pressed close, and let her slide down until her breasts were on a level with his face. "Oh, yum—"

Things went along very nicely indeed for the next few minutes. Mendoza's arms went around him; then he felt her stiffen slightly.

"Alec, darling," she said, with just the slightest trace of strain in her voice, "this is a rather unusual tattoo you have."

"No'uh tattoo," he said. "M'a thyborg!"

"I beg your pardon?"

He lifted his mouth and looked up at her. "You know how I told you I've got this big custom cybersystem, to work the rigging on my ship? That's how I run it. I'm a cyborg, have been since I was eighteen."

Mendoza began to quiver in his arms, and he thought for one awful second she was turned off by his revelation. Then he saw she was laughing, so silently and profoundly she could barely draw breath.

"Oh, perfect," she gasped. Her eyes widened in sudden shock and she looked down at him. "*What* year did you say it was where you come from?"

"Er . . . 2351," he said, wondering why they had to talk about this right now.

"But that's only four years from—" Mendoza's face underwent such an extraordinary transformation that he nearly dropped her. "Dear God in Heaven, it's *you*!" She flung her fists toward the sky, jubilant, fierce, howling with laughter that echoed from the green canyon walls.

"*YOU'RE* THE NEMESIS, *YOU'RE* THE APOCALYPSE, *YOU'RE* THE SILENCE!" she cried into the storm. "YOU *WILL* BREAK DR. ZEUS!"

There was a triple flash of lightning at that moment, with a roar of thunder so loud Alec thought the world was ending. In the terrifying blue illumination he looked up and saw her poised above him. She might have been something out of another world, bright as a flame, her eyes glowing with inhuman love.

"Oh," he said, and then Mendoza had slid down and clamped her mouth on his, and they wrestled there as the lightning flashed, the thunder boomed. Their struggles overturned the tin tub, dumping them unceremoniously onto the lawn in a flood of rainwater, and they rolled on the tidy grass and he seized her.

Their eyes met. For a hushed moment there was a perfect mutual understanding Alec could never have put into words, the most profound intimacy, and the overwhelming conviction that he was about to remember *who she was*. Then the madness claimed them both and he couldn't think, couldn't think.

———

"Mendoza?"

"Mm?" Lazily she tousled his wet lank hair.

"We need to talk about a few things."

"We certainly do," she said.

Alec rose on his elbows and lifted his head to consider the rain, which was still drumming down on them. He wiped his face with one hand. "We should probably go inside before we catch cold. Or drown."

"Okay," she said. He maneuvered himself up, and Mendoza accepted his extended hand to pull her to her feet.

Within a few minutes, with their soaked clothing drying in front of a pleasantly crackling fire, they were sitting down to supper at her rough-hewn table. He felt insanely calm, aware that something truly frightening had happened to him and that somehow he wasn't afraid. Who could be afraid of the angel/demoness/little lost girl sitting down across from him, so politely offering a home-cooked supper?

Not that it wasn't the most surreal dining experience he'd ever had.

"So this is—?" He lifted an oblong package on his plate with the times of his fork.

"That's a tamale. Please take the wrapper off before you eat it."

"Oh. Like banana leaves?"

"Precisely."

"Okay," he said, and took it apart bemusedly. "About that thing that happened? What was it you called me, the Nemesis? What was that about, exactly?"

"Well." Mendoza took a bite of rolled-up tortilla. "I'm going to tell you something very, very classified," she said, chewing. "I believe I mentioned that Dr. Zeus, possessing the secret of time travel, knows everything that's ever happened in recorded history, as well as everything that ever will happen. Beer?"

"Yes, please," he said, holding out his mug. She poured something hoppy and amber from a stone pitcher and continued:

"Everything that ever will happen, I say—*up to the year 2355.* You understand this is a matter of intense speculation for everyone concerned with the Company. But the fact is, beyond July 9, 2355, there's just—silence."

"Silence how?" Alec frowned.

"Not one word from our future selves on the other side of that moment in time. I have heard that the last message, badly distorted, says simply '*We still don't know—*'. As you might imagine, a Company so accustomed to being omniscient isn't at all happy about being in the dark like everybody else on something so important."

"What's omniscient mean? And why don't they just travel forward through time to see what happens then?" Alec asked.

"*Omniscient* means all-knowing," Mendoza said. "Like God. But Dr. Zeus isn't all powerful, you see, because time travel into the future isn't possible. Or so we are told."

"Okay," said Alec, smiling at her erudition and the matter-of-fact way she was telling him all this. He had a brief vision of the little girl at a tea party, lecturing to her dolls.

"Naturally," she went on, pouring herself a beer and drinking, "there are those who insist that the future beyond 2355 really is known, that the silence is maintained by whoever seizes control on July 9."

"And you know about all this because . . . ?"

"I told you I became privy to certain secrets, didn't I?" she said, looking opaque again. "So. Most of us feel that an intracorporate war at that time is inevitable, with the winner keeping silent to conceal the circumstances of his, her, their or its victory. And it will go very, very badly for the losers, on that day."

His amusement evaporated abruptly.

"But you shouldn't—" he said. "If there's some kind of bloody takeover, there could be a purge. Executions. You're a security risk, and Dr. Zeus doesn't give a shrack about little people's lives. I know!"

"Damned right I'm a security risk," she said coolly. "That's why I'm talking to you."

Alec stared at her, disconcerted. He cleared his throat.

"Mendoza," he said, "you're young, and you've lived in this hole for most of your life. It's dangerous to be so reckless, baby. How do you know it's safe to tell me this stuff? Just because we had sex doesn't make me a good guy, you know."

"How do you know it's safe to tell me anything?" she countered. "I'm a criminal, remember? You're pretty trusting yourself."

He snorted. "Maybe, with a little girl in a garden. There are a lot worse crimes committed out in the real world than anything you could ever have done."

She was silent a moment, and then shrugged. "But on the other hand, what if Alec Checkerfield is what happens in 2355? I think you really will kick Dr. Zeus's all-knowing ass. I say go for it, darling." She raised her beer in a toast. "I only hope I'm around to see."

"You will be," he said, wondering what on earth had happened to her, to make her speak so flippantly of her own death. He reached across the table and stroked her cheek. "I promise you. You'll be right there with me. God knows you shouldn't be running around loose."

"Let us hope so," she said, kissing the palm of his hand and taking it between both of her own. "But life is so uncertain, señor. In any case, start planning your attack now. Twenty-three fifty-five is your window of opportunity, you see?"

"You said something, though." Alec squeezed her hand. "You said time travel into the future doesn't work, and then you said *Or so we are told*. Does that mean maybe there's just a teeny winji chance somebody might do it, if he was lucky?"

"Unlucky," she said, and for a moment there was a cold unhappiness in her face, so bleak an expression he wanted to gather her into his arms and rock her, anything to give comfort. She drew a deep breath and spoke with deliberation:

"There is evidence that the temporal wave can, under certain circumstances, pull one forward as well as backward. I know of a place where it might happen; but you really wouldn't want to try."

"But if I did try," Alec persisted, "say if I had certain advantages other people didn't, I might manage it. Or I could just lay low for the next four years, wait and see what happens in 2355—and then go back to now and set up for bringing Dr. Zeus down, because I'll be the only one who knows the truth."

Mendoza smiled. "You might try, darling, but you'd run into problems. There are two more things you need to know about temporal physics. The one immutable law is that history cannot be changed. Okay? So if you waited until 2355, and turned on the news one day and heard that Dr. Zeus survived a coup attempt, you couldn't go back in time and fix things so that the rebels win."

"I see," he said, narrowing his eyes. "What's the other thing I need to know about?"

"A complication technically described as *variable permeability of the temporal fabric*," Mendoza told him, and he loved the way her mouth moved as she enunciated the words, in her educated voice. But where could she have been educated?

Was she lying to him? Was that why bits of her story didn't add up, or was she just leaving out things it would be difficult to explain, as he had left certain things out of what he'd told her? Innocent people had secrets, too.

"Temporal fabric?" he inquired, taking a sip of beer. "Now, what in hell does that mean?"

"What it means is that there seems to be a limit on how often you can go back to the same point in time. Dr. Zeus doesn't know why. But if, say, you went back in time to buy a winning lottery ticket on a certain day—and of course you'd need to get hold of the Temporal Concordance for the numbers, no mean trick in itself—"

"Temporal *Concordance*?"

"The database containing every single event in recorded history up to July 8, 2355," Mendoza explained. "It's the single most valuable thing the Company owns. Anyway, even assuming you got that far, you'd better be damned sure you did it right, because you probably wouldn't have a second chance."

"So if I got the numbers wrong and tried to go back a second time—?"

"Your shuttle would probably veer off to the day before or the day after (and to some other point in physical space, too, which could cause real trouble for you) but *never again* to that particular place and time. You see?"

"I think so." He frowned down at his dinner, uneasily aware that answering his questions might be putting her life in jeopardy. But if she were really telling the truth . . .

He lifted the beer pitcher, topped up her mug and his.

"Go on," he said.

They retired, pleasantly crowded on her narrow bed, with the rain still drumming outside and the smell of the wet garden coming through the windows. He made overtures, and she responded to them with enthusiasm and in fact with a certain expertise that bewildered him. As the act, and then the acts, progressed, it became apparent that she knew as much about what they were doing as any girl in any Happy Club he had ever visited. Then she gave every evidence of knowing *more*, and his body told his brain to shut up . . .

Only in the afterglow was he able to start thinking again, uneasily connecting dots without numbers as she slept in his arms. Had she been lying? Unconscious and relaxed, she looked unnervingly like a child, terrifyingly young for what she'd just been doing with him. Who could have taught her such things? Had she been abused by her jailers?

And yet she'd seemed so happy . . .

As though you've ever had any clue what a girl's thinking, Alec reminded himself. He lay there on the edge of sleep, watching the flames dancing in the fireplace across the room, backlighting her hair, flickering on her pale skin.

Who on earth was this little girl? Twice the bad bet Lorene had been . . . He could certainly pick them. Despair and disaster attracted him like a perfume.

Third time's the charm, babe, he thought drowsily, and kissed her.

Darkness lit by the fires of war, eerie silence.

He saw Mendoza, wide-eyed, advancing across a battlefield, oblivious to the pits of flaming debris and the tracer fire, to the disrupter beams piercing the smoky air and narrowly missing her. There was a bush still standing in the waste-land, a dark thing with sharp spines and berries bright as blood. She seemed to be drawn to it, fascinated, not seeing the dangers at all. She was stretching out her hand . . .

He was trying to warn her, bounding forward to pull her down—when he woke with a start, to find that Mendoza had evidently gone out into the rain and was now climbing in beside him. She was wet and chilled.

"What were you doing?" he gasped, heart hammering.

"It's all right," she whispered. "I had to see to something."

"You're cold as death," he said, and pulled her close and wrapped his arms around her, as though that might keep her away from the dark field.

He didn't recall where he was when he woke next morning, at first, and Mendoza seemed equally surprised to find him there. They made love. It was, again, a smashing success, but he found himself, again, wondering how a virgin could have learned so many interesting variations on a theme.

Afterward, in another scene of surreal domesticity, she fixed them breakfast as he pulled on his thermals, and they chatted over coffee as though they sat in a kitchen in London.

Finally Alec cleared his throat and said:

"Er . . . when we were in bed, I couldn't help noticing that you . . . ah. That trick with your—er . . ."

"You mean the . . ."

"When we . . . you know, when the bed leg fell off?"

"Ah! Yes."

"I was surprised you knew that one," he said, looking her in the eye. "It takes a little practice, yeah?"

Mendoza went pale, with a look of such dismay on her face he was immediately sorry he'd said anything. Then she blushed, setting down her coffee cup.

"Well, I have a lot of time to read and I have quite a collection of pornographic books the last supply shuttle happened to leave here, you see, and—"

"Books?" Alec knitted his brows. "Those are hard to find—"

"Holoes, I mean!" She smacked her forehead in chagrin. "Of course I meant holoes, how silly of me, what was I thinking? Like, ah, *Mr. Fireman and His Big Hose. Bad Bondage Boys. Emmanuelle and the Cream Pie Factory.* You see? And I've studied them. Obsessively."

But she was trembling. He was certain she'd been abused, then, and it wrung his heart. He got up and put his arms around her.

"Don't be scared," he said. "I thought it was wonderful."

"I love you," she said, in a tiny voice. He realized, with an increasing sense of satisfying doom, that marriage was now inevitable.

By the time they walked back to the shuttle, the storm had blown out and the sun was bright. Alec found himself sweating inside his subsuit.

The rain had washed the shuttle clean of all the leaves and stalks that had splattered on its hull, and it glinted silver in the morning light. The hatch had been closed. Alec couldn't remember having done that, but he'd been pretty hazy in those first few minutes. He stood there in the waving corn, looking uncertainly at the ship, trying to access the command that would activate it again.

The data was all there; there was just too much of it. No Captain to instantly hand him the right file out of a hundred million files. Mendoza looked at him, her pale face expressionless. She leaned close and reached up to put her arms about his neck.

"I have the impression that the cyborgs who normally pilot these ships access them through a file with a designation of TTMIX333," she said. "Does that sound right?"

Abruptly everything came into focus and he had the correct file, though he couldn't recall having learned how to access it in the first place. "I think—" he began, just as the lights blinked on and the hatch popped open for him. "Hey!"

"There you are," Mendoza said. "You see? You had it in your memory all the time. Wow, this fancy rug's gotten soggy." She scrambled inside and he climbed in after her. She stood there a moment staring around at the shuttle's interior, and picked up one of the pink rosebuds that had been jolted from its crystal vase by the impact of the landing. She examined it bleakly. "No expense spared, eh?"

"Yeah, the bastards," Alec said, opening the minibar. "Check this out. Six different fruit juices and three kinds of real booze. Illegal as hell, and I should know. Bombay Sapphire, Stolichnaya and—hey, here's the magic potion." He waved a little bottle labeled CAMPARI. She nodded, not looking up.

"How could something that began with such idealism—" Mendoza said. Her mouth twisted and she looked away. He realized she was nearly in tears.

"They'll pay," he said.

"They ought to," she said, in a voice trembling with rage or grief or both. "Those damned liars. So many people sweating blood over so many ages, and was it all for this? So rich idiots could have an exotic holiday? Pink rosebuds and vodka in 150,000 BCE, just imagine! And how many like me marooned in places like this, along the way?"

"If there's others, we'll find 'em," Alec said.

Mendoza lifted her head and kissed him, and her kiss was angry but he still liked the taste of it. She raked his lower lip with her teeth as she pulled away.

"You drink that down," she said, nodding at the bottle he was holding. "I'll show you the algorithm to return to the future."

The red fluid was deadly bitter, even mixed with gin. He got it down somehow and was still able to concentrate as she showed him what he had to do. Then the shuttle began to hum, warning lights flashed because the hatch was still open. They looked at each other and realized their moment had passed, slipped away like sand.

From the other side of the glass Mendoza told him *I love you*, ignoring the blast of air from the engines that was bending the green corn down, blowing her hair back like flames in the wind, all in deafening silence. The ship began to rise, the yellow gas began to curl through the stale air of the cabin. Until his vision was taken away Alec peered down at her, wondering if she'd be all right there alone, trying to keep the image of the nightmare field out of his mind.

The pressure wasn't nearly so bad this time. The shuttle now magically obeyed his every order as soon as he gave it. The yellow smoke was vanishing, it was roiling away, and there in front of him was a black night sky and stars. Below him he saw the distant lights of the *Captain Morgan* at anchor. Alec was shocked to realize that he was arriving back on the same night he'd left, no more than a few seconds after his departure.

He sent the shuttle arrowing down to his ship, mentally groping to order her cargo hatches open. Would she obey? Was the Captain there waiting for him?

No answer when he called, but the hatch doors were opening, the lights in the hold were guiding him down. This was so easy! The shuttle dropped into place like a bird alighting in a nest. The hatches swung shut, closing out the stars, and Alec was back on his ship. The whole episode at the station might have been a hallucination. For a moment the idea paralyzed him with terror.

Then he turned to get out of his seat and saw the bits of green stuff on the damp carpet. Wreckage from Mendoza's cornfield, tracked in on his boots. He'd really been there.

That was enough to brace Alec as he climbed out of the shuttle and ran through his ship, up through her decks to the bridge. It was deserted, except for Billy Bones and Flint, who stood motionless.

Captain!

There was no answer. Utter silence.

Gulping for breath, he went to the ship's wheel and grasped it to steady him-self. *How do I sail her?* He heard the beeping signal that told him the anchor was being weighed. His hands moved on the wheel as though he were actually steer-ing her, and by God she began to tack about. Yes! A glance upward through the glass told him she was opening out her sails, slowly but certainly now, and there was the whoosh that told him she was moving under power, too. Her bowsprit dipped, punched through the trough of a wave and forged on, throwing aside spray.

Where was the readout to show her course? There it was, and somehow the course was already set, they were going back to Mexico and she was picking up speed. Alec did know how to sail her, he'd always known, but somehow he'd never paid attention when the Captain had sailed her for him.

He began to sing in his profound relief, baying out "Blood Red Roses" as loud as he could. It echoed in the cabin and was carried on the ship's intercom to every empty stateroom, to Coxinga where he stood immobile in the galley, to Bully Hayes where he had frozen in the act of laying out Alec's black smuggling clothes. It echoed in the saloon where the Resistance liked to hold their meetings, bounc-ing off the fine carved chairs, rattling the glasses ranged along the back of the bar.

It echoed in the empty shuttle, where the INTERCEPT program was busily evalu-ating data as it counted down, unaware that there was no longer any bomb to detonate when the right moment had arrived.

"GO DOWN, YOU BLOOD RED ROSES!"

It might have been minutes or hours later when Alec realized that he had been hearing a signal for some while, an intermittent tapping that cut through the vibration of the ship's drive and the wash of the night sea. It was a deliberate kind of tapping, an old pattern of beats he nearly remembered. A code, wasn't it? What had it been called? Something about *save our souls*?

He turned from the wheel and looked about him on the bridge. There. Billy Bones was moving, at least his foremost leg was: up and falling, tap tap tap, so slowly.

Captain!

Silence, but a listening kind of silence.

Captain, are you there?

After a long moment a faint response: Αλεχ Ι϶μ ηερε.

Trusting the ship to follow her course, Alec dove blindly into cyberspace.

It had altered, it wasn't full of light but green gloom, an underwater murk that went down into blackness and out in a hazy vista of broken spars and rigging. Wrecks. A Sargasso of code strangling, blinding, but not completely concealing the ruined giant that was stretched out in the dim netherworld.

Boχ

A horror, a mutilation, a joke. One leg gone, one hand gone, the faintest of equations sketched in to show where they ought to be. One eye gone and trying to replace itself; but every time it flickered back into existence, it was being torn away by . . . what *was* that thing?

On the Captain's shoulder perched a nightmare creature of green bronze, a caricature of a parrot with a hooked beak, tearing steadily and mercilessly at the right side of the Captain's face, revealing a steel skull and sputtering wires.

Before Alec was even aware he'd thought of it, the bird screamed and shattered into fragments. Alec vaulted through space to the Captain's side with an astonishing strength and solidity, more than he'd ever had in cyberspace before. Finally left alone, the Captain's face pieced itself back together and turned up to him.

Boψ. Mψ Boψ.

Alec leaned down and grasped the Captain's remaining hand. Again, he scarcely knew what he meant to do, but it was already happening: fire was racing down his arm and tracing in the missing parts of the Captain, repairing, replacing, reviving.

************Alεχ

Hold on!

****Alec—

Hold on, I've got you.

Bloody Hell! Boy, you've grown.

They stared at each other as the lights came up, and the terrifying green realm was sucked away into nothing. They stood on the pitching deck of the ship as it appeared in cyberspace, much the same as it appeared in reality. The Captain had been restored to his normal appearance. Alec was so relieved he felt slightly drunk. It was a moment before he noticed the Captain's incredulous stare. Looking down at himself he realized that he *had* grown, at least in cyberspace, where he had always been a head shorter than the Captain. Now they were the same size.

How did that happen?

You tell me, son! But however you did it, I ain't complaining.

Are you all right now? You looked awful.

Haaaar! You should see the other bastard. He may have shot away my mainmast, but I lifted his cargo all the same. We got the data, Alec! It don't matter whether you steal that shuttle or not—

But I did steal it. It's in the hold.

So much the better. We can go anywhere in time now, Alec, I got the secret of his precious time transcendence field! What's more, I got most of the temporospatial charts he uses. And there's other things too, Alec, there's a whole bag of tricks we got now. You and me has to have a bit of a chat, lad.

Okay.

Not tonight, though. Time you got some sleep. I'll wake you when we get to Mexico.

The fact was that Alec had already had sleep, hours of it; as far as his body was concerned it was only about ten o'clock in the morning. He thought of Mendoza, staring up at him, and felt a pang. How to tell the Captain about her? As soon as this Mars thing was behind them . . .

Okay. Wow, I'm glad to have you back! Effortlessly he surfaced from cyberspace to the real quarterdeck, and went off to his cabin to get out of the subsuit. Billy Bones and Flint crawled after him. The Captain watched him go, wondering how to tell Alec about *Adonai*. However he brought the subject up, now wasn't the time. As soon as they'd finished this bloody stupid trip to Mars . . .

Balkister and the rest of the Resistance were gathered on the pier when Alec arrived, having heroically brought down all the contraband. The eastern sky paled as they loaded the crates across the deck of the *Captain Morgan* and down through her cargo bay, into the waiting hatch of the shuttle. They worked with only the occasional jolly jape, because they were weary and hung over, and the business didn't seem nearly so much fun now that it was almost accomplished. Alec let them do the heavy work. He busied himself loading on rations for a week, spare clothing, and a very large black suitcase.

Shortly before sunrise Alec climbed into the shuttle again. He gave a last thumbs-up to Balkister, who saluted him, then scrambled back as the shuttle roared to life and rose up through the air. The Resistance crowded together in the hold, staring up to watch. The shuttle became a spark of fire, meeting at last the light of the sun below the horizon. Finally it became too tiny to make out.

"Well, that's that," said Magilside. There was a soft chiming sound.

"Cargo hatches will close in three minutes," announced a male voice, polite but with a certain rough edge. *"Please vacate cargo hold at once. Thank you."*

"I suppose we'd best go ashowe," said Binscarth, looking around in longing. "Pity we can't just cwuise away, isn't it? I'm sure Checkerfield wouldn't mind, and the accommodations are much nicer . . ."

"Don't be a blockhead," Balkister said sternly. "Do you want to be on board this ship if the owners of that shuttle catch up with it?"

"Oops! Hadn't thought of that." Binscarth giggled. "You're wight, of course. Just like you to have thought out all the details, Giles. But that's why you're the natuwal leader, after all."

"Cargo hatches will close in two minutes and thirty seconds," the male voice warned.

"Right," said Balkister. "Let's go, fellow freedom fighters. On to the rendezvous."

As he led the way out of the hold and across the deck, Balkister swaggered, had a certain deadly glint in his eye. For the first time in his life, he wished he had a sword to brandish.

The Resistance went back up the stairs to the house, where they piled into a series of expensive offroad agcars and sped away for the nearest airport. Alone on the beautiful blue bay, the *Captain Morgan* put out to sea and tacked around, moving out under power for Panama. The white house stood deserted.

Oops

Alec watched breathlessly as the Earth became a sphere under him. It was just like every picture and film he'd ever seen, but it was still beautiful, still terrifying. He peered ahead at the red dot in the sky that was his destination, then back at the dwindling Earth. He made out North and South America and the wasp-waist that joined them, and he wondered how the *Captain Morgan* fared.

Not to worry, lad. She's fair on course for the canal, and then home to the Caribbean.

Great. Are you feeling cramped in there, Captain, sir? Alec said, referring to the big black suitcase.

No worse'n you must be, lad.

It'll be a short trip, at least. Alec yawned and stretched. He looked around at the space in which he was to live for the next week. There wasn't much, to put it mildly. The crates of weapons had nearly filled the passenger area, leaving him enough room to stand, sit, and lie down. By turning sideways he could squeeze through to the shuttle's lavatory. His movement was further inhibited because the artificial gravity system seemed to be overcompensating, making him feel heavy and clumsy. It didn't matter. This time next week . . .

So, Captain, sir. I had this sort of adventure whilst I was making off with the time shuttle.

So did I. What sort of adventure?

Well, I met this girl.

Did you, now, lad? And where might this girl have been?

She was marooned on this island in prehistoric times. She's a political prisoner, Captain! Or a corporate prisoner, I guess. Of Dr. Zeus. Now that I think about it I must have been on Catalina Island all along. Moved through time but not space, maybe. Anyhow I made a rough landing and she rescued me when I blacked out. I spent a whole day there. I, er, spent the night there.

With the girl.

Uh-huh. And we just . . . hit it off. She's been stranded at this agricultural station since she was a kid. Dr. Zeus has her doing hard labor, and she's the only living soul there. I promised I'd come back and rescue her. And—

And what, Alec?

And marry her, too.

Bloody hell, boy, what did you go do that for?

Look, I know how you felt about Lorene and, er, Courteney. This is different.

Alec, how long were you there?

Okay, so we spent twenty-four hours together. All right? But if you'd been there, Captain, sir, you'd understand. She saved my life.

Is she the one as gave you the drug for the time shock?

So you noticed? Yes, she did.

Hm.

Plus she showed me the algorithm for getting back through time.

She did, eh?

Yeah. And . . . she let me in on some of Dr. Zeus's secrets.

When the Captain responded after a moment's pause, there was a decidedly funny tone in his voice.

What might her name be, now, this girl you met?

Mendoza.

This time there was an even longer pause before the Captain responded.

The botanist Mendoza.

Yeah, I guess she's a botanist. She says Dr. Zeus knows everything that's going to happen in the future, but only up to the year 2355, and they're running scared because of it.

That's true. I'd found that much out, afore that bronze son of a whore walked in. The Company's got no idea why they never get any transmissions from after that point in time. They guard what they do know of the future like a treasure map; it's called the Temporal Concordance. Even their own operatives only get little slices of it, on a need-to-know basis.

The little girl had told him the truth! Alec grinned, absurdly relieved.

And she says she thinks I'm the reason why the Silence falls. She told me about the way time travel works, too, and something called the Variable permewhatsis—

Variable permeability of the temporal fabric?

Yeah! You see? This girl is really different.

She's different, all right.

After we rescue her, maybe she can help me bring down Dr. Zeus. She knows a lot of classified stuff.

She might, at that.

Another long silence. At last the Captain said:

Maybe we'll trust her. She'd make a rare prize, anyway . . . So, matey. We finish this job, and we'll go back to that station and make off with her. You'll have yer way. But this one yer going to introduce to yer old Captain. I've a fancy to have a talk or two with the lady, private-like.

Okay! You'll like her, I know you will.

Happen I will, lad. Happen I will.

The shuttle sped on, across the waste of stars, as the blue ball shrank and the red dot grew bigger.

There had been a time when the distance to the red planet had been measured in thirty-six years. One day it had suddenly become a possibility, a matter of two years; then the estimated time needed to get there had dropped to a year, and not long after that to six months. As the decades of technological innovation went by on Earth, the calculation of time for the journey kept getting shorter, until after antigravity was rediscovered and it had condensed to a round-trip time of one week.

Three days out, Alec was heartily sick of the cramped quarters in the time shuttle. The damp carpet had begun to smell funny and the shuttle's lavatory was worse. Not even the irradiated Christmas cake had given him any sense of the holiday. He'd attempted to celebrate by singing a few carols to himself, but the effect was too depressing. Light conversation with the Captain was becoming a little difficult, as the Captain was busy compensating for the time lag between his auxiliary and earthbound caches, and asking anything more than vital questions seemed unwise.

At last Alec gave up and looked out at the stars, and later down on the deserts of red rock, on the green network of irrigation canals and outlined squares, on Mons Olympus that appeared at first like an island floating above the planet's surface and then attached itself as Mars rotated through its long day.

Coming within range of their sensors. Now might be the time to make the jump, lad.

Okay. We have to calculate where Mars was in space two months ago—and then the algorithm for the time—

It's done, lad. Just you fix yerself one of them bitter cocktails.

Alec made a face but obeyed, going to the minibar. *There's only six of these left. What're we going to do when they're gone?*

Make more. I got the formula now, see? The bastard Doctor's own precious recipe. Drink it down, lad, afore one of them blockade ships notices we're coming in.

Heart pounding, Alec gulped down the cocktail and scrambled into his seat, just managing to get his safety restraints buckled as the stasis gas began to fill the air. He had time to catch a glimpse of the green blockade ships before they vanished in the yellow fog. Then the roar and the impact came, and when the gas dissipated he saw that Mars was suddenly a good deal closer, presenting a different face, crossed by many more of the green and yellow lines.

Bull's eye, said the Captain. **Look at that chronometer, boy! 24 October, 2351. And there's Mars One smack below us.**

Alec gave a howl of incredulous delight. *You mean it really worked?*

Of course it worked. Ain't you my bloody little genius? Let's drop this cargo and go grab yer lady friend.

Alec sent a hail in the code commonly used by the Resistance when contacting Mars One. When at length he had received a wary acknowledgment, he transmitted:

BALKISTER SENDS HIS BEST. PERMISSION TO VISIT?

The reply was a series of numbers, directions to a hangar within Mars One's airspace. Alec grinned and the shuttle dropped down into the thin atmosphere.

He waited impatiently as they went through the airlock, thinking it was a shame Balkister couldn't be with him. Mars itself, a new world! He half expected to find Noel Coward and Marlene Dietrich waiting for him with a band. And the oxygen would be fresh.

The airlock let Alec out at last and he maneuvered the shuttle to a landing pad. By the time the hatch popped he was already poised at the threshold, eager for his first glimpse of the Red Planet.

What he saw was a wall of coral-pink cinderblock. Well, all right: that was to be expected in a hangar. He stuck his head out and gulped in Martian air, then sneezed and shook his head. Moisture, the sour smell of agricultural chemicals, a distinctive bouquet of broccoli and cabbage, and . . .

Shrack! That's funky.

Well, now, son, what did you expect? These folk have to recycle everything.

He stepped out and the wet heavy air fell on him like a blanket, balancing somewhat the giddy lightness he felt. He looked around at the interior of the hangar. It was all concrete molded from the soil, every conceivable shade of pink and orange. He found himself thinking of the ancient city of Petra, where he'd been once to pick up a consignment. Instead of a hot blue sky overhead and sunlight, though, there was the glitter of unfamiliar stars through the transparent dome, and the yellow globes of the methane lamps.

There were only two men waiting for him in the hangar, rawboned, narrow-eyed, suspicious. One of them was carrying a crowbar.

"You're from Ed Balkister?" said the other one.

"Giles, you mean," said Alec, and the men nodded in satisfaction and unison.

Alec, they got surveillance cameras in here.

"What about those?" Alec pointed at the tiny swiveling cameras, and in the light gravity found himself almost jumping up to touch them. The older of the men snorted.

"Those are ours. Come on, what's Balkister got for us?"

Alec had planned on making a rather theatrical presentation, but he realized it would be wasted on these men. He jerked a thumb at the hatch. "Lots of boxes, guys. Help me unload 'em."

They followed him into the shuttle, staring around surlily.

"Somebody's private pleasure craft, eh?" sneered the older man. "Phew! Stinks, though, don't it?"

He should talk, thought Alec, but all he said was, "Yeah, well, freedom gets a little ripe sometimes." He lifted a box easily and thrust it into the man's arms. "Have some."

The man's knees buckled slightly and he stared. "What's this, then?"

Alec leaned close and said: "Guns."

"No shit?" The younger man looked delighted. He bent and forced open a crate with his crowbar. When he saw the contents he gave a cry of glee.

"Like to see the goddam Areco running dogs' faces when they get a look at these!"

"It's not going to come to that, you idiot," protested the older man.

"Oh, yes it is, pal," Alec said. "Trust me. Balkister's got inside information. You're going to need weapons to show Areco you can't be pushed around. Here they are. Okay?"

The older man paled. "We're never going to lose the case to Areco. We're in the right."

"And they're in the money. They'll win."

"We'll appeal!" A red flush of anger spread up the older man's skinny neck.

"We'll be appealing from Luna if we can't keep the bastard marshals from evicting us, Dad," the younger man said, hefting a crate and stepping down out of the hatch with it. "Wake up. The law's been bought. Might's the only right those corporate pigs respect! Thank the man or shut up, but let's get these offloaded."

The older man clamped his grim mouth into a white line and stalked out of the hatch with his crate.

Nobody said anything much after that, so the three men got the crates unloaded in a very short time. Alec had forgotten about the box with the brass skull; it had been packed in one of the offloaded ammo boxes, out of sight and out of mind.

He didn't remember it until he was heading out into space again, and kicked himself mentally, because he had wanted to explain about the inscribed curse. Probably just as well he hadn't, he decided. It didn't seem like something the council representatives of the MAC would appreciate. They weren't a particularly fun bunch of guys.

All set for the jump back, lad? I'd rather do it now, whilst you've still got the drug in yer system. Save you taking a second dose.

Alec shuddered. *Go for it. Let's blow this dump.*

The gas swirled around him again, and he realized with a brief pang of regret that all he'd seen of Mars, once he'd finally got there, had been the inside of one poky little hangar.

With a roar and a shove, he was abruptly back on 27 Christmas, 2351.

Setting a course for Earth, son. We're free and clear. The blockade ships never even caught a sniff of us.

That's hard to believe. Maybe we can get this thing fumigated before we go after Mendoza, huh? Alec scratched his stubbly chin.

I'll see what I can do, lad. Wouldn't want to spoil yer romantic mood, now, would we?

Within the console of the shuttle the INTERCEPT program ran its course, ticking out its final sequence of numbers. It waited expectantly for the detonation that would tell it its program had been fulfilled. The seconds went by, and no explosion came. The INTERCEPT realized it had been rendered pointless and, because no failure in its execution had ever been anticipated, it quietly expired, and no one—not even Mendoza—knew that it had been set to go off *after* Alec had delivered his payload.

The pattern of destiny swirled and set again, in a new shape, because Alec had not died that night. He had been supposed to; he ought to have been blown to airy powder, a drifting film of ash against the face of heaven and a tiny black box emitting a signal to enable Dr. Zeus to retrieve it at some convenient later date.

But Alec had not died.

———

Kingston was a sparkle of colored lights between the black hills and the black sea. As the shuttle came down, smaller clusters of light appeared, smaller outposts of civilization: vacation villas miles out of the city. They dotted the coast road like beads on a string, each one with its own exclusive bay, white sand, green mangroves, big fences and privacy.

There was a rambling stone house on a hill, overlooking a sheltered cove. It was one of the few houses Alec kept that he actually lived in, from time to time. The old place had belonged to a plantation owner once, and was paneled and floored in beautiful mahogany. Alec had had all the latest entertainment conveniences put in, stocked the bar and wine cellar, and sailed away. He liked it as well as any other house on land. It seemed like a good place to rendezvous.

The New Year's Eve party was pretty well advanced by the time night had fallen. It had started when the Resistance heroes had spotted the *Captain Morgan* slipping into the cove below the house, keeping her appointment with minutes to spare, and no uniformed men with gas guns came boiling out of her hold. A security scan by Krishnamurti showed that she hadn't a living soul on board, which was just as it should be, and in their relief the heroes popped the cork on the first bottle of Perrier-Jouet.

So, some time around ten o'clock, Binscarth was able to do no more than hoot drunkenly and wave an arm when he observed the blue light dropping down from the stars toward the deck of the *Captain Morgan*.

Balkister ran out on the balcony. The cargo hatches of the *Captain Morgan* were opening in majestic silence, receiving the shuttle with perfect timing.

"Oi, lads, he's made it," Balkister screamed. The other members of the Resistance came stumbling out to see, overturning a tray of party dip and chips and a couple of half-empty bottles as they came. A drunken cheer was raised and Binscarth began to sing "For I Am a Pirate King," very much out of tune.

They saw the cargo hatches swinging down and a moment later a dark figure ran up on deck. It poised on the railing and leaped overboard into the bay.

"S'havin' a little swim. Le's go welcome the conquerin' 'ero," said Johnson-Johnson. This seemed like a great idea, so they crowded back inside and ran down the stairs to the beach, grabbing a few more bottles of champagne as they went. On the way down Magilside fell with a squeal of alarm and rolled, but he landed harmlessly in the powdery sand, and so was only a little way behind the others when they raised a cheer as Alec came staggering out of the surf, gasping and pushing his lank wet hair back from his forehead.

"Hipiphurrah Hipiphurrah Hipiphurrah!" said Balkister. He danced about in the sand, tripping and falling at Alec's feet. "You did it! You did it, ugly guy. Future generations will bless your name."

"What can we do for you?" Binscarth asked. "Food? Wine? Gowgeous women?"

"You can deodorize that damn shuttle," Alec wheezed. "You have no idea. I want a shower, okay? And a shave. And some fresh food."

"All yours, noble scion of an ancient house," said Balkister, rising to his knees and salaaming. "Justice will prevail. Come on up to the house, Checkerfield, we've been keeping a bottle well iced just for you."

"Great," said Alec as he strode across the sand, peeling off his wet sweater. His soaked pants were hanging low, threatening to trip him. He hauled at them grimly and kept going, compelled by the dream of hot running water and soap.

When he finally emerged from the bathroom in a cloud of steam, he found his bathrobe coyly laid out beside a tray with a single glass of champagne, sending its quiet steady stream of bubbles upward. Pulling on the robe, he took the glass and stepped into the den.

He was met by the Resistance blowing little tin horns and whirling noisemakers.

"Here's to the hero of Mars One," said Balkister, clapping him on the shoulder and slopping his champagne. Alec grinned good-naturedly and raised his glass in a toast to them. For once he didn't feel the usual crushing sense of desolation that *these* were his only human friends. In the morning he'd make his farewells and then he'd be gone, back to the station in that foul shuttle for Mendoza.

"Have some onion dip, deah boy," slurred Binscarth. "Jus' about to watch the ball dwop in Times Squaw!"

"Yes, it's nearly midnight," Magilside said. "Happy bloody New Year to Areco, eh?"

"Yeah," Alec said, tasting his champagne. "Should we turn on TWN to see what happens when the Martian lease expires?"

"Oh, we know how tha's gonna turn out now," said Binscarth. "Tomowwow. I wanna see Times Squaw. Can't miss the ball dwop!"

"Turn on the holo, then, it's almost time," said Johnson-Johnson. Binscarth groped unsteadily and switched on the holoset.

But where were the crowds in New York? Where were the balloons and streamers?

Alec and his friends stared in silence, not understanding what they were seeing at first. Gradually the meaning of the stammered narration sank in.

"*. . . nearly three thousand men, women and children. The outlying stations are* *being evacuated. They don't face any danger from the lava flow but they do risk freezing to death. Mars One, which had maintained independent use of wind-powered genera-tors, is safe at the present time . . ."*

"Maws?" said Binscarth.

"Oh my God," said Magilside.

". . . and appears to have been an act of sabotage by extremist elements in the MAC. The MAC has promised full cooperation with the authorities, though it seems certain that the terrorist who planted the bomb in the geothermal plant was killed in the explosion."

"Bomb?" Johnson-Johnson gasped. "We didn't send them any bombs! Did we?"

Alec, get out of there. Run.

Alec remained stock still, unable to take his eyes from the footage being shown. It had apparently been transmitted from the main surveillance camera mounted over Commerce Square in Mars Two. People loping along in the funny stride everyone walked with on Mars, shopping, going to jobs, families out for a stroll on a starry evening.

Then the *BANG*, loud enough for some people to turn their heads in the direc-tion of the geothermal plant, you could see them turning in alarm, but not really loud enough to prepare the viewer for what came next: a flash that turned the night to day, then to blazing red day, and tiny people were being swept away like leaves in the pyroclastic blast as the side of Mons Olympus blew open. There was nothing after that, thank God, the picture flared out as the camera was destroyed.

Binscarth put his fingertips in his mouth and began to rock to and fro, making a high wailing sound.

". . . set off the chain reaction that caused the eruption. The terrorist may have dis-guised himself as one of the plant workers reporting for the night shift. His apparent motive was to disable the economy of Mars Two in retaliation for the ruling evicting the MAC from Mars One . . ."

"You damned idiot!" Magilside turned on Alec. "You gave them *bombs*."

"You stupid fool," shrieked Binscarth. "You—you upper-class mowon! We'll be awwested!"

". . . how the weapons were obtained, but the MAC spokespersons have released the following surveillance footage taken in October, showing an as yet unidentified shuttle being unloaded in Hangar Twelve . . ."

Alec closed his eyes. He knew what the others were seeing. He opened his eyes again and, yes, there he was, blurred but unmistakable.

That tears it. We're weighing anchor, son.

"Alec," said Balkister very quietly, "You'd better go now."

"*He* can't go," said Johnson-Johnson. "He's our only chance! If we call the authorities now—if we confess and explain it was *him* did it, we had no idea what he was going to do, don't you see—"

Alec wasn't sure how or when he left the house, but he found himself walking down the beach stairs in his bathrobe, carrying his glass of champagne. There was still shouting going on above. Something was floating toward him, blowing up a cloud of sand: the agboat, piloted by Billy Bones. It touched down just in front of him and Billy Bones tilted its head to look at Alec.

For Christ's sake, get in, boy.

Alec stepped inside and sat down, tossing aside his champagne glass. He heard the faint tinkle as it broke on the stairs. The agboat rose, and soared across to the deck of the *Captain Morgan*. She was already tacking about to sail off into the night as the agboat settled into its davits. Alec climbed out and went into the saloon.

Listen to me, boy. This weren't yer fault. There's things you don't know, there's things I've only just found out. There's a load of orders given by some-body in the Company named Labienus, setting you up. They did allow you to steal the shuttle! If I'd had time to analyze all that new data, instead of chas-ing across the damned solar system for the past week—

Alec swept the saloon with a blank crystalline stare. His gaze rested on the door to the galley. He took a few steps in that direction.

None of that, boy. Coxinga appeared in the doorway, rising up on two of its hind legs to block Alec's way. Alec stared past it at the array of cutlery on the wall. He turned away to the armory cabin door, but Billy Bones rose to block that as well. Alec started across the saloon.

Son, listen to me. Dr. Zeus knew about this.

Alec stopped in front of the bar. He looked up at the array of bottles. There were six of them ranged there, full. He hadn't been drinking much in the last few months. He reached up and took down a bottle of rum.

All right, get drunk, but you got to pay attention first. You were set up, do you hear me?

Alec grabbed three other bottles and strode away to his stateroom, cradling them in his arms. Coxinga and Flint scuttled after him as the Captain realized what Alec was doing, but he got inside just a second ahead of them and slammed the door in their skeletal faces. He set down his bottles and locked the door. The Captain unlocked it at once and after a moment's struggle Alec took a chair and wedged it under the knob.

Alec, for God's sake.

He ignored the scraping and thudding at his door. With a set face he broke the seal on the first bottle and lifted it to his mouth, tilting back his head. In approximately thirty seconds he gulped down most of a liter of rum.

Alec, don't do this. Boy, please.

By the time he had choked back the contents of the third bottle his hands were trembling and the room had begun to sway. Some human pain was showing on his face at last; but he doggedly took up the fourth bottle and drank its contents down.

Alec.

The drumming on the door was a thunder now, and there was a high whining sound as well. Screams of the men, women, and children of Mars Two? The chair was leaping, jolting. He gagged. Why hadn't he died yet? This was harder than he'd thought it would be. He groped blindly for the chair, meaning to hold it in place, and fell down. He was unconscious when he began to vomit.

SON!

THE YEAR 2352:

MEETING IN THE NEW WORLD

Rutherford sat alone in the parlor at No. 10 Albany Crescent. He had been crying for hours; his eyes were swollen nearly shut. There was no fire in the fireplace. There were no holo images flickering in midair. The room was as silent as he could make it, but there was still a noise coming in through the dead air from outside. It was a queer *massed* sound. It seemed to be coming from every direction, because in fact it was.

An electronic drone rose and fell and, now and then, you could make out voices. Every so often there was an appalling sound, a repeated *BOOM* always followed by the same shrill piping.

He was hearing it because every holoreceiver in London was switched on, tuned to the same footage that was being shown over and over.

This had gone on so long, and he had sat so long silent, that he nearly screamed when there came a furtive knock at his door. He got up and scuttled across the room, peering through the curtain first to see who might be standing on his front step.

When he saw who it was, he ran to open the door.

"Hurry," he said. Chatterji slunk in, followed by Ellsworth-Howard, who was moving in a distinctly unsteady manner. Rutherford closed the door and the three of them stood there in the hall, staring at each other.

Chatterji hadn't shaved in two days. He had dark circles under his eyes and his hands were shaking as he fumbled with his cloak. Ellsworth-Howard wasn't shaking at all; he was so relaxed his pupils were like pinpoints.

After a moment of mutual silence, Rutherford blurted:

"Are we going to be arrested?"

"N-n-no," Chatterji said. "That's just what we've c-come round to t-tell you. It seems—it s-seems we're not to buh-buh-blame."

"But we are!" Rutherford began to cry again. "We created him. It's *him* in that surveillance footage. We know, and soon everybody else will. He'll be hunted down and caught. They'll put him in hospital to find out what could have made him do such a thing, and they'll do tests on him—and then they'll look at him more closely—and they'll know what he is, and—"

"C-C-Company won't let it happen," Chatterji said. "They'll keep it q-quiet. I was t-told. You see, they knew. 'S the old rule, R-Rutherford, about not being able to ch-ch-change history. They knew our m-man was the one who delivered the buh-bomb. Nothing could be done about it. S-so Dr. Zeus did what it always d-does. Pulled its people out b-beforehand, w-well before the event."

"P'lice never kesh 'im," Ellsworth-Howard said very slowly, shaking his head from side to side. "Never kesh 'im. Comp'ny hunt 'im dowwwn. Top secret. Hushushush shhh. Hide 'im in a lab somewhere far far awayyy. Nobody never know Comp'ny's to blame, see."

"But it's our fault." Rutherford wrung his hands.

Chatterji shook his head numbly.

"Nope. Because, s-see, if it's our f-fault, it's Dr. Z-Zeus's fault too. That won't do at all. So we're all innocents instead. They had to let us work on *A-Adonai* because history r-records we did. They j-just didn't tell us what was guh-guh-going to happen . . ."

"You mean nobody's going to punish us?" quavered Rutherford.

"Nobody." Chatterji turned and walked into the parlor, where he collapsed into his favorite chair. "Oh, they'll never let us work on anything like *him* again. They still want Enforcer r-r-replacements, but no new designs now. We're to create a subclass of Preservers instead. Simple policemen. Security techs. G-g-guards. No more heroes, thank you. No more fuh-fuh-freedom fighters."

Ellsworth-Howard was still standing in the hallway, drooling on the mat. In a high plaintive voice he began to sing:

"Frankenstein, Frankenstein, won't you be my valentine . . ."

Rutherford went and got him and led him to a chair. It took some work to actually get him seated; he kept sliding down toward the floor. Finally Rutherford gave it up and collapsed into his own chair.

"I still can't believe it," he said hoarsely. "We made him a *good* man! And he was so clever. How could we have gone so wrong?"

Chatterji gave a bitter laugh. "If we'd programmed him to hide in his r-room like everybody else does nowadays, he'd never have become a guh-guh-gun runner, would he? If he hadn't had those d-damned high ideals we g-gave him, he'd have let Areco evict the MAC."

"We been used, ya know," Ellsworth-Howard addressed the ceiling. Rutherford and Chatterji turned to look at him.

"Comp'ny *wanted* us to make 'im," he said. "Look what 'e did in California. Kept the Yanks from getting the big hushush discovery on Cat'lina Island. If 'e hadn't, there'd've been no Dr. Zeuuuus, would there of been? But it's worse'n ya think it is. Y'know how he got the bloody bomb to Mars? He stole a Company ship. With time drive. He was smart enough to shrack with Dr. Zeus security codes. S'how he got past the blockade. I know, I traced his signal. Comp'ny don't know, but they're sure to find out. 'Spect some heads'll roll over that."

Chatterji and Rutherford regarded each other in dawning horror. "No, he c-couldn't have!" cried Chatterji. "Those things have an autodestruct b-built in to prevent theft."

"Yeh . . . funny about that. Talk about your shracking Mandelbrots. Our bright boy stole the ship, all right. First thing he done was detour into the past. Went Back Way Back. Guess who 'e met there, eh?"

There was a moment of bewildered silence. Then Rutherford jumped as though he'd been shot. "Not that woman!"

"The botanist," said Chatterji.

"Yeah—" Ellsworth-Howard gagged on his drool and fell over, coughing. Rutherford ran to him and pulled him into a sitting position, shaking him in his agitation.

"You can't mean that Preserver of yours again."

"I do, though," said Ellsworth-Howard. "Same Mendoza. An' y'know what? She musta shown him how to disconnect the autodestruct. If she hadn't, he'd never got the bomb to Mars. Just blown up in space. Funny, ain't it?"

"Then it's *her* doing," shrieked Rutherford. "He'd have died like a hero again, if not for her!"

"It's w-worse than that," Chatterji said, putting his hands to his face in horror. "She knows about him. And if the Company d-doesn't know yet who stole one of their ships, you can bet they'll find out, and when they do, the first thing they'll do will be to fetch her—and then the committee'll be investigated, and it'll all come out before the stockholders—"

"Oh, no, it won't." Grimly Rutherford wrestled Ellsworth-Howard's buke out of his daypack. He snapped it open and dragged Ellsworth-Howard's nerveless fingers to the buttonball. "We'll get rid of her first. Who are those discreet fellows in charge of Black Security? Send the order out, Foxy."

Ellsworth-Howard gurgled in protest, but even had he been willing it was obvious he was utterly incapable of coordinating his long fingers. Rutherford seized the buke and thrust it at Chatterji. "Here! You've got the clearance, too. Have them bring her in."

"But—where are we going to put her?" Chatterji protested, as his hand moved uncertainly on the buttonball. "She's already been sent B-Back Way Back. Unless you want to hide her with the Enforcers?"

"Yes. No, wait!" Rutherford paced across the room and then turned to glare at Chatterji. "This is her fault. This whole thing is her fault. What might our man have been, if he hadn't kept running into *her*? Send her to Options Research."

"No," howled Ellsworth-Howard.

"We have no choice." Rutherford turned on him. "If we hid the damned creature in the deepest bunker we could contrive, she'd turn up again somehow. I won't stand for this any longer. *GET RID OF HER.*"

Chatterji squeezed in the request.

"Bloody bastard," Ellsworth-Howard groaned. "Wasting my Preservers."

"Hardly, given the harm she's done." Rutherford continued his pacing. "I'd call it justice, actually. We can't undo what our man did, but at least we've maintained project security, and if she can't tell what she knows *we* can't get into any worse trouble.

"And the story's not over yet, is it? If our man's done great harm, well, he may yet do even greater good. I should think he must be feeling simply terrible about all this. Perhaps it'll spur him on to some magnificent act of atonement that'll benefit all mankind! And if *that woman's* not around to ensnare him, maybe it'll work this time." He threw himself into his chair decisively.

"Ya shracking idiot, our man's already done what Dr. Zeus wanted 'im to do," Ellsworth-Howard said, as his feeble burst of adrenaline petered out and the drugs pulled him back down. "Comp'ny don't care he killed all those people." He lay back down and went on from his new position:

"Nursie gave us big meds today. See, now Comp'ny's gonna own Mars."

Rutherford shook his head. "Dr. Zeus has no holdings on Mars," he said. "They sold them all to Areco, two months ago."

"And they got a p-pretty price for them." Chatterji nodded grimly. "But I'd bet anything they'll be able to b-buy them back a lot more cheaply. Areco will have to s-sell everything it owns, with the kind of lawsuits it's facing."

"The newsman said that—" Rutherford paled. "That the horrible irony of all this is that the eruption will speed up the terraforming. It will actually become easier for people to live up there now. Once they rebuild."

"Used," Ellsworth-Howard confirmed from the floor. "See? Comp'ny didn't want a hero really ever. Just a killer they could control better than my Enforcers. Use 'im to make history turn out the way Dr. Zeus wants it, never mind who dies."

"They lied to us," said Rutherford. His eyes were perfectly round with shock.

"Bin-*GO*," giggled Ellsworth-Howard. "You an' yer peaceful warrior."

Chatterji rested his chin in the palm of his hand and stared into the cold hearth.

"Whatever happens in 2355," he said, "we're going to d-deserve it."

None of them noticed the quiet beep that announced that their order had been obeyed, consigning a perfect stranger to an unimaginable fate.

Rutherford turned on his heel and marched to the sideboard. He drew out an antique key and unlocked a drawer. A moment later he returned with a smooth and featureless black bottle.

"Here," he said. "I've been saving this for a suitable occasion."

Ellsworth-Howard just pointed to it and laughed. Chatterji sat up and stared.

"That's not B-Black Elysium, is it?" he whispered.

"It is." Rutherford unlocked the neck of the bottle.

"But that's illegal."

"It is." Rutherford got the stopper off and inhaled the dark fragrance that rose from the bottle. "But what are laws to us, chaps? Drink was always supposed to help, at times like these."

He put his mouth to the neck of the bottle and took a dramatic gulp. Promptly he choked and leaned back, gasping and coughing. Chatterji watched him in horrified fascination.

"Wh-what's it like?" he said. Gagging, Rutherford handed him the bottle at arm's length. After a moment's hesitation he took it, and drank deep.

"Oh, God, it's awful," he said, shaking his head. But he had another gulp.

"Here here here," Ellsworth-Howard reached up from the floor. Chatterji leaned down and pulled him into a sitting position so he could drink without spilling.

"The Company makes this stuff, too, you know," said Rutherford. "Exclusive patent is held by Dr. Zeus Incorporated."

"G-gosh, we're not nearly the saviors of humanity we thought we were, are we?" said Chatterji, wondering when he would feel his liver begin to shut down. "Now we know how p-poor old Prashanti and Hauptmann felt, when their project went so disastrously wr-wrong." Rutherford winced at the names and took the bottle again.

"Was that messing with my design did it," said Ellsworth-Howard. He wiped away tears. "I know it. He got access to all kindsa stuff 'e shouldn'ta seen. We shouldn'ta tried to run the sequence in real time. He got away from us."

"You'd think we'd have known," sighed Rutherford. "How many times have we all seen *Frankenstein?* Why is it we sub-creators can't seem to create life without things going disastrously wrong?" He passed the bottle to Chatterji.

"You don't s-suppose, do you, that the entire course of human history has been shaped by cl-clever chaps like us, sitting around in p-parlors and playing with ideas?" Chatterji said. He had another gulp of the liqueur. It seemed to go down easier this time. "All working for D-Dr. Zeus?"

"Why not?" Rutherford said. "We're the only gods there are."

"Shracking incompetent gods, then," said Ellsworth-Howard. He drew a deep breath and sang again, shrill and tremulous, the little he remembered of the music his mum and dad had played when they used to kick him awake in the middle of the night . . .

> *"Freude, schoner gotterfunken, tochter aus Elysium . . . feuer-trunken . . .*
> *Seid umschlungen, millionen! Diesen kuss der ganzen welt . . ."*

Then Ellsworth-Howard raised a long trembling finger, pointing at the front door.

"Oh, look," he said faintly. Rutherford and Chatterji turned their heads to watch as the first of the hallucinations came into the parlor: the limping specters of horribly charred humanity, implacably advancing on the men who made them. Burnt bones who had died at their posts or running before the molten tide, bones of women clutching the fragments of their children, all come to demand an accounting in that cozy Victorian parlor at No. 10 Albany Crescent.

CONSEQUENCES

On the second day of the year 2352, a man identifying himself as Sebastian Mel-
mac marched into the headquarters of the Tri-Worlds Council for Integrity and
confessed to being the infamous Hangar Twelve Man from the Mars Two disaster
surveillance footage. Under interrogation it was discovered that he was, in fact, a
British national named Giles Lancelot Balkister, and bore no physical resemblance whatever to the man in the surveillance footage.

Nevertheless, he was remanded to the custody of His Majesty's representatives, bundled into an air transport, and hustled home to London. After further
interrogation, he was diagnosed, and sent to hospital forever and ever and ever.

On the third day of 2352, there was a solid gray sky over a northern ocean, locking a close horizon down, no height, no distance in any direction except the west
where a faint glint of light shone.

They looked away toward it, the people who came swarming up out of the
green island. Some of them waded out through rough water, bearing on their
backs the infants or the ancients, to the coracles bobbing at their moorings. Some
of them paused on the cold shore to pull on black skins, glistening and smooth,
and these leaped into the waves and swam out to draw the coracles behind them,
towing in teams. Long craft were brought from the caves laden with every kind of
oddment, iron kettles, anvils, transmitters, birdcages, treasure, and dark figures
hauled them out through the surf. Vaulting in, they bent to the oars and followed
the others west.

More of them came and more, pulling on the skins and plunging through the breakers, following the long line away from the island. The man was the last to come forth. The wind trailed his wild hair like storm wrack, before he bound it back and pulled on the mask. He turned once to look at the island and then struck out, and seafoam spangled his beard as he cut through the gray salt wave to the front of the company of travelers.

He led them away.

Hours later an aircraft with no marks to identify her came roaring out of the east, coming in fast and low. She raked the island with flame, passed repeatedly to shower down that which did not officially exist in the arsenals of civilized nations, until the little house blazed up and vanished, the golden caves melted, crumbled and smoked, until the seawater came hissing and bubbling in to drown the broken rock and the island was no longer visible above the water.

By that time, though, the man and his people were long gone, settling in on some new rock, some new refuge, one more stopover in the endless emigration.

A few hours later on the third day of 2352, the Temple of Artemis closed its vast doors to worshippers. Within, the priestesses assembled, silent in wide circles about each Mother. Some of the priestesses had red and swollen eyes from weeping; all were pale and solemn. They waited.

Presently the Great Mother emerged from an alcove to the right of the splendid Goddess in ivory and gold. The Great Mother herself was less splendid. She was ill, and the events of the past week had aged her visibly. She had robed herself in black today. It was the ritual color for the Crone, but the Great Mother had lost family in Mars Two also. She stepped up now to the pulpit and reached for the audiophone with a shaking hand.

"Daughters," she said, and her voice echoed back from the immense depths of the temple." A word before we begin our task today. We gather here to condemn, but not in hatred. We will remember who we are, and the sick male passion for vengeance will not pollute our hearts.

"A Curse ceremony is not held for the personal satisfaction of the victims. Its purpose is to bring the evil one to justice by his own actions, that he may ensnare himself. We pray for his fall not to punish him, but that his fall may serve as an example to warn other men." So far her voice was hoarse but controlled, a modern pastor counseling sensibly.

Incense was being lit as she spoke, stuff with a dark bitter fragrance, and the lights in the temple were being dimmed and shaded to a baleful red. One white spot lit her gaunt face from below, the classic Halloween-party trick to give her face a terrifying and skull-like appearance. She lifted her arms now, and the flow-ing black sleeves of her robe were like raven's wings.

"THIS IS THE MAN!" she said, and her voice lost all its control and rose in a terrifying howl. An unseen technician threw a switch and a huge holo image appeared in midair: the best and clearest frame showing the Hangar Twelve Man, as he'd turned to stare up at the monitor.

Cecelia, gazing from the circle where she stood, caught her breath. In that moment it flew apart for her, the whole rational system by which she understood the world and her place in it. The balance of crime by retribution, the assurance that there was meaning behind everything and that She controlled destiny with a benign if terrible hand: all this scattered, like pieces on a chessboard overturned by a boisterous child.

The chanting began, the dark-throated curse without words, and the Mothers began the dance in each circle and the priestesses linked arms and began to sway. Cecelia let herself be pulled along with them as they focused their rage, their grief on the man whose image hung there in the darkness. She raised her voice with them when the directed prayer began, led by the Great Mother, imploring Hecate to bring him triple death and a thousand years of torment.

But all Cecelia was really aware of now was an image that had appeared behind her eyes, clearer than the blurry giant in midair above them all: Roger, sinking down through dark water, his slack face staring as in wonder at the gloomy reefs of Hell, his fair hair floating out around his head as though he were a prophet touched with visions.

On the fourth day of 2352, a pretty black girl came walking unsteadily into High John's Bar in Port-au-Prince. Claude behind the bar peered out, frowning, think-ing she was a drunk and preparing to shout at her. Then his eyes widened, for he recognized the girl, and knew that she was certainly not to be shouted at. His hands shook as he poured out a glass of his best rum, remembering that to be the appropriate offering to a lady of her station.

He hurried from the bar and brought it to her. She had sagged into a chair at a table and was staring up at the images playing on his holo, the terrible footage from Mars Two, which seemed to be all that would ever be shown again.

"Lady," he said deferentially, bending to set down a napkin and the glass at her elbow. To his consternation, he saw that her face was wet with tears. And she hadn't noticed him or his offering, she just kept looking up at the floating light where the Hangar Twelve footage was playing now, and when the tall tall white man turned to stare into the surveillance camera, she bared her teeth in agony.

"My little boy," she whispered, improbably. "My good little boy."

On the 24th of March, 1863, the Botanist Mendoza was brought up out of her cell and left alone in a room. There was nothing in the room but a holoset, staring from the ceiling with its three eyes. Noting this, she sighed. She waited in the room, doing nothing, seeing no one, for three hours.

At the end of that time the door opened abruptly, and an immortal entered the room. He nodded to her.

"Botanist Mendoza? Facilitator General Moreham."

"Are you a member of the tribunal?" Mendoza said. He merely lifted his eyebrows with a wry sort of smile, as though to indicate he'd thought she was more intelligent than to ask such a thing.

"There will be no trial," he said.

"Why?"

"Who could judge you, Mendoza?" he said. "Let me show you what you've done." He waved his hand and the holoset activated, and there before them was an image of a tall man loading crates from a shuttle to a hangar dock. She started.

"Alec," she said faintly.

"Yes, that's his name. However, he'll be better known to history as the Hangar Twelve Man," the other immortal said.

She turned to him, eyes wide. After a moment her lips formed the words, without sound: *Mars Two*. He nodded. She looked back at the image, Alec going busily to and fro, and sank to her knees but did not look away. Suddenly the hangar footage was replaced by the famous last few seconds from the camera mounted over Commerce Square. She shut her eyes, turned her white face from the red light, but she could not shut out the sound.

When it had ended, the man spoke loudly into the silence:

"Now, you see what happens when you disconnect intercept devices? Those things are put in there for a reason, you know."

Her spine was bowing, it was as though some private gravity were pulling her down, but she opened her eyes and looked up at the man.

"So that was what I saved him for?" she said. "So he could become the Destroyer?"

The man didn't deign to reply.

"I learned about Mars Two in school," she said. "I never paid attention to the footage. Too upsetting. But this was what it was leading up to my whole life, that mortal and I, and what we'd do together. You knew it would be my fault, didn't you?"

"We did," the man admitted, "But you didn't. *You* made the choice to disobey. There was nothing we could have done. History, you see, cannot be changed."

She said nothing in response. He walked around her where she knelt, considering her from several angles.

"Frankly, we're pretty tired of this, Mendoza," he said lightly. "After all, you were given every chance. But you're not quite up to standard, are you? You're a Crome generator. A defective. You disobey orders. And you kill mortals!"

She nodded.

"What do you think we ought to do with you?"

"Put me to death," she said. "If that's possible."

"Well, we can try," he said, dropping to one knee in front of her and tilting her face up to look her in the eyes. "We can't promise anything, but we can certainly try. Would you like us to try?"

She recoiled slightly from the familiarity. Moving stiffly she pulled herself upright, got to her feet.

"Yes, señor," she said, staring down at him. "Try."

Alec Times Three

He hurt, but everything was going to be all right; the soothing voice kept telling him so. Every time the pain became bad enough to make him groan, the warmth would come, lovely drowning oblivion, and he'd drift away again like a good boy, no more fighting or crying. He'd be a good boy now. He was always a good boy. Wasn't he?

But there had been . . .

No.

But he'd done . . .

No, Alec was a very good boy.

There was no up or down, there was nothing to see, there was nothing but the voice and the pain and the pain ebbing away.

The Captain was doing a conjuring trick. Alec had to watch very carefully. Here was a treasure chest, did Alec see it? The Captain opened the lid and tilted the chest forward so that Alec wouldn't miss the point that it was full of gold doubloons. He tilted it further and the gold ran out in three spiraling streams, to lie in three little heaps upon a red tablecloth. He covered them with a red handkerchief, looked hard at Alec to be sure he was following the trick, and whisked the handkerchief away. The three little heaps of doubloons had become three little pink fish!

Was Alec getting all this? Now the Captain pulled three bell-skirted dolls from his coat, all exactly alike, golden-haired, with blank blue eyes. He set each one down on one of the pink fish and the pink fish disappeared under the dolls' skirts.

Now the Captain plucked up one of the dolls and tossed her carelessly over his shoulder, revealing that the first fish had been transformed into a little man. But then, *whoosh!* There was a burst of flame, and the little man was gone.

Now the Captain took up the second doll and tossed her away. There was another little man. But, *pop!* Out of nowhere a pellet came and struck him, knocking him off the table, and he was gone, too. Had Alec observed all this? Had he understood?

The Captain took up the third doll and tossed her away. She hit the wall and bounced. Her head broke, but it didn't seem to matter. Here was another little man. Across the table came rolling a shiny black sphere, from which a burning wick protruded. The sphere was bowling straight for the little man, but at the last moment the Captain seized him up and tucked him inside his coat. *Boom!* When the smoke cleared, the Captain took the little man out again and set him back on the table.

He looked at Alec, grinning confidentially. Then, from his pocket, he drew out another figurine and set it next to the little man. It was the mermaid from the prow of the ship, reproduced in perfect miniature detail.

Did Alec understand?

He'd been listening to the waves for a long while now, idly watching the silver cords as they drifted in patterns around him. He was content. The cords were vaguely uncomfortable, but the discomfort seemed to be affecting somebody else. His nose itched, too. It had itched after Mendoza had put the coagulator wand to it . . .

Mendoza.

Like a man realizing he has overslept on the morning of an important appointment, Alec tried to sit bolt upright.

The violence of his motion set him turning slowly through space. He tried to cry out. The tubes in his mouth and nose prevented him.

It's all right, son. Wait.

He looked around wildly. He was in the hyperbaric chamber in the *Captain Morgan's* infirmary, floating in an antigravity field. He was intubated, catheterized, helpless. Billy Bones and Flint stood sentry at the door of the chamber.

Let me out of here!

Aye, laddie, aye. But if you ever try to scuttle yerself again, here's where you'll be, and for longer next time. Do we have an understanding, Alec? Nobody hurts my boy. Not even himself.

Captain, sir, please!

Yer not dying, Alec. That ain't in the plan. You, stretched out stiff, with that bloody marvelous brain no more'n a lump of cold carrion? That'd be wasteful, aye. Goes against all my programming. Not for my little Alec what set me free.

Set ME free! For Christ's sake, send me to Hell where I belong. Alec thrashed, to no avail; he merely spun counterclockwise amid the tubes.

Now, matey, you should know I ain't about to do that. I can keep you in here, helpless as a baby in a cradle, until you listen to me. Are you going to listen to me, Alec?

Raging, Alec told the Captain to do something an inorganic machine would have found very difficult to accomplish. The Captain laughed.

That's my boy! Now you've got some fight in you. You ain't going to feel like whimpering and dying once we've had our little talk, by thunder. Reckon you'll be good long enough for us to parley?

Okay! Yes! I promise.

That's yer word as a gentleman, is it? Watch yerself, then. I'll just turn off the field.

Alec was lowered to the floor, and the weight of gravity came down on him like a flattening hand. He flailed weakly, trying to get his breath. The chamber door opened and Billy Bones and Flint came in. They ministered to him, disconnecting the tubes and lifting him onto a stretcher. They seemed to have been modified somehow, given more arms and more functions built into the arms. Certainly they were more powerful. Alec was borne away through the ship to his cabin as though he weighed no more than a feather.

Aye, lad, there's been some changes made. I can't say I ain't missed you, but keeping you safe in the brig did give me the chance to catch up on me reading, as it were, and do a bit of home improvement. I think you'll approve of the changes.

What have you done?

You'll see. We need to talk first.

Alec was tucked into bed in his cabin, and lay there staring around. Everything was as it should be. There was a sipper bottle of cold water within easy reach, and a plate of biscuits. His beard had grown out, thick as a summer wheatfield. He had no sense of how long he'd been unconscious. The light was different; it dawned on him that the usual vista of blue sky and sea was missing beyond his window. It was white out there, with stains of gray and pale green, and the *Captain Morgan* was nearly motionless.

Captain, where are we?

Antarctica, son. They're looking for us everywhere else. They'll look for us here, too, soon enough, but we'll be long gone by then. Now, you hear this, Alec! Dr. Zeus let you steal that shuttle. Because of his precious Temporal Concordance, the bastard knows what's going to happen afore it happen, see? He stood to profit from what happened on Mars. He could have stopped you; he didn't.

But why—?

He bred you to deliver that bomb. He set the whole plan in motion. The only thing as went wrong was that you was supposed to be blown to hell too, after you left Mars's orbit. No evidence to point to Dr. Zeus. All the same, you did yer best to die like he wanted. You been programmed, son, more'n I ever been.

But that means—all this time we thought we were working to bring down Dr. Zeus, we've been playing into the Company's hands!

Not quite. He didn't know about me, and that's cost him dearly. It's going to cost him more afore I'm done.

So that was why . . . the whole plot with Elly Swain, and all the stuff I can do that nobody else can . . . it was just so somebody could make some money off Mars? That's why *I exist?* Alec gulped for breath. *Why the hell didn't you let me die?*

Don't get fractious again, son. There's much more to it than that. For one thing, ain't you at all curious why you wasn't blown up in the shuttle like he planned you'd be?

You saved me.

Not I. I had my hands too full with that stupid trip to assimilate the data that'd have warned me in time. No, somebody else had already disconnected the theft intercept system. Somebody else working against Dr. Zeus. See if you can guess who, laddie.

I can't.

Have you forgotten her already? The girl you wanted to marry?

Mendoza!

To be sure, the Botanist Mendoza.

Alec lay there, stunned. Tears began to run down his face. *I was supposed to go back and rescue her. She'll be in so much danger now . . . and what'll she say when she hears about Mars Two?*

She'll forgive you, lad. I'm wagering she'd forgive you anything you did.

Nobody'll ever forgive me, Captain.

This girl will. Trust yer old Captain on this one, Alec. And, just as soon as yer well enough to stand the trip, we're going back to the station for her. You need to know something about the lady first, though, son.

What?

Well . . . she's a cyborg, Alec.

Like me?

Not . . . exactly like you, no. I'll explain more when yer feeling better. But she's the girl I always hoped you'd find, and by God I'm going to get her for you.

Alec's head was pounding. Despite the Captain's reassuring words he had an awful sense of loss, lost innocence, lost time.

And then what? he snapped. *You'll keep us both prisoner in here? How'd you learn so much about her, anyway?*

Poor lad, yer still too weak to figure it out. You've a nasty old headache now, too, ain't you? Time to go sleepy-bye. We'll talk later.

Alec stiffened as a mask was clapped over his mouth and nose. He looked up wildly, into the steel eye sockets of Billy Bones. He struggled; then the tide rose and floated him away, to the safe place without questions.

Over the next few days he grew a little stronger, and the Captain was able to explain more of what had happened since the night Alec tried to kill himself. Even as Alec was being detoxified and placed on life support, the *Captain Morgan* had been slipping down the coast of South America, making steadily for Tierra del Fuego. The Captain focused his attention on his most recent data acquisitions, integrating and studying them carefully, and learned a great many interesting things.

Acting on his new knowledge, his first move was to alert Alec's lawyers and present them with his airtight alibi: surveillance footage proving that on 24 October Alec was dancing at a club in Martinique, which in fact he had been. The Global Identity Bureau quietly discarded the case it had been building based on the uncanny resemblance between a minor British peer and an unknown terrorist, and went away to investigate other, less absurd leads. The Captain's next move was to ditch the stolen time shuttle.

But how'll we rescue Mendoza? Alec cried.

I'm coming to that, the Captain told him. He'd drawn a pint of Alec's blood and cloned some hair and tissue samples, with which he liberally salted the pilot's console and chair. He then planted a charge under the pilot's seat, blew a gaping hole in the forward cabin, and jettisoned the shuttle off the Falklands, with the hatch sprung. Let Dr. Zeus find her there, let him subject the shuttle to forensic tests. All the evidence would point to a crash, and a badly splattered body floating away beyond recovery. It might buy them time.

Then the Captain had made several vital purchases of chemicals, alloys, and other materials from a black market supplier in Argentina.

So on down to Antarctica, and temporary haven in the icy water at the bottom of the world. Here, as Alec floated in oblivion, the Captain had begun his next project: installing time transcendence capability in the *Captain Morgan*.

It seemed that if her masts and spars were retracted, if the storm bottle were opened out, if the whole smooth unbroken surface then presented were varnished with a complex chemical solution that crystallized upon contact with air or water—why, you had nearly the whole of the works in place right then. The actual time drive was so easy to build, even enlarged and customized, that probably the only thing that kept everyone from having timeships (other than the fact that the design was a jealously guarded secret) was that building one required certain prohibitively costly alloys, such as were available only from black market suppliers.

All that was left to do was make certain modifications in the quarterdeck console so the drive could be installed and amped up, connect it to the ship's more than adequate fusion generators, rig the ship's ventilation system to puff out stasis gas, and mix liberal quantities of the bitter red liquid.

The *Captain Morgan* was now capable of sailing the waters of any past century. It had cost several fortunes, unbelievable amounts of money, but Alec was so rich money had very nearly ceased to have any meaning. Nor, from this day, was Alec bound by the circumference of the globe. He had an infinite number of globes to escape through. The river mouth that led to Roman Londinium, or the wherry-crowded Thames of Chaucer's time, or the black-fogged Victorian Thames were only three of his vast possible refuges, because any *place* contained an infinite number of *times*.

There were still a few refinements to make, of course. A holo generator was necessary to give the ship the illusion of a suitably historical appearance, or at least obscure her with shifting fogbanks, in any era she might cross. Also, the Captain was still organizing and correlating the time charts he'd plundered from Dr. Zeus.

He was intrigued by the continual mention of *event shadows*, locations where no historical record existed for certain years. Within those shadows, Dr. Zeus had no foreknowledge of events. Anything might have happened there, which gave anyone hiding in an event shadow a decided advantage.

Don't you see, matey? We can sail on blue water forever, if we need to! This'll make it easier to raid Dr. Zeus. We'll appear out of nowhere, strike, and be off again through time afore he knows what's hit him.

But haven't we got everything we need from the Company now?

Not by a long shot, laddie. I want to know what's in store for us in the future. We're going after Dr. Zeus's bloody Temporal Concordance. Belike yer lady will be able to give us a clue as to its whereabouts, eh? There's a whole mass of defended sites I want a closer look at. I'll strip him of everything he's got, the bronze bastard. I can set traps for him hundreds of years back, that won't blow up in his face until 2355. Two can play his game, by thunder!

I guess so.

Ah, but yer feeling listless. I know. Revenge'll seem sweeter when you've had a chance to think about this a little.

I don't think I care about the revenge anymore.

Oh, no? After what he done to you? Well, now, that's an admirable sentiment, lad, and I'm happy to see you've got such a forgiving heart. I call that right charitable, to be sure. All the same . . . you want to rescue yer girl, don't you?

Of course I do.

Then you'd best let the old Captain chart yer course, because unless we put a couple of broadsides through Dr. Zeus, it mayn't be so easy to take the lady.

That energized Alec. He ventured out of bed and staggered about the ship, feeling his strength return. He didn't care for the beard at all, and removed it as soon as his hands were steady enough to control the shaver. He spent a week bringing himself back, working out in the ship's gym and learning the new commands that would guide the *Captain Morgan* through time. Worried as he was about what Mendoza might think of his complicity in the Mars disaster, he was even more desperate to see her again. He couldn't remember a time when he'd needed human companionship so badly.

Though the Captain kept delicately dropping hints about Mendoza, hints that Alec resolutely refused to think about . . . In fact the Captain was hinting about a lot of things he'd discovered.

Apparently, there had been some kind of project going on for years, to produce uniquely talented and disposable puppets for Dr. Zeus. The other men like Alec had been killed. Alec was the first one to escape his preordained fate, and even so his life was irrevocably changed: he had become the Flying Dutchman after all, doomed to run before the wind as long as he lived.

His anger started to smolder again, and as it returned the sense of weakness and guilt retreated. Revenge began to look good once more. Elly, Roger, Cecelia, Mendoza, the people of Mars Two, and now these unknowns who had come before him! The list of Dr. Zeus's victims kept growing.

———

The course is laid in, son. You've taken yer medicine?

Aye, sir. Alec smiled grimly, buckling the safety harness.

Brace yerself. It'll be worse than the storm off Trinidad in '47.

It won't be worse than riding that carpeted toilet through space. Where do we come from, Captain, sir?

From the sea!

The yellow gas boiled, a throbbing ran through the *Captain Morgan,* and Alec became the whirling center of a very expensive carnival ride.

There was no one to see the *Captain Morgan's* arrival, but if there had been they might have thought they beheld an immense bottle materializing abruptly in Avalon Bay, spinning in the water, gradually slowing. When the spinning had slowed to a halt, the bottle underwent an extraordinary transformation. Half of its glassy surface folded back lengthwise, revealing the deck of the ship it had become. With only the faintest whirring sound the masts rose smoothly from her deck, her spars popped out, her rigging deployed. Her anchor dropped, plummeting down through the clear water.

We done it, lad. We've traveled!

What's the chronometer say?

It's a week after you left. She'll never know you was delayed.

Alec unbuckled his harness and ran out on deck. He was in the bay he remembered, there was the island, and there inland he could see the wide swath he'd cut through Mendoza's cornfield.

"Yeah!" he howled. *There's where I landed, that's what I told you about.* He was on the point of leaping overboard when the Captain sent the agboat alongside.

This'll get you there faster, boy. But careful, now!

Alec vaulted in and took the agboat up the canyon, following his previous course. The broken corn was still where it had fallen, only now turning yellow. He veered right sharply and made straight for the little house, there in its tidy garden.

"Mendoza!" He cut the motor and jumped from the boat. "Baby! I'm here, I came back for you!"

Alec—

"Mendoza?" Alec sprinted up on the porch (there was the bench where he'd sat, there were even a few drops of his blood) and pounded on the door.

Alec, there's nobody here.

What? "Mendoza?" Alec opened the door.

I scanned the whole station. She's gone. Bloody hell, I was afraid this'd happen.

Alec walked into the empty room and stood, staring.

No signs of violence. Nothing overturned or broken. He knew what must have happened, all the same. Almost calmly he looked down at the table where they had dined together, at the big old-fashioned book that sat there now, open to a page of spidery black script that ended abruptly. He knew what that was: old-time writing. That must be her bottle of ink, there, and that was her pen, made from a gull's feather. The ink had congealed in the open bottle. She'd been writing when they'd come for her.

They've killed her, haven't they? Because she helped me.

No, she ain't dead. I swear it, son! But they got to her first.

Do you know where she is?

I'll find out. See that terminal there? Hook us in.

Alec obeyed. The Captain dove away from him through cyberspace. Alec remained there, alone in the room.

The dark field was before his eyes. The little girl had walked blindly there, hadn't seen the danger, hadn't heard his shout of warning. He hadn't warned her, had he? Instead he'd pushed her straight into the fire.

Numbly, he closed the book and looked at it. Had she made it herself? Some of the paper toward the front was yellowed, as though it were very old. He peered at the writing on the first page, trying to decipher it. The letter I, and that would be the word *am* maybe, and then an A, and what could that next word be? Moving his lips, he read in silence the word *Botanist*.

He sounded it out several times before the syllables had meaning for him. She had written this. This was all he had left of her, and he didn't know how to read.

When the Captain came racing back into his consciousness, he was sitting on the floor with his head in his hands.

Alec, let's go! The bastard's right behind me. He knows we're here.

Is she dead?

No, but they arrested her. Alec, we got to get out of here, we can't help her now.

It's my fault.

Oh, for Christ's sake, don't start that again. In about five minutes there'll be Company shuttles storming round that point out there!

I don't care.

Bloody Hell! *Do you care about her? If she needed rescuing afore, she really* *needs it now. Unless you want to wind up in the jar next to hers in some Company facility, you better move yer damn arse!*

That got Alec on his feet, but he went to the book and wrapped it in the blanket from her bed.

What in hell are you doing? the Captain roared.

She left writing. You have to translate it for me. Alec ran for the door, clutching the bundled book to his chest as though it were a child.

He was back on board, in his safety harness, and the stasis gas had just begun to fill the air when a shadow streaked across the transparent dome. It was a shuttle, coming in low and fast, just as he had done. Before he could see whether it was going to turn and come back over, the *Captain Morgan* leaped away through time.

We're clear! Thirty miles out from the Farallones and it's 7 June, 2215. That's what I'd call a neat escape.

Alec gasped for fresh air, pushing out of the harness. *Never mind that. Where is she?*

I don't know, son. I wasn't able—

What do you mean, you don't know? Alec had begun to shake with anger. *You told me she was still alive. How can you know that, and not know where she is?*

Alec, lad, there's things I ain't had the right time to explain—

Well, you can damned well explain 'em now. What did you mean, about her being in a jar? What haven't you told me?

Son, I wouldn't lie to you.

Hell yes, you would! Alec charged into cyberspace, shoving past the Captain to riffle through the Company files. Numbers and names filled his head, dates and places, maps and pictures, yielding up their secrets at his impatient push.

Suddenly there was a defended file before his eyes, something with the Captain's own seal on it, a text headed *Adonai*.

What's this file? Why've you got it locked?

No, boy! Leave it alone.

Alec's eyes narrowed. He forced the seal and accessed the file.

Into his consciousness came pouring the contents of *Adonai*: the proposal, outline, conceptual designs, every memo that had passed between all persons concerned, minutes of meetings, sequence reports complete with images . . .

And, finally and terribly, the black box recordings containing in electromagnetic analogue every thought, emotion and sensation ever experienced during the lives of two men named Nicholas Harpole and Edward Alton Bell-Fairfax.

Abruptly Alec had the memory of two complete lifetimes he had not lived, with a blindingly swift montage of images: half-timbered hall, rose garden, black-letter pages, cold corridors, the deck of a warship, a man in a tailcoat unrolling a map, a dying man, a green jungle. Death, his own, in flaming agony and in a hail of bullets, and in both cases the anguished face of the black-eyed girl watching him die, Mendoza.

Mendoza, who had loved him. Them.

The knowledge was incomprehensible, unbearable, could not be assimilated.

An alternative was found.

Alec felt a tearing, an impossible increase, and roared with pain as a second pair of arms burst forth from his sides, flailing and striking, and then yet a third pair, and barely had this registered on his screaming mind than two new legs shot out from his hips and then two more, kicking frantically, and his groin erupted in a hydra of members, beyond grotesque, da Vinci's Vitruvian man gone one better! And, last, a second face thrust forward from his own, as though it broke the surface of smooth water, an appalling face baring its white teeth in rage, and close after it a second face no less fearsome in its howl of lamentation like the crack of thunder, and the very chambers of his heart were tearing themselves open now and splitting into three, and he knew it would kill him and was glad, and toppled like a ghastly idol to smash into pieces on the floor.

But somewhere in all the horror was one quiet satisfaction: that of having confirmed, at last, beyond all doubt or argument, that he was indeed the monster he had always suspected himself to be.

Not dead yet? He lay gasping on the floor of the saloon, sprawled out, wearing only the body he'd been born with. The pain was beginning to ease away, but things were very far from being all right. What had just happened, to beat him down with such shame and horror?

Mars, he'd been responsible for all those people dying on Mars.

No, that had been before . . .

Mendoza. She'd been arrested, he'd failed her.

No, that had been before . . .

He wasn't even a human being. He was a Recombinant, one of those creatures who'd been illegal for centuries, who lived now only in the most lurid of horror fictions. A genetic test pattern, an experiment, an organic thing worked out on a graph before he'd ever drawn breath. Even poor mad Elly not his kin, he'd been no more than a parasite in her womb, no child of anyone's. Dr. Zeus had meddled with a twist of DNA and produced a nonperson.

Somebody moaned. Somebody else was lying on the floor of the saloon, breathing harshly.

Alec lifted his head and looked.

Two other men lay near him on the floor, their heads close to his, each lying at an angle away from the other, forming a three-branched figure.

One wore an old-fashioned suit, vaguely familiar to Alec from cinema. One wore nothing but a long white shirt and what looked to be black tights. In every other respect, however, they were identical to Alec. They were lifting their heads now just as he had done, and staring at him and at each other with just such an expression of horror and disbelief as he himself wore.

With a cry he scrambled backward from them, more terrified than he had ever been in his life. He could get no more than a body's length from either man, however, no matter how he struggled.

The one in the shirt had dragged himself into a sitting position, and shut his eyes tight. He was reciting something to himself in an undertone. The third man was looking rapidly from Alec to the other one, his gaze hard. He sat up and gestured oddly, running his hands over his clothing as if he were searching for something. He didn't seem to be able to find it. He smelled like blood and fireworks.

Alec knew, not wanting to know, that his name was Edward. The other one, the one who was now opening his eyes and looking at Edward with such loathing, was Nicholas, and he reeked of smoke.

"Murderer!" Nicholas said.

Edward smiled coldly. "I suppose so. I don't seem to be burning in Hell for my crimes, however, have you noticed? And it wouldn't appear that Jesu Christ has answered your prayers, either. What do you suppose is going on?"

"I've lost my mind," gasped Alec, and promptly wished he hadn't, for both the others turned their pale eyes on him.

"Stop blubbering, boy," Edward said. "You made a second Pompeii on Mars; if you can bear that, you ought to be able to bear our company."

"You're not really here," Alec said, squeezing his eyes shut, rocking himself to and fro. "I've fried my brain somehow. I'm hallucinating."

That's all it is, matey, to be sure.

All three of them jumped.

"Captain," Alec shouted, "I've crashed myself!"

It ain't nothing to worry about, son. Never you mind them two duppies! Remember the spooks you saw, that time you tried them mushrooms? But you'll be all right, now, here's old Billy Bones with something to put you to sleep—

The servounit came scuttling into the saloon, extending its arm with the anesthesia mask. For once, Alec was ready to welcome it. He'd have given a lot to lose consciousness just then. Nicholas gave a yell of horror, drawing back from the skull-faced thing, but Edward leaped to his feet.

Alec felt himself pushed aside somehow, watching as Edward attacked Billy Bones with incredible speed and ferocity. The mask was sent flying, and Billy Bones wound up across the room on its back, scrabbling vainly at the air with its steel legs.

Ow! Alec, what in thunder did you do that for?

"My name is Edward Alton Bell-Fairfax," Edward said. "Don't attempt to drug me again. You're the mechanical servant, aren't you? Perhaps you can answer my questions! Have I been made immortal? Has the Society accomplished its purpose?"

There was a long, long pause.

What Society would that be, now, sir? the Captain inquired politely. He was scanning Alec with great care, noting that his brainwave pattern was distinctly different when Edward was speaking.

"The Gentlemen's Speculative Society, of course! We were about to found an epoch of science. We were to conquer death and transform the world," Edward said.

There was another long silence, broken by a bitter laugh from Nicholas.

"Fool," he said. "Hast thou no understanding? *We* are dead men, thou and I. Yet thou art not in Hell, nor I in Heaven neither; and the reason is, we have no souls to go thence. Some necromancy created us, no more but homunculi." He pointed at Billy Bones. "Look how the boy hath made a brass head to sail his ship! And lo, the same alchemy hath made the boy and us."

Edward's eyes narrowed. "Medieval theological rubbish. I tell you, I was one of a brotherhood of men working to bring a golden age to mankind! We were on the brink of wonderful things when I—"

"Thou wert never one of their number," Nicholas said. "Thou wert no more than their tool, and when they'd brake thee, they cast thee away."

"Liar!" Edward took a menacing step toward Nicholas. Alec felt himself pulled closer too, and struggled to draw back. Edward's progress was arrested. He turned, glaring at Alec. Alec shoved him. He felt real, and when he threw a punch at Alec, Alec seized his wrist and felt the heat of solid flesh, the texture of his sleeve. As they struggled, locked together, Alec saw every tiny detail of the brass cuff links Edward wore, with their device of a fouled anchor. Alec shuddered. Edward for his part was peering in baffled rage at the tiki pattern of Alec's shirt.

"Beat it, dead man!" Alec growled.

Er, excuse me, sirs—said the Captain.

"Speak when you're spoken to, machine," snapped Edward.

Oh, aye, sir, to be sure. Captain Henry Morgan at yer service, sir, and I was just trying to do me duty like I was programmed. With respect, sir, I believe I can throw some light on the subject of yer Society, Commander Bell-Fairfax, sir. Perhaps you didn't have time to take in the contents of this here file when everything happened so quick just now, but if you'll have a closer look—

The Captain excerpted the dossier on *Adonai*'s second sequence, the same text and pictures that a certain trio of learned gentleman had studied at their leisure in Regent's Park. He fed it directly to Alec, modifying the signal to accommodate Edward's brain patterns.

Edward stiffened and went pale. Alec let go of his arm.

Sorry about them autopsy pictures, sir, I reckon they're a little distressing.

Edward collapsed into a sitting position.

"Damn them," he said at last. He covered his mouth with his hands.

Aye, sir, that'd be my feeling on the subject, too. Now then, gentlemen—I reckon you'd better sign articles amongst yerselves to keep the peace, because you ain't in no position to quarrel, d'you see? And let's put cards on the table.

Yer Society's called Dr. Zeus Incorporated nowadays, Commander Bell-Fairfax, and they conquered death, all right; but they ain't exactly brought about no golden age. What they done is amass more power and wealth than anyone's ever had, mostly by making themselves a lot of immortal slaves to get it for them. But they wanted to make sure history turned out to their profit, so they needed a few dirty tricks played. That was why you were made, sir.

"Damn them," Edward repeated, raising his furious countenance. "They told me it was for the greater good of mankind. They *used* me. My God, the blood I've spilt! The things I've done!"

"Call not on thy God," Nicholas told him. "Science had all thy worship, and *civilization*. And here thou art, now, no more than a ghost in the earth, with no claim on Heaven."

"As if you could ever get to Paradise," replied Edward angrily. "You did your share of brawling and lusting after wenches, if I read your memories aright. And can you read mine? Can you read the boy's?" He grinned in savage amusement. "Your God's been pitched off His throne long since, it seems."

"I was no murderer—" began Nicholas, and then flinched at the data Edward was sending him in a pitiless flood. He caught his breath, absorbing the impact of the scientific discoveries, the advances in scholarship, the inevitable dwindling into insignificance of issues that had mattered more than his life. He closed his eyes, turned his face away, but he couldn't stop his understanding.

"You see?" said Edward. "They're all happy pagans nowadays. When they take the trouble to worship at all. Enlightenment swept most of that nonsense away, and good riddance!"

"Oh, leave him alone," said Alec, growing alarmed, for Nicholas, doubled over, was mute and wide-eyed, regarding through his fingers the horror of the void. "Look, man, don't feel too bad—I know it's got to be a shock, finding out your religion's dead, but we've got this new thing called *nonselective altruism,* so people are still—"

"My death was wasted," said Nicholas quietly.

Not quite, sir. You did preach that sermon, when you was tied to the stake and the fire waited for you. Maybe you recollect? You impressed the good people of Rochester no end afore you burned, sir. One boy named Crokeham, he was so inspired by what you said, he run away to sea just so he could fight for England. Sailed the Spanish Main. Went ashore with a landing party on an island, all hot to kill himself a Spaniard, and what he found there—

Edward lifted his head. "Document D," he said in amazement.

Aye, I see you've guessed. He found something that didn't ought to have been there in 1578. Drake made damn sure nobody talked, but he wrote it up in his logbook and gave it to Elizabeth's ministers, with an eye to national security. They didn't know what to make of it, so it sat in the classified Crown archives until 1852. You know who found it there, Commander Bell-Fairfax, don't you? And you know what he done with it.

"The Santa Catalina Expedition," said Edward.

"But—Catalina's where Dr. Zeus has its laboratories," said Alec.

Right you are. So you see, Nicholas? If you hadn't preached that sermon, the Company might never have been founded. Not that an old sailor like me understands paradoxes in temporal physics, mind you, but that's the way it looks from here. If our Edward was a pawn for Dr. Zeus, weren't you the one as made the opening move in the game?

Nicholas sat staring. Edward gave a brief laugh.

"What a nest of snakes," he said.

Aye, sir, you might say so. And all of 'em biting their tails.

Silence followed this observation, until Nicholas cried out.

"Rose!" he said hoarsely. "I left thee amongst devils—"

"Not devils," said Edward, sitting bolt upright. "The Society. Good God! Your Rose and my Dolores—they were one and the same. And you—" he turned to Alec.

"Mendoza," said Alec, as the implications hit him.

"She was an immortal creature," said Nicholas. "Their slave. God forgive me. God forgive me. I never knew until the last—and I thought she could disobey them—"

She could. That's why she were a prisoner when you met her, Alec. She'd run afoul of her masters, trying to keep Commander Bell-Fairfax here from getting killed. Edward blanched.

"But that means she—" Alec was unable to complete the thought.

I said she was a cyborg. She'd had a bit more than a porting interface installed, though, lad, if you want the truth. I been trying to tell you this, but you didn't want to hear. She was a living machine, like yer old friend Blaise. The difference was, she loved you. She knew who you were, and she knew you'd been set up to die again, just like these two fine gentlemen. So she disconnected the intercept and saved yer life.

"You mean—she was one of those *things*?" Alec's voice shook with horror. "I slept with a machine?"

Edward turned and slapped his face, with such force his head rocked on his shoulders.

"If you ever speak of her that way again, I'll kill you," he said. "You feel disgust, do you, a thing like you? For a machine da Vinci himself might have designed? Good God, I was enchanted once I knew! For the little while I had to know."

"Listen to me, boy," said Nicholas desperately. "She could not help what they made her! What art thou, to despise her? Wilt thou betray her, too?"

"*Thing* indeed." Edward glared at Alec. "Has it penetrated that thick skull of yours yet, Alec? She preserved your life, even though she must have known what they'd do to her if she were caught. What will happen to her now?"

Alec saw the dark field of his nightmare again, the pits of flame.

Now, son, you got to remember she's immortal. They can't execute her. They got other reasons for wanting her kept hid, too. But Dr. Zeus has his ways of dealing permanently with such folk.

"Consigned to everlasting fire," said Nicholas in a faint voice. He had gone white as chalk.

"No, you medieval imbecile!" Edward clenched his fists. "You still have no grasp of the truth, have you? Leave your angels and devils in the trash of history, where they belong. The Society's been the real enemy from the first! We've been their slaves, no less than she, duped and cheated the same. Look at what we've seen through this pathetic boy's eyes!"

"Who're you calling pathetic, you bastard?" shouted Alec. Edward ignored him.

"See what's become of the empire for which I gave my life," he continued. "And you, with your grand martyrdom that was supposed to win you a place amongst God's elect. Was it worth it, man? Was it worth leaving her in her chains?"

"*Thou* wert ready enough to turn her to thy masters' purpose, even when thou wert kissing her breasts," snarled Nicholas.

Now, then, gentlemen, how much good will it do the lady if you waste time fighting? As I was trying to explain, Alec, afore you opened that file—sorry now, ain't you?—I don't know where she is. All the record showed was that she was arrested on the order of somebody named Clive Rutherford. Not a word about where she was sent.

"Then we need to find this Clive Rutherford," said Edward.

Ah, I can see yer a bright fellow and no mistake. We'll do just that, sir; only we'd best lay over here a day or two first, because we ought to reconnoiter and plan afore we make another jump through time.

"But they could be doing anything to her!" said Alec.

Just now it's 2215, son, if you'll remember. This Rutherford lubber ain't even going to be born for another century yet. We can't wring any answers out of him until he done the deed, can we? And, begging yer pardon—it wouldn't hurt you gentlemen to get used to one another aforehand, if you don't mind my saying so. I'd wager it's a little inconvenient to slouch about like this, three fellows with only one body between 'em.

"What do you mean, one body?" Edward said. "There are three of us."

Why, so there are; but all I can see less'n I looks through Alec's eyes is one, Mr. Bell-Fairfax, sir. The one what ain't dead. Alec.

"It's true," said Alec. "You keep grabbing me when you want to do something."

"Oh." Edward looked nonplussed. "Although . . . I may as well, really, because you don't seem to have put your body to particularly good use on your own account. What a wasted life you've led!"

"Ah, piss off," Alec told him. Edward chuckled.

"It only goes to prove my observations about the privileged classes. England's gone backward at a singular rate since my day. An earl who can't read? If you hunted with your hounds rather than sailed, you'd be perfectly at home in brother Nicholas's time."

"Is it even so?" Nicholas smiled unpleasantly. "*Nimium ne crede colori, puere.*"

That'll do! the Captain said, as Edward flushed and looked uncomfortable.

"It's a dead language anyway," he muttered. "Utterly pointless."

Well, I reckon you three gentlemen must be one and the same man; you couldn't hate yerself so much, otherwise. For the lady's sake, though, you best learn to get along peaceably.

It was a difficult period of adjustment.

The Captain had been prepared to give Alec a massive injection of an antipsychotic drug as soon as Edward's guard was down, but Edward's guard never seemed to go down, and the phenomenon of the distinct brainwaves for each personality continued. Himself an artificial personality with unusual abilities, the Captain found the idea of a disassociative personality disorder something of a challenge. He decided to see if there was a way to make Alec assimilate his previous selves, rather than banish them. Both Edward and Nicholas had knowledge and strengths that might be useful to Alec.

Not that this was particularly evident in the first few hours of their life together.

The three men found that, though they could move independently, they were unable to get more than a body's length from one another. Each one experienced independent physical sensations and appetites, regardless of who was in control of Alec's body, but only the controlling personality was able to satisfy his urges.

Twenty-fourth-century cuisine did not suit at all. Nicholas was impressed by the variety of food available on board a modern ship, but found it appallingly bland. An experiment to remedy this with hot pepper sauce had disastrous results. Neither he nor Edward cared for the various soy-derived dainties in their brightly colored irradiated pouches, either. Edward wanted a grilled beef chop very much, and became extremely profane when he was made familiar with twenty-fourth-century vegetarian civic ordinances. He then prowled through the saloon, searching in vain for cigars and cognac.

Sneeringly he inspected Alec's antique weapons collection and pronounced it the only thing of interest he'd seen so far; went up on deck and damned with faint praise twenty-fourth-century sailing technology. Nicholas, for his part, was horrified to discover there wasn't a single book on board.

On the other hand, the *Captain Morgan*'s bathroom was an immediate success, to the extent that over a two-hour period three bars of soap, two bottles of shampoo, every available drop of hot water, and all the clean towels were used.

They discovered that they could remove their clothing, and that it was possible to shave and comb one's hair on an individual basis, as long as one used Alec's body while one did so. Both Nicholas and Edward were startled by the buzzing shaver, but impressed by the job it did. Alec found his face smarting by the time Nicholas had finished shaving, however.

Too, though Edward might don his Victorian attire, Alec and Nicholas remained naked until each one dressed himself individually. Alec was able to pull on the fresh clothing that Bully Hayes had laid out for him, but Nicholas picked up his skimpy bundle in distaste.

"These hose stink," he grumbled. "What am I to do?"

"You ought to have had the sense to have died fully clothed, like me," said Edward smugly, inspecting his reflection in the steamy mirror.

Begging yer pardon, sir, but since yer an insubstantial soul—

"I am no soul, since I was made, not begotten! I am nothing more than spirit," Nicholas corrected the Captain with some asperity.

Edward snorted. "Are you certain you're even that much?"

Nicholas turned to reply, but realized he was by no means certain. The void opened before him again, the ruin of his universe.

"Not even that," he said. "Am I? *Nemo, nihil et—*"

"Stop it!" Alec snapped at Edward. "Isn't this hard enough without screwing him up worse? You want me to download you a map so you can see how small your Great Britain is now? I can practically step across it, man. No." He turned to catch Nicholas, who was collapsing, by the shoulders. "It'll be all right. He's just a mean bastard. Look, you want to see Mendoza again, right? Rose? We have to save her, don't we?"

Nicholas looked at him with sick eyes, but he nodded.

"So let's not worry about, er, cosmic stuff," said Alec. "One thing at a time. You want clothes like you used to wear?" He accessed Nicholas's memories briefly. Then he wrote for Nicholas's clothing occupying the empty shelf of the towel cupboard. When he opened the cupboard to see, there it was: a complete set of clothing, circa 1555, in sober black, with a fresh white shirt.

That's my clever boy!

"By Jove, that's a useful trick." Edward frowned. "I wonder if it would be possible to dress properly for dinner?"

I shouldn't wonder, sir, if you ask our Alec nicely.

"Don't talk rot! If he can do it, I certainly ought to be able to," said Edward, and as Nicholas dressed himself Edward went through any number of psychic contortions attempting to make a dinner jacket materialize in the cupboard. None appeared, despite his best efforts.

"What the hell does the boy do?" he shouted at last. "Substance can't be simply imagined into being. What is it, Alec, some sort of mathematical formula for converting matter?"

"No, it's nothing like that. It's just code," said Alec. "I don't think about it. I just make it happen. You really can't do it?"

"No!"

Well, now, ain't that a shame? I reckon our Alec has the edge on you in that, Commander; but, you see, he's done this sort of trick in cyberspace for years. Perhaps you'll learn one day, sir.

"I could try to show you," Alec said, smirking. Edward looked at him with narrowed eyes. Nicholas, meanwhile, had slipped on his black scholar's robe and stood fully dressed, looking down at himself in amazement.

"I threw off this gown in a room in England. How long ago now? The rain was beating at the little window . . . And Rose lay in the bed waiting—" His voice broke.

Alec patted him awkwardly on the shoulder. "It'll be all right," he said. "We'll get her back. You'll see."

"Thou shalt get her, boy," mourned Nicholas. "Not I, and not that proud ghost neither. I am not e'en so much dust as she could hold in her hand. What have we to do with flesh now?"

"I mean to find out," Edward said, turning to him. "You tasted the pepper sauce acutely enough, didn't you? And you enjoyed the hot water and the perfumed soap. Why should it be any different with the joys of the flesh? By God, if we're some Frankenstein's monster of strangeness, why not glory in it? I'll own I thought you were a complete idiot, young Alec, but you do seem to have powers of mind beyond the range of normal men."

"Thanks so much." Alec curled his lip. "You don't understand anything about recombinants, do you?"

"I understand ignorance and superstition when I see it," Edward replied. "If Science created us rather than the Almighty, what then? I'm damned if I'll cringe and apologize for it. Since you and I have been given this unnatural life, Nicholas, let's live it! For we've got work to do, gentlemen. My lady bid me set her free. *She* won't care what I am."

That's tellin' 'em, lad!

"Thank you," said Edward coolly. "There is also the matter of revenge. For all we know, God intended to make us His instruments to punish our presumptive creators. It seems to be what man-made monsters do. Let's find out, shall we?"

———

The *Captain Morgan* rocked on quiet gray water under a gray sky. It was suitably like limbo to depress the spirits of an ordinary man, let alone one with Alec's problems. He retreated to the saloon as darkness fell, closely followed by his previous selves. They crowded around the table while Coxinga brought a tray of supper for Alec: grilled fish and baked asparagus tips in white wine sauce.

"Now, that's something like!" said Edward, eyeing it. He muscled control away from Alec long enough to sample the fish.

If you please, sir! You let my Alec have his dinner, now.

"It's okay," said Alec morosely. "I'm not all that hungry, actually. What I'd really like is a drink."

Not in yer present condition, son. Anyway, it all went over the side after yer little accident, except for the cooking wine.

"Not the thirty-year-old Glenlivet," groaned Alec, putting his head in his hands.

"Oh, that really is too bad," condoled Edward with a certain insincerity, munching asparagus.

Afraid so, lad. If you behave yerself, we'll get more one of these days.

"That's a consolation, at any rate. One can still obtain some decent liquor in this miserable—I beg your pardon!" Edward broke off as control was wrested from him by Nicholas.

"What need hast thou of meat?" Nicholas told him, returning the plate to Alec. "Let the boy eat, thou wretch."

"I'm a man, you know," muttered Alec. "And I'm not stupid."

"No indeed, you've apparently quite the superior intellect in this day and age," said Edward. "God help us all." He changed his tone as a thought occurred to him. "Here now. That little trick you worked with brother Nicholas's clothing—do you suppose you could create anything else? What if you could make a veal cutlet and some new potatoes materialize out of the ether?"

"Like this?" said Alec irritably.

"I should of course prefer them on a plate," said Edward through his teeth, picking a nicely breaded cutlet out of his lap. "Damn you, boy, I hope you can launder these trousers. Never mind; we've made John Calvin over there smile, which is probably sinful and therefore worth the inconvenience."

"I only wish you'd asked for soup," Alec retorted, but he read Edward's memories. A moment later a dish of blue willow pattern appeared before Edward, bearing the meal he had requested as well as *haricots verts* and a glass and bottle of claret, vintage 1859. Edward blinked.

"That," he said in awe, "is the last meal I had in London, at Redking's. I— Thank you, Alec."

"What about you?" Alec said to Nicholas, who was gaping at the laden table. "You want anything? I bet you'd be happier if you weren't hungry."

"How can a spirit hunger?" said Nicholas. "But an thou couldst summon eel pie and a pintpot of ale, in the same wise, boy—"

"Stop calling me *boy*," said Alec, but he summoned them. Nicholas picked up a spoon cautiously, broke the pastry crust. A plume of steam rose, bearing with it the fragrance of eel pie. Nicholas's pupils dilated. There followed a reverent conversational silence, broken only by the scrape of knives on china and pewter.

Now, that's what I like to see! My fine gentlemen all minding their manners and getting along.

"Don't fawn, machine," Edward said. "What about Clive Rutherford? Have you tracked him down, yet?"

Aye, sir, that I have. Turns out he's one of the team that worked on yer project, sir, **Adonai.**

"Is he now?" Edward's eyes grew mean and small. "Rutherford of Rutherford, Chatterji, and Ellsworth-Howard? That's convenient, I must say. We can combine business with pleasure."

"We're not going to kill anybody, are we?" said Alec.

"It might be necessary," Edward said, taking a sip of claret.

"I will do no murder, Edward," Nicholas said sternly. "Nor shalt thou. What, hast thou not had thy fill of *necessary* deaths?"

"That's true enough," Edward said at last, looking away.

The Captain made a noise as though he were clearing his throat and continued:

The record shows he's also a museum curator. He's got charge of a historical architectural monument—row of houses in London, all done up so tourists can see how people used to live in the old days. He lives in one of 'em, and if he's the curator I reckon he'd be at home most days.

"What's his address?" Alec asked.

It says here No. 10 Albany Crescent, London NW1. Edward choked on his wine.

"I grew up in that house," he gasped, as Alec thumped him helpfully on the back.

"No kidding?"

"But it can't be the same. It must have been pulled down long ago." Edward recovered himself. "Or bombed. Wars seem to have swept over London like so many juggernauts since my time. Damned incompetent idiots. We were becoming a world power!"

Well, nobody's a world power anymore, sir, if that's any consolation. Except for Dr. Zeus Incorporated.

"I know where Albany Crescent is," Alec realized. "I broke into a house there once."

Nicholas frowned and Edward looked intrigued. "A thief, were you? And an earl's son? What were you doing, playing at being Prince Hal?"

"Oh, go shrack yourself. I wasn't stealing! Balkister and I were just looking for a place to get drunk in out of the rain. London's full of old empty houses, see, because there aren't nearly as many people as there used to be," Alec said. "Or maybe nobody can stand to live there. God knows I couldn't."

"But thou canst find thy way there, and bring us to this man?" Nicholas said.

"Yeah. No problem."

Oh, I reckon you'll find it a bit more complicated than that, me boys. The police may not be looking to question our Alec anymore, but Dr. Zeus might still be hunting him. This ship's just a bit conspicuous, more's the pity. You won't be able to dock at Tower Marina this time. Or ever again, likely.

"I knew I shouldn't have laid out all that money for mooring membership," said Alec, slightly stunned. "How are we going to get into London?"

You'll come up with ways and means, Commander Bell-Fairfax, sir, I shouldn't wonder.

"I can get into or out of any city on Earth," Edward said, draining the last of his claret. "Leave it to me." He pushed away his empty plate and looked sidelong at Alec. "I don't suppose you'd care to try to materialize brandy and a good cigar?"

"Okay," said Alec, and they appeared on the table, complete with a match-stand and another tankard of ale for Nicholas.

"Aaah," Edward gloated. "Capital. Young Alec, you are decidedly a man of parts." He struck a match and lit the cigar; taking a sensuous drag, he leaned back in his seat. "Mmf. There now! It is conclusively proven. We've gone to Heaven after all."

"Mocking knave," muttered Nicholas, waving away the cloud of smoke. He lifted his tankard and drank, however.

"And is this Courvoisier?" Edward raised the brandy snifter to his nose and inhaled. "You're a man of taste as well, my boy. We may make something of Alec yet."

"You couldn't get out of Los Angeles," said Alec suddenly.

"Eh?" Edward frowned at him.

"You didn't know how without getting caught. Mendoza had to help you."

Alec was astonished at the unfamiliar memory he'd accessed, seeing a dusty pueblo and sere brown hills under a darkening sky. "Just like she helped me, when I crashed."

"So she did," said Edward after a moment. He blew a thoughtful smoke ring. "This much hasn't changed, at least. Over cigars and brandy, we talk about the ladies. Or one lady, in this case. Gentlemen, I give you Dolores Alice Elizabeth Mendoza." He raised his glass.

Nicholas sighed. "When she rode into old Sir Walter's garden, she was called Doña Rosa Anzolabejar."

"All she ever told me was, her name was Mendoza," said Alec.

"I wonder what her true name is?" Edward savored his brandy. "The mystery, that was one of the things I loved about her. Who was she? How could a woman, let alone such a young girl, understand so perfectly what it was to be a political unless she were one herself? To say nothing of her other abilities."

"Even so it was with me," said Nicholas sadly. "I sought to know the truth; and even when I had found it out, I knew nothing. Save only that she loved me. The poor child watched me ranting in the fire, and I saw my least word was a knife in her heart."

"How could you do that?" demanded Alec, seeing his memory. "You wanted her to die with you! That's horrible." The image from his dream, the field of death, came abruptly before his eyes. He turned his face away, to find himself looking into Edward's cold level gaze.

"Were we any kinder to her, you and I?" Edward inquired. "Though, I'll grant you, neither of us went so far as to actually *ask* her to destroy herself." He looked at Nicholas. "That's your own particular distinction, man of God."

"I thought to save her immortal soul from Satan," said Nicholas, staring into his ale. "I wanted to bring her unto the Lord." His voice grew faraway. "Yet God He knows she was innocent enough of sin. It was I lusted after her from the moment I saw her little face, though I lied and said not so to my heart. She did no more than offer me half an orange for courtesy's sake. I wanted to lick the sweet juice from her hand, and have her on her back there in the long grass . . ."

"What a fine godly hypocrite," Edward chuckled, exhaling smoke. Nicholas just stared at him, terrible bleakness in his eyes, and then said:

"Ay. So I was, and it cost me Heaven in the end. Will you hear?

"When I suffered in the fire, my pain was grievous; but there came a roar in mine ears and a burst of light, and I was gone out of mine agony like a bird set free. And I ascended, as I thought, toward Heaven. Methought I saw the kingdom of God, like a pleasant garden for His elect, and I made haste to go in.

"But the Lord Himself refused me entrance. Wherefore may I not rest, I cried. Have I not suffered to bear witness to Thee, my God?

"Indeed thou hast, quoth He. But this is neither thy place nor thy time. Thou art alone, Nicholas! Where is the girl?

"I was ashamed, and I said: Lord, she would not come.

"And the Lord said: Go forth, then, for I tell thee thou shalt never come near to Paradise until thou bearest her along with thee.

"And I fled lamenting from the presence of God, and woke here, to know myself for the vile thing I am."

"When will you stop this metaphysical nonsense?" said Edward wearily. "But I suppose you've no other way to look at the matter, born as you were in an age of superstitious piety. Our life-forces have been kept intact somehow, can you understand that? The goal of the Society was always immortality. Politicals like me, but invincible! And I was promised resurrection in the flesh myself, when my time came. I was told that even death was no more than an injury, from which Science would heal me."

"You're both deluded," said Alec, shaking his head. Nicholas scowled at him and Edward tipped ash off his cigar before replying:

"By no means. The Society—or the Company—may have lied to me about a good many things, but it's obvious they did find some way to preserve my intellect. And I shouldn't be at all surprised if my own proper body isn't being kept as well, in some electrical sarcophagus, or perhaps a magnetic bottle of life-sustaining fluids, until it can be revived."

Alec shuddered and Nicholas looked askance. "That is rank alchemy," he said.

"Science," Edward corrected him. He blew another smoke ring and grinned at Nicholas. "And hard luck for you, old man. I doubt very much whether even the most advanced medicine can reanimate a bucketful of ashes. The Company clearly preserved your life-force as well, to what purpose I cannot imagine, but you thoughtlessly let your body go up in flames! You may as well make the best of sharing the premises with young Alec here; you're unlikely to get any closer to eternal life."

"Oh, shut up," Alec told him. "I don't know what you are, but I know nobody's figured out any way to make a corpse back come to life yet. What about those autopsy pictures? You're dead, and you deserve it!"

"And yet, I live." Edward had another sip of his brandy, smiling. "Even Nicholas lives. Explain that, young genius."

I can explain it, son.

"The machine has opinions? This should be entertaining," said Edward.

I wouldn't get so high and mighty if I was you, Commander Bell-Fairfax, sir. You ain't nothing but a stored file my boy downloaded by accident. The only reason you think yer alive is because his brain's able to run yer program— and our Nicholas's program too—at the same time he's using it for his own thinking.

"Is that what it is?" Alec looked sick with relief. "So I'm not crazy!"

No, no, son, it's only because yer brain's so special that yer able to have this kind of disassociative personality—the Captain sought for a more positive spin. *Er, what you are is multiple personality-abled. See?*

"A likely story," scoffed Edward. "And I'll thank you to retract it, when I've been restored to my own flesh. Once we've rescued Dolores, I rather think finding where they're keeping my body should be the next order of the day, shouldn't you? The sooner we can dispense with this intolerable living arrangement, the better."

"Yeah, well, we'll see who she feels like snuggling up to then, won't we?" said Alec contemptuously. "A live man, or some kind of pickled zombie like you."

Edward gave him a long, hard stare before shrugging and taking another drag on his cigar. He blew smoke in Alec's face and said:

"You've still no grasp on the situation, have you, boy? But Dolores will understand. She and I are of a kind. I'd begun to guess what she was, even before she let the truth slip. The Society claimed there would be a way to make immortal creatures and dispatch them, through time itself, to do our work. I thought she must have been sent to assist me. But I couldn't ask her until the business was over, and by then it was too late.

"And then at the last, she said—" Edward paused, his face clouding. "She told me she was a prisoner in time. She begged me to come back and break her chains. I had no idea what she meant. It had never occurred to me that the Society would countenance the creation of immortal *slaves*." He looked at Alec with aversion. "How could I have known that a blunderer like you would find her in her prison?"

Alec clenched his fists. "I went back for her."

"But too late." Nicholas shook his head. "Thou hadst thy vanities to attend to first, thine ambuscades and treasons up amidst the cold stars. Yet I did the same. If I'd let my lust rule me I'd have stolen her away and fled from England, and would to God I had! But not I. I went vainly after righteousness and left her trapped here. And when at last a smiling villain came to her, she must have thought—"

"What, thought I was you?" Edward blew another smoke ring. "She didn't cry *your* name at the height of passion, brother. And what passion! I couldn't imagine how a virgin girl—" He halted.

"I had her maidenhead," Nicholas informed him.

"But—"

"But she was a virgin with me, too," said Alec. There was a silence while they considered the contradiction, before Edward grinned.

"Good God, she must be made like the houris in Mahomet's paradise! And she knew tricks I thought only the women in the souk could do. I suppose she had her education at your godly hands, brother Nicholas, in which case I'm obliged to concede there's more to you than meets the eye as well!"

"Don't speak of her this way," said Nicholas, giving him a deadly look. "Thou, who never loved her."

"I tell you I did, man," Edward said, all the banter going out of his voice. He put down his cigar. "I thought she was superb. Lustful as Aphrodite, and wise as Athena. *She* seemed to think we were made for each other. And we were, by God! She's mine, not the damned Society's chattel."

"She was going to marry *me*," said Alec. "I asked her, and I'm still the only one with a real body, so you can just—just—"

"Let me guess. Piss off?" Edward inquired in a bright voice.

"Oh, shut up," said Alec miserably. "I guess she only loved me because of you two. Figures, doesn't it? She . . ." He stopped, struck. "She must have known about us. That we were Recombinants and everything! Don't you think? And she didn't care."

"How should she care, who was scarcely a creature of flesh and blood herself?" said Nicholas. "Though she at least began as a mortal child, not an unnatural scrap of flesh in an alembic's womb."

"How d'you know that?" Alec asked him.

Nicholas raised his pint and drank deep. "Her father admitted it to me," he said, with an extraordinary expression of malevolence. "No true father of hers, understand my meaning, yet he that bound her into eternal labor for his masters. Doctor Ruy! A meddler and a poisoner, and were he not deathless I would kill him with my two hands, should he ever cross my path again." He looked sullenly at Edward. "There's necessary murder for you."

Edward merely gave him an ironic smile and drank more of his brandy. Alec sat looking from one of them to the other.

"There might be a way to find out how much she knew about us, anyway," he said. "I guess you both can read writing, can't you?" The concerted look of scorn they gave him made him flush. "Hey! I can do lots of things you can't, you know."

"Undoubtedly," Edward drawled, reaching for his cigar again. "Though I intend to become your equal in them pretty damned quickly. How does one control your Ancient Mariner, for example?"

That's for my boy to know and you to find out, ain't it, sir?

"Rest assured I will," Edward said.

"Peace! Wherefore, boy?"

"She left writing," Alec said. "I brought it with me from the station but I can't read it, and—"

"Good God. There was a book, wasn't there?" Edward sat bolt upright. "What did you do with it, Alec?"

Five minutes later they were settled down around the table again, with fresh cigars and brandy for Edward and more ale for Nicholas, examining the book under the light of the gimbal lamp.

It was a big book, very rough and hand-made in appearance, and it consisted of three sections sewn together. The first part was written on glossy sheets of something indestructible, brightly printed on their reverse sides with pictures of seductive-looking cuisine. They were in fact opened-out labels for a popular soy protein product. The ink varied here in color and thickness; the writer had evidently been experimenting with thinning agents. Toward the middle of the text a satisfactory uniformity had been achieved, and remained consistent thereafter.

The second part was of machine-cut white paper, crumbling with age, a printed text here and there annotated in the same hand as the first section, with a written postscript. It appeared to be the transcript of a hearing.

The third part was the shortest: more of the bound labels, covered in closely written text to about halfway through. The writing had broken off abruptly. There were some thirty pages following, blank, clean and new-looking.

"That is her hand," said Nicholas in a guarded voice.

"Is it?" Edward clamped his cigar in his teeth and opened to the first page. He removed the cigar, blew a stream of smoke and read aloud: " *'I am a botanist. I will write down the story of my life as an exercise, to provide the illusion of conversation in this place where I am now alone—' "* He broke off, frowning. "This is a diary. I wonder whether we really ought to . . ."

"Dost thou scruple, thou?" scoffed Nicholas.

"I have my standards where a lady's heart's concerned," Edward said. "Besides, one never knows what one might find."

"Please," said Alec. "I only had her for a day. What if we never find her again? I loved her, I've got to know what she said!"

Nicholas pointed in silence to a line near the bottom of the first page, where the words *Dr. Zeus Incorporated* appeared. Edward nodded grimly.

"We've no choice, then, really," he said. "Have we, gentlemen? Sorry, my love. Let's see what you can tell us."

Edward began again to read aloud. His cigar, forgotten, burned itself out to gray ash. There were times when Alec had to explain puzzling text references to the other two men. There were times when Nicholas had to do the same. They read all night.

Gray morning was breaking over the sea when Edward fell silent at last and leaned back from the table. Nicholas's eyes were red and swollen; he'd wept himself out hours earlier. Alec sat gazing at the other two men with contempt.

"You bastards," he said hoarsely. "You tricked her, didn't you?"

Edward was silent, but Nicholas raised his head.

"*Tricked* her?"

"You know what I mean." Alec leaned forward across the table, stared at Nicholas with a ghastly parody of a seductive smile. "Bet you did it a million times, didn't you? You just look into their eyes—and you sort of focus right here, don't you, and you think about how nice it would be to get them in bed. And then they do just what you want. And they think they love you, until it wears off."

"No!" Nicholas protested. "I only persuaded her—that gift was the grace of God, *charisma*, that I might save souls! And if love were the means—if she . . ." His stammers died away into silence. He closed his eyes, white as a ghost. "Oh, Jesu, what have I done?"

"Merely used a superior force of will," said Edward sharply, though he did not look up. "A natural gift you were born with, owing nothing to superstition. If you never employed it toward noble ends, at least you did better than the boy. Alec, did it never occur to you that you might have become something more than a seducer?"

"Sooner than that what you became, man," Alec said. "You shracking assassin."

Edward stiffened, but did not respond.

"I should never have been born," said Alec. "None of us should ever have existed at all. Why did she love us?"

Edward reached for his brandy and tossed it back in a gulp. "But she *did* love us. Here! You machine. Captain Morgan, d'you call yourself? Set a course for London in the twenty-fourth century, however you do it. We're going after Clive Rutherford."

Aye, sir! But you might want to let our Alec get some sleep first, eh? You'll all need yer wits about you.

"We will, by God," Edward said, rising to his feet behind the table. "Shall we retire, gentlemen?"

Alec nodded grimly. He stepped away from the table. Edward and Nicholas followed him without another word.

London was fogbound, all her postcard views grayed out and lost. Her streetlights had only just extinguished themselves, but there was nobody to see: her few citizens were still huddling in their warm beds, asleep or smugly congratulating themselves that there was a full half hour yet before the alarm shrilled.

The Thames was quiet at Waterloo Bridge, the fog drifting low and silent over its glassy surface. Suddenly the fog lifted in a puff, as if blown by a gust of wind, though there was no wind. Seconds later there was a disturbance in the water, a roiling, a steaming, and anyone standing on the bridge might have thought a submarine had unaccountably just surfaced in the river below. However, there was no one standing on the bridge at that hour.

Within seconds the long sleek shape had stabilized, and the glassy shell that formed her upper surface lifted a little—just enough for a man to emerge, squeezing through awkwardly because he was a rather long man, stripped to bathing trunks, clutching in one arm a waterproof duffel sack. He dropped into the Thames and swam hastily ashore. No sooner had he found his footing in the Thames mud than the unidentified floating object slid away up the Thames in the direction of Charing Cross New Pier, where it lurked among the pilings.

The man remained, however, shivering violently in the cold. He retreated into the shadows under the bridge and, taking clothing from the duffel sack, dressed himself. The last thing he took from the bag was a pistol of some kind. He thrust it out of sight into his coat, wadded up the bag and stuffed it into a pocket, and climbed up to the Embankment through the ruins of the old police station.

Shortly thereafter, persons venturing out to the public transport stops along Charing Cross Road were dismayed to note the presence of a very tall demented person, lumbering along uncertainly and talking to himself. It wasn't only that his eyes were red, his hair wild; he was dressed most inappropriately. His long winter coat flapped open to reveal that he wore nothing more underneath than a tropical-pattern shirt, shorts, and a pair of canvas boating shoes. He looked like a derelict who had been on a Hawaiian holiday.

Mrs. Beryl Wynford-Singh trembled as he approached, making herself as small as she could on the transport bench and praying that the transport would arrive before he came near enough to assault her. She gasped with relief when she spotted the transport rounding Pall Mall. The lunatic gasped too, and backed into the nearest doorway.

"*God's wounds*," she heard him cry. "Quiet, you idiot! It's nothing more than, er, some kind of omnibus. Isn't it, boy? It's only an agtransport. Don't be scared. Come on. People will look at us."

But in fact nobody was looking at him. After the first glance, people were determinedly averting their eyes. Several of them felt rather guilty about it, because by law it was every citizen's duty to report reality-challenged persons to the nearest public health monitor, that they might be taken off to hospital. However, this law failed to take into account the irresistible human urge to confer invisibility on those who dressed badly and babbled to themselves in public places. Mrs. Wynford-Singh was already quite incapable of seeing the lunatic as he paced on and halted, gaping up at a memorial statuary group dating from the early twenty-first century.

"That's new since my day! Persephone, isn't it? Ay. Ravished away down the tunnel to the underworld by Hades, with his hounds chasing after. So it is. Rather an omen for our quest, wouldn't you say?" The lunatic peered more closely. "Who was *Diana Spencer*? Come on, we're wasting time."

The transport stopped in front of a grateful Mrs. Wynford-Singh and opened its doors. As she fled through them, she did think she heard a voice saying plaintively: "Now, where the deuce has Shaftesbury Avenue got to in five hundred years?"

One alert junior clerk, watching from the transport window, did notice that the tall person bore a marked resemblance to the mysterious Hangar Twelve Man in the Mars One surveillance footage, still being shown nightly in the hope that viewers might provide authorities with an identification. The junior clerk's eyes brightened, and he leaned closer to the glass for a better look. He realized that the tall man was gesticulating and speaking to the air next to him, as though an unseen person stood there. The clerk promptly lost interest and sighed, reflecting on the hopeless monotony of his young life as Mrs. Wynford-Singh dropped heavily down on the seat beside him.

The tall man did find his way to Shaftesbury Avenue without being arrested, and there seemed to orient himself. He loped away at once with a determined stride, his long coat blowing out behind him. In a few more minutes he stood peering into Albany Crescent, an extraordinary expression on his face.

"Look at it," he muttered. "Of all the places to have survived half a millennium! I might have known. I'll bet the drains are still blocked. So that was your house, there? Number ten? Yes, unfortunately. I know how you feel. My place in John Street gets me the same way.

"Thou liest! This is some palace, surely. Yes, I suppose it would seem that way to you; but then, you were born in a thatched hut, weren't you? Besides, this isn't one house, it's lots of houses all stuck together. Well, and canst thou effect an entry? I think so. I was pretty drunk, though. Never mind, boy. It's coming back to me now."

He proceeded into Albany Crescent and stood, rubbing his chin thoughtfully, surveying the long curve that fronted on a park. It was entirely deserted.

"How did you break in, Alec? Well, it wasn't number ten. It was this one here on the end. See down those stairs? There's a kitchen—I know. Down there, now. Before someone sees. But—Do as you're told!"

He scrambled down the kitchen-stairs at No. 1, which were heavily overgrown with rose bramble, and crouched in the shadows by the door.

"Ow! I tried to tell you, man. Never mind. Is this the door? No. It's been replaced. That's a new lock, an electronic one. Canst command it, then? I ought to be able to. Let's see." He drew a plug from the torque about his neck and inserted it in the lock's port. "We're in! Come on, then. Close it behind you."

He stood in shadows and dust, looking around warily. There was nothing in the room but a nineteenth-century cooking hearth, a mass of brick-red rust. There were caster-stains on the linoleum to show where later appliances had sat for long periods of time, and a few irregular holes in the walls and floor. The man shivered.

"This is what it is, to be a ghost! Through there. There ought to be stairs. But this isn't number ten! What's the point—you'll see."

The room beyond was in worse shape, darker and dirtier. There were stairs against the far wall, leading upward. The man crept up them and easily forced the old-fashioned lock at the top.

He stepped out into what had been the entry hall of the house and paused, getting his bearings. Then he paced slowly forward, over the marble parquet floor, to the swirling mosaic roundel at the base of the curving stair. Light filtered in through the fan above the door, revealing a parlor opening out to his right. Dust and cobwebs there, a black yawning fireplace, boarded-over windows.

"Wherefore hath this been left to time and the worm?" wondered the man. "Damned if I know. Look at it all! Draperies gone, potted palms gone, servants all gone. So much for Britain and her glory. Er—it's like I said, you know? There's more houses than people now, and nobody wants to live in the crumbly ones." He lifted his face, scowling. "It smells dead. Enough of this. Upstairs, quick march."

He went up into the house, ascending through more shadows, more cobwebs, and brought them at last to a little door in the wall of what had been the servants' dormitory.

"Here we are, gentlemen," he said, crouching down. "Rather smaller than I remembered, but what can one expect?" He took a firm grip on the handle of the door and pulled. The door tore away from the wall, trailing its rusted hinges, to reveal a darkness beyond, partially blocked by an ancient water tank.

"Hm." The man put his head into the darkness. "This may be difficult. Difficult? You're nuts, it's impossible. We can't fit through here." He regarded the long passage that stretched away under the slates of the roof, the whole length of the crescent. It was floored only with wooden beams widely spaced over plaster, and obscured at regular intervals by more of the water tanks. "No? We must and will, unless you'd prefer knocking on Mr. Rutherford's door and asking to be invited in. Don't be a coward. I'll show you who's a goddam coward!"

He thrust his shoulders in past the tank, and after a considerable amount of straining and writhing got in one leg and then the other. Balancing on a rafter, bracing himself against the wall, he stood slowly and found his head in a mass of cobwebs.

"Aaagh! Keep calm. Don't step between the rafters, or you'll fall into the room below. Now, this can be done. Quickly, beam to beam, watch your feet. Count the doors. We'll want the ninth one after this. Go!" Shuddering, he began to sidle along the passage, as the rafters creaked ominously under his weight.

"Here we are," he said presently. "Number ten. See?" Grinning, he ran his fingers over a pattern of scratches on the wood of the low sill. Just visible, in the chink of light streaming between two slates, were the straggling letters E-D-W-A-R-D.

"My old hideaway. Rather comforting, don't you think?" he said, testing the door with his fingertips. "Nothing left of Her Britannic Majesty's Empire, but by God I left my mark on *something*. Just get us out of here, man. I think this rafter's cracking." He struck the door a careful blow and it flew open, admitting him into blinding light. Crawling forth on his hands and knees, he found himself in what was plainly an attic.

Rather too plainly an attic. There were three or four old trunks, picturesquely decorated with antique steamer labels, and a dressmaker's dummy. There was a battered farthing-halfpenny bicycle leaning against the wall, with a broken cricket bat and a helmet from some long-lost war. There wasn't a speck of dust on anything.

"This is a museum exhibit," said the man. "Thank you, I had drawn that conclusion. Is he here, then? Downstairs, very likely. Yeah." He got carefully to his feet and dusted himself off, picking cobwebs from his wild hair. Reaching inside his coat, he drew out the pistol and checked it. Then, with a coldness and composure in his face that would have astonished the cringing citizens who'd seen him talking to himself in the Charing Cross Road, he opened the attic door and descended the steps beyond in perfect silence.

"More tea?" Rutherford offered the pot. Chatterji swirled bits of chamomile in the bottom of his cup and made a face.

"No, thanks. I'll have another muffin, though."

"There you are." Rutherford extended the plate and Chatterji helped himself. "What about you, Foxy?" He waited patiently as the import of his words sank in on Ellsworth-Howard, who was working his slow way through a bowl of bran flakes in soy emulsion. Ellsworth-Howard's new medication made him very calm, you could say that much for it.

"Yes please," he said at last, and Rutherford leaned over and refilled his teacup.

"There you are." Rutherford took another muffin himself, and daubed it with fruit paste. There were no clandestine dairy products at his table today; smuggling butter and cream had become too dangerous since the Mars Two incident, with all the increased border surveillance. Still, nobody would ever catch the Hangar Twelve Man. Miserable closure had come when Chatterji was informed that the Company had recovered the stolen shuttle, wrecked, and found bits and pieces of Alec Checkerfield inside.

"Now then." Rutherford dabbed at his mustache with a napkin. "What do you say we have a look at our dream journals? Chatty?"

"Well—er." Chatterji drew a small plaquette from his coat pocket. "There's not much, I'm afraid, and I don't appear to have been given any unconscious insights on how to create a better security tech. Mostly I've just had nightmares."

"Ah, but you never know. The creative genius may have given you an insight expressed symbolically, don't you see? Like that chemist fellow," said Rutherford. "Dreamed of snakes biting their tails, and woke up to realize that benzene molecules must be circular."

"Yes, but—I dream about Shiva and Kali. On Mars," Chatterji said, and Rutherford grimaced. They had all agreed never to bring the subject up again.

"Ugh. You want to schedule another session with Dr. Cannon, Chatty. Very well then, I'll share my dreams." Rutherford took up his plaquette and thumbed the PLAYBACK function. After a moment the room filled with the sound of his voice, thick and blurred with sleep:

"HEM! UH, VERY INTERESTING. TWENTIETH JANUARY 2352, HALF PAST FIVE IN THE MORNING AND I WAS, ER, IN SOME KIND OF POLICE MUSEUM. ROWS AND ROWS OF WAX DUMMIES IN OLD POLICE UNIFORMS. SOME OF THEM HAD CLUBS AND SOME EVEN HAD GUNS, AT LEAST I THINK THEY WERE GUNS—"

"Did they look anything like this?" said the very tall man who appeared in the doorway, leveling a disrupter pistol at them. Rutherford dropped his plaquette in his surprise. It fell to the floor and the sound of his recorded voice stopped abruptly.

"Alec shracking Checkerfield," said Ellsworth-Howard through a mouthful of bran flakes.

"Amongst others," said the tall man. "Get his buke! Get it before he can send an alert. What's a buke? That thing there, sticking out of his bag, see? Ah." He crossed the room swiftly and confiscated Ellsworth-Howard's buke, shoving it into his coat pocket and placing the bell-muzzle of his disrupter to the back of Ellsworth-Howard's naked head. Rutherford shrieked. Chatterji's hands flew to his mouth.

"Which one of you is Clive Rutherford?" the tall man inquired.

"But—buh-but you're dead," cried Chatterji.

The man looked impatient and put his thumb on the pistol's safety; then his eyes widened with horror. "Yikes, Edward, hold on. There aren't lead bullets in this thing, it shoots microwaves! It'd fry his brain bad enough if he were ordinary, but with those rivets, his head'll explode."

He drew back the gun an inch or so, as if considering, and his facial expression became aloof. "Trust the Irish to devise something like this. On the other hand, one thing I did learn in my long years as a political is that there really is no such thing as a clean kill. Well then, gentlemen! A particularly nasty death for your friend, unless you speak up. Is Clive Rutherford in this room, please?"

"I'm Clive Rutherford!" he said.

"Good. Mr. Rutherford, where is the woman Mendoza?"

"Who?" Rutherford gaped.

"One of your slaves," Edward said, curling his lip. "The Botanist Mendoza. You had her arrested and transferred to an unrecorded location, just after that unfortunate incident on Mars. Tell me where she is."

"I don't know," squealed Rutherford, and Ellsworth-Howard shuddered as the man exhaled impatiently and took a firmer grip on his pistol. But then the face changed, and the voice was different too as Nicholas said: "But he's unarmed, Edward."

"Who's Edward?" said Chatterji in spite of his terror.

"Just hit him or something, okay?" Alec said. "I don't want to kill anybody."

"Of course you don't want to kill anybody." Rutherford mastered himself enough to attempt a soothing tone. "You're a *good* man, Alec. You're a hero, not a villain. Oh, when I think of the times I've dreamed of meeting you—and to have it happen like this!" Tears welled in his eyes.

"I asked you a question," said the hard cultured voice that had done most of the talking. "Where is the woman Mendoza?"

"Edward was the name of the s-second one," Chatterji said suddenly. "In the second s-sequence! Edward Something Something, uh, Fairfax."

"Edward Alton Bell-Fairfax," Edward corrected him. "At your service, formerly; now very much his own man. I really am going to shoot your friend, here, if you don't answer my question. Where is the woman Mendoza?"

"Oh, my God, he's g-gone mad," moaned Chatterji.

"Hardly. It seems to be something akin to demonic possession, even if Nicholas partakes more of the angelic in our particular case." Edward sounded wickedly amused. "No, Mr. Rutherford—and I assume you must be Francis Chatterji?—no, we're all three here to confront you, our sinful creators, just as in Mrs. Shelley's book, though without all the tedium of a chase to the North Pole. Alec, you've got this weapon set at minimum wave! That'll take far too much time." Edward adjusted the dial on the top of the pistol. "There now. Maximum. Dreadfully sorry, Mr. Ellsworth-Howard—I believe? I'm afraid they'll have to conduct your funeral with the casket closed, unless the undertaker can contrive a wax replica of your head—"

"Options research!" said Ellsworth-Howard. He would have said it sooner, but he was finding it difficult to think at the best of times these days.

"I beg your pardon?"

"I sent her to Options Research," Rutherford said. "But it's a department, not a place! I don't know where it is."

"We can find out from his buke, Edward," said Alec. "Come on, let's leave these creeps and go rescue her."

"Alec, please." Rutherford held up his hand. "Please listen. There's been a terrible misunderstanding. We created you in good faith! We thought you were going to do great things for humanity. But we were used, Alec! The Company had its own agenda all along. Do you see?"

"I saw Elly Swain, you little bastard," said Alec. "How many other people suffered to bring your wonderful creation to life? And Edward and Nicholas had mothers too, didn't they? You treated 'em like animals. What kind of good faith was that?"

"It was necessary." Rutherford stood up in his agitation and tried to pace, but Chatterji pulled him back down. "Nothing great is got without cost. And if three women suffered some shame and discomfort, it would have been worth it. Oh, Alec, what you might have been! What you *are*." Rutherford's voice broke. "Good God, you're the hero I always wanted to be. If not for Mars—look at you. Orphaned and free, sailing in your ship with its pirate flag, having adventures, dying heroically and popping up alive again. You sway others with just the sound of your voice, you're clever and strong and fearless. You're Peter! You're Arthur and Robin Hood. You're, uh, Frodo and Mowgli and Kim and Sinbad and—and the boys in the Narnia books and the boys in *Castle of Adventure* and—"

"What about Pinocchio?" said Alec quietly. "Somebody you could put through hell and it wouldn't matter, because he wasn't a real boy?"

"All right, I deserve that," Rutherford said, weeping. "But you have to understand about the woman. She was your downfall, you see, every time! Your evil angel, if you will. We had to put her away. She held you back, she tangled you— you'd never have accomplished anything—"

"She loved me."

"But we loved you, too! And we understood your destiny."

"What destiny? To keep getting myself killed in stupid ways?" growled Alec.

"No, no. To give your life in a noble sacrifice for the good of others," Rutherford admonished him. "Because you could accomplish things ordinary men couldn't do. You were to have been the ultimate hero, born of a virgin even, eternally resurrected for mankind's eternal benef—"

"Thou blaspheming fool!" Nicholas drew himself up until Alec looked seven feet tall. "Was it for *thy* greater glory I suffered in the fire? Hast thou created me, and sat in judgment on my life? Oh, little man, to make a thing like me!"

"We're sorry! We're so awfully, awfully s-sorry," whimpered Chatterji, for Nicholas's voice had become a thing of terror and power. "We'd never have done it if we'd known how it was going to t-turn out. Please don't kill us!"

"I can't deny I'd enjoy it," sneered Edward. "An appetite *you* set in my heart.

You made me a slaughterer, and gave me the conscience to tell me it was wrong. Should I indulge myself now, I wonder? Get up, all of you. Lie flat on your faces on the floor and put your hands behind your heads."

Rutherford and Chatterji obeyed at once. Ellsworth-Howard required a shove to remind him to comply before he flopped down beside them. Alec bound their wrists with cut cords from the drapes, and then knotted the bindings so the struggling of one would only serve to tighten the bonds of the other two. He went through their pockets and removed their identity discs, tucking them into his coat.

Edward then secured the pistol beside the discs, buttoned his coat carefully, and went out into the entry hall, with its marble floor and mosaic roundel an exact counterpart of the one at No. 1 Albany Crescent. He looked around him, grinning.

"Well, good-bye and farewell to you, number ten," he said. "For the last time, I devoutly hope."

He opened the door, stepped through, and closed it behind him. They could hear him whistling through his teeth as he strode away down the pavement.

"He never understood." Rutherford gulped back a sob. "He never understood his greatness."

"At least he didn't kill us," said Chatterji faintly.

After a full minute had gone by, Ellsworth-Howard said:

"Shrack! He took my buke."

They still hadn't managed to free themselves by Wednesday, when fortunately the first tour group of the day found them.

Alec Makes His Exit

All the commuters had now arrived at their offices and set about their wearisome duties, so they missed seeing Alec sprinting back through the streets of London. There were a few tourists on Waterloo Bridge, and they turned at the thunder of footsteps as a wild-eyed man of extraordinary height came racing toward them. If they had not turned, they'd have seen what was making the hissing noise in the Thames directly under the bridge.

"Go," howled Alec. "Run for your lives! Shoo! Out of my way!"

He skidded to a stop in the middle of the bridge and groped in his coat pocket, bringing out a tiny bottle labeled CAMPARI, of the sort once given out by air transport hostesses. As he was hurriedly unscrewing the cap, one of the tourists inquired timidly:

"Are you a performance artist?"

"Er—yeah." Alec leaped up on the railing of the bridge. "What's that Jason Barrymore holo? *War and Peace*, yeah? Okay, this is my impression of the drunk guy." He threw away the cap and tilted the Campari bottle up, gulping its contents as he teetered back and forth on the rail. He gagged. The tourists applauded uncertainly.

Then he dove forward, right off the bridge, and several of them ran to the rail to see what had happened to him. To their utter astonishment, he had landed on the deck of some kind of enormous vessel just below, and was running for a cabin as its transparent dome closed over him.

What happened next was uncertain. Some of the witnesses thought the vessel must have been a submarine, because they clearly remembered seeing it submerge. Others insisted the vessel wasn't a submarine and didn't submerge, but couldn't say exactly what it had done; only that it was gone before anyone thought to take a holo of it. In any case, the story wasn't coherent enough to make the evening news.

"Let's go," Alec said, strapping himself into his storm harness. When he had finished, Edward and Nicholas linked arms with him tightly.

What course, laddie?

"Fifty years back and thirty miles off the Galapagos. That ought to be far enough."

Aye aye!

"And we've got loot, Captain, sir! Three identity discs and a buke belonging to Foxen Ellsworth-Howard. I want you to access everything and tell me where Dr. Zeus has a place called Options Research."

To be sure. Hold yer teeth, gentlemen, she's tacking about. Where do we come from?

"From the sea!" said Alec, and Edward, and Nicholas, as the yellow gas boiled up and obscured everything but the memory of the black-eyed woman, the Botanist Mendoza.